THE GATOR
LEAVES NOTHING BEHIND
PART II

THE DISTURBING HISTORY SAGA

KAMI BOLEY

www.boleybooks.com

16477 Live Oak Drive

Prairieville, LA 70769

Published by Boley Books LLC

Printed in the United States of America

ISBN: 978-0-9975217-7-1

ISBN: 978-0-9975217-6-4 (eBook)

To surviving histories and building futures . . .

For all the souls and bodies damaged by domestic violence—
May your scars heal and may you find equanimity and all its
synonyms.

Contents

Friday
December 11, 1959

I look around the room at all the progress Mary made throughout the day—relieved that she couldn't have been gone from the house for long—when my eyes land on the bookshelf and the envelope I'd forgotten existed. My thoughts explode,

That fucking envelope!

To anyone else it's innocent-looking enough, sitting snuggled between a dictionary and a Bible, but to me it's a caustic sight that bores an excruciating splintery hole into my skull; a vessel that no doubt contains the answers to questions I've refused to consider. A paper sarcophagus which came to me sealed for a reason and which I never opened.

I don't want to know!

It may be the alcohol, or the shock of facing an old demon I'm not prepared to do battle with just yet, but I lose my cool and draw from the evil in me that I have come to embrace.

There is no excuse for what I do next.

I raise my hand and damage the one person in the world I never intended to harm. I grab that fucking envelope from the shelf and subdue its retribution beneath my arm, and in a blind rage I spit out words I can't remember, desperate to slam the bedroom door and lock out all prying eyes. I sit in contest with that damned legal-size, caution-yellow envelope staring back at me from my pillow. I linger on the bed a moment longer, still glaring at that stupid envelope, but I know it's me I hate. When I decide to reach out and lift it up, it seems heavier than it did before, as if I can feel the weight of the information inside.

I shove my finger beneath the top flap and rip apart the seal on my dreaded history . . .

Tuesday
December 23, 1958

Vinny suffers a pang of guilt for not being around when Old Joe's eyes turned the strange white-blue color that plunged his sight into darkness, as if he could have protected him from that evil somehow. Under Vinny's covert surveillance the old man sits, a relaxed sentry; he guards the entrance to the same seedy Brown Bomber Bar in Gretna, a glorified drug-slinging pool hall, just like the day they first met. Vinny studies Joe's dull, haggard face—the lines of worry, the wrinkles you get when the world has its foot on your neck, and the sagging skin of heartbreak. He sees that his beleaguered friend has finally started to earn the "old" in Old Joe.

Old Joe suddenly senses a presence; he frowns, and his swinging leg suddenly goes still.

"Where's Christmas?" Vinny asks as he approaches Joe, hearing the familiar crack of a cue ball as it strikes against a tight rack of solids and stripes.

Joe's sightless eyes brighten at the sound of a familiar voice. "Probably taking a dump in the lot down the street," he replies. His dark, leathery skin creases in a broad smile. "That dog you give me thinks she queena da block."

"Ole Black Joe, what's new?" Vinny asks, grabbing his old friend's extended hand. Joe's dry clubbed fingers painfully bend to fit the curves of the young man's grip.

"Hey, Vin, man, not too much new round here. Same ole shit," says Joe.

"Never shit where you eat—right, old man?" Vinny pats him on the back with dubiosity.

"Yes, suh," Joe laughs. "You sure been missed round here. What's been keepin you away so long?" He takes an inquiring sniff. "A woman, by the smell of it. A nice one, I bet." He takes another sniff. "Maybe even *the* one."

"What makes you say that?" Vinny asks, as if the man's blindness allows him to smell another person's soul.

"She don't smell like the others. Not like dried-up flowers. More like a spring cloud," The old man smiles and lifts his sightless eyes toward the sky. "Like a angel."

"Get outta here! What you know 'bout clouds, old man?" Vinny investigates, sniffing his own sleeve. "Probably just hotel soap."

"If it is, can you bring me a bar? I haven't had that scent round me since I was yo age."

"Would you like to take a ride to go and meet her?"

Joe's smile fades. He bites down at the corner of his lip, slowly shakes his head, and says, "We been friends a mighty long time. Why you want to play me like dat, Car-lean-o?" Joe lowers his head in resignation. "I know why you here. I'm going ta meet an angel, all right . . . but it ain't yours."

"Let's go for a ride and talk." Vinny reaches out to lead Joe to the car.

Joe jerks away, leery of his advance. "I need to do this at my own pace. You can at least give me that," he says and purses his lips with mistrust.

Vinny's chin lowers to his chest and he lets out a long, low sigh. "I know you didn't do it, Joe. I want you to tell me who did this and we'll just go wet a line like we did in the good ole days. All right? Can you do that, my man?"

Joe rubs the middle of his forehead and closes his eyes—still as dark as ever that way, Vinny figures, but it does shove a tear out onto his leathery cheek. Instead of voicing anything resembling information, he licks his lips and whistles for Christmas. A dark shadow from down the street grows larger, imminent, as the dog happily heeds the call of her master. Joe slaps his leg and Christmas falls in line, ready for orders and panting. She snorts and licks Joe's hand as he presents it to her.

"We ready to go now . . . lead the way," Joe says solemnly.

Vinny sees that the team of Christmas and Joe have learned to work together with no need of a bulky harness as they follow him easily to the car. Vinny opens the door of the Thunderbird and tilts the front seat to give the dog access. "The back seat's all yours, girl." Guarded, she looks up at Vinny. She whines and sits on the cement next to Joe.

Joe puckers his lips and kisses the air twice. "It's okay, girl, go on." She hesitates but ultimately decides to listen, climbing gingerly onto the immaculate backseat cushion.

Trying to ignore the whelp's claws on his custom leather, Vinny applies a pair of dark, unlined leather gloves one finger at a time. "Your turn," he says and protects Joe's head as the old man lowers himself into the passenger side of the car.

Once behind the wheel, Vinny finds himself unable to turn the key; he rakes his gloved fingers through his hair instead. "Are you going to talk to me and fix this, Joe? You need to let me fix this."

"Drive," Joe barks. A sheen of sweat rises on his face as he feels his way around to crank open the vent window. Christmas snores, the engine purrs, Vinny hides his eyes behind aviator shades, and they pass gray moss-hung cypress trees and bright green palmettos that stretch as far as only his eyes can see. The tires roll until the smell of swamp mud fills the dank December air.

After the engine dies, in the new quiet Joe can hear the subtle voices of wildlife in celebration—a chorus of tweets, buzzing, and croaks. Joe knocks a knuckle against the tempered glass. "Betcha them cows is walking around in the fields right now."

"I believe that's true," Vinny nods. "You were always good at knowing when the fish are hitting," he says and stretches his arm over the shoulder of the seat.

Joe, on wire-taut alert, listens to the irritated drumming of Vinny's leather-covered fingers, an eerie leather-on-leather sound behind him.

"You know . . . we could go hook us a ton of bass," Vinny says, almost to himself. He inhales a long breath and adds, deceptively light, "Right after you tell me who's been skimming the till."

Awakened by the front seat voices and the absence of the engine, Christmas becomes ready and restless to explore, fidgeting and whining in the backseat. Vinny frowns at the break in his interrogation and decides to let her exit the car. He steps out and releases her from the backseat jail. Nose immediately to the ground, she departs on a tantalizing trail of discovery. Joe takes the dog's initiative to wander, to experience the feel of fertile and mushy ground beneath his feet.

Vinny stalks close behind. His eyes soften and a gentle smile plays at the sides of his mouth as he recalls the first time he and Joe went fishing together—in this exact spot—Vinny watching the old man hunt down the scents of slime and lunker bass.

"Don't you need me to lead you or something?" Vinny asks.

"Lead me?" Joe pauses and flaps his lips like a horse. His blind, frustrated eyes dart around as if to find a better path, then he marches forward with arthritic knees. "Ha! I know my way from here, fool. It's you who better step careful, Jack, cuz you never know when roots is gonna sneak up an knock you on yo face."

"What did you call me?" Vinny falters. "You're the one that can't see."

"Am I?" Old Joe huffs. "And you're the one who refuses to."

"To what?"

"To see!"

"To see *what?*"

"When she took my eyes she gave me the sight . . . and I don't want to look no more. I worry for the fruit of your tree, boy."

Vinny takes a step back. "The what of my *what?*" He tries to shake loose the confusion in his head. "What are you talking about? 'She' who? What has gotten into your crazy black ass?"

Old Joe stops, turns his pale eyes to Vinny, and jabs his gnarled finger into the young man's muscular chest. "I want you to remember that there are worst things than being Black, boy. You need to pay attention to the color of your *heart.*"

Vinny begins to feel almost manic; the skin around his eyes bunches up; his heartbeat quickens. "You know I don't want to do this . . . but your tight-assed lip is leaving me no choice."

"You always has a choice," Joe says with an overwhelmingly strong desire to turn back time.

"You know how all of this works!" Vinny yells, the cords standing out in his neck. He freezes, his eyes pinwheeling, the rogue ocean wave of realization washing over him. "Why'd you do it, Joe? Huh?"

"That don't matter an iota. Explanations don't matter to Carlos, not to you, and certainly not to me. We're men that don't care about reasons, ain't we?"

"You knew it would end like this," Vinny says, swiping off his aviators and squeezing his eyes closed.

"I'm tired. I'm not gonna put up any fight. I ain't had no lunch and the sugar got me weak."

Before he can lose his nerve, Vinny clamps a gloved hand behind Joe's neck and pulls him in for a bear hug, the warm comforting embrace of an old friend. A strained whimper escapes Vinny's lips as the hug becomes tighter, tighter, far too tight, more like that of a child that doesn't understand the frailty of being when picking up a new baby animal and loving it so hard that he squeezes all the life from it, to render it joyless and limp.

Suddenly Joe's eyes spring to life with the vision of Beulah, his lost love, returning to forgive him and take him home.

Joe struggles only slightly near the end, against the sharp jagged edges of bone piercing his lungs, the last survival instinct, feeling the sunlight warm on his face for the last time.

Wednesday
December 24, 1958

"**H**ey, **Mary, Vinny** just pulled in," Jason says, without missing the slightest bit of the holiday evening program on the television screen.

Mary runs outside, still shoeless, to breathlessly greet Vinny. "You just missed us opening presents," she says, and steps on something squishy. Instantly grossed out, Mary warily inspects the underside of her toes, rethinking the whole no-shoe idea.

Vinny emerges from the car, droopy with disappointment at Mary's words. "I thought everyone on the planet waited for Christmas morning to do that stuff."

"We always open presents on Christmas Eve. It's tradition. Mama doesn't like missing all the action on Christmas morning, with us trying to get breakfast out of the way and all. It's just easier to have it after supper Christmas Eve, when everybody's awake and less cranky."

No less droopy, Vinny says, "I have all the presents in my car, but I didn't wrap them yet . . . I was going to do that tonight."

"Less mess for me to clean," Mary says with a grateful grin.

"That's what *you* think." Vinny rubs his non-existent beard.

She narrows her eyes in suspicion. "What's that supposed to mean?"

Vinny's eyebrows raise and his lips pull back in an exaggerated smile. "Wait till you see what I brought for the boys."

"What have you *done?*" she says, forgetting the mess on her toes and dancing from side to side to see into the car.

"Take a look for yourself," he says, stepping out of her way. "It's in the backseat."

Mary peers into the shadowy car through the rolled-down window, then back at Vinny in confusion. "I don't see anything." Just then, she is accosted by a large pink, wet tongue. She reels backward, spitting and wiping away the slobber, and now she clearly sees her assailant: a black Labrador retriever with shining eyes and a wagging tail, popping her furry head out of the car to lick any human in reach.

"He's so friendly," Mary laughs.

"The truth is, *she* wasn't meant to be a present. I had a friend who recently passed away and no one wanted the poor old thing. I didn't want to see her go to the pound."

Mary pets the dog's freshly washed fur, her keen nose detecting the faint scent of some medicinal flea shampoo. "They will love him . . . I mean, *her.* What's her name?"

"I haven't the foggiest . . ." Vinny lies.

"That's okay. The boys would probably change it anyway. Should I send them out here to the car, then?"

Vinny attaches a leash to the dog's collar. "I think so. It might make your mom happy if we keep her outside for now."

Mary bounces inside and the dog whines at seeing her go. Vinny rubs behind the pup's ears and gives her a short pep talk. "Don't be afraid, old girl. These are good people. They won't hurt you. And don't worry about the whole name thing. We all have to change our names when we start over in a new place."

Inside, Mary turns off the television and equips the children with shoes and jackets to brave the evening air, announcing that Vinny has a Christmas surprise for them in the car.

As soon as they enter the porch, Jenny screeches, "It's a puppy! A real-life *puppy!*" She sprints down to Vinny, opening the car door to coax the dog out.

"Not exactly, kiddo," Vinny says, carefully handing Jenny the leash. "She's a little older than a puppy, but she has a few miles left in her." He opens the trunk, where he has stored the remaining gifts. "The problem is, we forgot her name."

"Her name is Christmas," says Sarah, rubbing the dog's snout.

Mystified, Vinny cocks his head, looking much like the confused adult dog. "Are you sure about that?" He looks to Sarah with caution, swallows, then shouts, "Get the ball, Christmas!" throwing a baseball he purchased as a gift for the boys.

The dog cuts loose after the ball, dragging the tether behind her, and returns the slobbery sphere to the children, who reward her with hugs and lots of praise.

"See? Told you so," says Sarah triumphantly, removing the leash before the dog chokes herself.

The kids take to the dog right away, not giving much notice to the parade of store-bought trinkets Vinny has hunted and gathered for them.

"I would have guessed the Slinky or the hula hoop would have been the biggest attention-getters," Mary says, shaking her head as she and Vinny sit side by side on the front porch, along with Norman, her father, in his favorite rocking chair, watching the kids play in the porch light.

"I would have put my money on the sports equipment or the board games," Vinny says.

"That baseball sure is catching hell," says Norman as the kids play fetch with the dog.

"If it makes you feel better," Mary says, trying to ease Vinny's disappointment at being outdone by a pooch, "Barb there hasn't let go of her Raggedy Ann doll since I handed it to her."

"I guess I'm going to build a Lincoln Log house for Mr. Potato Head all by myself," Vinny says loudly, to draw the attention away from the dog—but to little effect.

From behind the screen door, Vivian settles the matter with a holler: "It's time for everyone to come inside! It's chilly out there! Charlie, make a bed for that mongrel on the back porch with a pillow and some old blankets."

"Wait! Mary didn't get *her* present," Sarah says.

"That's because I don't need one." Mary gives Vinny's hand a little squeeze. "I'm happy just as things are."

"But I saw it," Sarah insists. "It has a red bow."

Mary turns to Vinny. He shrugs, having no idea what Sarah is talking about.

Norman sighs dramatically, admitting, "I was saving it for last on purpose." He dances his lanky body into the house to get Mary's gift. He's hidden it behind the small tinsel Christmas tree he picked up on sale last-minute at Woolworths.

"Who wants eggnog?" Vivian asks, walking into the kitchen to stir the creamy mixture on the stove. Mary and Vinny follow her, eager for a serving of the homemade brew. Vivian wants everyone to get a good night's sleep, so she has secretly added a fair amount of rum to the recipe.

Norman enters the kitchen with Mary's gift. Her hand covers her speechless mouth and her eyes fill with tears of gratitude; he gently lays what looks like a small suitcase down on the table in front of her.

Unbuckling the case, she lifts the top to reveal a brand-new, turquoise-blue portable typewriter.

Norman watches his daughter's reaction closely. "I couldn't figure out how to wrap it, so I just put on a bow. I hope it's the one you wanted . . ."

Her head begins to slowly nod her answer: Yes, it is the exact model she lusted after in a store window almost a year ago. She never once asked for it—because the price tag alone gave her the answer. But Norman must have seen her face, must have known her desire for it was strong.

Mary's fingers caress the keys affectionately, as if to make sure they are real.

Charlie enters the kitchen and hands her two packs of opened paper, one just plain office stock and the other a fancy linen stationery.

"I bought these special, with my own money, when we went to pick it up." He removes a sheet from the top ream and loads it into the typewriter. "I had to check that the ribbon was good before we took it, because it was the window model."

Overwhelmed by the sentiment of the offering, Mary whispers, "It's the best present ever." She hugs her brother briefly, then falls into her father's arms and buries her face in his shirt, partly out of love and appreciation, partly to hide the tears starting to form in her eyes. "Thank you so very much," she says, her voice muffled by the linen cotton blend.

"I just wish I coulda got it for ya sooner," Norman says, patting her silky mane with his loving, callused fingers.

The family drinks every drop of the potion that Vivian has prepared, rum and all, before taking part in another tradition: lining the front room floor with pallets to sleep on. They only perform this ritual on Christmas Eve—or on the rare occasions when the outside temperature drops below freezing and they need heat from the wood-burning stove that sits in the corner of the room. Since the temperature has only dropped into the forties this evening, the small fire currently flickering in the corner stove is mainly for the ambience.

The darkened room falls quiet, except for an occasional shift or crackle of the dying fire, embers barely aglow.

"You never told me you wanted a typewriter. I would have bought one for you," Vinny whispers sleepily, and yawns as the long day and the rum finally begin to take their toll.

"That's the point," Mary inhales sharply, unable to resist yawning herself. "I needed it to come to me this way. Please understand that it's more precious to me with my father's sweat on it."

Thursday
December 25, 1958

"*You lied!* Jason said there's no such thing as Santa Claus!" Jenny protests, using full volume–despite the fact that most of the house is still hibernating in the front room.

Mary bolts upright, rubs her eyes, and attempts to focus. "What is the problem?"

"There is a pile of games and toys in here," Jenny says, pointing at the evidence.

"Vinny brought those in last night while you were all out playing with the dog. Now be quiet so we can rest," Mary says, turning over to go back to sleep.

"All right, but how do you explain the truck outside?" Jenny says, encircling herself with the hula hoop, but still not sure how to get it started.

Mary's eyes pop open, and she darts to the window for a look, hurdling sleeping bodies like a track star.

Sure enough, there is a truck outside.

Jenny gives up on the hoop and opts for a coloring book instead.

Mary lunges over to Vinny, shaking him awake. "Someone's here," she says. "I don't recognize the truck."

"A friend drove it in for me last night." He stretches out from an awkward position and hopes his morning erection goes unnoticed.

The implications of his words strike Mary like a knuckle punch. "I told you not to go overboard," Mary says slowly, still in shock.

"I didn't. It would have cost me just as much to have the old one fixed. I swear. I got that one at an auction real cheap, and it came with tools. Some place was going out of business or something." He shrugs.

Mary's brows pull in as she taps a conflicted finger against her lip. "I'll go and start the coffee. Come and get me if Dad wakes before it's done," she huffs, and rolls up the abandoned bedding from the floor.

"I'll come help. There's a big meal to prepare for," Vinny says, following her lead. "Right after I visit the facilities."

By the time he comes back, most of the house is up and involved in some form of food preparation, including Norman, who has not been made aware of the large present outside. Luckily, the town crier is still occupied, crayon in hand, her dangling feet lightly sweeping back and forth across the dog, who's napping under the table. Occasionally Jenny stops to embed her toes in Christmas's soft, warm fur, a massage enjoyed by both.

"Coffee is ready. Why don't you two men go have yours out on the porch?" Vivian suggests. She wants to clear some space in the kitchen, and is completely oblivious to the near heart attack she has just caused her daughter. Mary shoots a panicked look over to Vinny.

Norman being Norman, he instantly catches the sense that something is awry. "Woman," he says, "it's too chilly this time of the morning. The sun hasn't even woke up all the way yet."

"It will get our blood going," Vinny says. He throws on a light jacket and takes both cups of freshly poured caffeine.

Mary takes her father's coat off the peg by the back door and hands it to him.

"I have the feelin I'm not wanted round here," Norman says in a huff. He heads for the porch, close behind Vinny and the warm coffee.

Vivian is the only one who isn't the least bit interested in what is going on; she has too much to do (and take credit for).

As soon as the men are on the porch, Mary turns to everyone in the kitchen and places her finger to her lips for them to keep mum. She tiptoes behind Norman to see his reaction as he steps out into the dank morning air. He has no reaction whatsoever. He stands there and quietly sips his warm chicory.

Perplexed, Mary emerges onto the porch after waiting patiently for him to speak. "Merry Christmas, Daddy," Mary says timidly. She stands beside him and studies his face. It is the face of a man who can't find the words, either because he is happy or is too polite to say them—she can't tell which.

"Vinny tried to get your old one fixed, but this was a better deal," Mary says, trying to figure him out.

"A deal . . . or a steal?" asks Norman, and takes another swig of his coffee.

Mary frowns, never having heard her father with such a nasty tone to his voice.

"I got it at an auction," Vinny says, nervously staring into his cup as if it were poisoned. "It came with tools and everything. Only a hundred dollars more than the cost to fix the old one."

"Stole off the back of some other working man in debt, no doubt," Norman says. He throws his last sip onto the dirt and holds the cup out to Mary with pain in his eyes. Her cheeks burn as she removes the cup from his work-worn hands.

"I wanted to buy one new, free of any history," Vinny stammers, "but I promised Mary I wouldn't. I can take it back or . . . or sell it."

Norman ponders the offer. He eyes the truck, clears the scorn from his throat, and turns to Vinny. "Son, you did a real good thing for this family. I thank you and I apologize for what I said." Norman reaches out to shake Vinny's hand, placing his other hand on the younger man's shoulder. "My pride just pinched me there a bit is all. Chalk it up to a cranky old man gettin kicked out of a warm house first thing in the morning on his day off."

"Yes, sir, I understand," Vinny says, handing his leftover coffee to Mary, who comforts him with her eyes.

Norman softens and looks for a way out of the situation; he spies his eldest on the porch, ill equipped for the temperature. "Get your shoeless self inside before you catch your death, young lady! And tell the spectators that breakfast won't make itself."

Mary stabs her father with a look of warning, afraid of leaving them alone at this point; she's not sure if the rejection has completely left him.

"If you want, we can go for a quick spin before breakfast," Vinny offers, and hops down off the porch.

Norman hesitates, sees Mary's warning expression, and turns to Vinny. "Maybe you should give me the tour first. I don't know if I can locate all the bells and whistles on a newer model." He descends gingerly down the porch steps, having been wounded by sleeping on the floor.

Inside, Mary deposits the cups in the kitchen sink and hears the dog whine at the back door.

Vivian is startled by the engine roaring to life outside. "Where does that man think he's going without his biscuits?"

"They're just going to test drive the new truck," Mary says, pulling the biscuits out of the oven and putting a ham in its place.

"What happened to repairing the old one?"

"Don't worry. Vinny was the one to pay for it," Mary says, before her mother gets too worked up.

"Well . . . your dad deserves something nice. And for Christmas, no less." Vivian eyes the dog that appears to be doing a little dance at the back door. "Will someone please put on some shoes and take that flea-bag for a walk before it pees in my house?"

Several children volunteer for the job.

"One of you bring some eggs in from the coop," Vivian adds as they file past her.

When breakfast is ready, Mary goes outside to get the men. They are sitting on the tailgate of the truck, talking and laughing as if nothing uncomfortable has happened between them.

As the three of them enter the kitchen, Vivian fusses, "We are going to have a pow-wow about that mutt later." They glance at each other, eyebrows raised, accepting the invitation to Vivian's butt-chewing with quiet resignation and filling the empty seats at the table.

As the meal comes to an end, Vinny notices that all the children have left a little bit of food on their plates—an odd occurrence in a house that has a mandatory plate-cleaning rule. He says, "Did I forget to mention that I deposited two large bags of dog food on the porch?"

Before he can finish his sentence, the children gobble up the rest of their breakfast.

Vinny laughs. "I'm going to feed the dog. When I get back, I'm going teach you all how to use that hoop."

Christmas swiftly earns her place in the Poche household. Before Vivian can oust the poor dog and render her homeless, she witnesses Christmas protecting little Brandon by blocking his access to an electrical outlet. Accustomed to guiding a blind man, Christmas uses her keen senses to avert the wobbly walkers Brandon and

Barbara, helping to keep their curious fingers safe from harm. In doing so, she not only earns herself a spot in the family, but also a cozy bed near the front door. Which suits Christmas just fine, as it reminds her of waiting patiently by her old master on his wooden stool.

Gayle, ever Mary's best friend, trots over to the Poches' house for a Christmas Day visit and watches Vinny's expert hula hoop demonstration in the front yard. The children have already eagerly lined up for their turns.

Gayle applauds graciously. "I never would have guessed that you had such a talent, Vin!"

Vinny bows as the rest of the children cheer him on and hands the hoop over to Sarah. "I have many skills that I tend to keep secret, for they might make me famous, and I don't like crowds." Vinny buffs his knuckles on his shirt. "Oh, I almost forgot. I got you something, pipsqueak." He leans into his car, reaches into the glove compartment, and hands an envelope to her.

She gives him a suspicious look as she tears it open to reveal a card announcing a one-year subscription to *Hot Rod* Magazine. "This is *awesome!* Oh, I can't wait to show Chick. It really wasn't necessary, but I'm glad you did." She reads about the free offers that come along with the gift, then adds, "I was hoping to steal Mary for a little while so we could go over some details for the wedding. You know, maid of honor, flower arrangements, that kind of stuff."

Vinny's eyes cloud over and his throat tightens. "I suppose."

"Great!" Gayle bounces and hugs his neck. "I'll go get her."

Distractedly, he mentors the promising hoopsters, watching Mary cross the road to Gayle's house without so much as a wave in his direction.

The girls have an exhaustive conversation about what kind of this will go with that, laughing in Gayle's kitchen, until Mary sees the time and realizes she needs to get home. But when she gets up to leave, Gayle stops her.

"You can't go yet. You haven't met my Christmas present."

"Met?" Mary asks. Intrigued, she follows Gayle to her bedroom.

"My mom said something about how I don't even know how to take care of myself, so on and so forth . . ." says Gayle. "One thing led to another. You know me and my big yapper—next thing I know I have this fish tank in my room. At least they let me pick which one of the little buggers I have to remember to feed every day."

"What did you name him?" Mary asks, tapping on the glass in front of a large-eyed goldfish.

"The Little Bopper," she says, and demonstrates her fish-flake sprinkling skills.

Gayle's parents are out delivering holiday meals to some of the older, less fortunate of the community—so the three loud knocks on the front door startle the girls.

"Well, it ain't Santa." Gayle shrugs and goes to the door, Mary close behind, giggling. The opening door reveals Vinny wearing a hard smile.

"It's time to come home to your family. Your mother sent me to fetch you," he says, eyes boring into Mary's.

Gayle is taken aback by the coldness behind his words, and the way he seems to purposely avoid acknowledging her presence. He has an uncanny ability to channel the worst parts of Vivian's nastiness, Gayle has noticed (and Mary as well), as if she has somehow possessed him.

"Is . . . something wrong?" Mary asks, her smile falling into uncertainty.

"Your mother is angry. She said this is a day meant for family, and you have been here over two hours."

"But *Gayle* is family, Vinny. I'm sorry we lost track of time. I was about to come home . . ."

Before she can finish, he moves to the side of the doorway to direct her outside to join him. Mary's first instinct is to buck, but there is something in his eyes that warns her not to.

Better pick my battles . . .

She quietly obeys, looking at Gayle with sorry-filled eyes as she joins Vinny on an eerily silent walk back home.

Upon reaching the house, Mary walks over to her father's rocking chair. She sits woodenly and looks out at a sun that, it seems to her, decided to droop way too early.

Vinny looms nearby for a while before daring to speak. "Are you coming inside?" he asks finally, looking at her firmly planted feet.

"I need another minute," she says harshly.

"Are you mad at me?"

"Yes!" she says, louder than she meant to, then recants with a softer "No," and winces. "Not nearly as mad as I am with my mother. I just can't understand for the life of me why you would follow her commands like that."

"While you were gone I listened to what she had to say. It made a good bit of sense to me," Vinny explains, his hands shoved deep in his pockets.

"Oh, really? Please enlighten me. What did my mother say that made you march over and treat me so rudely, like I'm some disrespectful child—and in front of my best friend?"

Vinny's pockets seemed to get deeper. "Your mother said the two of you were closer before Gayle came along. She told me that Gayle has ways of manipulating, poisoning you against her. Of keeping you from spending time with your family."

"That's what she believes? Is that what *you* believe?" Mary's blood is boiling. "That woman has no one but herself to blame. *She* is the manipulator in this scenario!"

"I'm not sure it's all her fault, Mary. I've seen Gayle's ability to pull your strings, too."

Mary's jaw drops. "When? What are you saying? I have no idea what you are talking about!"

"It's subtle. You're just too close to see it."

"So I guess this means you're on my mother's side now," Mary snaps.

Vinny bends down and places a hand on her knee. "No such thing, my love. I will always be on your side. Yours alone."

"Prove it."

Vinny falls to his knees, hand still on Mary's. "I want to! Let me take you away from here. You can be free of anyone's influence for a while . . . clear your head."

"That sounds nice in theory, but I can't do that, not right now. I know where you're going with this, and I'm just not ready yet."

"Is there any better way to prove that I am on your side than to make you my wife and take care of you for the rest of my days?"

Mary cradles his face in her hands. "Okay. I believe you."

"So does this mean you forgive me?" Vinny asks.

"I guess. I really can't blame you for trying to assimilate."

Vinny's brows knit together.

She guesses he doesn't understand. "Trying to be part of the family, silly."

"Oh." Vinny stands up, brushing himself off. "Don't do that," he warns.

"Do what?" Mary asks, blanched by his tone.

"I know you're smart, but don't use your complicated words to rub everybody's nose in it."

"I'm . . . sorry. It's just how I talk. I wasn't being malicious," Mary blurts, then bites her lip.

Vinny takes in a deep breath and flashes his eyes. "If you weren't so damn cute, you'd be in trouble. Now get inside before I put you over my knee," he teases, tapping her hip when she makes a move for the door. She squeals with surprised delight, figuring it's better to quit before you lose your adorability.

Wednesday
December 31, 1958—New Year's Eve

"**I get to** *stay up till miiidniiight,*" Jenny taunts Margene in the living room.

"*Maaa*-ma!" Margene calls out. She runs into the kitchen and starts a formless game of hopscotch around the table, waiting to be acknowledged.

"For sweet heaven's sake, what is it now?" Vivian hollers back in frustration. She doesn't even bother to lift her eyes from the Christmas edition of the Sears catalog, which she is perusing for the fifth time since it arrived.

Undeterred by Vivian's ugly tone, Margene whines, "Mama, can I stay up for New Year's, too?"

"You can all stay up and watch for UFOs, for all I care!" Vivian scoffs.

Full of flap and flurry, Margene runs to tell the others the good news.

Vinny and Mary are sitting on the front porch around an unleveled fold-out table, playing a grueling game of Pedro with Jason and Charlie. Vinny is shuffling the cards for a new round when Margene thumps her way through the screen door and lets it slam shut behind her to grab her audience.

"Guess what—Mama said we can stay up all night and watch *UFOs* if we want to!"

"That's wonderful, little bit," Vinny says. "I know just what we need to celebrate." He gives Margene's head a rub and perches her on his lap before dealing out a fresh hand.

"What—a UFO to watch?" she says, igniting laughter amongst the players.

"No, honey, better. You're going to love it, I promise," Vinny says, separating his hand, thinking of the sparklers and other pyrotechnics in his trunk ready to light up the night sky with flaming color.

"Vinny?" asks Margene, watching the cards move around strategically.

"Yes?" Vinny tosses the discards in the community pile.

"What's a UFO?" she asks, followed by more laughter.

"It's something that you see in the air and you're not quite sure what it is."

"Oh, like a bird you never saw before . . . or a new kite?"

"Yeah, something like that."

She wiggles loose from Vinny's lap to look him in the eye, hands on her hips. "How we gonna watch for em in the dark?"

"Just make sure to be a good girl and get your nap this afternoon, so you don't fall asleep before all the fun starts."

"Okie-dokie, smokie!" She scampers off, fully trusting that tonight will be full of excitement.

Vinny glances at Mary, a smile on his lips. "Where did she get that from?"

"Where you think? Same place Jenny did—sounds like Gayle to me," Mary says, taking a sip of iced tea.

Vinny's eyes turn down, along with the corners of his mouth. "I don't want her around teaching our kids all that nonsense."

Mary freezes mid-swallow. Her throat is suddenly thrown out of order by his presumptions, sending her into a fit of chokes and gasps. *"Kids?"* she finally manages after clearing her lungs enough for proper oxygen exchange.

He avoids eye contact, studying his hand carefully, pulling out a trump and throwing it into the center of the table.

Unmoving from her expectant gaze, she completely ignores her turn and waits patiently for any response other than his lopsided grin.

"Haven't you ever thought of having kids?" he asks, as if that alone will be enough to resume the stalled game.

The boys sit back in their chairs for the duration. It's like someone has just rung the bell on round one; they have the look most boys get on their faces when they discover a playground fight at school, ready to choose a side, jeering at the opponent until the duty teacher arrives to break it all up.

Seeing this, Mary says, "Boys, I think we should take a break. Go on inside and make yourselves a snack."

"We're good—aren't we, Charlie?" Jason says, not wanting to miss the show.

Mary gives Charlie the look that he associates with a thirty-five-inch wooden stir paddle that Vivian calls the Board of Education.

"I'm going to raid the pantry," Charlie says, winking at Mary. "I thought I saw a stash of cookies in there."

"Not if I get em first," Jason says, scrambling to beat his brother to the door.

Alone with Vinny, Mary slaps her cards on the fold-out table. "Do you not see that I already know what it's like to have kids? What makes you think I would jump off that cliff?"

"Having your own will be a different experience, I'm sure."

"Nope," she says, shaking her head vehemently, "*I'm* not so sure! And I won't be sure for a very long time. I have no interest—"

Vinny distracts her rant by patting her hand, still splayed on the table. "You will . . . someday . . . you will."

Mary's knees instinctively slam closed in self-preservation and she thinks,

The threat of fire and brimstone isn't nearly as effective as the threat of dirty diapers and screaming infants in deterring me from fornication.

Tuesday
February 3, 1959

here is an unusual calm in the Poche house at six-thirty on this particular Tuesday morning—except for the *tippy-tap* sound of the nervous dog's nails following Mary's every move. The empty kitchen is haunted by the lovely scent of oatmeal and cane syrup Mary stirred earlier for a household that remains in bed, stricken down overnight with a nefarious case of the stomach flu. Many of the bowls Mary has retrieved are in much the same condition as they were delivered. Regardless of the uneaten portions, there is constant traffic to and from the porcelain confessional. Many prayers will germinate in this bathroom—some thanking God and some begging for His mercy. And rumors will fly for many weeks about individual fault with the meal preparations the night before—but because there had been too many spoons in the pot, the full blame will never find a solid place to stick.

Mary is the only one who is not amongst the infirm, having somehow managed to skip the tainted culprit. Throughout the night she imagined restless spirits forced to roam the halls of the old house, muffled moans and groans that disturbed her sleep—until one of these "restless spirits" entered her room, looking an awful lot like Sarah seeking her sister's assistance.

Mary considers herself lucky to have been spared from such a horrible experience. It's not until Vivian tells her to stay home from school to take care of the ailing malodorous bunch that she realizes she hasn't been spared at all. Struggling with sleep deprivation, Mary keeps herself busy with many ablutionary tasks, but avoids the bathroom at all cost, and instead dawdles in the kitchen until she runs out of options.

She decides that washing dishes in a sink full of warm, sudsy water is the next best thing to a bubble bath. It lulls her into a better state of mind—until the telephone rings.

She quickly sets a freshly rinsed breakfast dish in the drying rack next to the sink and frantically dries her hands with a dishtowel on the way to the device, which loudly summons her from a side table next to the couch. She catches it just after the third ring.

On the line blubbers an unintelligible female voice in obvious distress.

Mary stands erect with concern and asks, "Who is this? You're going to have to calm down. I can't—are you all right?" in an attempt to console the woman long enough to decipher her liquidy rant. "I am so sorry, but I don't understand—"

"He's dead! They're all dead!" shrills the now familiar, teary voice.

Mary swallows hard. "Ga . . . Gayle? Is that you? *Who* is dead?" She tries to stay calm despite the grisly possibilities. Her knees begin to buckle, so she picks up the phone base and takes a seat, with it in her lap.

Instead of an answer, there is a *click*, followed by a hollow void of sound.

"Hello? Hello!" Mary's voice is heavy with panic. She presses the hook switch down long enough to reset the dial tone.

"Shit!" She drags the finger wheel over the numbered faceplate as quickly as it will allow. "Come on . . . come on," she mumbles, waiting for the connection. No luck–a busy signal. She hangs up the phone, leaves it on the cushion beside her, and begins a distressed search for her shoes to head over to Gayle's house. She scrubs her fingers through her hair just as the phone beckons again.

Mary dives to catch the handset as if it's a fumbled ball in the last play of a state championship football game. "I'm here! I didn't mean to–"

"Didn't mean to what?" Vinny asks, his voice thick with suspicion. "Who have you been on the phone with? I've been getting a busy signal."

"I think it was Gayle–she was crying and . . . and I'm not sure what's going on."

"I was calling to tell you I just heard on the news there was a plane crash in Iowa. Everyone on board is dead."

Mary's fingers scrub her scalp again of their own accord. "Oh, my God! That must be what she was trying to tell me! Who was on the plane?"

"On second thought, maybe I should wait and tell you in person."

"Everyone over here is blowing chunks. I'm already so frazzled– just spit it out!"

"Ritchie Valens, Buddy Holly, and . . ." Vinny trails off.

"And?!"

"And the Bop man."

"The Bopper . . . The Big Bopper . . . *Our* Big Bopper?" she quickly repeats, waiting for Vinny to verify the entertainer's identity.

"Yeah. They all died, including the pilot."

"I have to go to Gayle! She needs me."

"I'll come by this evening with plenty of ice cream and tissues to treat the ill and the heartbroken."

"Thanks. That will be great. Oh, and a couple loaves of bread too, please. See you soon." Mary hangs up.

"I love you," Vinny says solemnly into the void that follows.

Christmas whines when Mary opens the front door and is met with a blast of chilly morning air, reminding her to grab a housecoat—and it's a good thing she does. The school bus bounces down the pockmarked road, unaware that it will be denied its usual cargo today.

"I don't think that outfit will pass the dress code, missy," says the bus driver, after opening the folding glass door.

"I wish that was all I had to worry about today, Mrs. Brignac. Neither of us will be going to school today, I suspect."

"Is it about the plane crash? I heard about it when I went to pick up my bus. It's a shame. I'm a big Holly fan myself," she says with reverence. "I didn't take you for the kind to get this worked up," she mentions, looking at Mary's haggard state.

"Well, the truth is that my whole family came down with a bug last night."

"There's no shame in admitting you care about music, young lady."

"No, really."

"If you say so, dear. I'll see you tomorrow, in something more . . . appropriate."

"Yes, ma'am." Mary pulls her coat tight, watching the school bus leave without her. As the bus engine roar fades, Mary hears muffled yet clearly agonized wails from the Gautreaus' house, and quickens her pace.

Shirley answers the door after only one knock and pulls Mary inside. "She has been inconsolable. I hope you have better luck than we did."

Mary climbs the stairs to Gayle's room, where she finds her friend sprawled across her bed, staring at the ceiling, her face all puffy, red, and leaking. Mary stands frozen—what can she possibly say to undo the pain that twists Gayle's face up in ugly torment?— until their eyes meet, launching Gayle into another crying jag.

"Why, why, why, Mary?"

Mary lands on the bed, pulling Gayle into her arms like she does when a child wakes from a nightmare. "Shhh," she says to soothe her best friend, fighting back her own empathetic waterworks.

"It's all my fault," Gayle sobs.

"No, honey . . . these things happen . . . don't be silly . . . shhh . . ."

Gayle hiccups. "Where do you think he is now?"

"I don't know for sure. None of us will . . . until we follow."

Gayle jerks away in confusion. "Down the commode?"

". . . aaand somehow you lost me," Mary admits.

"Mom came to tell me about The Big Bopper and the plane crash," Gayle sniffs. "But I was already crying because the Little Bopper was limp and floating on his side when I got up. I called to tell you about everything, but then I heard Dad trying to flush him before I got to say goodbye!" Gayle cries, putting her wet face in Mary's housecoat.

"Oh, that is awful! I am so sorry. What an incredibly bad day this is turning out to be," Mary says, petting Gayle's hair. "Please don't be mad, but I can't stay. I really need to get back. Everyone over there is painting the bathroom walls."

"Eeew!" Gayle turns her face up and runs the length of her forearm beneath her pink nose. "Poop or puke?"

"Sadly, both. I sure could use some help if you're feeling up to it."

"No way, José—but I wish you much luck with that."

"Figures." Mary rolls her eyes and slides out from under Gayle, letting her friend's head thump unsupported onto the bed. Mary watches her pout. "You gonna be okay, snail?"

"Yuck. Only my dad calls me that."

"Gayle the Snail . . . why does he call you that, anyhow?"

"He said I looked like a snail when I was a baby trying to crawl in one of those drawstring nightgowns."

They both laugh trying to picture it.

"That sure is a lovely sound," Shirley says, entering the room with two short glasses of orange juice.

Mary stands. "I'm sorry, but I can't stay. My family needs me."

Shirley blocks the door and holds out a glass. "Not until you drink this juice you're not, young lady."

Mary takes the glass and knocks it back like a cowboy in a saloon, grins, and hands the glass back to Shirley.

"I have a chicken boiling on the stove to debone and make a big pot of soup," Shirley tells her. "Gayle and I will bring it over as soon as it's done."

"And how did I get volunteered for cleanup duty?" Gayle grumbles to her mother.

"You need to learn to do these things if you are to raise a family."

" 'Raise a family'?" Gayle says, throwing herself flat on the bed in a pool of self-pity. "I can't even keep a *goldfish* alive."

Mary pats Gayle's dangling foot good-bye. "The soup will be greatly appreciated, Mrs. G."

"Anything else we should bring with us?" Shirley asks, watching Mary inch toward the doorway.

"Elbow grease . . ." Mary pauses to think. ". . . and bleach. Lots of bleach." She taps the doorframe and disappears down the stairs.

Despite the soup and the extra help from Gayle and Shirley, it is nearly dinnertime before the aftermath of lunch is completely mopped up and disinfected.

"The end of round two," Mary says. "The hard part should be over now." She sets some coffee to percolate and collapses into a chair at the kitchen table, joining Gayle and Shirley, who waved the white flag a full half-hour before Mary.

Too tired to exchange war stories, all three just sit and enjoy the lull with droopy eyes. A new energy rouses the caregivers when Vinny arrives with much-needed morale boosters: bags filled with bread, milk, tissues, ice cream, and a fresh-baked king cake, all of which he begins to unload.

"I sure could use a piece of that cake right now. With some coffee," Gayle says, salivating.

Shirley rises to help but Vinny stops her.

"Ladies, please sit. I can only imagine what you've had to endure today. Let me serve you a treat." Vinny cuts even slices into the colorful, creamy glazed ring, places each cinnamon-y piece onto a small plate, and hands the first section to Shirley.

"May I have a slice of justice, please?" says Gayle.

Vinny looks at Mary to decipher.

"She means a purple piece."

"I didn't know the colors meant anything," Vinny says, and grants Gayle's request.

"Last year the girls had that question on a social studies quiz," Shirley explains. "Apparently, the gold represents power, the green is for faith, and the purple is for justice."

"And the baby—what does the plastic baby mean?" asks Vinny.

"Some say it's lucky, but no one wants the *baby*," Gayle says, looking underneath her slice for the signs of a hidden not-so-lucky prize. "If you get the piece with the baby, you have to buy the next king cake."

Shirley shakes her head. "To tell you the truth, I'm always afraid of someone choking on the dang thing. Where's the luck in that?"

Vinny offers a piece to Mary and she gives him a *No-thank-you* smile that barely holds back the sourness in her throat. After the horrors she has faced with long plumber's gloves for most of the day, she is left with no appetite.

"What are you planning to feed the natives?" he asks.

"Toast," she says definitively.

Fat Tuesday
February 10, 1959

Every year, approximately forty-seven days before Easter, crowds of people gather along the streets of Houma to experience a cultural phenomenon known as Mardi Gras. The Krewe of Houmas is loading up this year's colorfully festooned Paris-themed floats with beads, booze, trinkets, and more. Their annual voyage will take them from the air base service-road past the viewing stand near the courthouse.

"Can you believe the turnout?" Mary asks Gayle. They are strolling down the street, visiting with the smiling faces of kids young and old who line the parade route on Grand Caillou Road.

"I guess you still think this is weird, huh?" Gayle asks.

"What? The fact that these people are all here to beg for baubles and doubloons from masked men on the side of the road all day? Naw . . . that's not weird at all. We'd better get ourselves back to the staging area before we get in trouble."

"You're such a rule follower," Gayle cracks. "I wanted Chick to see me in my uniform before I get all messed up in this wind."

"We should have asked where they would be standing. The route is miles long, and it's about to start." Mary is interrupted by the piercing squawks of police vehicles rolling slowly down the street to announce the impending approach of the main event, and to clear and smooth a street-wide path between the hordes of merry-makers.

"Too late—that's our cue!" Mary grabs Gayle's hand and they hotfoot it all the way back behind the Terrebonne High School banner, where the coach has already begun giving directions.

"Ahem . . . I'll repeat for those of you who can't seem to stay put. We are to look for hand signals to know when to perform, so pay attention at all times. I know the crowd can be distracting. Don't let that get in the way of our performance, ladies."

The percussion starts to play a steady drum cadence fit for marching.

Mary smiles watching Gayle pinch her cheeks and nervously smooth her uniform.

"Don't fret Gayle! You'll look fine," she says, her feet finding their left, right, left rhythm at the end of her row.

"A fine couple of dancing monkeys, I'd say," Veronica jeers in passing, bumping Mary from behind. "Excuse you!"

If it had been another time or place, Gayle would have followed her blood-lust instincts, but luckily the irritated coach intervenes. "Move it along, bête noire!"

Mary wonders why a person's native tongue seems to win out when emotions run high. She has never heard the phrase before, but imagines that it must have been just ugly enough to leave Gayle with a satisfied grin. Unable to let it go unexplored, Mary asks for some clarification with only her face.

"I don't know for sure, but my gramps used it for 'pain in the ass,' " Gayle says with a shrug and a pivot, keeping in step with the line, turning onto the main thoroughfare.

"Smiles for miles, ladies!" As a last reminder, the coach reveals two imperfect rows of tobacco-stained teeth, poking her fingers into nonexistent dimples on either side of an exaggerated grin.

All the practice makes performing second nature for the groups—and makes it easier to search for friends along the route. It is a mile or so before Mary sees several familiar faces in a row, waving and calling out in excitement. Looking at her loved ones celebrating, it is hard to believe that all of them were so sickly such a short time ago. Her mother looks not only restored, but also better than before, having lost more than just a few pounds around her middle during the vexation. She wears a frock that has not seen the light of day since a pregnancy or two ago. The sickness-induced weight loss has given Vivian a boost of inspiration to continue down a diet-seeking path.

"Wowza, Mrs. V!" Gayle shouts her approval, drawing the attention of the coach who turns to march backward long enough to frown in Gayle's direction. She then blows a whistle to signal the bandleader to proceed with the next song selection.

The youth in the crowd, recognizing "Jailhouse Rock" from the first few iconic beats of the intro, cheer, sing, and dance along as the mobile performance steps ever forward.

Saturday
February 14, 1959

"That son of a bitch and his Goddamned brother!"

With the sudden roar of Carlos's voice, Vinny holds the payphone handset away from his ear to protect his tympanic membrane. He waits for a patch of silence, looking around the public booth for possible eavesdroppers, before daring to endanger his ear again.

"Your line clear?" Vinny asks him. "Better watch it."

"Fuck em if they can't take a joke!" Carlos lashes out. He sucks his teeth in disgust. "Nah, we good. Did a sweep already."

"We can't fix it today. Don't let em get you riled. It's what the Kennedys want. A subpoena is just an invitation to the dance—so we spin em, and spin em hard," Vinny coaches.

"Yeah, you right," Carlos says, with his cogs set in motion. "Yeah, you right," he repeats, becoming more calm and calculated.

"Better keep your eye on Cuba, too. I bet our friends in Florida are having a fit."

"The Junior is just as pissed as me ova all dis shit," Carlos confirms.

"I have no doubt," Vinny says over the sound of the brief, impatient honking at the corner red light that has turned green.

"Where you at, anyways?" Carlos asks.

"Houma."

Carlos laughs. "You still sniffing up that baby's skirt?"

"She's no baby," Vinny says, thinking of her shape. "It happens to be Valentine's Day, so don't forget to send the missus some candy and flowers."

"Is it? Thanks for the save. For dat, I sure hope you land yourself that flower. Or at least a little piece of candy," Carlos chuckles.

"If we're done, I have plans," Vinny says dryly.

"Don't get sore. Since when did you get so sensitive?"

"Time just isn't something I like to kill."

Carlos snorts. "Yeah, I know. I hope to add a couple names to your list soon. Right now, they're untouchable."

"No one's untouchable," says Vinny.

"Hmmm, I think I'm gonna keep you in my pocket for now. Momo's got Ruby covering Cuba. Oh, and don't go sayin 'untouchable' in front of Momo. He has a new beef over some show gonna air in the fall. Wants to put Desi Arnaz in a box."

"The Outfit issued a paper on it?"

"No, just ol Sam Giancana blowin steam or showin off for some dame. He musta went through all the good-lookin broads in Chicago. Now he's got his nose all ova LA . . . him and Blue Eyes trading em like baseball cards."

"Listen, I got a good-looking morsel waiting on me. Talk to Wasserman and I'll check in tomorrow."

"Sounds like a plan," Carlos says, then hears an abrupt *click* as the line goes dead. Carlos is no stranger to the fact that Vinny is not a fan of saying any kind of goodbyes, so is not taken aback nor offended by the lack of proper procedure.

Vinny holds the phone lever down long enough to disconnect from business, releasing it for a fresh dial tone. He rotates the finger wheel with the pep of a starving man dialing up a steak. The connection is made and it takes three rings for Vivian's voice to accost him unexpectedly.

"Poche residence," she says heavily, sounding bothered, or just plain angry from the constant ache of her rumbling midsection, fed only with low caloric offerings.

"Good afternoon, Mrs. Viv. May I speak to Mary?"

"Oh," Vivian says in a much lighter voice. "Hi, Vinny. She's attending a meeting for the SAT test."

"Can I come by and leave a present before she gets home?"

"Yes, of course . . ." Vivian starts, then discovers she is talking to a dial tone.

An hour later, Mary returns home. She bounces out of Mrs. Tisdale's slightly rusted first-generation Studebaker and into the house.

Vivian sits in the kitchen, slurping on a second helping of thin, flavorless cabbage soup as she flips through a circular. A Lux Soap ad featuring Elizabeth Taylor gives her a bite of jealousy which only deepens when she looks up at Mary's flawless face—no Lux needed. "Vinny called earlier and said he was going to drop by, but never showed," Vivian says pointedly, feeling instant vindication. "So how'd your thing go?" she asks with no real interest.

Mary sighs. She grabs a glass out of the cupboard and replies, "Apparently there was no better way to study for this test than to take this practice test to see where we're weak. I'll know more after she grades them." She pours a glass of cherry Kool-Aid and drains it in two healthy gulps. "My brain hurts . . . I'm going to lay down a few minutes."

"Suit yourself," Vivian says, barely listening, and snaps the page of the circular.

Upon opening the door to her room, Mary's breath catches, discovering that Vinny did indeed pay a visit.

"How in the world?" she asks the twelve long-stemmed roses standing tall in the vase atop her dresser; the bright crimson blooms fill her room with a dazzling fragrance.

Carefully, she lifts one rose out of the vase, knocking a note to the floor. As she rubs the velvety petals across her cheek, she reads Vinny's words.

A room full of these could never compete with you. Show them what a real flower looks like, throw on that pink number and I will pick you up at six.

All my love,
Vinny

At ten minutes to six, a freshly decorated Mary descends the staircase. She hears Vinny's voice assuring Norman that no rules will be broken this evening—that is, until he is made speechless by the pink dress accentuating Mary's trim waist.

Vinny's loins stir, his wild eyes drawn to her exposed neck, shoulders, and wrists moving toward him; he forgets all mention of rules as he places a hand in the small of her back to guide her out of the door and into the meticulously planned evening: candlelight, rose petals sprinkled on a stark white table cloth, soft music in the background . . . all while Mary looks over the Valentine's Day menu.

"Filet Mig-non," she says, leaning over and unwittingly pushing her cleavage forward—a delight not missed by Vinny. "I've never heard of this fish. I was hoping for something other than seafood."

Vinny covers his amusement with his hand so as not to laugh. "My darling, it is a steak, and it has a French sound. I don't know that I am the best person to teach it to you. We will ask the waiter. I can vouch for the cut of meat, though—I think you would enjoy it."

Mary sits upright, raising the menu higher, enough to hide her face, which has become warm and pinker than her dress.

"I'm not as cultured and worldly as you might think," Vinny says. "I only know that information because I had a friend who was a butcher when I was a child."

Her delight in his willingness to talk about himself overshadows her brief bout of embarrassment. "Did you work for him?"

"No, but he did teach me a few things."

Even after all of Vinny's efforts—the flowers, the meal, even actively engaging in every conversational whim Mary tosses his way over the course of the evening—the last thing Mary expects is for him to reach for the big backseat prize on the way home.

Parked in a secluded area, Mary enjoys the thrill of his kisses with her eyes closed—but her eyes pop wide open, revealing the steamy car windows, after he runs his thumb firmly over the pink material covering one of her aroused nipples and Mary's body responds, her panties becoming warm and wet.

She pushes Vinny away. "We should stop. It's not right."

Vinny abides her wishes like a true gentleman, without any hesitation or hostility. He nods and escapes the body-heated car to cool off, to straighten his mind and his clothes.

Mary suddenly feels abandoned. She steps out to join him. "Are you mad, Vinny?"

"No. Why would I be mad?" he says, reaching down to smooth her skirt.

"Because I wouldn't . . ." She trails off, shrugging one bare shoulder.

"You're a good girl, Maggie, and that's a good thing to be," he says, brushing a loose lock of dark hair away from her face.

"Are you sure you're not mad?" she asks again.

"Do you want me to be mad?" He opens the passenger door for her.

"No," she says softly, and returns to the front seat.

On the ride home, with no conversation and the radio turned off, she can hear the subtle changing sounds of the car's engine as Vinny's foot presses down on the gas pedal—sounds she had not noticed before. Mary thinks of Gayle's ability to recognize what those mechanical sounds mean, and wishes she had the same ability to read the subtleties of Vinny.

"Goodnight, my love," Vinny says, kissing her hand before leaving.

Mary stays on the porch, watching his taillights, then looks all around at the perfect night—a perfect night she feels like she has ruined. He did nothing to indicate a disconnection, but she feels it, like a joint pulled from its socket. The tears come and she runs to the telephone.

"Did he get mad?" Gayle's concerned voice follows the tearful explanation of the matter.

"I'm not sure," Mary says.

"Did he *act* mad? Did he *sound* mad?"

"No. In fact, he said he wasn't mad at all."

"Well, there you go! So what are you crying about?"

"I don't know. Maybe he was—"

"Just being nice? Isn't that what he's supposed to be?" Gayle says, finishing Mary's thought. "Since when do you not believe everything you're told?"

"Huh?" Mary says, lost in her tears.

"The man said he wasn't mad. Maybe he isn't. And maybe you're all upset about nothing. I wish I had a neat Valentine's Day date to tell you about!"

"I'm so sorry that Chick had to be offshore this week," Mary says, peeking out of her self-absorption.

"He said he'll make it up to me, but he sure doesn't know how to plan like Vinny does. You should get some rest. Things might feel different in the morning."

"Thank you," Mary sniffles.

"No, thank *you*! This makes *me* look like the sane one," Gayle says, sparking some much-needed laughter before they say goodnight.

Sunday
March 22, 1959

With the Valentine's Day misfire behind them, a pleasant month's worth of calmative blandness helps Mary trust the stability of Vinny's resolve once more. All is right with the world . . . in Mary's eyes.

"I'm sorry, but I might not be back in time for Easter," Vinny says, after receiving orders to take care of some pressing business.

"Where are you going this time?" Mary asks as she wipes down the kitchen table, removing the crumbs from the evening meal, tempted to wipe a crumb from the experimental facial hair Vinny has been cultivating.

"I have to see a man about a cigar," Vinny says, making eye contact with thirteen-year-old Charlie and smirking, which causes the stray crumb to fall away.

"I've never seen you smoke cigars," Mary says. She shakes the rag out in the sink and rinses it while Barbara tugs at her clothes, wanting to be held.

"It's like saying 'I gotta see a man about a horse,' Mary," Charlie says, proud of his comprehension of the guy code. He fills the sink with hot water and adds a dash of Palmolive.

"Because that makes so much more sense," Mary says and purses her lips, acclimating to the vagueness of Vinny's answers. She finally gives in to the insistent tugs and picks Barbara up.

"I'll bring back a couple of those new Barbie dolls everyone is talking about," Vinny offers, planting himself back in his seat.

"What for?" Mary asks. "We have one of our own right here!" She squeezes little Barbara's cheek, then her side, making the tot squeal with delight. She sits next to Vinny and bounces Barbara on her knee. "I hear those dolls are hard to come by right now. Don't go to too much trouble," she says.

"It's no trouble at all," Vinny says and softly tugs on one of Barbara's springy ringlets.

Charlie turns from the sudsy sink. "Yeah, Mary, don't you know Vinny has friends in the entertainment biz? He can probably snap his fingers and get ten of whatever you want, like that." Charlie attempts to snap his own fingers, but the friction doesn't take with all the soapy water.

Vinny swallows, a pulse visible in his neck, and gives a snort of dismissive laughter. "Who told you that nonsense?"

"Started working with the school paper. I saw you in a few pictures developed from last year's assignment on the set of *King Creole* hanging up in the darkroom. What was it like working with Elvis?"

Mary gasps, her face awestruck. "How *exciting*—why didn't either of you mention this before?" She stares at Vinny. "Did you really work with *Elvis*?"

Charlie shrugs and looks to Vinny with panic, having unwittingly betrayed the recently established bond between them.

Vinny winks at Charlie and shakes his head in denial. "Nah, I just ran a few errands for some of the crew, it really wasn't that big a deal."

Mary shakes her head, still a bit shell-shocked from such a revelation no matter how low-key Vinny tries to play it. "I'm going to go put this one down." She kisses Barbara on her pudgy cheek. "But when I come back I want to hear all about this," she says, pointing a finger of inquisition at the secretive males.

Vinny smiles at her and raises his hands, declaring innocence. He shoots a glance at Charlie who quickly follows suit, soapy foam dripping on the floor. When Vinny hears the creak of Mary's footsteps up the stairs he moves next to Charlie, who stands frozen. Vinny reaches into the sink, pulls the plug, and turns the hot water valve. He dries his hands and says, "You're going to get me those photos—*and* the negatives . . . do that and these will be the last dishes you do by hand."

Tuesday
March 24, 1959

Vinny is wearing a common dark-gray, single-breasted wash-and-wear suit. He adjusts his cheap felt fedora over the pair of black brow-line eyeglasses on his nose.

"Taxpayer dollars hard at work," he remarks under his breath, walking up to the opulent Senate building, which is faced with expensive limestone and marble, grounded by peppery granite.

He enters the light-filled rotunda, greeting all the busy people who pass with a polite shallow nod, the day's headlines tucked neatly beneath his arm. His dull black shoes pivot as he scans the area, estimating how many guns could be in the vicinity—not that there is any gun play on today's docket. Merely precautionary. A good habit to have. Detectable in the air is the faint musty smell of lies cleverly disguised as the truth.

"A higher breed of crooks," he says to himself, smoothing his thin mustache as he climbs one of two marble staircases to the caucus room—just to have a visual map to access if anything were to go astray.

Standing at the top, he pretends to check his cheap wristwatch for the time, just as Carlos enters the building with Wasserman, followed by aggressive members of the press.

Vinny crosses to the other staircase, leaving them to the process of the law, but waits at the ready if the law tries any funny business. He knows that, unlike La Cosa Nostra, the men who make the laws can be much more ruthless and unpredictable behind their veil of so-called "righteous causes."

Much sooner than expected, Carlos emerges from the caucus room with an inflated chest and a high chin—clearly, his second stonewalling session with US Senate has been successful enough—and he exits the building like the victor of a high-stakes cockfight.

Carlos decided long ago that being seen with Vinny in public wasn't the best of ideas, so neither man acknowledges the other—not that Carlos could easily recognize Vinny out in the wild. Fading into the background is a skill Vinny has long mastered, just like an obedient child, not to be seen or heard until called upon to report. A good student of many clever sources over the years. He knows words mean nothing, and sentences often end with a bullet.

Late due to gathering intel (and a large bottle of scotch), Vinny slips into the back door to a private dining room of a friendly D.C. restaurant and joins a cozy table of trusted cohorts. Few of them know him by anything other than "Gator." And he likes that just fine. Your name is not as important as your ability to keep the cash and favors flowing.

The Florida representative asks, "What is the fallout of the junk freeze last month in the big city?" He passes Vinny a basket of newly delivered bread wrapped in a cloth.

Vinny listens for the answer as he spreads a soft, buttery layer across the bread with a knife.

"Looks like the cops got about thirty-two pounds of our last shipment. More importantly, they pulled twenty-seven of our guys off the street," admits the New York City representative.

"Any that would talk?" Carlos asks. He glances at Vinny cracking the seal on the bottle of single malt as if he were breaking its neck, and pushes his empty water glass toward him for a fix.

"I guess there's always that chance," says NYC. "We're gonna monitor the situation with utmost caution."

Carlos rubs the fingers of his right hand against his thumb in slow, analytical circles. "See that you do, and pull out any weeds—all twenty-seven if you have to," he says, his face as sour as his empty belly. He slams his fist down on the table. "Omertà!"

The reverence of this invocation gets the moment of silence it deserves. A silent toast is made once everyone has a glass in hand.

Vinny sighs, looking at a menu. "I was hoping to hear how today went."

Carlos grabs some bread, dropping his foul mood. A large immodest grin spreads across his face, as easy as the butter over his slice. "I respectfully decline to answer on the grounds it may tend to incriminate me," he says, eyes twinkling with mischief.

Mickey Cohen cackles as his feet drum against the floor. "I still can't believe that asshole tried to ruffle me with that fuckin question about the lights!"

"About the lights?" Vinny asks with a cheek full of bread.

"Yeah, that son of a bitch had the nerve to ask me . . . 'What does it mean to have someone's lights put out?' "

Mickey shoves his tongue in his cheek, amused, watching Hoffa clap as he holds back the laughter. "Tell em what you said," Hoffa squeaks, wiping the corner of his eye.

"I says . . . 'Lookit, I dunno what you're talking about, I'm not an electrician . . . I got nuthin to do with electricity.' " Everyone at the table roars with hysterical laughter.

The meal is ordered, served, and eaten, rowdy stories and joyful noise filling the room, before Carlos, Cohen, and Hoffa, proud courtroom veterans, completely finish each account of how deliciously defiant they had been under oath.

"I don't think this is over," Vinny says, pouring another sip of smooth amber warmth down his throat.

"Me neither. Dis ain't ova by a long shot," Carlos replies, his eyes fierce, pushing his glass over for another hit.

Good Friday
March 27, 1959

Mary spreads layers of old newspaper out on a picnic table in Gayle's backyard. "When in Rome," she mutters.

Using the outdoor hose, Gayle's father James fills up a large stainless steel basket nestled inside a stock boiling pot set on a propane burner stand, then tosses the nozzle aside in search of fire. Gayle takes the hose to rinse an aluminum washtub full of live crawfish. James picks up a carton of salt and pours some of it on top of the squirmy lot.

"Is the salt to season them?" Mary asks.

"No, it's to help them purge," James says. "At least I think that's what it does."

"It's one of those 'monkey see, monkey do' situations," Gayle laughs. "We don't know for sure, but we do it anyway. Kinda like the church thing."

James frowns at Gayle as he twists a piece of newspaper to use to light the burner.

Chick arrives just in time to provide the two forms of fire needed, handing James his trusty Zippo and a stuffed cheesecloth bag the size of a brick. James tosses the magic bag filled with allspice, bay leaf, coriander, mustard seed, cayenne, and black pepper into the pot, then ignites the blue flame underneath. It roars like a small jet. Mary giggles, imagining the pot taking off like a rocket.

"Did you get everything on the list?" Gayle asks Chick.

"Yes, dear," he answers politely, just like his future mother-in-law instructed him to do.

Gayle kisses his cheek and runs into the house to help Shirley prep the vegetables.

Mary follows Gayle, but at a much slower pace, fascinated by the cooking process that is completely foreign to her—eyes glued to the tub of death-row inmates trying to climb to freedom.

In the Gautreaus' kitchen, Gayle immediately digs an ice-cold Coke out of the back of the refrigerator. Shirley is rinsing silk strands from freshly shucked corn. "I still can't believe you've been here all this time and never attended a crawfish boil," she says to Mary, and gives her a handful of dripping ears.

Mary shrugs. "Until I met Vinny, most of the meals I ate were ones I prepared myself," Mary says. She lines up a knife on an ear of corn and leans on it over a cutting board on the kitchen table. "Cut these in thirds?"

Shirley nods. "Oh, that's right—not all teens are strangers to the kitchen." She hands a bowl of rinsed red potatoes to Gayle, who makes an exaggerated sneer. She puts down her Coke and takes the bowl out to the guys, who are standing guard around the pot.

James lifts the lid to check the water.

"Haven't you ever heard that a watched pot never boils?" Gayle says, handing her father the potatoes.

"You girls better get crackin! This thing is gonna be bubbling in no time," James says, carefully drowning the spuds in water just shy of a rolling boil. "I need the onions and the corn next," he adds, coughing from the spicy steam.

Less than an hour later, James drains and pours mounds of bright red, juicy hot crawfish and veggies atop the layers of newspaper. "Everybody dig in!"

Chick, an expert crawfish peeler it turns out, demonstrates his skills to Mary in quick fluid motions. "Don't be afraid of em, they're delicious." He tosses the carcass in a nearby trashcan. Tackling the piles of food, James, Shirley, and Gayle prove they are no strangers to the art form.

Mary attempts to break the shell open—not as cleanly as Chick, but she is able to eat the meat from inside the tail. It tastes like nothing she's had before, so spicy it makes her lips tingle. Chick rips through five while she struggles with the first one. She is grateful when he tosses a few her way.

By the time Mary becomes more proficient at peeling the crawfish, she is nearly full. She directs her attention to a piece of corn and digs in. It has soaked up so much spice that she steals a sip of Gayle's Kool-Aid, but it doesn't stop her from attacking the rest of the kernels.

"You won't catch Vinny eating this," Chick says matter-of-factly.

"Why not?" Mary asks, grabbing a small red potato.

"Too messy, and . . . and," Chick says, searching for the right word. "Too common."

"Common . . ." Mary repeats. "Yeah, it's not like him to dine with the rank and file." Looking at everyone around the table chowing down, she is unable to imagine eating this way anywhere but here, with the nonjudgmental.

"Speak for yourself," Gayle says before sucking a crawfish head. "I am the height of class." She discards the small crustacean skull in the trash.

"Sometimes we call em mud bugs, just to keep the fancy and the squeamish away from em," James explains, holding a crawfish with exceptionally large claws.

"More for me," Gayle says. She squeezes a boiled onion until the inside layers pop out, and drags a piece through a dip made from mayonnaise, ketchup, garlic salt, and paprika.

Shirley peels, filling a bowl with meaty tails.

When Gayle reaches into the bowl, Shirley smacks her hand away.

"Yikes, Mom!" Gayle laughs. "What happened to worrying about your only child starving?"

"This is for the crawfish cornbread I'm feeding you on Easter Sunday," Shirley says.

"Yum! You may proceed," Gayle replies, adding a freshly peeled crawfish to the bowl.

Shirley smirks. "So glad to have the blessings of Your Majesty."

James shakes his head at Chick. "Son, I hope you know what you're doing! Not too late to change your mind."

"Too late for my heart, though," Chick says. "The little thief took it and won't give it back."

Gayle smiles with a funky, seasoned finger to her dimple.

Cleanup is easy as rolling the soiled newspapers into the trash, a squirt of Joy liquid soap, and hosing everything down. Shirley is the first one to wash her hands with the outside spigot.

"I think I hear the phone, Mom," Gayle says, washing the stink from her own hands.

Shirley disappears into the house and returns shortly. "It's Chick's cousin. Lester." She pauses. "But he's calling for Gayle."

Gayle senses an apprehension in her mother's voice. "Oh, Mom, don't be ridiculous!" she says, passing her in the doorway.

Shirley's eyes find Chick.

"It's nothing to worry about, Mom," Chick says. "Lester wants advice on that house we've been renovating. Picking colors and stuff—you know, a woman's touch."

"Oh, I see," Shirley replies with a sniff.

Mary hears the sniff. Moving close to her friend's mother, she asks, "Are you all right?"

"Chick called me 'Mom,' " Shirley whispers.

"How sweet!" Mary gives Shirley a hug, and they ascend the back steps and go inside together.

"Speaking of sweet," Shirley says, "let's make an ambrosia to put in the fridge for dessert." She pulls out a large mixing bowl and hands Mary several different containers of fruit to open.

Gayle, still in conversation with Lester on the phone, sees the ingredients on the counter and hops with excitement, pointing at the bowl when the guys enter the kitchen.

"No, you should not put down any linoleum," she says into the receiver, getting back to business. "It is simply too much maintenance. My parents are always having to fool with theirs"—she waves her hand in the air—"waxing and whatnot."

Shirley stops whisking the whipped topping and looks at James, who is frozen in his tracks.

"Is that right?" Gayle says, eyes narrowing. "Only once a year if needed?" She repeats Lester's advice loudly before listening to him explain the flooring choices.

Her parents go on about their business, knowing that Gayle has finally caught on to their "waxing" ruse. Mary gets it, too, and giggles as she dumps the opened cans of fruit into the bowl.

Gayle hangs up the phone. "*Eww!* The two of you are *gross!*" she yells, running to her room.

In a shared look of public humiliation, James and Shirley hang their heads, then go upstairs to talk to Gayle about the role that sex plays in all marriages—her own impending marriage included.

Chick sits down at the kitchen table, clueless. "What's happening?"

Mary sits down beside him and quietly explains that Shirley and James would find Gayle something to do for a few hours nearly every week, so they could "wax the floors" without her underfoot.

"Oh," says Chick. "*Ooohh!*" He covers his mouth, laughing, finally getting the gist.

Wednesday
April 1, 1959

"**Because I am** such a fool for you," Chick says to Gayle, defending his choice to apply for a marriage license on this Fool's Day afternoon, right after picking up the girls from school.

Finding a parking place proves difficult, considering it is before five o'clock on a workday in the center of the business district. The Impala rolls slowly down Main Street toward the courthouse. Chick, Gayle, and Mary have to circle the block twice before they spot a red Buick pulling out. Chick squints in the warm afternoon sun as he waits patiently to slip into the parallel parking spot, just a block down the street from the courthouse.

Out of nowhere, a matronly dressed middle-aged woman appears at Chick's open window. His features unwrinkle themselves as her cool shadow eclipses the sunlight from his face. His vision takes a moment to adjust in her silhouette before he is able to see the older woman's face clearly. She intentionally waits for Chick to recognize her hate-filled eyes before she spatters his face with her thick, sticky phlegm.

Just as stealthily as she arrived, she is gone in a wrathful haste.

"What in the hell is her problem?" Gayle cries, mopping up the overspray that has ended up on her arm and skirt. "It's not like we stole her spot! She wasn't even in a car. Did *you* see a car?" she asks, turning to Mary, who is following the trail of the offender as she slips inside a nearby office building.

Peering through the wet mess, Chick quickly maneuvers into the parking space and cuts the engine.

"No, there was no car," Mary answers, watching the office building door as it closes, worried the woman is going to return with backup.

Gayle turns to Chick. "Why didn't you defend yourself?"

He is still stunned, cleaning the yuck off his face with a buffing rag he always keeps in the car for emergency touch-ups.

"Because I deserved it," he says, to Gayle's dismay. "And more."

"What did you do to that woman?" Gayle asks softly, afraid of where this path might take her—considering the man who will become her husband in less than a month has obviously been keeping a huge secret.

"It's not what I did to *her* . . . it's what I did to her son." Chick's breath is shaky from fighting off his overwhelming emotion. He knows that what he is about to say could take away all of his plans and ruin him in the eyes of his future bride.

"What happened?" Mary asks, in a gentle nudge for him to reveal the rest of the mystery.

"I killed her son," he says, as plainly as if he has announced what he has had for lunch.

"You . . . wh . . . *what?*" Gayle replies, shaking her head, shaking off the words that just don't fit right in her ears.

Chick's face begins to lose its hue. The girls can almost smell his distress as he takes a long, ragged breath, preparing to dig up his buried past.

"I used to run with a rough crowd when I was younger," he starts. "I always felt like I had something to prove. One day we were goofing around at the racetrack and a guy challenged me to a game of chicken. You know . . . where you drive full speed at each other until one gives up and turns."

"Yeah, we know," Gayle says impatiently. "Go on . . ."

"Well, we were headed for each other at about fifty miles an hour, and neither of us turned. He never had a harness installed in his car. No one I know races without one. He was thrown . . . died instantly." The girls watch an old ache of sorrow steal away Chick's good humor and fill him with regret.

"How's that your fault? He asked for it!" Gayle says, looking to Mary for support. Mary leans forward and places a caring hand on his shoulder.

"I should have turned. He was only fifteen," Chick says, staring fixedly at the rag he is twisting, much similar to his insides.

"You couldn't have known that! You didn't mean for it to happen," Mary says from behind him, her eyes moist.

"If I could give him back to her, I would. I thought going to prison would pay back my debt, but it hasn't—not enough for his mother to forgive me." Chick's gaze rises to meet Gayle's.

Her eyes blink rapidly in disbelief. "Jail? You were in *jail*? For how long?"

"It wasn't jail. It was Angola. There's miles of difference." Chick pauses, gives his forehead another wipe, finds the courage to finish what he started. "I served about a year, with good behavior, for involuntary manslaughter. I got out when I turned nineteen. If I had served the maximum sentence, his mother might have eventually forgiven me. But during the trial, they revealed that her son had suicidal thoughts and had written a goodbye note to his best friend. That fact alone reduced my sentence. My lawyer said he could get the charges dropped. But I dismissed him, and met with the district attorney to plead out and take it like a man—even *he* didn't want to charge me. I wouldn't have been able to hold my head up if I'd gotten off scot-free," he concludes, watching Gayle's face twitch in silence.

"You did a very noble thing," Mary says. "Does Vinny know?"

Chick looks at her in the rear-view with large eyes; the blood leaves his face and the remaining spittle blends in with his ghostly complexion.

"I can keep a secret," Mary says, trying to ease his anxiety.

"That makes one of us," he murmurs to himself, waiting for Gayle to react.

With vague alarm, Gayle says, "My parents can't know about this. They might stop the wedding."

"You still want to marry me . . . after finding out what I've done?"

"I can't *not* marry you! You are the spark that makes my engine go vroom," she says sweetly, reaching over to wrap her small, forgiving hands around his cheeks as they begin to regain color.

Chick closes his eyes with relief. A single tear that he has been desperately holding on to slides down from the corner of his right eye and pools around her thumb.

Gayle leans in to kiss his trembling lips. "You are the one for me, Chickster."

Mary claps her hands to remind them that she is present before she witnesses something that might require therapy later on. "Shall we go round up this marital paperwork before the office closes? Or before you consummate the marriage right here, two weeks early?"

Chick turns his watch to check the time. "Oh, yeah! We better get a move on," he says, and rushes them out the car.

"Vinny and your parents should be meeting us here. We have to go finalize the details of the menu with the caterer. It's where we get to taste-test everything, so I hope you guys are hungry," Chick says, rubbing his belly as they approach the courthouse steps. "Out of all the wedding stuff, I've been looking forward to this night the most." He reaches out and opens the heavy glass door.

Mary passes first, then Gayle stands still in the doorway for a second before walking inside, her brown eyes jerking in Chick's direction, her lips in a wry little smile. "Even more than the wedding night?"

"Well, not quite . . . but almost." He gives her a playful swat.

Mary is glad to see everything back to normal between them, and ignores the receptionist's look of disapproval as they enter the courthouse lobby.

"Can I help you?" she says with a condescending sneer.

"Yes, we are here to get our hitching papers," Chick says, giving Gayle a squeeze.

"The Department of Motor Vehicles is in another building, but if you are wanting a marriage license, it's down the hall and to the left," she says dismissively, pointing them away from the desk with her No. 2 pencil.

"Why do all adults seem so miserable?" Gayle says, her voice echoing down the hall. "I hope I don't become like *that* once we get married. It's like that movie *Invasion of the Body Snatchers*. As soon as you hit a certain age, they come along and change you into a certified grump who doesn't enjoy fun or anything related to it."

"What that lady needs is a Melon Ball cocktail," says Chick.

"You really are hungry, aren't you?" Mary asks.

He snickers. "Who's talking about food?"

"Poor Mary!" Gayle *tsk-tsk*s. "They already got to you."

"Very funny. I'm laughing on the inside. My mind just doesn't stay in the gutter all day like some people I know."

Friday
April 17, 1959

T he makeshift dressing room in the church smells of old lady, fresh roses, and nerves.

"Are you sure you want to go through with this?" Chick asks Vinny, securing his boutonnière in place with a pin.

"Shouldn't I be asking *you* that question? If you're still jumping off this cliff, I'm giving you a place to land," Vinny says, jingling a set of keys in Chick's direction. "Nothing to make a big deal about. I got a good deal on it at auction."

"It's a house, Vinny. You're giving me a house," says Chick, still unable to comprehend the gesture.

"It isn't a mansion," Vinny scoffs. "Look at all the work you and Lester had to do just to get it ready to move in. Didn't you think it was weird that Lester wanted Gayle's opinion on everything?"

"I just thought he wanted it to be modern. You know she's always flipping through magazines."

"You can pay me rent if it'll make you feel better. But I think you should save all your dough. That gal . . . I mean *wife* . . . of yours has expensive taste."

"*Wife,*" Chick repeats, as if the wind has been knocked out of him, reaching out to a nearby chair. The enormity of the responsibility is sinking in.

A knock at the door summons them to take their places at the front of the aisle.

"Speaking of . . ." Vinny says. "I think it's time."

Standing up in front of the pews full of invited guests makes Chick very nervous, even after Vinny joins him.

The night before, everyone made a practice run of the procedure, knowing where to walk, where to stand, when to light candles, when to kneel. The thing they had not practiced was how it was going to feel: how Chick's legs would turn to rubber, how his bottom lip would quiver when he sees Gayle looking like an angel, her beautiful face surrounded by a white, lacy veil.

The love in the room is palpable, undeniable, infectious throughout the ceremony, and at last the pastor announces, "I would now like to introduce . . . Mr. and Mrs. Clarence Bourgeois!"

Beneath the afternoon glow of the stained glass window, after a ceremonial (yet still passionate) kiss, Gayle's face beams up into Chick's teary eyes and the entire congregation gets wrapped up in their long euphoric embrace. Her flouncy, tea-length hemline swings and sways as he takes her hand and proudly presents his smiling bride to a room filled with loved ones, casual friends, and rarely seen relatives. No one seeing Chick and Gayle in this moment—the joy in their sparkling eyes, two devoted hands blissfully clasped together—could ever doubt the validity of the young couple's vows.

Mary isn't sure if it's the formal ceremony, being the center of attention, or perhaps the bridal gown—but she sees that Gayle's posture is more upright, her gait more graceful. Mary contemplates her recent *Body Snatchers* statement as she watches a sophisticated Gayle "Hello" her way down the corridor with Chick, greeting total strangers who share her family tree on faraway branches, making their way to the reception hall.

Once they're inside, Gayle sheds her shoes, shouts, "Let's get this party started!" and heads to a row of tables topped with metal chafing dishes.

Mary is relieved to see that Gayle is the same nut in a different shell—but it's a horror for Shirley, who wants more wedding photos taken before Gayle can reach the saucy meatballs.

"Please get her shoes!" Shirley pleads, zooming by Mary, running as fast as an Olympian in her princess heels to stop Gayle.

Performing one of her last duties as maid of honor, Mary happily hunts for the discarded footwear, knowing that you can take the shoes to the bride, but you can't make her wear them.

Reluctant pictures are taken and many congratulations are given as the bridal party rushes through the remaining formalities for the sake of hungry wedding guests. Mary spies her siblings and frowns at them—piling high plates with a sample of everything in line, then walking slowly as if on a tight wire to their table in the corner of the room to sit with Vivian and Norman, who are nearly finished with their conservatively portioned meals. Mary is too wired and distracted to sit, so she just picks a few finger foods left on the plate she fixed for Gayle.

"The boys went out for a smoke. I'm going to the bathroom," Gayle tells Mary. "Mom wants us to mingle! You get started."

"I don't know how," Mary admits, listening to the sound the layers of Gayle's dress make when she moves.

"You ask strangers a bunch of nosy questions, and then they ask you a bunch of nosy questions," Gayle explains. "It's fun."

Mary knows that to succeed in life, she must learn strong conversational skills, and practice is key. She boldly walks up to a young wedding guest with a pleasant face and says, "Hi."

"Hi," the girl responds.

Mary searches for something else to say to make the exchange less awkward. "Can I get you some punch?"

"No, thanks, Mary. My friend is bringing me some," she says politely.

Mary is embarrassed that she cannot place this girl.

"Are you enjoying your violin lessons?" the girl asks.

"Oh, yes. My teacher makes it fun."

"She ought to, for all the money she gets!" the girl snorts.

"Rose is sweet," Mary defends, "and doesn't charge me a cent."

"You mean she doesn't charge *you*. Bobby Vicknair works for my dad at the music store to pay for your lessons. Trust me, Rose gets plenty."

Mary wears a horrified look. "Pardon?"

"I'm sorry! I thought you knew," the girl says with remorse. She looks across the room. "Here comes Bobby now. You two should talk."

Mary turns to see Bobby, so handsome in his suit and tie, walking toward them with two cups of punch.

"I don't have anything . . ." Mary struggles, in immediate need of fresh air. "Please excuse me."

Gayle returns to the reception hall just in time to see Mary slip out of a side door and decides to follow.

"Mary?" Gayle calls, looking around in the empty breezeway.

"I'll be there in a minute!" Mary's upset voice carries from around the corner of the building.

Gayle's bridal gown rustles as her bare feet pound the concrete, heading in the direction of Mary's voice. She finds her maid of honor leaning against the wall, hands on her knees.

"Are you okay? What happened?"

Mary glares up at her. "The mingling was not fun."

"Is that all? Let me show you how it's done," Gayle says, hooking Mary's arm with her own.

But Mary pulls free. "How come you never mentioned inviting Bobby?"

"Mom made out most of the invitations—you know that! I would've needed a good excuse not to."

"Are we moving the party out here?" Chick asks, walking up with best man in tow after spending several minutes searching for his new wife.

"Girl chat," Gayle says. Mary straightens herself.

"Can we join?" Chick asks. "Vinny has something he wants to tell us without the crowd."

Three minutes later, Gayle runs back into the reception hall and up to James and Shirley, burbling, "I have a house! Vinny bought us a house! Best wedding gift I could have ever imagined!"

Vinny endures the gushing gratitude of Gayle's parents while Chick helps Bobby move a table for more room on the dance floor. Mary, feeling snubbed by several of her closest friends, swimming in a myriad of emotions, is thinking about how the path beneath your feet is forever changing to challenge your choice of shoe.

The bright overhead lighting dims, followed by the sharp squeal of a microphone blast through a portable speaker system.

"The tunes are about to start!" announces the hired deejay, twirling a twelve-inch record between his hands. Mary's eyes meet Bobby's, staring him down while she kicks her left shoe off, the shoe landing in the same corner where Gayle's discarded ones lie.

Mary starts twisting next to Gayle as the harmonized voices of the Everly Brothers sing about a boy who is both bird and dog. Mary turns around to burn a hole in Vinny, kicking off her right shoe, aiming it to land at his feet. He tosses it in the corner and joins her on the dance floor, pretending not to notice Bobby's presence or the defiance in her eyes.

Thursday
June 18, 1959

You never notice how loud the ring of a phone is until you hear it rip through your slumber and up your spine. The first ring creates a panicked urgency not to allow a second, or—heaven forbid!—a third.

Vinny makes a mad dash into the kitchen on the first ring, his sleep-fogged brain hiding the blasted phone's location until he can triangulate it—in the front room, on a side table—with the second ring.

He grabs the receiver from the cradle.

"Hello . . . yeah . . ." Vinny says into the receiver. "I would ask how you found me here, but I already know." Too early in the morning to be good news. "Wait . . . I need you to repeat that a little slower . . ."

Mary sits up from the place on the couch she snuck to after her folks went to bed, listening to Vinny's end of the sleep-interrupting call.

"You say Joe died yesterday—are we talkin the barber, or Joe Jr., here? There's a huge difference. And are we sure it was a heart attack?" He pauses for the person on the other end to answer his questions.

Mary decides to get up and make coffee, seeing this conversation may continue awhile and Vinny will not be lying back on his mat beside her.

"I should have been called on May 29th, then! I know it's in New York state, you putz, but why Johnson City?" Listening to the caller's ramble, he pinches the bridge of his nose. "We all know how much he loved that place in Apalachin," Vinny says, eyeing Mary as she passes by to heat the kettle. "Yeah, yeah, that makes sense. He always did like a square deal, I guess. Whatever helps the family get through . . . We corresponded through the channels from time to time, but I ain't put eyes on him since the big barbecue in '57. Yeah, I'll be ready . . . No, just me," he tells the caller. He shoots Mary "the look," one which she recognizes all too well from growing up under Vivian's roof, one which infers *Do as you're told and mind your own business.* She breaks the gaze, returning to the job she knows best—making breakfast.

Vinny wraps up the call with, "It should be a short trip, if it was just his bum ticker . . . a bow to the royals and home again. All right, see you in an hour or so."

He turns to Mary with a tightened throat. "I have to go. Plane to catch. I need to go pay my respects."

He heads to the bathroom upstairs, and in slightly more time than it would've taken Superman to change in a phone booth, he arrives downstairs looking fresh and dapper in tailored Italian silk from a zippered garment bag he keeps in the car.

Mary casts a pat of butter in a pan. "Was he a friend?" she asks him as he searches for his few belongings.

"I'm only going to tell you this once: don't question me about my work," Vinny replies, not looking at her and slamming the door behind him.

Mary's heart sinks and her eyes fill with tears at receiving less than a loving goodbye from her man.

Charlie walks into the kitchen, yawning. "What's up? What are you doing?"

"I thought I would give you a break today since I was up," Mary says with a sniff.

"Everything all right? Where's Vinny?"

"He had to go unexpectedly. Someone he knew died."

"Oh, I'm sorry. You okay?"

"Yeah," she said, laughing through her tears, "I'm just being a silly girl."

Half an hour later, Mary is sitting at the kitchen table, feeding the twins yams for their breakfast, when the phone rings again. She lets Charlie answer it.

"Poche residence," he says, then, "Mary, it's for you."

"Who is it?" she whispers.

He shrugs, giving her the handset. "Some girl."

She holds the receiver to her ear and adopts a formal, business-like tone. "With whom am I speaking?"

"Hi, Mary, it's Rose. I'm calling again about continuing your violin lessons."

Rose's voice sounds nervous, Mary notices. She rolls her eyes and plops on the couch.

"Oh, hi, Rose," she says. "I already told you, I have absolutely no intentions of having any more music lessons—with you, Bobby, or anyone else. I'm done."

"You'll have to tell that to him yourself," Rose says, followed by muffled sounds.

"H . . . hello," Bobby's voice cracks. All he can hear for some time is Mary's angry breath, which is more than he had hoped for.

Finally, she says, "Hello. Still having Rose do your dirty work, I see."

"I would've called myself, but you have a nasty habit of not taking any of my phone calls. I really don't understand what I did wrong. *Please* . . . talk to me."

Mary thinks. Her ankle goes to work bobbing her knee up and down. She says nothing.

"I need to see you. Can I come over?" he asks.

"No," she replies, wrapping the curly cord around her hand. "That's not a good idea."

"I miss you! This is killing me," Bobby pleads. "Can't we at least be friends?"

"Friends don't lie and hide things from one another," Mary says, the tears returning easily. Her heart yearns to hug him, or knee him in the groin, she's not sure which.

"I'm guessing Vinny is some kinda saint then, huh?" he says, then wishes he could suck the words back in.

Mary slams the handset down into the cradle, scaring Barbara. "Shhh," she says, rushing to her high chair to soothe her. "It's okay . . . it's gonna be okay."

Mary doubts her own words, feels the twinges of truth, is tired of clinging to righteousness . . . hopes to acclimate to a world of grayish compromise and concessions.

Sunday
July 12, 1959

Vivian, still wearing her new burgundy church dress so she can flaunt her weight loss, asks Vinny, "What will the birthday boy be doing this evening?"

"Hm . . . a movie might be nice—but I sure don't want it to be that nun movie."

"I thought you liked Audrey Hepburn," Mary says, rinsing the lunch dishes.

"Seeing her as a nun might ruin her for me."

"I thought you said Two-Man was throwing you a party tonight," Mary says. She picks up a dish towel and dries her hands.

"He is," Vinny says, "but I didn't think you would want to go if it wasn't at Mosca's." He winces. "It's at the Beverly Country Club in Jefferson."

Norman raises his eyebrows, but doesn't look up from the broad sheets of the *Houma Daily Courier*.

"Why wouldn't we go? It's your party!"

"There . . . won't be cupcakes and ice cream, Mary," Vinny says, consciously respecting Norman's parameters.

Mary throws down the dish towel. "I think I can handle a grownup party."

"I'm guessing this 'grownup party' will go past midnight," Norman wonders aloud. "Don't you have school or something?" he asks Mary.

Vivian places a hand on his shoulder. "It's summertime, dear—and it's Vinny's *birthday*."

"Fine," Norman growls. Flinging his paper down, he leaves his seat at the kitchen table to smoke his pipe on the front porch.

Vinny looks at Mary. "Do you still want to go?"

"Yes! I think we should."

"Go ahead and get dressed, then," he sighs, looking at his watch.

Once Mary is out of a quick shower and in her room, she can hear two male voices quarreling outside in the cross-breeze, one clearly her father's.

"She *is* still a virgin!" Vinny's voice carries through her open bedroom window. "I can't believe after all this time that you still don't trust me!"

There is a pause before Vinny's car door slams, the engine roars, and his tires kick up loose shells as he tears down the road.

Still beaded with water and wrapped in a bath towel, Mary runs downstairs and onto the porch. She stares at Vinny's fading trail of dust. *"What did you do?!"* she screeches at her father.

Calmly, Norman puffs on his pipe, rocking in his chair. "Don't you worry. He's coming back. Like a damn lizard tail, that one." He shakes his head.

Mary stares at him, unbelieving. "He only wants to have a family. Why do you have to keep pushing him away?"

"Something is off with that boy and I can't put my finger on it," Norman says. "Until I do, I can't trust him."

"Can't you trust *me?*"

Norman stops rocking. He grips the bowl of his pipe, drops his hand and eyes to answer. "You need another coat or two."

"It's ninety degrees out here!" Mary stomps her naked foot, confused and irritated.

"You are an unfinished plank. Without several coats of varnish, you won't last a week in the weather of 'grownup parties.' " Norman stabs toward the road with the bit of his pipe. "And that boy is a storm waiting to happen."

"I'm not some ignorant piece of wood! I've been tested—I have the highest scores in the parish. And I think I can make my own educated decisions from now on!"

Norman flinches when the screen door slams behind Mary. His daughter is forging ahead, preparing to join the adult world . . . or at least look the part.

At 6:25, Vinny honks the horn, engine running, still too angry to face Mary's father. Norman sits on the porch, helpless, and considers getting his shotgun to do what he should have done the first day and run him off. Mary emerges and glares at her father, reminding him why that wouldn't work.

Vinny hops out of the car to graciously escort Mary and secure her in the passenger seat. "You look smashing," he says, still adamantly ignoring the man on the porch.

"You look pretty good yourself." Mary watches her twenty-one-year-old Adonis walk back to the driver's side. "Where did you go this afternoon?"

"I got dressed at Chick's place," he says, and throws the car in Reverse.

Mary sees her father stand up on the porch, pleading with his eyes for her to get out of the car. But she feels too pretty and too proud to give up the potential for fun this evening. Fluffing her petticoat, she asks Vinny, "Aren't Chick and Gayle coming to the party?"

"Nope," he says, snorting. "They've turned into old married fogeys."

Arriving at the country club, Mary is awed by the Beverly's fancy white pillared plantation exterior. A valet opens her door and escorts her around the car, handing her off to Vinny, who tosses him the car keys.

Walking up the steps, she feels like Cinderella at the ball wearing a silver-blue ballerina-length party dress.

What do I do when the clock strikes midnight?

she thinks, and giggles to herself.

Another man opens the large front door, revealing the spacious interior, filled with laughter and activity. Mary frowns—all the other females within sight are wearing skin-tight sheath dresses barely to their knees.

"There you are!" A woman holding a drink clings to Vinny's neck. With disgust on his face, he peels her away. "Happy Birthday, honey," she slurs, undeterred and unsteady on her feet.

Camille appears, batting her smoky cat eyes, dark blonde hair teased and varnished into an elaborate updo, waistline and hips hugged by a sheath dress just like the others, hers a sparkling silver. "Darling!" she cries, and kisses each of Vinny's cheeks like in the movies. She steps back to evaluate Mary, and smiles condescendingly. "Oh, how *quaint*."

Vinny whispers in Camille's ear, and winks at Mary.

"Come with me, kid," Camille tells her. "I have a bag of tricks in the other room." She takes Mary's hand and leads her to a quiet space to add some finishing touches to Mary's lips and eyes.

"Now look to the left," Camille says, dragging a brush through Mary's top right eyelashes. "Now look at me," she says, her hand placed lightly beneath Mary's chin, making a final inspection. "All done."

Back in party central, Two-Man and Vinny are catching up.

"Yeah, I've been meaning to ask you about that middle of yours." Vinny dauntlessly rubs the tall man's Buddha belly. "What happened to the washboard?"

Two-Man narrows his large brown eyes, tucks his thick bottom lip, and coolly runs his large hands over the faded sides of his buzz cut. "Don't be fooled," he says as he shadow boxes a three-punch combo, landing a light jab on Vinny's chin. "I might be in a different weight class, but I can still take you in or out of the ring."

"Of that I have no doubt, big guy," Vinny laughs.

"I'm retired, remember?" Two-Man says. He playfully tugs at his collar, shrugs his meaty shoulders, and adds, "I'm a lover, not a fighter."

Vinny raises his eyebrows. "How's that workin for ya?"

Mary returns anew, her feminine warpaint expertly applied, and notices several dirty looks thrown her way from other women upon entering the room.

Vinny's eyes light up when he sees her. He wraps his arm around her, which elicits more dirty looks.

"I am so glad you guys decided to come," says Two-Man. "I can get you a Shirley Temple if you'd like, Mary."

"Nah," laughs Camille, "fix the lady a *real* drink!"

"I think a Shirley Temple will do fine for now," Vinny says, patting Mary's hip.

The party is in full swing now. Mary feels more comfortable with the company and surroundings. She takes little sips of champagne from a coupe glass she is offered by a man with a tray. Someone rolls out an enormous cake and starts the crowd singing "Happy Birthday" to Vinny. At the end of the song, there's a *pop!* and all eyes are drawn to the top of the cake, where it has burst open. The crowd cheers with delight. Before Mary can see the gift inside, she loses contact with the ground as Vinny scoops her up and they slip behind a large and heavy tapestry, swiftly disappearing into a hidden alcove that leads to a private poker room.

Successful in abducting her from the crowd, he sets her down. Mary feels bewildered, special, as if she is being secretly inducted into the *Illusionists' Code*. Before she can utter a word, he kisses her full on the lips, pressing into her. Inhaling his aftershave, every muscle in Mary's body releases; her brain is left numb, his mouth on her ear, her neck, her chest. His fingers entangle her hair and gently tug her head back.

"I want you," he says in a low, sultry growl, before engaging her full, parted lips again.

"I want you, too—but not now, not like this," she whispers; she enjoys his strong hands pawing at her, but she can hear the crowd begin to question the birthday boy's whereabouts.

"There's a room," he says, picking her up.

She swats his chest in protest, laughing nervously. "You're insane!"

Vinny puts her back down. "I thought when you got into the car tonight, you were choosing me."

"I *did* choose you," she says, her lips quivering.

"Then what is it? Is it that boy?"

"What boy?"

"That music boy . . . Bobby," he says, rubbing his neck. "The one that keeps calling your house."

"No—" Mary says, with wide eyes and another uncomfortable laugh. She reaches for Vinny's shoulder but he recoils. "It's just too scary with all these people around. I want my first time to be private and special, Vinny."

He considers this a moment while his head cools. "You're right. I don't know what got into me." He takes her hand and puts it over his pounding heart. "I love you, and I promised to wait until you were ready."

"I love you, too," she says, kissing his cheek. She can hear the beginnings of a song with a good dance beat. "Now let's enjoy the rest of your party!"

They reappear, smudged and mussed, into the room filled with revelry. Those who catch sight of them approve of their disappearance with laughter, winks, and upward thumbs. Mary is shocked to see that the present from the inside of Vinny's cake is a young woman dancing atop a short table, jiggling and shaking to the music; the woman is wearing the briefest bathing suit Mary has ever seen.

She frowns and looks at Vinny, who holds up his hands feigning ignorance. "I chose you," he says, performing a rock step and agilely guiding Mary through a few Latin-y swing dances.

Finally they collapse on a couch, sweat dripping, to sit the next song out. Two-Man waves Vinny over to the bar.

"Stay here," Vinny tells Mary. "I'll get us some water."

"Yes, please." Mary fans herself, looking around at all the misbehaving adults.

Kansas is far, far away indeed,

she thinks, and giggles to herself. Perhaps she's had too many sips of champagne.

By the bar, Vinny shoves a cigarette in his mouth. Two-Man flicks open a Zippo and holds the flame to the end while Vinny puffs.

"Thanks for the save." Vinny exhales smoke from his nostrils, looking like a sweaty, sexy dragon. "For making the girl put on a swimsuit."

"That's what good friends do," Two-Man chuckles. "What else can I do ya for?"

"I could use a couple favors," Vinny says, and takes another drag.

"You name it. Twenty-one is a big year, kid." Two-Man slaps a hand on Vinny's back and downs a whiskey shooter.

"It won't be until fall. Will you still be around?"

"I can make it so," he says, tapping the bar for another shot.

"Can I get a couple talls of water to go along with that?" Vinny asks the bartender as he pours, handing him a five-spot. He turns back to Two-Man and tells him, "I need some of that magic dust."

"Which powder are we talking about?" Two-Man asks, ready to throw the whiskey down his hatch.

Vinny gives the bar a jab with his toe. "The one that makes the females more cooperative."

Two-Man's whiskey spritzes from his face. "Well, I'll be a monkey's uncle," he says, wiping his chin with his sleeve.

"Don't give me a hard time about it. Can you get it or not?"

"I can get it," he snickers, "so *you* can get it."

Vinny's eyes flare. The bartender slides two glasses of water to him, and he starts to walk away.

Two-Man stops him. "Come on, I'm just fuckin with ya. What was the other thing?"

"Remember the scarecrow?"

"Yeah." Two-Man rubs his chin. "That Vicknair kid?"

"That's the one," Vinny confirms. "I want you to teach him a lesson he won't soon forget."

Monday
August 10, 1959

"**B**low them lights out already!" Vinny shouts.

"I'm fuckin trying to!" Chick says, winded as he hovers over his Betty Crocker birthday cake.

"Don't *spit* on the damn thing!" Gayle says, pouring a short glass of water from her kitchen faucet and handing it off to Mary.

"I'm sorry," Mary says to her. "We saw them at the market when we bought the present and thought it would be funny." She plucks the trick candles out one by one and douses them in the glass of water.

"It *is* funny," Gayle says. "I just don't want him to ruin the first homemade cake I ever baked by myself." She stabs the lopsided sheet cake with her brand-new orange serving knife.

"What a nifty little gadget," Mary says.

"Mom invited me to go along to a Tupperware party," says Gayle. She drops a piece of cake onto a paper plate and hands it to the first victim—her husband, the birthday boy. "I think I'm going to be a sales consultant," Gayle continues. "I can have parties and sell Tupperware from home." She plops another piece down and hands the paper plate to Vinny.

The guys look at each other, daring the other to take the first bite.

"It's not *poisoned*," Gayle tells them. She hands Mary her slice, then licks her finger. "See?" She takes a bite from the piece she's served herself.

"Hey, this is pretty good," Chick says.

" 'Mix with water and eggs,' " Gayle recites. "How could I flub that up?" She tosses the box into the trash bin.

They all look at one another, remembering the time she put salt instead of sugar in an apple pie for the church bake sale.

"We're sure sorry we didn't go to your birthday party, Vinny," says Chick. He is already cutting himself another piece of cake, and Gayle smiles, proud of her small success. "I've been so beat from work, I just can't stay up that late anymore."

"You didn't miss much," Vinny lies.

"I bet." Chick says, knowing better. Mary has already informed Gayle all about her peek into the private pleasure dome in Jefferson Parish.

Fortunately, Gayle is enjoying her stint as a newlywed and no longer craves the excitement of the wild—just that of her marital bed. Which is why she keeps the evening short and sweet, practically shoving her guests out of the door just after seven o'clock.

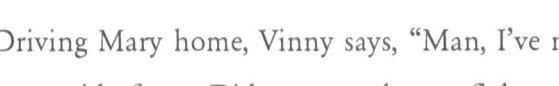

Driving Mary home, Vinny says, "Man, I've never seen her so eager to get rid of you. Did you guys have a fight or something?"

"No . . ." Mary smiles knowingly. "She wants to get pregnant."

"Ahhh," he says. "I see. But school starts next month. She can't go *pregnant,* can she?"

Mary shakes her head, more than a bit disapprovingly. "School never was much of a priority for her. She would gladly quit to stay home with a baby."

Mary shudders at the thought.

Saturday
September 5, 1959

Vinny casually tugs at his sleeve, releasing a small amount of a powdery substance. It fizzes in the tall, fluted champagne glass destined for Mary's lips. Like a seasoned Motown artist, he spins away from the bar and glides to their table, where Mary sits enjoying the last bite of their one-year anniversary celebratory feast.

"What is this?" she asks with an apprehensive smile.

"A toast, my lady . . . to our wonderful first year together." He hands her the delicately stemmed glass and they share a cheerful *clink!*

The bubbles tickle her nose and she swallows an ample amount of the sparkling wine.

"It has been such an incredible year," she says. "So much has changed."

"For the better, I hope."

"Oh, yes! I feel so . . ."

". . . happy?" Vinny says hopefully.

"Yes, I *am* happy," she says, and takes another swig of alcohol.

"Happy enough to spend your life with me?" Vinny asks. He places his still-full glass on the table and gets down on a well-adorned knee, his hand smoothly revealing a small black velvet box.

Mary gasps, her hand finding her face to cover the little smile of pleasure that she could not otherwise hide. Her head feels light and buzzy as she searches for an answer. She looks around at the other patrons in the restaurant, who have all stopped their activities to witness the proposal.

Vinny opens the box to reveal a European-cut diamond ring with a petal motif at its shoulders, giving it the look of a dazzling flower.

"It's a vintage design. If you don't like it . . ." His eyes are steady, soulful, even though his body is shifting uncomfortably as he awaits her answer.

"I love it . . . and I love *you*," Mary says, with tearful eyes and a sniff. "Yes. *Yes*, I'll marry you!"

Vinny slips the diamond ring on her finger before she has a chance to change her mind. She feels her feet leave the floor as he lifts her in a spin that catches up with her head and ends in a long, lippy kiss. Cheers from throughout the dining room add to the joy and excitement of this unforgettable moment—one of many unforgettable moments she will soon share with her husband-to-be.

"One more toast for the road," Vinny says. He plucks his glass from the table and raises it to the restaurant's patrons. "To my future wife!"

The room cheers with renewed vigor. From the corner of his eye, he watches Mary take the last of her dose, and they set their fluted glasses down to leave.

The night is electric. Excitement builds in the bodies of the couple as they cuddle in the backseat on their taxi ride to the Monteleone. A rush of blood fills Mary with enough heat for her to remove her wrap in the lobby of the hotel. She lets it fall to the floor unceremoniously and reaches for her dress zipper.

"Honey, no," Vinny chuckles. "Wait until we get to the room." He retrieves the fabric and waves to a guy at the front desk.

"The room?" Mary giggles. "Just the two of us?" She bites her lip and stumbles into the open elevator.

Vinny steadies her, pulling her body close to his. "Just you and me, doll," he purrs, touching her plump bottom lip with his thumb.

Feeling the heat again, and giggling even more, she fans herself using her skirt. Vinny slides his hand beneath her slip, running his thumb along her vertical smile, warm and wet through her thin cotton panties. His eyes are trained on hers; her pupils dilate. Her body responds to his soft touch, her hips slowly undulating. He licks his lips, watching her mouth fall open.

The elevator stops and opens on their floor. Vinny pets her skirt back down and takes her hand to lead her to his room—to his bed. Mary's mind doesn't argue, resist, or allow a thought over her body's pulsating scream for more of his touch, his mouth, to have his skin on hers.

Hours later, blindly reaching for a glass of water on the bedside table in the early morning light sends Mary's head swimming. When the glass is empty, she opens her eyes to see her dress from last night crumpled on the floor. She stares at it bleakly.

Wrapping herself in a sheet, she crosses the room to the window and stands looking out over the Mississippi. The river looks altered somehow from this height ... or maybe just her perception has changed. She looks upon the river as it is, still no thoughts to jumble and confuse her mind.

When she hears Vinny say "Come back to bed," her body responds. She lets the sheet fall away from her shoulders, revealing the soft, supple flesh of her breasts, and eagerly returns to the satin playground where she has lost her innocence.

Monday
September 7, 1959

"I'm married and** you're engaged, Mary. It's perfectly healthy to talk about this stuff," Gayle fishes. She knows her best friend, can smell that there is something amiss, and wants to know more.

Walking ever closer to the condemnatory school building, wearing her invisible cloak of shame in silence, Mary hides the racy details of what has transpired with Vinny over the weekend. She is unable to fully understand or explain what happened without revealing that she is thrice a wicked fornicator.

I would gladly toss the cloak, tattered morals, and all
of my clothing aside to only feel and not think.

Gayle plays with Mary's hair, looking for evidence of passion on her neck as they walk. "So ... a perfect gentleman, huh? All weekend?"

Mary stops to listen. "The campus seems different," she says, referring to the eerie calm of the breezeway leading to the main school building.

"No Ettes," a male voice says from behind the building. A boy steps into view, taking a last drag on a cigarette.

"Really? No kidding? We just saw them last week," says Gayle.

"Yeah," the boy confirms, exhaling smoke with the single word. "They all transferred to Vandebilt, the private Catholic school."

"Even Veronica?" asks Gayle.

"Yep. All Vandy candy now."

"Good riddance!"

The boy snorts. "Most guys around here don't agree. That's why it's so quiet—they're all in mourning."

"But not you?" Gayle says.

He drops his cigarette and crushes it beneath one foot. "I don't mind doing a little work for my rewards," he says, and disappears into the building.

Mary turns to Gayle. "Who was that?"

Gayle shrugs, pulling the door open for Mary. "No idea. I only know him as the bearer of good news."

"Good news, indeed! The fires of tyranny are vanquished!" Mary's voice echoes in the hallway.

"Well, now," Gayle smirks, letting the door slam behind her. "I guess *someone* did their summer reading assignments."

"I suppose this means we'll have to change all the formations we just learned in cheer squad," says Mary, not the least bit regretfully. "Wonder why it was so sudden."

Bobby appears from around the corner, slipping a bit on the freshly buffed floor. "You are never gonna believe what I just heard!"

"That the fires of tyranny are vanquished?" Gayle says.

"Huh? Uhh, no," he replies. "Veronica and her kind have vacated! Gone."

"Do you know what happened?" Mary asks. "I mean, why so sudden?"

"Well, at the last PTA meeting, they announced we're supposed to imminently integrate all the public schools."

"Is that all? Let them run." Mary snorts derisively. "They can't buy their way out of the changes that are coming."

"We lost some key players," says Bobby. "The coach is furious. Now Vandebilt has a fighting chance against us on the field."

"Won't we gain any *new* players in the process?" Gayle asks.

Bobby nods. "We did. We spent the whole weekend training and helping the new guys learn the playbook."

"This could be good," Mary says. "Shake things up, get us motivated."

"We'll find out soon enough," says Bobby.

He turns Mary by the shoulders toward the main entrance, where two athletically built male students with dark skin timidly enter the hall into a silence of stunned disbelief, punctuated by a few loosed books and pencils that drop to the floor.

To everyone's discomfort—and to some students' disgust—Mary charges over to greet them, disarming the boys with a warm smile. "Welcome to Terrebonne, gentlemen."

Gayle shrugs and pats Bobby on the shoulder. "Gotta hand it to her, Bob, she's good at making friends."

His concerned eyes turn to the sour faces in the hall and adds, "And enemies."

Friday
September 11, 1959

Having just finished the final refrain of a song about beating the Terriers, Gayle and Mary step off the bus and look over at a group of Vandebilt girls ready to cheer for the home team.

"You girls got a problem with Vandebilt?" one of the Ettes says to them, loud enough to get the attention of a made-over Veronica, who charges over with hands on her hips. She displays her brand-new royal-blue-and-gold cheer uniform while swinging her Jean Harlow hair. The uniform is a new look for her. Back at Terrebonne, she could never hold her grades high enough to make the cheer squad.

Bobby steps in front of Mary, shielding her from any venom emitted by the peroxide-blonde harpy.

"It's a fine school," Mary replies over Bobby's shoulder. "They just aren't picky enough about the people they allow to enroll."

"Only if you got the money, honey," Veronica sneers.

"That's what all the prostitutes are saying," taunts Gayle.

Veronica snorts and snaps her fingers, signaling her girls into formation. "Are you ready?" she barks.

"Ready, okay!" the rest of the squad barks back, happy to perform a prepared welcome cheer.

"One, two, three, four!" Veronica shouts.

"We'll watch your Negros hit the floor!" the squad yells back. In practiced unison, the Terrier squad continues:

"That's all right,
That's okay,
You will pump our gas someday!
We've got spirit,
We've got rule,
We've got the money to buy your school!"

The nasty reception doesn't stop here, but continues on the football field. Mary is not surprised at children without fully formed brains who treat each other with malice and cruelty. It is the adults who jeer and spit whom she cannot understand or forgive. But all their hate combined cannot secure a victory for the home team against the tenacious Terrebonne Tigers. Not everyone at Terrebonne is happy about the changing landscape of the student body—but when it comes to a football win, those individuals choose to temporarily turn a colorblind eye.

Friday
October 2, 1959

Mary and Vivian wake up with violent stomachs. Nauseated and unable to see herself cheering for the Tigers at tonight's home game, Mary calls the school to warn them of her absence. She then immediately turns to her duties in the kitchen—the children don't have her sickness, and are likely starving.

"Go back to bed, Mary. We have this under control," Jason tells her, pouring juice for the smaller ones.

Mary, ever doubtful of her siblings' ability to have anything under control without her, looks to Charlie, who gives her a confirmative *Aye-aye, Captain* salute with the spatula he is using to push eggs around in the skillet.

Before she can resist, her stomach presents its own argument, and her embarrassed feet carry her up the stairs. She is unable to make the toilet, so she settles for the sink, rinses her mouth, averts her gaze in the vanity mirror, and shuffles weakly back to bed.

After school, Bobby straggles behind. Swinging his helmet, he ambles from the locker room to the staging area in the stadium. In his head, he is already making an immaculate reception.

A massive shadow stealthily swallows him into a corridor within the belly of the stadium hall, knocking the helmet from his hand. It skids along the cement, coming to a halt against the wall.

The large figure hugs Bobby painfully tight from behind and whispers in his ear, "You were warned to stay away from Mary. Now you will suffer—and it's your own fault."

Bobby doesn't move or speak. He's frozen with fear. Overpowered from the start, he goes limp, with no idea of what comes next.

"You *asked* for this, right?" the figure demands with a shake. *"Right?"*

Bobby slowly nods his head, not knowing if he is permitted to speak.

"That's right! And don't you forget it!" The figure shoves him to the ground and is gone faster than anyone that large should be able to move.

Bobby stays on the ground for a moment, then picks himself up, retrieving his helmet. *Was that . . . it?* he wonders. Somehow, he doubts the "suffering" is over.

Just before the game starts, Bobby arrives at the back of the bunch behind the banner held by members of the cheer squad. He sees Gayle. She locks eyes with him and can tell something is terribly wrong. His lips move frantically, trying to tell her something.

The coach looks puzzled at Bobby's disheveled state. "You ready, boy? 'Cuz this is your shot! A scout from LSU is up there in the stands waiting for a show!"

Bobby, still stunned, just nods slowly. He secures his helmet and waits for Coach to blow the whistle. The team rips through the banner and takes their places on the field. Bobby temporarily releases his fear so he can focus on the game. He makes two impressive receptions in the second quarter, despite—or perhaps because of—the many random disturbing thoughts that tug at his brain.

Late in the fourth, victory for his team assured, the rest a pure formality as he lines up for the next down, Bobby looks up at his opponents . . . into a new pair of eyes. These eyes are dilated with purpose above lips set in a sneer. The snap is made. Bobby tries to avoid the truck of a player, who is coming straight at him for a head-on collision, but it is hopeless. Bobby now knows what the large figure meant by "suffering." The play is over, the clock runs out—and Bobby is on the ground, crushed beneath the truck.

"Watch whose girl you snake around next time, Bobby Boy," the player growls as he rises from Bobby's contorted leg.

Gayle rushes to Bobby on the field. When she gets close enough to see his twisted limb, she passes out. The scout from LSU is on the sideline, a hand over his mouth, watching the medics peel Bobby off the field and onto a stretcher. Coach Grabert is hovering next to Bobby, making sure they don't injure his player further.

"Sorry, Coach," Bobby manages between pained sobs.

"You got nothing to be sorry for." Coach Grabert's voice cracks, running the back of his hand across his eyes. He walks beside the stretcher as it is rolled off the field to the ambulance standing by.

One of the medics snaps an ampule of smelling salts. He waves it beneath Gayle's nose, rousing her from unconsciousness. As Gayle comes to, she can hear Brenda Vicknair's hysterical crying over someone's ineffectual consolation.

"Wait!" Gayle's voice travels to the stretcher faster than her revived legs can get to him.

Bobby winces trying to twist around to see her.

"Don't move," she says, reaching out to him. "Please be okay."

"I need to see Mary," Bobby says hoarsely. He begins to gasp for air. The medics slide the stretcher into the ambulance, and one of them slips an oxygen mask over his face.

The coach lifts Brenda on-board to sit beside her injured son. Her attention is entirely focused on each word uttered and each action performed by the medics.

"My husband is a doctor at Terrebonne General," she tells them.

"I will bring her to you! Don't worry," Gayle calls to Bobby just before the doors close and the ambulance rushes off, flashing and screaming into the night.

Earlier that evening, Norman sits in the chair on the front porch to witness the dying of the day. Mary knows this ritual well. Her stomach feeling much better, she takes advantage of the freedom to join him, stepping quietly onto the squeaky wood. She parks beside his feet and let her own swing freely off the porch edge.

"It sure has been a lovely day," she says. She hugs on her father's leg like she used to do before she could reach his knee.

Norman makes a happy grunt, chewing on the bit of his pipe. She lifts her head to look at him. He winks back at her, smoothing her hair with loving fingers.

Mary's eyes return to the sky ablaze with the rich, fiery color of the gathering dusk. Her lungs fill deeply with the sweet fragrance of cane becoming sugar in the nearby mill. No fields burn this evening, leaving the breeze clear and crisp.

She thinks,

If time were my friend, I could linger in this moment for an eternity.

A moment or two later, her leg endures the rude prick of a mosquito that has found itself a tasty snack. "No matter how cool it gets around here, somehow the pests survive," she says, rubbing the itchy spot on her shin.

Norman agrees with a sleepy nod. A chill wind blows sharply, rustling what is left of the leaves on the pecan tree, and the wind chimes tinkle their reply.

"Hey, Pa, I thought you wanted to catch the premiere of that new show, *The Twilight Zone*. It will be on soon."

"I s'pose I won't be watchin anything 'cept the inside of my lids without some coffee," he slurs sleepily.

"I'll go brew some for you. Wouldn't want you to miss it." She hops up to kiss his balding head. "I'll come and get you when it's ready."

"I love you, Mary. You make me proud," he says to her back as she leaves.

"I love you more for showing me how," she responds through the mesh of the screen door.

As Mary enters the kitchen, she finds Charlie, busy rinsing and loading the dinner dishes into the crowded grid of the Hotpoint dishwasher. She waits patiently to use the faucet to fill the percolator. She sets the contraption up to brew coffee like she's done so many times before, always trying to find the secret to the perfect cup of java. She has never been a huge fan of the hot brew, but she must taste it each time because her father will never complain. Once, it was almost thick enough to eat with a fork—and Norman still asked for a second cup as if nothing were awry. She knew then that a father's love must be deep and wide.

"His program will start before that coffee is ready, you know," Charlie says, rinsing the last of the dishes.

Mary knows Charlie may be right, but she has to reduce the heat under the spurting percolator, careful not to burn.

"I'll go get him," he says. "I know you want to keep your hawk-eye on that pot."

"Tell him it will only be a few more minutes. He's so tired today." Mary adjusts the heat again.

Charlie kisses his sister's cheek, then goes to find his father a prime seat in front of the television.

Mary hums as she confidently reaches for a mug and the sugar jar. As soon as she places one of two ample spoonfuls of granulated sweetness in the mug, Charlie's hand covers it.

She smiles in exasperation. "Stop clowning!" she starts to fuss.

But when she looks up, she sees in Charlie's face that he is not. His eyes are wide and wild.

Something's wrong with Pa,

she thinks, and her feet move before she gives them permission, carrying her to her father on the front porch. Mary's legs give way, her throat tightens, and both hands cover her mouth to hold back a horrified scream at seeing Norman's pipe lay dejected on the porch beneath his limp fingers, his eyes locked in a frozen stare where the fading sun was several moments ago.

"Da—Daddy?" she mutters. Shaking with grief, blinded by tears, Mary crawls next to his lukewarm shell and reaches up to close the lids on his twinkle-less orbs, unable to stomach their cold gaze. She desperately clings to her father's leg. "Daddy . . ." she sobs, her tears absorbing into the fabric of his faded jeans. "Daddy, don't leave!"

But Norman is no longer there—just the body he has left behind.

Charlie, still in a state of shock himself, knows that Mary needs this minute before he alerts anyone else. He walks slowly behind her and puts his hand on her shoulder to lend her some strength to bear the unbearable together. When he hears the children stirring inside, he swipes his tears away, clears his throat, and straightens his back like a newly crowned king. "We have to be strong for the others," he says numbly, more to himself than to her, and adds, "He's watching . . . we must make him proud."

Mary nods weakly.

The screen door flings open. "That silly program is on!" says Vivian, emerging from the house. She freezes and the door slams behind her. "What's going on here?"

Charlie goes to Vivian and holds her arms gently. "Mama, he's gone."

"What the hell are you talking about? Move outta my way!" Vivian pushes past Charlie to where Mary still has her face against a hand that so many had depended upon.

Vivian kicks Norman's work boot and screams, "Get up and come watch your show! You've been going on and on about it—like ta made me crazy!"

Mary flashes angry warning-eyes at her mother for touching him in such a way. She wipes her snotted nose and says between clenched teeth, "Don't!"

Vivian's face becomes red and wet with crescive fear. Determined to wake everyone from this hellish dream, she kicks his boot again and adds in that same obstinate voice, "Right now!"

Taller than she was this morning, Mary rises to her feet. "Back off, Mama! Go call someone."

Vivian slaps Mary's face, hard. Nevertheless, she turns to do as her daughter instructed and rushes through the sea of children who are now spilling out of the doorway, triggering a symphony of tears.

Gayle arrives at the Poche house still wearing her cheer uniform from the football game. Mary doesn't register that her friend no longer lives across the street, or that the only call made was to the coroner, whose vehicle has already pulled away with Norman's body.

"Something *terrible* has happened!" Gayle yells—meaning Bobby, of course, though Mary doesn't know it—jumping out of the Woody before it comes to a complete stop. She runs to Mary, who is standing alone on the porch.

"My daddy!" Mary crumples on the porch and weeps once again. "He's d-*dead*!"

Gayle pauses, halfway across the front lawn. She stares at her best friend, suddenly disoriented, then a choked sob bursts from her throat. "No! Oh my god, *no*!" Gayle rushes to embrace her friend there on the porch. "I am so ... so *sorry*, Mary," she cries, squeezing her own eyes shut against the salty tears. Gayle pulls Mary in tight to weather the next debilitating wave of grief.

Shirley leaves the car and tries to join the moment, but Gayle quickly shoos her away. Rejected, Shirley points to the Gautreau house and sets the car keys down gently next to the newly licensed driver on the porch. Gayle nods in understanding. She watches her parents walk to their house to make a few urgent and necessary phone calls.

After a long period of hugging and swaying, Mary pulls away to wipe her drippy nose with her sleeve, for lack of a better option. Gayle stares at her, as she does whenever there is something serious to say but she cannot find any serious words.

"Out with it," Mary says.

"I can't, Mary. You're in so much pain already. It just feels wrong to pile on," Gayle says, then checks out her wet, slimy shoulder.

"N-nothing you say can possibly make things w-worse." Mary takes a calming breath. "If I'm strong enough to continue breathing right now, I can handle anything. Just, please . . . don't drag it out."

Gayle draws a long, haggard breath. "Bobby was hurt real bad tonight at the game. He's in the hospital."

Unresponsive, Mary hugs herself and begins to rock.

Gayle continues, "My mom thinks we should go to the hospital to show our support. Everyone else rode the bus there from the game."

Mary shrinks, her knees pulling up close to her heart. "I don't know if I can face anyone right now."

"I understand if you can't . . . and Bobby will understand, too. I just wanted you to know." Gayle glances furtively at Mary and adds, "And there's something else."

"Please, no more bad news." Mary clutches herself tighter, pressing her face to her knees. "I'm drowning, Gayle."

Gayle fights the urge to sob again. "I know, but . . . Bobby tried to tell me something right before the game. He looked like he'd seen a ghost."

Once again, Mary is unresponsive.

Shirley returns with James, walking with somber faces into the driveway to offer assistance and words of encouragement. They both look upon Mary in her upright fetal position. Shirley bends to kiss her on the head and rubs her back before entering the house to help Vivian with the children. James shoves his hands deep in his pockets and grasps the lining.

"I'm sorry about your dad," he says quietly. "Norman was a wonderful man. We all loved him. His loss will be felt a long time. But there isn't anything you can do for him now." James clears his throat and glances at Gayle's pleading face. "There's a young man who is hurt, afraid, and could use his friends right now. No one will blame you if you don't go. But might you regret it later?"

Shirley looks up when she hears the screen door bang open and sees Mary charging up the stairs. "What happened?" she asks James as he enters the kitchen.

"She's just changing her shirt," he answers.

"Where in the hell does she think *she's* going?" Vivian asks.

"A friend from school was taken to the hospital this evening and Gayle was coming to get her." Shirley drops her eyes and inhales. "Before we knew about Norman," she adds.

Charlie walks in the back door after a long session of petting Christmas. He's holding Norman's pipe. "Is Mary all right?"

"Your father isn't even cold yet and your sister has just decided to do whatever the hell she wants!" Vivian yells, throwing her hands in the air.

"They won't be gone long," Shirley says apologetically. "James and I will stay and help. We'll do anything you need us to." She turns her face up to James, who places a hand to her back and nods.

Vivian forces herself back against the cabinet, folds her arms, and stares hatefully at Mary, who is moving slowly, like a ghostly version of herself, into the kitchen. "Are you really going to leave your family at a time like this?" Vivian asks, grabbing hold of the counter, knuckles turning white.

"I'm losing my mind right now, Mama," Mary says, damming an ocean of tears behind her large eyes. "Please don't force me to think."

Charlie rushes to hug his big sister.

Full of spite, Vivian says, "Selfish! Pur-dee selfish is what you are."

"Leave her alone," Charlie says with authority. He looks his mother in the eyes. "I'm the man of this house now, and I say she can go."

Vivian throws up her hands. "It's a damn mutiny around here!" She stomps out of the house, followed by a loud yelp from the poor dog that accidentally gets in her way.

Gayle honks the horn in the Woody.

"Probably worried about missing the last of the visiting hours," James explains of the honk. "You should be going, Mary."

Charlie, still holding his sister, nods and gestures her back out to the porch. "Don't worry about it. Just go," he tells Mary as he walks her out to the car. "Gayle behind the wheel of a car—will this nightmare ever end?" he says, opening the passenger door for his sister.

Mary can't help but smile at his attempt to make her laugh and gets in with Gayle.

Making sure she is all inside, Charlie shuts the car door. "Bring her back home safe, as soon as possible," he tells Gayle in a voice she's surprised to hear sounds ten years older.

"Yes, sir," Gayle says, turning off the radio. "And I'm a good driver, by the way." She cranes around to check behind her before rolling in Reverse. "Sheesh, there's a new sheriff in town," she says, waving goodbye to Charlie as he stands in the beams of her headlights.

Mary can't find any joy for Gayle's new accomplishment. She makes no sound in the shadows as the hot salty tears flow freely upon her grieving face. Terrebonne General Hospital waits for her down the road, housing more horrors to come.

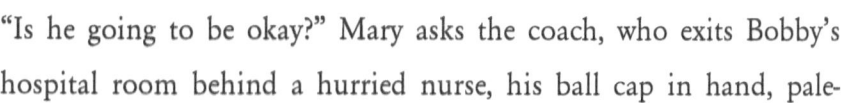

"Is he going to be okay?" Mary asks the coach, who exits Bobby's hospital room behind a hurried nurse, his ball cap in hand, pale-faced, eyes red with worry.

"It doesn't look good," he says, staring at the floor.

Mary feels the floor drop and she dips to follow. The coach's athletic training kicks in with a cat-like reflex, and he breaks her fall.

"I'm so sorry," he says, fanning Mary with his cap. He looks sheepishly to Gayle as she kneels beside them. "That was stupid of me. Bobby is going to live, Mary. But he'll never play football again—the doctor says Bobby's knee was obliterated. Couple of cracked ribs, too. His mother and father are downstairs in the waiting room, telling everyone the news."

Mary struggles to get up. "I have to see him."

The coach helps to put her on her feet. "The nurse told me to leave because she just gave him a sedative. His surgery is scheduled first thing in the morning." The coach looks into Mary's determined eyes, then searches the halls for the nurse. "I'll stand watch while you go in, but only for a minute."

With a silent thank-you, Mary sneaks into the semi-private room. Through an opening in the first curtained cubicle, she sees a figure wrapped in gauze, like a Halloween mummy, one arm hanging from a sling apparatus. The fingers on the suspended arm point her to the next bed, where she finds Bobby lying in a tremendous amount of pain, unable to move for fear of more.

"You came," he whispers.

"Shhh, don't talk," she says, stroking his head. "Just rest."

"I have to tell you something," he slurs, his focus seeming fuzzy. He knits his eyebrows together, straining to remember what was so important.

Mary kisses his cheek and he relaxes.

"I love you, Mary," he says, eyelids drooping. "Stay with me."

"I'm here." Mary holds his hand and begins to hum a lullaby until he falls into a heavy dreamless state, not to awaken again until after his surgery the following morning, to the nightmarish reality of a long and painful recovery . . . for both Bobby and Mary.

Friday
October 16, 1959

"I'm very sorry** for your loss," the doctor says, his stethoscope like ice on Mary's chest.

Her face hangs slack and somber, non-reactive to the cold metal disk through the thin examination gown. A nurse with a salt-and-pepper bun stands in silent witness by the door. Her gaunt face is kind and full of concern.

"Thank you," Mary says, weak with grief.

"Open," he says, coming at her with a tongue depressor. "Say 'Ahhh.' " He must see all he needs to, because he tosses the wooden stick into the trash and begins to test her reflexes. "Lie down, please," he asks robotically.

Mary complies, just as robotic, shifting the noisy paper on the table. His poking and prodding makes her uncomfortable, especially with the fullness of her bladder.

He sits on a rolling stool, pushes back from the exam table, looks at her chart, and makes several notes.

Mary feels uneasy in the silence; it allows her to imagine what it is like on a morgue table. "Can I sit up now?"

"Oh . . . yes," he replies, preoccupied by his paperwork. "It says here that your main complaint is that you haven't been sleeping since your father passed away. That was . . . two weeks ago?"

"That's correct," she says, righting herself and feeling a slight spin of the room.

"The nurse here will take some blood and get a urine sample . . . just to make sure there isn't something else going on," says the doctor, waving errantly at the nurse. "I will see you in my office when you're finished."

The nurse moves closer and hands Mary a small plastic jar. "I'll show you to the restroom after you've dressed, dear," she said. "We'll get the blood after your sample."

With her thin fingers, the nurse places a small Band-Aid over the cotton wad that blots the needle puncture on Mary's arm. "There . . . all done," she announces with a kind smile.

Mary does not see the kindness; her eyes are still closed, her body feeling green around the edges. "I don't feel so good," she moans.

"Oh, dear . . . let me get you some juice." The nurse flees and returns with a small glass of Vitamin C, so fast that Mary feels as if time has become fluid around her. "Please drink it all, then I will show you to the doctor's office. Have you had lunch?"

"No . . . I haven't had much of an appetite lately," Mary replies, in spite of a snarl from her midsection.

"I'm sure I can find you some crackers. I know you're upset, but you need to eat," says the nurse, who looks as if she could use a meal slightly more than Mary. She gently guides Mary down the hall to a small office filled with books and a large wooden desk. She reaches into one of the desk drawers and gets a small package of saltines. "Have these with your juice, dear. That should settle your stomach for now. The doctor will be in shortly."

Just being in a room with rows and rows of knowledge puts Mary more at ease than she has felt since her bedrock crumbled. She puts the cellophane wrapper in the empty drinking glass and sets it on the desk. Unable to deny her nature, she is drawn to the wall of reference manuals. Her fingers walk across their spines until she finds one by Dr. Max Gerson. The book looks new, yet the spine gives easily when she opens it. There are notes scribbled on almost every page. Mary finds it odd that a general physician is so interested in alternative treatments for cancer. She is quite amused reading about how to give yourself a coffee enema, considering that at first she doesn't know what an enema is.

Suddenly she hears the doctor's voice in the hall near the office door. She scrambles to put the book back on the shelf before the door opens.

Luckily the doctor is still eyeing her chart as he enters the room and shuts the door behind him. He takes a seat across from her. "Well, Mary, everything seems normal. I'm going to prescribe a mild sedative, but only use them if you truly feel you need them. Adhere strictly to this dosage. Overuse could be bad for the baby." He tears a slip of paper from his prescription pad and hands it to her.

"Baby?" Mary has not considered the twins to be babies anymore, and is always careful to keep things like this out of reach.

"Ah, yes. I ran a routine pregnancy test and it came out positive. You should make an appointment with an obstetrician to get a second evaluation," he says, closing the chart.

Mary feels her chest hitch with panic. "Could . . . could the test be wrong?"

The doctor clearly does not see how his words are affecting her. "Not likely, but it's always good to have a follow-up appointment to be sure. Besides, it will give you a better idea of what your due date will be." He rises from his chair to shake her hand. "Good luck, and congratulations to you both."

"Thank you for taking good care of me on such short notice," Mary says. Her panic is only being held in check by the relief that Vinny convinced her to see this doctor in New Orleans, instead of one at home.

The doctor opens his office door for her. "Don't worry," he tells Mary. "I'll give Vinny the name of a good obstetrician. You'll be in good hands." She stands and freezes, rigid, a mounting uncertainty in her veins. Taken aback by the candidness of Mary's stare, the doctor pauses to study her, seeing the reflection of his own fears about life and death, the affliction of mortality, in her glassy eyes. "Beginnings can sometimes ease the pain of endings," he says thoughtfully.

After giving him a slow, tentative smile, Mary walks out and her eyes water, surrendering to her new reality.

Sunday
October 18, 1959

Two half-empty cups of coffee are all that lie on the table between mother and soon-to-be grandmother—that and the heavy silence.

Mary is holding onto the table, waiting for the grenade to explode, seeing as she pulled the pin a moment ago.

Vivian is no stranger to surprise pregnancies. She is actually a little relieved that it is not hers for a change. It's Mary's second revelation that has her searching for answers in her ceramic mug. She lifts it to her mouth, takes a sip, and slams it down hard enough to challenge its integrity, which—this time, at least—holds.

Vivian's voice fills the kitchen. "You most certainly will, young lady! It's the only option you have!"

"Mother . . ." Mary takes a steadying breath. "When and if I get married, I want it to be on my terms—not forced because of an unforeseen mishap."

" 'Unforeseen mishap'? Is that what you're gonna name my grandchild?" Vivian snarls.

Mary blanches at her own poorly chosen words being used against her.

Vivian slams her hand on the table this time instead of the frail mug. "You need to stop acting like this was some accident. You know damn well how this happened and now you need to make it right!"

"I need more time to think about my choices," Mary replies.

"I see only one choice here. Don't you love Vinny? You must have loved him six weeks ago—that's how far along the doctor says you are," Vivian digs. "Besides, I can't raise another child."

"*I* raised your children," Mary says matter-of-factly.

"In a family, everyone has a duty, Mary. You will learn that soon enough," Vivian answers in her arrogant tone.

"I agree," Mary says, setting her elbows on the table and clasping her hands, as if to arm-wrestle herself. "I just don't know what *yours* is."

Vivian gasps; her face contorts, inhaling the four winds of Lucifer, and she rises from her seat with an intensely fevered stare. She bares her teeth to her first born. "You will rue this day. Oh, of that I promise you . . . you know-nothing little bitch!"

Horrified, Mary flinches and claps her hands over her ears when Vivian launches these fiery words—along with her coffee mug, which shatters into ceramic fragments that skitter every which way over the tabletop and to the floor. "Marry him, don't marry him, I really don't give a shit anymore! Pack yourself a bag and go shack up with whoever you like . . . 'cause I'm rolling up my welcome mat."

Mary rubs her temples, afraid the outburst isn't over. "You're kicking me out?" she cries.

"You need a dose of the real world, little girl . . . *then* we'll see who needs who around here."

A canvas bag hastily packed with its contents bursting over the top hangs from one of Mary's shoulders, her arm protectively wrapped around a coveted vase as she descends the staircase. Only a shade or two calmer but remorseful for nothing more than her broken cup, Vivian is in the doorway of the kitchen gathering up the ceramic chips—all that is left of her favorite mug—with a broom. Unable to make eye contact, Mary slowly walks to the front door with sobs trapped in her throat. She hesitates, standing in the mouth of the opened screen door, searching for a way to apologize.

Vivian places a hand on her hip and sighs. "Go on . . . fly, birdie, fly."

Saturday
November 14, 1959

"**I** **am excited**," Mary says to Vinny, unconvincingly, desperately trying to find her new normal. As they drive, she balances a brand-new pair of swim goggles on top of a notebook in her lap.

"I hope you take good notes. I've never known him to give away his recipes before," Vinny says, as the car ambles into the empty restaurant parking lot.

"Oh, I will! He promised to teach me how to make your favorite meal . . . start to finish." Mary leans over to give Vinny a quick kiss, then opens the passenger door.

"I have a few errands to run, but I'll be back for the finale," he says before she pushes the door shut. He lingers, smiling as he watches Mary walk in the bright morning sunlight—carrying his budding seed, discreetly growing within her perfect body—into the small building.

Twenty minutes later, in the Mosca's kitchen, Two-Man removes the last of several whole Roma tomatoes from boiling water with a slotted spoon and plunges them into a large bowl of ice water. He places a new batch of tomatoes in the pot and drapes a fresh apron on Mary.

"Always prepare, measure, and chop everything in advance," he explains, handing her a knife and placing a large Vidalia onion on a cutting board. "We're going to hone your knife skills. Having quality tools is key. You must have a sharp blade, so be sure to keep your thumb and fingers outta the way." He demonstrates the significance of cross-, tap-, and rock-chopping.

"Spill all of your best secrets . . . or else," Mary comically threatens, wielding the stainless steel chef's knife. She feels silly in her apron, peering through swim goggles, but she's ready to hack at the onion and dice it into submission.

He chuckles at her appearance, but continues his instruction, shaking his head. "Fresh ingredients will make the best red gravy you've ever tasted," he says, peeling the skin and the seeds from the tomatoes with quick precision and placing the vine-ripened flesh in a bowl.

"I thought we were making a spaghetti sauce."

He responds in a thickened motherland accent, the fingertips of one hand bunched together. "You must have-a de good red gravy to make-a de good spaghet." Two-Man shakes his bunched fingertips and kisses them apart, resembling a small explosion.

After removing the second batch of tomatoes from the heat, he moves to the twin cutting board alongside Mary to smash four cloves of garlic with the blade of his knife, after which he minces them into fine bits. She covets his technique, listening to his excited, labored breathing. She slices eight ounces of mushrooms and a bell pepper, replicating the nuanced knife-rocking maneuvers.

He grabs a bowl topped with a crank handle. "This little fella is called a food mill. I wanted to show you how to use it—because I'm sending you home with it and all the other tools you need to start cooking with style. My gift to you."

"Really?" Mary reaches up to hug his thick neck. "Thank you so much!" She pecks him on the cheek.

Two-Man teaches her to use the food mill to separate the second batch of warm tomatoes from their skins and seeds in short order, leaving her with a fresh sauce base. "You can make the best mashed potatoes with this thing, too," he says as he rinses it off in the sink.

A deep pan sits on a stove-top flame. Into the pan he pours olive oil from a tall green bottle, scraping the garlic, onions, mushrooms, and bell pepper off the cutting board. "A pinch of salt and a pinch of black pepper," he says, tossing in the seasoning. He then pushes the ingredients around the pan with a wooden spoon, smoothly sautéing the onions into translucency. "Vinny likes ground beef in his gravy, so I browned a pound of it just before you got here." Two-Man makes an exchange, sliding a deep pot from the back of the stove and removing the lid; he tilts it for Mary to see the contents. "No secret here. Just strained, brown, and loose."

He usually makes a joke about liking his women this way, but considers the comment too crass in mixed company.

"Dump in the sauce you just made," he continues. On top of the meat, he squishes apart the flesh of the few whole tomatoes he separated earlier. "I like to add texture to my sauce—plus, it's fun. Try it."

Attempting to keep up with his trance-like dance, she pours the sauce and takes the plump tomato heart, feeling it slide apart in the grip of her small hands. She lets the messy pieces fall into the pot, which is already starting to bubble.

He stirs the mixture, splashing in a bit of red wine before pouring an ample swig for himself. Then he tosses in chopped sprigs of oregano and basil and stirs it up again.

"Now we put in the rest and let them all bathe together while we talk about the befores and afters," he says, banging slivers of onion from the spoon on the pot edge. He covers the pot and lowers the heat.

"I have to admit, I don't know much about salads or desserts," Mary says. "I've had a limited repertoire."

"This one is easy," he says, pulling the large salad bowl out of the refrigerator. "I threw this together in seconds." He sets the bowl in front of her and tosses the salad around with tongs. "You can use any kinds of lettuce you want, and any brand of pickled veggies to tang it up. Vinny won't care. Just don't forget the lumps of crab meat—he'll turn his nose up without it."

Mary bites her lip. "Can I have a few minutes to write this all down?"

"Sure. Holler if you need me to repeat anything," he says, peeking at the sauce and waving the aroma to his nose.

Mary finds a pencil by the phone and quickly scrawls several notes to herself. He reads over her shoulder to see if she misses anything important. "Oh, and I know I told you fresh is best, but in a pinch, canned tomatoes can work. Just don't tell anybody you did . . . or that I said it was okay."

"How long does the sauce simmer for?" Mary asks, bouncing the eraser end of the pencil on her cheek.

"Red gravy is usually finished along with the pasta, but with the meat sauce, it takes an hour or so," he says, checking the sauce again, this time with a taste and a stir of the spoon. "Oh, and if it's too acidic, don't use sugar, use bits of carrot."

She adds this tip to her notes while he fills another pot with water at the sink and puts it on a separate burner on the stove.

"This is for our pasta," he explains. He pours an unmeasured amount of salt in his palm and tosses it into the pot. He rinses his hands in the sink and turns the oven to four hundred degrees. He turns back to Mary. "For some recipes I don't like short cuts, but for baking I make exceptions."

Mary learns the value of a box of Flako pie crust mix and a can of Lucky Leaf cherry-pie filling. She brushes the top of the raw pie dough with egg wash before stabbing a few steam vents in its flimsy skin.

"My shortest of shortcuts is to grab myself a fresh pie from Hubig's if I'm in New Orleans." He laughs as he places the pie on a baking sheet in the preheated oven. "Always let the pie sit a bit before serving, or you'll burn the shit . . . I mean *crud* outta your mouth."

Sadly, somewhere in Kansas right now, another girl with the last name Clutter is also teaching someone how to bake a pie, and riskily samples a slice before letting it cool on the last day of her short life.

"Good, our pasta water is boiling," Two-Man says. Next he removes long, dried, anorexic sticks from a box and lays them in the bubbling pot. "Ronzoni noodles are my favorite—next to my mama's spaghetti, of course."

"How long do you leave those in?" Mary asks, picking up the pencil.

"No more than ten minutes, so we'll use a timer," he says, winding the analog ticker beside the oven. He stirs the sauce and says, "If you have all of your tools and ingredients handy, and make good use of your time, it doesn't take all day to cook Vinny's favorites. And if I know my boy Vin, he'll gladly eat leftovers, so don't be afraid to make plenty."

Shortly after the chime of the timer's bell, the pasta is drained and the pie sits finished on a cooling rack.

"Now *we* can cool, too," Two-Man says, tossing the oven mitts on the counter. "There isn't anything left to do before we plate our spaghetti with a sprinkle of Parmesan."

"Shouldn't we clean up?"

Two-Man looks at the dirty dishes. "Nah, help's coming any minute now." His face brightens. "*I* know what we can do." He pulls Mary out of the kitchen and seats her in a chair in the middle of the unlit dining room. "Stay here," he tells her.

Mary follows him with her eyes as he excitedly prances out of the room. She looks around the dim room and imagines how later this evening it would be filled with couples and families, filled with food, laughter, and joy. Her mind tries desperately to not think of loss, and instead of taking baby steps into love, strength, and perseverance.

Her mind is helped along when Two-Man reenters the room and, upon seeing him, Mary laughs in delight.

When Vinny shows his face ten minutes later, Two-Man is playing the accordion and Mary is clapping to the peppy Italian melody. Both are enjoying the fact that Johnny is now in the kitchen cleaning up the mess.

"Hey, I thought this was a cooking lesson!" Vinny laughs. His eyes shine with adoration for the family he is creating for himself, glad to see a genuine smile on Mary's face—the first one since the second day of October.

Two-Man finishes his tune and carefully places his instrument on an empty tabletop. "Lesson's over, which means . . . time to eat!"

"That was *amazing*," Vinny says after the meal. He leans back in his chair, patting his temporary paunch beneath a large napkin he has tucked and draped across his shirt for stain prevention. "I thank both master and student."

Two-Man beams at Mary. "You have passed your test with flying colors, my young chefling. Soon you shall be a culinary ar-*teest*."

"The true test will be if I can replicate all of this on my own," Mary says, touching her new notebook of gourmet guidance as if to absorb its knowledge through osmosis.

"I'll gather up your gifts in a box and bring them out to the car for you," Two-Man says. He hugs Mary and adds, "My little honorary Dago."

"An honorary what?" she asks, pulling back to see his face.

"Forget I said it. It's just a bad joke," he says, releasing her and waving it off.

"I'll help." Vinny pulls the large napkin from his shirt and covers his empty pie plate with it. "Go ahead to the car," he says to Mary, "and I'll be there in a few."

She picks up her things and heads out to Vinny's car, Two-Man's bad joke wiped clean from her thoughts.

After the restaurant door closes behind her, Two-Man asks, "What's on your mind, Gator?"

Vinny looks around, rubbing his neck. "I'm thinking of getting out."

Two-Man walks behind the bar to pour himself a shot of whiskey. "You mean like a temporary stand-down?"

Vinny doesn't answer.

"You do know that no one gets completely out—unless . . ." Two-Man slams the drink into the back of his throat, then holds the back of his hand to his lips until he is sure it goes down.

"Have you ever considered it?" Vinny asks. "Being removed?"

Two-Man coughs. "Like . . . rubbed out?" he asks in an alcohol-husked voice.

"Not *dead* . . . erased."

"No. I like my face way too much to go that route," Two-Man says. He looks at said mug in the mirror behind the bar, then raises his eyebrows. "I guess I might, if it was a choice between that and the joint." He turns back to Vinny. "Wait—tell me you're not thinking about doing that."

"No—but have you known anyone that *has* done it?"

Two-Man turns his face back to the mirror, contemplating this. "I think it might be like an urban legend kinda thing. I don't know that anyone would want to completely lose their identity all the way down to what they see in the mirror."

Friday
November 27, 1959

On the sidewalk in the heart of Houma, Mary fills her lungs in a soft afternoon breeze, beneath large, rustling oak trees near two small concrete goldfish ponds, her hair tucked in an elegant twist, her knocking knees on a path to Vinny—the path leading into the courthouse . . . the path to becoming a married woman.

Close by are several benches lining the sidewalk, and they beckon, serene places to sit and think. But thinking times are over and the decisions are already made—like the purchasing of the palest of stylish blue dresses, almost white. Almost.

Gayle runs down to her from the courthouse steps with a small bouquet of pink and white carnations. "Everyone is in place. The judge said five minutes." Gayle gets a closer look at Mary's complexion. "You okay?"

"I just needed some air," Mary says, a hand wandering unconsciously to her expanding waist.

Gayle hands Mary the bouquet and walks around her, inspecting her dress and hair for needed adjustments. Finding none, she asks, "Ready?"

"No," Mary says. She takes a deep breath, looking up to the sky for any sign of her father. Storm clouds stare back at her, off in the distance, above her clear blue.

"He's there, Mary." Gayle puts a lace-gloved hand on her shoulder.

Mary lowers her head. "Looking down on the mess I'm making."

"Is that what you think? That starting a family is making a mess?"

"I just don't know if I'm doing the right thing."

"We already went over this, Mary. I know you think your father didn't want this for you, but he didn't know about the baby. Don't you think that changes everything?"

"Oh, yeah, I think it changes everything, all right," she replies, a little too prickly for Gayle's particular soft spot concerning her own barren womb.

"What I wouldn't give for the wonderful changes you're going through," Gayle says, touching Mary's stomach. "Now, are you gonna march your cold feet up those steps, or do I have to bring the judge to *you?*"

A jag of lightning flashes, splitting the blue sky in two, as the door to the courthouse lobby closes. Mary and Gayle cling to each other at the loud interposing boom of a thunderclap. The storm is approaching faster now.

Wednesday
December 9, 1959

After a long, uninhibited night of exploration in a pool of luxurious silk-like cotton, Mary pops up on her elbows and looks around the Honeymoon Suite and out the window, her eyes drawn to the opulent vivid blues of the Caribbean Sea. She reaches over to touch the sprawled bronze sinews of her husband's back as he sleeps. Drawn to his broad, warm shoulders, Mary presses her body against him, fitting the serpentine curves of his body to her own. Vinny stirs, then the two twist and rotate until he is spooning her in the expanding bright light of day.

"I can't believe we have to leave all of this tomorrow," Mary sighs.

Vinny pulls her tighter and kisses her neck.

" 'In Xanadu did Kubla Khan a stately pleasure dome decree,' " Mary whispers. The scent of tropical salty air and exotic flowers tantalizes her nose.

"What is that ridiculous nonsense?" he whispers back, continuing to kiss along the seductive curve of her shoulder.

"Just an old poem from my childhood." Mary lowers the sheet to reveal more of her skin for him to kiss. "You hungry?"

"Starving," he says, rolling her onto her back and looming over her with a devilish twinkle in his eyes. Mary giggles and Vinny continues his explorations.

Thursday
December 10, 1959

Boarding the plane to leave their island paradise, they are welcomed into the first-class cabin by a smiling, well-costumed stewardess, seemingly plucked from a magazine, ready to pamper them with amenities galore.

Once Mary is settled and feels the plane rocketing off the runway, she sits forward to touch the window and say a last goodbye to her honeymoon, to the lush green of sleeping Piton peaks, to the long nature walks with adorable wildlife, and to all the breathtaking moments and views of St. Lucia.

Where in the heck am I going now?

she thinks, her brain shaking loose of the honeymoon's dying euphoria.

She turns away from the window, to Vinny. "Are we going to live in your suite in New Orleans?"

"No," Vinny smiles, laying his head against the back of his seat.

The passing stewardess slips a small pillow behind his head for added comfort, for which he thanks her. Mary looks pensive, and offers a brief smile to the uniformed woman while receiving an identical mini-pillow. She waits for the stewardess to leave, then lowers her voice to say, "Please tell me we are not going to live with my mother."

Not that that's an option anymore,

she reminds herself.

"Don't worry," he says, rolling his head to the side to face her. He lifts his eyebrows at her sudden distress. "Chick is boxing up our stuff to help us move into our place. I set up the bedroom before we left. The rest should be there by now."

". . . '*Our* place'?" Mary falls against the seat, stunned; she hugs her pillow, not sure whether to feel elated or mad. "We have a *place*? Why didn't I know about this?"

"A surprise gift to my bride." He interlaces his fingers with hers and lifts her hand up to his lips. "You were so troubled after the funeral." She can feel his warm breath on her sun-kissed and now husband-kissed hand.

"True . . ." she says. "Well, can I at least know where it is? Or is that a secret too?" she adds, getting excited in spite of herself.

"It's only a secret until we arrive—but I have another one that I can tell you about."

"More secrets?" Mary asks, feeling a pressure change in the cabin as the plane lifts farther into the sky.

Vinny smiles at her. "I took on a short job at a shipyard. I start tomorrow morning."

"Ha, ha, very funny."

Vinny blinks at her, showing no sign of comedy.

Mary sits forward again. "Wait . . . are you serious?"

He nods. "I want to try it out for a while. To see if I like it."

"What would you do at a shipyard?"

"I can read blueprints, and I've done some welding before," he says.

Mary shakes her head in awe. "There are so many things about you that I still don't know."

"Good—then it will take a while for you to get bored with me."

"I can't imagine I'll ever be bored when it seems there is a surprise around every corner," Mary says, tucking the pillow in the curve of her neck.

The stewardess returns and asks, "Can I get you lovebirds something to drink? We have water, coffee, tea, soft drinks, and alcoholic beverages available."

"Do you have ginger ale?" Vinny asks and holds up two fingers.

Mary frowns—she would have preferred a Coke, despite how Vinny feels about her prenatal nutritional needs.

"Yes sir, coming right up." The stewardess is off in a flash and returns momentarily with two fizzing glasses of sweet ale over ice and small square napkins bearing a center logo. "Will you two be having the beef or the chicken for lunch today?"

"We will have the roast beef, thank you," Vinny says, taking the glasses and passing one to Mary.

Once the stewardess is gone, Mary asks him, "What if I wanted chicken?" She takes a sip from the glass, feeling the tingly mist on her nose until the ice slides onto her face and dribbles out the side. She dabs her face with a napkin.

"Did you want chicken?" he asks.

"No, but that's not the point," she replies. She puts her glass down and stands up. "I'm going to the restroom. Is that all right, or should I wait for you to come wipe me?"

Vinny ignores her tone and looks up at her beautiful scowling face. "For the price I paid, you should let the stewardess do it if she offers."

Mary rolls her eyes and finds her way to the currently unoccupied, tiny, unpleasant lavatory, and shuts the troublesome folding door behind her.

In her icy absence, and against his better judgment, Vinny lifts a finger in the air to flag the stewardess.

She promptly responds to the gesture. "Is there something I can do, Mr. Carlino?"

"Can you bring my wife a Coke, please? I think she's tired of me ordering for her." He hands her Mary's abandoned glass.

"Sure," she says, bending and lowering her voice, "but if I were her, I'd let you, and never get tired of it." She winks and turns to fetch the new drink.

Mary opens the bathroom door and sees Vinny with raised eyebrows watching the stewardess twist away to her station. Letting her pregnancy paranoia take hold, Mary marches through the aisle in a huff.

"Ahem," she says, taking her seat.

Vinny looks at her, finally cutting his gaze away from the retreating stewardess.

Mary wants to knock that woman's hat off and destroy her well-placed curls.

"She's getting you a Coke, my love," Vinny says innocently.

"Good, and hopefully a straw this time," she replies with cranky disdain.

After the meal, Mary yawns and snuggles up with an airline blanket to take a short nap.

Vinny is relieved—hopefully she will wake in a better mood.

One connecting flight and an hour's car ride later, Vinny and Mary pull up into a familiar driveway.

"We aren't taking their house away, are we?" Mary says, sitting in the car, camera full of blissful memories in her lap. A naked outdoor bulb comes on, lighting the way for Chick and Gayle to greet the returning newlyweds.

"No, honey, just give me a minute." Vinny steps out of the car.

"I'm too tired for a visit," Mary whines.

"Surprise!" Gayle shouts, opening the passenger door. She takes the camera from Mary and pulls her from the car, then hugs her tight while Chick grabs her suitcases from the trunk.

"I don't understand . . ." Mary says. "Are we moving in with you?"

Gayle holds her at arm's length, smiling, then turns Mary slowly around to face the streetlight on the corner. She points to a newly restored house with gray asbestos siding and white trim. "We're *neighbors* again!"

Vinny turns, suitcase in hand, to see Mary's reaction to the modest one-story abode.

Expressionless, she walks slowly after them to the corner lot—diagonal from Gayle and Chick's house—to get a closer look at her new home in the partial light of the humming street lamp.

Ahead of her, Chick carries the suitcases inside the house and turns on the lights. Mary sees two windows come to life, like a pair of strange eyes awakening to her presence.

Vinny lowers his case to the sidewalk and reaches for her hand. "I know it isn't big and fancy, but it has two bedrooms and all new appliances."

Mary lowers her head and begins to cry.

Vinny lifts her chin. "I'll fix it. I'll phone a realtor tomorrow."

She gazes at him through the tears running down her face. "Fix what? You gave me something I can finally call my own. Thank you. *Thank* you!" Mary wraps her hands around his face and pulls him in for a kiss.

Vinny lifts her growing body with ease in his strong arms, his mouth still on hers. Without detection, Gayle snaps their photograph with a flash cube. She winds the camera and sneaks another suitcase in the house, not wanting to interfere. She'd take more from inside.

Vinny carries his bride to the door and over the threshold.

Gayle calls, "Say cheese!" as she documents the event. After capturing several homecoming photos of the smiling couple, she winds the camera again and finds the roll won't budge any further. "We're certainly glad to have you home, but we also know you're tired and need to rest," she says, depositing the camera on the kitchen table atop a small stack of paperwork. She hugs Mary and Vinny goodbye and adds, "I have school tomorrow, but we want the two of you over on Sunday, okay?"

"Yeah, we all need to catch up," Chick says. He hugs his friends goodnight. Letting go of Mary, he says to Vinny, "I put the stuff on the grocery list in the fridge and the pantry."

"Oh, and Mary," says Gayle, "I put your missed schoolwork assignments on the table. I figured you would want to turn them in on Monday."

Then, just like that, she and Chick slip away to enjoy their relaxed evening at home and allow their friends to unwind in their own.

Three hours later, still in her clothes, in the dark of her bedroom, Mary listens to the new nighttime sounds, looks at the new lights and shadows dancing along the smooth newly painted surfaces, thinks of the bathroom that she doesn't have to share with a handful of others.

"Thank you, thank you, thank you," she says, throwing her arm over her tired, almost-drifting spouse.

"No need to thank me," he says, kissing her wrist. "I love you. Just do one thing for me. Don't leave the house while I'm gone tomorrow. Can you do that for me?"

"Yep," Mary agrees. Her own eyes are feeling heavy now. "I have plenty to keep me here and busy the whole weekend."

No more talk, no more kisses—just sleep.

Sleep and dreams.

Friday
December 11, 1959

All morning is spent involved in the piddling that a new wife enjoys. Mary has dusted, arranged, swept, and mopped, removing all traces of the previous owners' funk. As she unpacks, she finds just the right places for all of their belongings, and happily decorates a freshly wiped bookshelf with her dictionary and three almost-due library books.

She revels in the new surroundings that provide her with a sacred experience: silence. In a house with eight children, silence was never afforded for more than a moment or two, especially during the day. In fact, when she finally does come across the radio, she cannot bring herself to turn it on. The only sound she is willing to endure at this point is the sound of her own humming and the whisper of her slippered feet as she continues to assemble the kitchen, where later today she will prepare her first official meal as a *bona fide* married woman.

The next box Mary opens contains a combination of hers and Vinny's belongings. Mindlessly she places a large, sealed legal-sized envelope with his name written on it beside her books on the shelf. The envelope no doubt contains boring property papers or the like.

She is eager to unwrap the next possession, which she has longed to display—so much so that it makes her squeal with delight as she rinses, dries, and carefully places it as the centerpiece on her dinette set. It is the glass vase that Vinny procured for her at the autumn festival on the day they first met. She suddenly remembers that day, that moment, and laughs to herself; she clearly recalls the desire to decorate her own home with this very carnival glass.

A true love story, come full circle,

she thinks to herself, her lips spreading in a gentle smile.

The sunlight passes through the window and hits the glass, projecting rainbows throughout the room, and fills her with a sense of peace. Peace that she has made the right decision for her and the life yet to enter the world.

The next item in the box is a wall clock, telling her it's time to wrap this up if she is going to have a proper meal prepared for her hard-working man when he comes home. Luckily, all the wedding presents she needs were in the very first box she unpacked. According to her inspection of the groceries Chick picked up for them, she has everything needed to make a huge pot of perfect spaghetti sauce just like Two-Man showed her. He even somehow located a Hubig's pie. The only thing Chick overlooked was the lump crab meat for the salad.

Surely Vinny wouldn't mind if I just went to the store and back in the pursuit of a perfect first meal?

Mary grabs her purse and walks down to the local grocery store just a few blocks away. Mr. Ledet, the owner of the store, doubles as the butcher, and he is also a member of the church her family attends. She feels his detail-gathering eyes on her as she enters the store; she hopes he pays more attention to the slicer before he loses a finger.

Catching sight of her own reflection in the theft-deterrent mirror makes her aware that she is wearing yesterday's clothes; her hair is mussed, and she quite possibly forgot to brush her teeth before leaving the house.

> *Breaking all the rules of decorum in one day*
> *hopefully does not lead to many more like it.*
> *I'll be the cliché of the pregnant wife who lets herself go.*

"Well, hello there, Mary," he greets her at the counter. "I didn't recognize you at first. You're wearing your hair different or something."

Embarrassed, she smooths her hair. "Sure is windy out today," she says, almost apologetically.

Mr. Ledet nods. "So sorry about your dad. We'll all miss him somethin awful."

"Thank you for that . . . and the sandwiches you sent for us after the service. It was much appreciated."

"How's married life treatin ya?" he asks, clearly privy to all the wagging tongues in town.

"Just fine, thank you. It would be even better if you could find me about a half-pound of lump crab meat," she says, conscious of the small amount of cash in her possession, hoping it will cover the expense.

"Good choice," he says in a cheerful manner. "We just got some crab in fresh this morning. I'll wrap that up for you in a jiffy. Will that be all you're needing today?"

"I think that will do it. I don't believe I have enough money for anything else," she says, unable to help eyeing some large pristinely white daisies that might bring the right amount of cheer to her new accommodations.

Her gaze doesn't go unnoticed by Mr. Ledet. Not only does Mary find out the crab meat is on special, but her order also happens to include three freshly cut daisies that will put a finishing touch on her plans for this evening.

Preparing a meal was never so much fun before. No tripping over little ones, no running or yelling, no finding ways to make food stretch for growing boys. While the sauce simmers, she spruces up with tooth-polishing, a shower, and application of a red pinched-waist, cleavage-revealing dress that won't fit much longer due to the progression of her delicate state.

After stirring, tasting, and adjustments have been made, her masterpiece now sits on the stove, ready for serving. She surveys the room to make sure her beau will be pleased when he walks in. Standing at the table, she fluffs the flowers as if they were a dozen instead of only three.

Now it's only a matter of minutes before Vinny is expected—time to make the salad. She unwraps the thick white butcher paper and proudly sprinkles in the crab meat she was explicitly told to add by Vinny's favorite culinary expert.

After fifteen minutes pass, she becomes concerned that the food will be wilted by the time he finally arrives—and just then the car pulls in. She pinches her cheeks for added color and smooths her dress, her heart pounding with excitement.

Out of the corner of her eye, she spots a small treasure on the floor—one she had almost completely forgotten about. It must have fallen out of one of the boxes. It is the pink baby sock she used as a bank on the day she met Vinny.

So that's where you were,

she thinks,

I sure could have used you at the store this morning!

She grabs the sock and stuffs it under the cushion on the couch to deal with later, not wanting to abandon her roost for more than a second.

At that moment, she spies her husband leaving their neighbors' driveway headed home. "Thanks again," Vinny calls. He waves at Gayle across the street and swaggers through the door with a paper bag in hand, his overalls unzipped to the waist, revealing his white undershirt. He plops himself at the table. She can smell the stench of alcohol on him and immediately knows why he is late for dinner. She pretends not to mind as she quietly delivers his food and then stands back to seek his approval.

"How was your day?" she asks nervously, sensing something is wrong.

He has a cold, cocky smirk on his face and he hasn't taken his eyes off her since he entered the room. She is a little disappointed that he hasn't seemed to notice she has made him two of his favorite dishes. They stare at each other in silence. Her inexperience keeps her from making the first move, afraid of wrecking what is supposed to be their first night of normal wedded bliss.

He takes a deep, haggard breath and opens the paper bag. "What you been doing all day?" he asks, pushing the food away with a sweaty, unopened six-pack of bottled beer.

Never before in the history of knowing Vinny has she seen him with beer. They've had a couple of casual drinks of celebration on occasion—one, after all, led to the loss of her innocence—but not beer, and not as if getting drunk were the goal. He has a wild look in his eyes that puts her senses on full alert.

"I unpacked several boxes, put things away, cooked . . ." she lists cautiously.

Vinny interrupts her. "I thought I told you not to leave the house. Mr. Ledet said you came by the store earlier today, looking *pretty* as a *picture.*" He says these last words with a hint of sarcasm as he opens one of the snub-necked bottles of Pabst Blue Ribbon.

"We didn't have any crab for the salad. I didn't think you would mind," she replies, presenting the bowl of salad as proof. "I know how much you like it."

"I do like it just the way you fixed it," he agrees in a softened tone. He gets up and shoves the rolled-up paper bag atop the five remaining amber bottles in the fridge. "Please continue. What else did you do?"

"I cleaned," she says hesitantly, not knowing the correct answer—a test she has not studied for.

"You ... *cleaned*," he repeats, looking around, as if he is disbelieving.

He takes a slow walk around the room in an impromptu inspection. She follows, hoping he will be impressed with her progress. He pauses in front of the envelope on the bookshelf, drops his head, squeezes his eyes shut in what Mary can clearly see as anger, then yanks the chair he had been seated in and drags it haphazardly across the floor to the interior doorway to the bedroom. He climbs onto the chair; slowly and dramatically, he wipes the top of the door frame with his hand. His hand now has a layer of dust that has been accumulating no doubt since the house was built some twenty or so years ago.

Her eyes widen at the sight of the thick, ashy film that had earlier escaped her notice, now filling her with shame. How could she have *missed* it?

He descends the chair and observes his hand a moment out of interest, as if he has never seen the grayish powder before in his life. She stands there nervously, trying to think of something to say, something to end the awkward silence.

Before she has a chance to utter a word, he raises his open hand and it comes down on her face with a force she could only imagine a boxer enduring inside the ring. The blow sends her reeling backward onto the floor with the residue of dust smeared upon her horrified face. The shock wave fills every ounce of her being.

He moves the chair back to its original place at the table, grabs the envelope from the bookshelf, and tucks it beneath his arm as if to keep the contents from escaping. Mary, still on the floor, cowers as he passes, not wanting to receive any more of his apparent rage. Never in a million years would she have thought this man, who had been so kind and loving toward her all this time, could possibly be capable of harming her in such a way without even a hint of conscience.

From the open bedroom door, Vinny's razor-sharp tongue yells, "When we took our vows, you promised to obey. I don't know who taught you how to clean, but you damn sure didn't pass that class, did ya?!"

Adding insult to her injury, he tosses her pillow and a blanket outside the bedroom, landing atop her head. The door slams shut, followed by a sharp click of the lock.

Once the shock wears off and Mary can review the scenario with a level head, she begins to weep.

I need to learn how to be a better wife,

she tells herself.

I should have listened and stayed home.
I should have done a better job of cleaning.
I don't know what to do now.

"Daddy, I need you," she whimpers quietly to the ceiling.

She picks herself up off the floor and proceeds to pack up the food she put so much love into preparing, leaving the streak of dust on her bruised cheek as a reminder. Her penance for neglecting her post.

In this distressed moment in her life, Mary needs to feel the safety of her father's presence, but he is no longer here to lend his wisdom or his shoulder. She didn't cry at his funeral, but the flood that comes this night more than makes up for that. The tears continue to come in waves, her body heaving until she passes out from exhaustion.

Before the tears. Before the locked door.

Vinny looked around the room at all the progress Mary made throughout the day—relieved that she couldn't have been gone from the house for long—when his eyes landed on the bookshelf and the envelope he'd forgotten existed.

That fucking envelope! his thoughts exploded.

To anyone else it was innocent-looking enough, sitting snuggled between a dictionary and a Bible, but to Vinny it was a caustic sight that bored an excruciating splintery hole into his skull, a vessel that no doubt contains the answers to questions he's refused to consider. A paper sarcophagus which came to him sealed for a reason and which he never opened.

I don't want to know!

It may have been the alcohol, or the shock of facing an old demon Vinny was not prepared to do battle with just yet, but he lost his cool and drew from the evil in him that he's come to embrace.

There was no excuse for what he did next.

He raised his hand and damaged the one person in the world he never intended to harm. Vinny grabbed that fucking envelope from the shelf and subdued its retribution beneath his arm, and in a blind rage spit out words he can't remember, desperate to slam the bedroom door and lock out all prying eyes. He sat in contest with this damned legal-size, caution-yellow envelope staring back at him from his pillow; lingered there on the bed a moment longer, all the while glaring at that stupid envelope, but he now admits, *It's me I hate!*

When he finally decides to reach out and lift it up, it seems heavier than it did before, as if he can feel the weight of the information inside. Vinny shoves his finger beneath the top flap and rips apart the seal on his dreaded history. As Mary dissolves in a fresh puddle of her tears beyond that locked bedroom door, he dumps the contents out onto the mattress: mostly papers, then a key lands heavily on the bed his wife so lovingly made up earlier, making this moment all the more unbearable.

Vinny pushes aside legal documents until he sees a folded handwritten letter. As he carefully unfolds it, a photograph falls out and floats like an autumn leaf before it lands on the floor. He looks down at the image in profound confusion. The lovely milk-chocolate face that stares back at him is one he has seen before in person; in fact, he was the last person to have ever seen that face before her last breath. He remembers the spicy scent of her skin, and how she gently touched his face as she lay dying.

Vinny picks up the photo and turns it over so that the ghost cannot accuse him any longer. On the back is written, *To my little man, love Mama.*

He looks at the birth certificate that bears a name Vinny cast away, along with his humanity, so long ago. Beneath that, beside "Mother," it says *Beulah Laveau;* beside "Father," it says *Unknown;* and beside "Race," it says *Negro.*

Nothing about me is what I thought it was . . . I'm the guy that always had it all figured out . . . turns out I know nothing at all. What happens if Mary finds out the monster I really am? . . . I kill people for a living . . . I'm a goddamn Negro . . . I killed my own mother . . .

Who the hell am I?

For a moment in the predawn darkness, it is as if Mary is back in her old bedroom with a leak in the roof. The annoying drip she feels is warm, unlike the freezing raindrops she is used to. It feels much like tears, their salt stinging the abrasion across her cheek. *Drip, drip, drip* come the tears upon her face—only the tears are not hers. The sensation arouses her reluctantly from a much-needed slumber. It takes a minute for her puffy eyes to adjust enough to make out the shape of him hovering over her. Her head fills with the memories of last night and she instinctively pulls away—except she can't, because Vinny is holding on desperately to her hand.

"I am so sorry. Please say you forgive me," he pleads thickly through his tears. He looks as if he hasn't slept at all. "I understand if you're afraid. I'm completely at fault, Mary. I shouldn't have done or said those things to you, especially when you went to so much trouble. I don't know what came over me. Let me make it up to you somehow. I'll do anything."

She has never seen a grown man in such a state before. She isn't sure whether to be lovingly compassionate toward him or stand up, be enraged, and demand he be held accountable for his alcohol-induced outburst. She can hear the judge's voice in her head saying "for better or worse."

> *Maybe this is the "worse" he was referring to.*
> *Perhaps you have to experience the "worse" . . .*
> *if you are ever to appreciate the "better."*

While she mulls this over, he continues to writhe in the pain of her silence.

"Say something . . . yell at me . . . hit me. Do whatever you need to do to me," he begs, putting her hand to his fear-stricken face.

"I need you to calm down and discuss this with me," she says coolly, trying not to get sucked into his emotions. "I have so many questions that need to be answered before I can even begin to take the next step."

Vinny nods, letting her hand fall away from his face as he settles beside her. "You have my full cooperation."

"Can I trust you?" she asks, and pauses to sit up, needing to gain some insight into his psyche. "After last night, I don't even think I know who you are, or what you're capable of. Who are you?"

"I'm still the man you fell in love with. I just made some bad decisions," he says, watching the slow, disbelieving shake of Mary's head. "Please let me explain. When I got off work, some of the guys offered me a drink at a bar on the way home. I didn't want to be a jerk on the first day, ya know? So I went and had a couple rounds before leaving to come home. I stopped at the corner store to pick up some cigarettes and a six-pack to keep in the fridge. When I found out you'd left the house . . . I lost it. I kept thinking of all the things that could've happened to you, to my baby . . ." His eyes flash down to her belly, then back up to her gaze. "It scared me. When I got home and saw you in that dress, looking so pretty, I got crazy thoughts that you might have had someone over or been out with someone else. I was furious. I never meant to hurt you. I love you so much. I know how wrong my actions were."

"Is that what this has all been about?" she asks with just a sliver of amusement. "I had no clue how silly and jealous you could be. I can assure you that I didn't wear this dress out of the house. In fact,

I hadn't even taken a shower until I got ready for you to come home. I went to the store exactly how you left me this morning. If Chick had purchased everything on the grocery list, I never would have had to leave the house, and we could have avoided this whole mess!"

At that statement he gets up, walks over to the fridge, and returns with the rolled-up paper bag, which appears to be empty, its brewed contents removed. He sheepishly lays the bag at her feet. "He didn't forget."

She opens the bag to reveal a half-pound of crab meat still wrapped in its unfamiliar brown deli paper. She giggles and begins to relax.

He embraces her and tenderly brushes the hair from her face. "It'll never happen again," he says softly as he examines her wounded cheek.

"Promise?" she asks soberly, searching his eyes for the truth.

"I swear it," he vows, and kisses her forehead. "Does it hurt?"

"Not much anymore. I think my feelings were hurt more than my cheek."

"Tell me how to make it up to you," he says, leaning in and holding still with expectation.

She pulls away from him. "You need to talk with me before you jump to conclusions and get angry—not to mention the alcohol probably didn't help your frame of mind."

Vinny listens, swallows, and nods as she speaks. "I worry so much about you and the baby when you're out of my sight," he says, rubbing his temples.

"You have to learn to trust me, and I'll learn to adhere to your wishes. If we're always trying to work toward each other, we're bound to meet somewhere in the middle," she says, rivaling that perennial optimist in *Pollyanna*.

"You're right, of course," Vinny agrees. He gets up and digs out his First-Aid kit for a tiny tub of salve. "You should put some makeup on that tomorrow when we go to dinner."

Thursday
December 17, 1959

Mary shoots up in bed when she sees the amount of light flooding into the bedroom window. "Vinny, you're late for work—and I forgot to ask for a ride to the baby doctor!"

Vinny scoops his wife back into the coziness beneath the warm sheets. "You won't need a ride," he says, his voice muffled by the cocoon of blankets. "I took the day off to drive you to your appointment. So is this a doctor who *is* a baby, or a doctor *of* babies?"

Mary giggles and lets herself fall back to sleep for a few more minutes.

Later that morning, after her examination, Mary shifts around in her chair next to Vinny in the doctor's office, waiting for the update on her pregnancy. Unlike the last office she visited, this one is closer to home, but, unfortunately, there is no soothing wall of books to peruse.

Suddenly the doctor bursts into the room as if he is in a tremendous hurry, reading from her chart and taking a seat behind his desk. He says, "All is well with both you and the baby. I'll be seeing you again next month, unless you call with an issue." He finally looks up from her chart. "Also, I want to assure you and your husband that we keep all of our clients' records under lock and key. Our staff is under a professional obligation to protect your privacy."

The doctor opens an expensive-looking cigarette case on his desk. After fishing one out, he closes the case and taps it lightly on the shiny surface before placing it back down on his desk.

"Thank you so much," Mary says, watching the doctor search for a lighter. "We were worried. Word gets around, and I'm still in school."

"Oh, I'm sorry—would either of you like one?" he offers, reaching again for the cigarette case.

Neither of them takes him up on the offer, but Vinny does lean over to provide a flame to ease his fidgeting. "You know, my wife calls those cancer sticks."

"Bunch of nonsense." The doctor exhales his smoky, toxic breath through his nostrils. "I recommend them all the time. They calm the nerves, see, and the data has yet to prove to me a link between cigarettes and cancer."

Vinny snorts and looks to Mary for her reaction. She wears a mask of indifference as she holds her breath.

"I want another doctor," Mary says, walking along the sidewalk with Vinny to complete the day's errands. "I like the one I went to before."

"I don't think he does babies," says Vinny.

A male voice behind them yells, "Watch it, nigger!"

Vinny spins around, a weird, suddenly visceral reaction to a word he has himself used on an occasion or two. He sees a large white man angrily walking by a young black man holding an upright broom, paused in the process of sweeping the front of a shoe-repair store. The frightened young man stays perfectly still, as does Vinny, until the grumbling threat of a man turns the corner and is out of sight.

"Do you know that man?" Mary asks.

"No," Vinny responds. Mary notices that he is holding his stomach. "I need to make a phone call. Can you go in the bank and deposit this check for me?" Vinny shoves the contents of his pocket into her hand.

She stares down at the enigmatic numbers on the check. "But I've never done this before . . ."

Vinny rubs the back of his neck, one hand still on his stomach. "I already signed it and filled out a deposit slip. Just hand it to the teller and they'll give you a receipt."

Outside of the bank, Mary looks back at her husband's fading figure. Stepping into the lobby, Mary takes her place third in line. She smells the bank teller. The young woman's perfume, a lingering odor of home permanent solution and Aqua-Net, reeks from behind the partition even before Mary sees her ash-blonde hair in a coiffure that would make Doris Day herself proud.

Mary's turn comes and she steps reluctantly forward.

"Good morning. What can I do for you today?" the teller asks.

Mary smiles and slides the two slips of paper over the laminate countertop between them. The teller inspects the slips while humming a tune, quickly recording a handwritten receipt. Still clutching the receipt, she pauses to unload a scripted pitch upon her new customer.

"Would you like to open an interest-earning Red Sock account today?" She points to the shelf display with the picture of a red boot stocking with a fuzzy white top.

"I don't think I have enough to open an account. I'm not even sure if I'll have enough to get all the things on my Christmas list," Mary explains, taking the receipt.

Undeterred, the teller continues. "There's no minimum deposit, and it will prevent that exact dilemma from happening next year. You can deposit money all year long in small increments, and by next December, you'll be well prepared to do all of your Christmas shopping," she reasons, barely taking a breath during the spiel.

Mary's eyebrows pull together, leery of the woman's astute sales persona. She is about to stand her "thanks, but no thanks" ground until a familiar voice fills her head with an urgent plea.

Take de money you got wit you now an place it in de red sock!

She breaks into a cold sweat. Instantly, Mary knows resistance isn't an option.

The teller becomes concerned at her customer's sudden color change and upper lip beading with perspiration. "Ma'am . . . are you all right?"

Silently Mary moves like a proficient sleepwalker. Without looking, she reaches into her purse to retrieve the small pink sock she placed there less than a week ago, and hands it to the teller. "Morning sickness . . . it'll pass," she says weakly, after releasing the tiny package onto the counter.

"How sweet," the teller says in response to the joyous news. "I have some saltines in the back—and some water if you'd like," she offers, raising an eyebrow at the contents spilling out of the sock. She gives it a shake to make sure she hadn't missed any.

Adding up to twenty dollars and fifteen cents, an amount that once seemed like thousands now looks quite meager on the counter of a bank.

"No thanks. I'll be all right," Mary says with a half-hearted smile, wanting to complete the transaction before any further embarrassment can occur.

"By this time next year, you'll have plenty to spend on baby's first Christmas . . . that is, unless you want to roll it over and have even more for the next year. Just fill out the top of this form," the teller says, handing Mary a yellow piece of paper.

Mary easily fills out each line of the registration—until she comes to the option of adding another person to the account.

"Suppose I want to keep this a secret . . . a secret even from myself?" Mary says, folding her lips into a hard line.

The clerk winces as if she has been poked before a look of sly recognition covers her face. "Ahhh, I got your number. I know exactly what you should do," she says slowly, glancing at the bank manager, and turns the paper away from Mary.

"You do?" Mary asks, thinking her façade must be as thin as the oniony sheets of paperwork.

"I have the same problem," the teller replies, lowering her voice and looking around to see if anyone is paying any mind to their conversation.

"You do?" Mary repeats, like a parrot that only knows one phrase. She has to stop herself from raising a hand to the cheek Vinny hit. Is it still red?

"If you know the money is there, you'll be tempted to spend it, right?" says the teller, proudly nodding her head as she fills out the next section.

Mary relaxes. "Yes, exactly."

"I put down for them to not issue a statement to your home. You will have to come here to get your balance information. Just sign here and you're all fixed up."

Mary puts the pen to the paper and scrawls her new name, which has not become second nature to her yet.

"Thank you so much for your help." Mary turns for the exit a bit too quickly, as if she has just committed a crime.

"Anytime . . . and congratulations on your baby!" the teller calls out—a little too loud for Mary's comfort.

Friday
December 18, 1959

"**M**ary Poche**,**" barks a muffled female voice over the intercom, halfway through the second-period class. "Please come to the office . . . Mary Poche."

Clueless as to what this could be about, Mary gathers her things and nervously leaves the room. Her cautious footsteps echo in the empty hall as they carry her to the dreaded principal's office. The door to the outside office where the secretary works is kept open during the day, held by a rubber wedge doorstop. Mary slows her steps as she approaches the entrance, but she can't slow her heart.

The plump secretary sporting a beehive is a familiar face, though not from this venue; she is a respected member of Mary's church. Inches above her, the secretary looms just inside the doorway, arms crossed, waiting, it seems, to pounce on Mary; she wears fashionable cat-eye glasses, through which she casts a hard, disappointed glare, reminding Mary of what boys do with ants and a magnifying glass.

"Go on in, Miss Poche. He is waiting for you."

Mary timidly knocks and enters the inner sanctum of the principal's lair, leaving the door unsealed out of childish fear.

"Mary Poche?" he confirms, looking up from her thin, immaculate file. "Please have a seat."

Mary looks at the two chairs in front of his desk as if this were a test, not wanting to choose wrong. She figures you can't go wrong with right. She sits in silence, wrapping her lips over her teeth and biting down hard enough to make them numb.

He closes the file and puts his elbows on the desk, placing his interlocked hands to his mouth while he studies Mary's face, looking as though he might be praying to the educational gods.

"It has come to my attention," he starts, then clears his throat, looking at the partially open door, "that you may be in violation of our student code of conduct."

"How so, Mr. Dubois?" Mary says, checking her clothes and shoes for something she might have missed. "I assure you that I am in compliance."

"Well, someone came across some information that you may be in the family way, and we simply cannot have one of our students parading their lack of morality in our halls."

Mary gapes at such an accusation. "But, sir, I am *married*. Certainly there is no lack of morality in that."

He nods, but his frown remains. "Yes, I'm aware by your absences that you just recently returned from your honeymoon."

"I promise you that I made up for all the classwork I missed and completed all my tests. I'll continue to study hard to maintain my perfect test scores." She is sure to put a slight emphasis on the word *perfect*.

He sits back in his chair, lowering his prayer-like hands to his lap. "Yes, I know all about it. Mrs. Tisdale just left my office singing your praises . . . which is all the more reason for you to understand that everyone in this building knows how these things happen, and we can all count to nine."

Speechless, Mary turns ashen, her blood on pause.

"I'm afraid that you can either voluntarily discontinue attending this school year, or I will be forced to expel you until the matter is resolved."

Mary has not prepared herself for this—the sudden death of her educational journey. Everything she's worked toward up till now, all her efforts washed away in a flood of social shame. Her tears come, but she swats them away in anger. "Why are you doing this to me?"

"Young lady, I have done nothing to you. You did this to yourself," he says, standing up to see her out. "I'm doing you a favor. These kids can be so cruel."

"More so than the adults?" Mary asks, rising to leave.

He is blanched by her dig, but he collects himself swiftly. "Come to me next year if you would like to return, but for now, I think it best if you clean out your locker and return any school property currently in your possession."

Mary hangs her head. "Next *year?*"

"You could just take the GED test," he suggests, reaching to lead her out of the office.

Mary recoils and looks at him, horrified. "How will I get into a top-tier school with a GED on my application?"

"My dear, you are delusional. How do you think you will go further than a GED with a child on your hip?"

Mary's nostrils flare; her body quakes with rage. "Four, thirty, eleven!" she shouts, throwing her books down at his feet.

As she walks away, he follows her into the outer office. "What's that supposed to mean?" he asks.

Mary spins around. "That, sir, is my locker combination. You will find everything you want to take away from me is well within your reach. I'll be damned if I will assist!"

The secretary scowls at Mary with bulging eyes.

Mary wheels on her. "Take that dictation, you malefic battle axe . . . locker number eighty-seven!"

The secretary's mouth drops open when Mary kicks the doorstop free and the door slams shut.

It takes hours for Mary to walk home from school in the cool December breeze. She stops every once in a while to indulge in hysterical bouts of crying right there on the sidewalk, to wallow her once well-sought future dissolving in a chilly puddle of her tears.

When Mary finally reaches home, she drags her drained body to collapse in her bed and closes her red, puffy eyes—until she hears the high squeal of a school bus stopping for a moment; then it roars, picking up speed, resuming its student-delivery route.

Mary sits up and feels her head throb with pain. Rising from the bed, she stumbles to the kitchen in search of aspirin.

A loud knock comes and Mary yelps, a hand flying to her startled chest. She spins around on wobbly legs to discover Gayle's forehead pressed against the kitchen door's glass panel, trying to see inside. With a huge breath of relief she opens the door and Gayle rushes in with various personal items from Mary's locker.

"I thought you might like some of this stuff," Gayle says, and places Mary's things on the table. "Now tell me what happened!"

Mary sits down. She touches a pack of colored pencils on top of the music book Bobby gave her. "How did you know to get these?"

Gayle shrugs. "I felt . . . *weird* after they called you to the office, so I got a hall pass for the bathroom to wait for you by our lockers. The maintenance man showed up looking for your locker . . ." She gets a look of spritely malevolence on her face. ". . . so I led him to Veronica's."

Mary bursts out a guffaw at this, despite her swollen eyes and throbbing head.

Gayle continues, "When the bell rang, I went in your locker, got your stuff, and put it in mine, while he struggled with the combination over at Veronica's old locker. I figured someone would show up eventually and inform him of the mistake."

"Nice diversion," Mary says, not wanting to talk, wishing she could come up with a diversion of her own. She gets up to pour a glass of water and reaches for a bottle of pain reliever.

"Spill," Gayle prods, sitting down to wait for the scoop.

"I got kicked out," Mary says. She takes the large bottle of aspirin and thumbs off the lid, which flies and lands in the sink. She taps three into her hand, uncaring about the mess.

"Can they *do* that?" Gayle asks, getting up to fish the lid from the sink. She reapplies it to the bottle while Mary swallows her dose.

"It's done," Mary says. She suddenly wonders if the aspirin will hurt the baby.

"Isn't there something we can do? We can't give in that easy!"

"I don't seem to have a choice." Mary swats the aspirin bottle off the counter onto the floor. "Oh, wait, I do. The principal told me to take the GED," she says sardonically, kicking the bottle; it skips and rattles across the kitchen floor.

"Is that such a bad idea? Wouldn't that make you eligible to start college next year?" Gayle asks, rescuing the bottle from Mary's abuse.

"Maybe. If I wanted to go to a *community* college," Mary says, leaning against the counter.

Gayle walks back over to her friend. "Listen. Figure out what it is that you want to be, and then we can make a plan to get you there. It'll be okay."

"He was right." Mary stares at the floor with pained, watery eyes.

"Who, Dubois? Right about what?"

"Even if I knew exactly where I wanted to go and exactly what I wanted to do, I'll be someone's mother soon . . . and that won't leave any room for me and my dreams." Mary pulls a chair out, crumples onto it with her head in her hands, and begins to sob.

"Oh, honey," Gayle soothes in a gentle tone, "it's going to be okay. I promise."

Mary bleakly shakes her head from side to side, silently and self-destructively wanting some addictive vice to turn to in this moment—anything to offer some temporary reprieve from this terrible feeling of dread.

Sunday
December 20, 1959

T he toilet flushes and the faucet turns on.

"Stay with me," Vinny says, reaching across the warm fragrant sheets where Mary slept.

"I can't." She appears briefly in the bathroom doorway. "I need to go to church."

Vinny enjoys seeing her nude silhouette beneath her flowing silk nightgown. He feels himself grow hard at the sight, and wishes she would come back to bed. "Why?"

She turns back into the bathroom. "Because it's what *good* people do. You should get up and come with me." Her voice echoes off the porcelain interior. She loads up her toothbrush with paste.

He calls back, "I'm not a good person."

Mary considers this while slowly stroking her teeth and gums with a hard-bristled toothbrush. She pauses to say, "Sure, you are. We're all sinners, and all deserving of our place in heaven."

Vinny laughs. "Boy, they really have you washed in the blood of the lamb, don't they?"

Mary spits frothy white foam into the sink. "I'm not going to have this discussion if you're going to poke fun at my beliefs."

"I just want you to know that I've *been* to heaven—and it's about to leave me, to go congregate with a bunch of self-righteous old biddies who only go to church so they can look down their noses at everyone else for what they do and think."

"You're wrong about those people. They care about each other's salvation."

"If you say so." Vinny turns over in the bed, pulling the covers up over his shoulder.

On the church grounds, as Mary approaches the breezeway, she can surmise by female voices speaking in hushed tones that there is gossiping afoot just beyond her sightline.

"Everyone is talking. Isn't it just a terrible shame?" she hears a woman's voice saying from around the corner.

"That's what happens," says another voice, giving her disapproving two cents, "when a family no longer has a man to guide them."

"*I* heard she couldn't be married in the church because she already has a bun in the oven. She went and *trapped* that poor young man . . . got him by the short-and-curlies."

At first Mary wants to giggle at the woman's remark, until it dawns on her that they are most certainly talking about her. About her bun and her oven. About *Vinny's* "short-and-curlies." Infuriated, she turns the corner to confront them.

"Whom are we trashing so early this morning, ladies?" she says coolly, arm folded over her worn Bible.

The astonishment suddenly masking their harsh faces rats them out completely.

Mary looks each of the three silent women in the eyes. "My, aren't we the good Christians we hear so often about? Full of love and compassion."

The women regain their composure, dusting Mary's intrusion off their creaseless church dresses. The most outspoken of the three takes a sanctimonious stance. "Some offenses are worse than others, young lady. It's the *Lord's* job to forgive you of your sins, not mine." The portly woman turns and walks away, and her friends follow, nodding primly to one another.

"Well, harping on others doesn't exactly make you an angel!" Mary says. She wishes she could have come up with something better on such short notice than the tired line she'd stolen from Gayle. With the hopes of acceptance by her church family dashed, and unable to face the rest of the congregation, Mary decides to head back to the arms of a man who didn't want her to leave in the first place.

When she gets home, she strips away her Sunday frock and slips into bed beside Vinny, who hasn't moved an inch since she left.

"Wow, that was the quickest sermon on record," he says, popping one eye open to check the time, thinking he may have slept well into the afternoon.

"All the sinners stayed in bed today," Mary says, slightly overwrought with hormone-induced emotion. "You were right . . . I should have stayed here with you."

He turns over to place her fretful head on his shoulder and embraces her. "You want to talk about it?"

"No . . . it'll only get me more upset. I just want to lay here with you for a while before I have to get up to make lunch."

"How about I take us to get a big juicy steak for lunch so you don't have to cook?" he says, giving her a squeeze.

A tear slips from Mary's tired eyes. "That sounds wonderful . . . *thank you*."

"For what?"

"For loving me."

He audibly inhales before responding, "No, I thank you for giving me happiness I didn't know existed." He breathes before rolling to a position above her and begins lavishing her with soft kisses. "Let me show you my gratitude."

By the time they are able to leave the house, both are in great need of a high-caloric meal to replenish all the energy spent this afternoon.

Sunday
January 3, 1960

aking full advantage of her ample leisure time and the Christmas spoils, Mary utilizes a brand-new Singer sewing machine, spending her holidays getting ready for the baby. She finds many easy sewing projects to fill her days and restless nights, making curtains, crib sets, clothes, and more. Reading craft books from the library, she also learns how to crochet.

Having no clue as to the sex of the love that is growing and stretching the confines of her insides, she sticks to gender-neutral color choices. Her hands pull silky woven yarns from the softest skeins she could find, cautiously chaining the meticulous first row of a mint-green and white afghan. *Meet the Press* is on the TV, and her ears absorb newly announced candidate John F. Kennedy explaining why he thinks personal wealth has no bearing in the presidential race.

Vinny wanders into the room and kisses Mary on the head. "You know I don't look good in green," he whispers teasingly.

She smiles, silently counting out her stitches, chaining one, turning the foundation, and yarning over to begin the eighth row of the pattern.

He watches the TV screen for a minute, then walks into the kitchen, opens the refrigerator, and examines the contents. He gathers supplies to construct two thick sandwiches. "I'll make you a juicy BLT if you let me turn the station."

"For breakfast?" she says, and then shoves her long aluminum needle into the skein to hold her place. She gets up to help with the bacon. "Aren't you at all interested in who might be next at our nation's helm?"

"You really think whoever's in that house on Pennsylvania Avenue runs the country?" Vinny takes a sharp knife to a bright red tomato, making several even slices.

Mary stares into space for a moment before turning off the TV. She removes a pan from the cabinet and sets it on a lit burner, opens a package of bacon and distractedly lays several slices across the heating metal surface. "So if the President doesn't run the country, then who does?"

"You shouldn't worry your pretty head about such things," he says, breaking off layers of crispy lettuce.

Mary frowns. "If you know something, I want to know, too." She untwists the colorful bag of Wonder Bread and drops two slices in the toaster. After pushing the lever down, she watches the Nichrome ribbon wire inside the toaster glow hot and thinks,

When I pull the lever I make a difference . . . right?

The bacon crackles in the pan and Vinny answers the call, flipping the slices over. "Why don't you sit down, Maggie? I can get it from here."

Mary's perception of her own reality has gone wonky, like she's needed glasses all these years and got a glimpse through windowed lenses that provided a pansophic view like that of Tolkien's Eye of Sauron; Vinny's words have spawned an existential unrest. She glances around the room, looking for an answer to her sudden irrational thoughts of being out of control, and falls into a chair at the kitchen table.

"Mag? You okay?" Vinny asks. He pours and hands her a short glass of orange juice.

"I might be if you can explain to me why you don't believe in the election process."

He sighs and says, "I really wish I hadn't said anything." He places the finished bacon on a bed of paper towels. "I had no idea it would cause you to unravel." He removes the toast that sat cooling after having popped up moments ago, reloads the slots, and pushes the lever down. "Don't pay any attention to me . . . believe what you want to believe." He unscrews the yellow lid of the Duke's mayonnaise jar, dips a butter knife inside, and spreads a thin creamy layer across the crisp surface of the toasted bread. He piles the sandwich high and adds a pickle spear to the plate before delivering it to Mary.

"Yum . . . thank you," she says.

As soon as Vinny is finished building his own meal, he sits down to join her at the table. "Do you feel better now?" he asks, then digs his teeth into a perfect blend of flavors.

"Much." She crunches her way through the kosher dill. "I didn't notice how hungry I was until I took that first bite," she says, enjoying the last one enough to lick the bacon grease from her fingers. She gets up to rinse the plate. "What do you think about me going to take the GED?"

"I thought you were done with all that now. What's the point?" he asks with his mouth still full.

"There's a testing date coming up, and I'd like to go ahead and take it. For some peace of mind."

He shrugs petulantly, swallowing. "Sounds like you're gonna do whatever the hell you want. I know you don't really care what I think about it."

Mary stares at him. "That's not true. I was hoping you'd be supportive of me."

"I probably would be if I thought it would end there, but it won't, will it?" Vinny, with convincing melodrama, hangs his body over his empty plate and mutters, "Next you're gonna want to go off to college and leave me and the baby in the dust."

"Is that what you think?" She rushes to embrace him. "I wouldn't do that!"

"Promise?" he asks, lifting his head to search her comforting eyes.

"Of course! There must be ways I can get educated and have a family. *Men* have done it," she reminds him.

But that still doesn't convince him. The hurt is still clear in his eyes. "I don't see why you can't just be happy here at home. Don't I provide everything you need?"

"Yes, honey, you give me plenty," she says. "But knowledge is something I can only get for myself. It has nothing to do with wanting material things."

With a curled lip Vinny rubs his tongue along his sharp teeth, a patient, calculating, indomitable hunter.

Monday
March 7, 1960

"**B**ut my report is supposed to be about the evils of communism," Gayle says, wishing she hadn't mentioned the assignment to Mary, who is newly licensed, on the relatively short drive home from school. "How is finding out about some foreign country going to help me?"

Later, she follows Mary blindly, a researcher who knows her way around the public library as if she were an employee. On a fact-finding mission, Dewey Decimal number in hand, Mary rubs her itchy belly beneath the adjustable waistband of her quarter-length Butterick-patterned maternity pants. She hunts in the reference section, searching for a book about a small Asian country called South Vietnam, recently mentioned in the news. She pulls a world geography book out of its slumber to sit atop an encyclopedia—but even these two behemoth tomes combined will not offer up enough food for her thoughts.

Gayle lags behind Mary's trajectory toward the nearest table. She glances around and finds none of the moldy-smelling books in the nonfiction section of any interest. "Why are we here, looking up some place we've never heard of, when we could be celebrating Elvis coming home from the Army and looking good as ever?"

Mary opens the stiff, rarely used book-binding and drags her finger through the glossary section. "Why do you think Elvis is more important than Eisenhower sending thirty-five-hundred men to the other side of the world?" she asks, flipping through pages and pages with one hand and playing with the collar of her smock top with the other.

"Are you investigating for the *government* now?" Gayle asks, a little too loud.

"No, I'm going to help you write your report. *I* want to know why I should be so afraid of communism," Mary replies, jotting quick factoids on a slip of paper with a short eraserless pencil. "I'm uncomfortable being told what to think and believe. I want to know for myself, to make up my own mind."

"Shhh," the librarian hushes the girls' conversation.

In retort, Gayle looks around with her hands in the air, as if to point out the absence of anyone else in the room to be offended by the noise.

Mary lowers her voice. "You better start paying attention to what these governments are up to. What they do can affect our lives in countless ways."

"How can it affect us when it's so far away?"

"I'm sure some people thought Europe and Japan were faraway places, too."

"How did we go from communism to war?" Gayle snorts. "Pregnancy has made you so paranoid!"

Mary looks up from the book to glare at her best friend. "Do you ever read anything besides those car magazines?"

"None of the things I put in my head make me this upset! Why would anyone want to read about that stuff? I just want to write a stupid report that says whatever will get me a passing grade."

"Don't you ever want to know things just for the sake of knowledge?"

"Sure . . . just not *this* stuff." Gayle plants her hands on the table and leans toward Mary. "You seem to think knowing all this stuff will make some kinda difference. Take a car, for instance—do you think understanding how an internal combustion engine works will change the road you're on?"

Mary contemplates the theory, surprised at her friend's apt metaphor.

"Furthermore," Gayle continues, "if the *driver* doesn't even have to know those things, what do you think we can do from the backseat?"

"Well said. I may see your point now." Mary twists her wedding ring around and around her finger. "So . . . if a government wants a war, the citizens are just along for the ride."

Gayle smirks at the serious look on Mary's face. "Can we just wrap this up and get some food? I'm *starving*."

"Just let me skim this next section and we can go." Mary digs in her wallet for her library card and places it atop a political philosophy book. "I want to borrow this one."

Gayle rolls her eyes and drags the book off the table. She brings it to the grumpy librarian with overly teased brown helmet-hair seated behind the front desk. The woman doesn't look up from stamping new stacks of donated arrivals when Gayle presents the book for checkout by plopping it on the counter. Ignoring Gayle and the mistreatment of the book, the librarian continues with her task. Gayle clears her throat. The woman lifts only her eyes to peer at Gayle like an angry owl through her bottle-thick glasses. Seemingly against her better judgment, the librarian sighs heavily and inspects the library card.

"Hmmm," she utters, as if deciding whether or not to sign and date the return card.

"Is there a problem?" Gayle asks.

"Acing the GED test did not win her any celebrity privileges around here," the woman replies steadily. She slips the card back into the pouch glued to the inside cover. "She needs to do this *herself* next time, and not send her . . . lackey." The librarian slams the book shut, lifts her nose, and pushes it to Gayle.

"What's the big deal? You can see her plain as day from here. Besides, if she isn't famous for making perfect scores on the test, then how do you even *know* about it, hmm?"

With a dismissive snort, the librarian returns to her duties.

Gayle takes large strides to the table where Mary is still seated taking notes.

"I know, I know . . . I'm almost finished," Mary says, one hand's finger on a passage which her other hand is copying with shorthand-like scribbles.

She closes the book and stands up. "Oh, I need to visit the little girls' room before we leave. Also . . . I promised Bobby we'd stop by the music store today."

"Ugh . . . hurry up, already," Gayle says. She picks up the books Mary left on the table and places them on a nearby sorter cart.

The librarian grimaces in her direction and Gayle sticks her tongue out defiantly before leaving to wait in the car.

Mary parks in front of the music store, with its whimsical black-and white-piano-key awning and windows decaled with various musical notes. Gayle takes the last scrumptious bite of the take-out burger she so patiently waited for over a grease-stained paper bag in her lap.

"Don't touch anything. I mean it!" Mary hurries to open the doors for Gayle, who holds her ketchup-contaminated fingers up in the air as if in surrender.

"What happened? Everyone okay?" Bobby asks, looking at Gayle's reddened fingers. He walks toward them, supported by crutches in a well-practiced three-point sequence.

"*Food* happened," says Gayle. "I need a sink before Mary has a conniption."

"The restroom's in the back on the left," he says, pointing with one of his crutches. His eyes are firmly planted on Mary.

Mary embraces him. "How are you healing? Did the second knee surgery do the trick?"

He sighs as she releases him. "My own Florence Nightingale," he says. "It looks better than it did, but it's still fused." Bobby sticks out his stiff left leg. "I exchange these stupid things for a cane next week."

"Well, that's progress, at least. You still have a couple months before graduation. You're going to walk across that stage yet!"

"You mean *limp* across it," he laughs. "I suppose there's a silver lining to my black cloud."

"Oh, yeah? What's that?"

"Good ole Uncle Sam won't be itching to send me off to fight anywhere. I'd be a sitting duck."

Gayle returns from the restroom. "I disagree. I've seen you on those crutches at school. You're lethal."

Bobby laughs again. "It's a good thing my ribs don't hurt anymore, or you'd be dangerous, too."

Mary jumps, feeling her fetus move, and places both hands on her belly. With wide-eyed excitement, she grabs Gayle's and Bobby's hands to experience the moment. All three giggle at the simple yet amazing entertainment.

Bobby still has his hand on her belly and looks deeply into Mary's eyes. "Are you safe? And happy?"

Gayle excuses herself from his awkward intensity with a simple "I'm going to go wait in the car," and walks out of the store.

Mary looks down, away from Bobby's penetrating gaze.

"The reason I ask is that I have some news," he says, taking his hand from her belly so he can grasp his crutch again. He moves to pick up a thick legal-sized envelope from the reception desk and hands it to Mary.

She turns it over to see who the fat packet is from. "LSU!" She looks up at his proud, handsome face. "You got in!"

He nods. "It's a full academic ride. Looks like all that recovery gave me plenty of time to study."

"Oh, congratulations, Bobby! This is so great! I'm going to miss you up there in Baton Rouge," Mary says, peeking inside the envelope to pull out the acceptance letter. The words on the paper read too simply to encompass the profound opportunity being laid at his feet. To her eyes, it is like viewing the Holy Grail—even if it doesn't have her name on it.

"You won't *have* to miss me." Bobby hands her a photograph of a small, pale-yellow garden home.

Mary looks at bright pink azalea blooms beside a porch with a swing. "What do you mean?"

"My parents bought this house near campus as an investment property. You could come with me, there's a program—"

"Whoa there!" Mary shoves the picture into the envelope, slaps it against his chest, and releases it. "Bobby ... stop. I'm already married and pregnant, if you hadn't noticed."

His hand rises to his heart to catch the envelope. "But are you *happy*, Mary? I'm not asking you to run away with me. I'm asking you to consider running toward the future you used to want. This house has two bedrooms in it—one for me . . . and one for you and the baby."

Mary steps away and covers her face with her hands, speaking into her palms. "Why are you doing this?"

"I want you to know you still have choices."

She peeks through her fingers. "Don't you see? I already made my choice."

"Was it the one you truly wanted—or the one you felt you had to choose out of necessity?"

Mary lowers her voice. "It doesn't matter what *I* want anymore."

"How sad for you to believe that," he says. He reaches out over the distance Mary has created between them and takes her hand. "I will always be available to you as your friend, if nothing more."

Mary pulls her hand away. "It isn't fair to keep you in the wings, waiting for a time that may never be."

Bobby sighs. "And that is where *my* choice lives."

The door to the store opens and two rowdy boys enter and make a bee-line to the piano, followed by a haggard mother trying to keep them from disrupting the peace. "Be careful, boys," she pleads, looking to Bobby for help.

He smiles back at her. "Be with you in just a moment."

"It's getting late," Mary says to him. "We need to go anyway." Mary starts for the door, and Bobby follows, hobbling.

"Think about what I said, okay?" He flinches, disturbed by the boys banging on the piano keys.

"Only if you promise to mend." Mary touches his warm cheek and leaves for home.

After helping Gayle write a thought-provoking, slightly subversive essay that will either get her a good grade or a one-way ticket to the principal's office, Mary soaks in a warm bubble bath, permitting herself to imagine a life in Baton Rouge filled with learning, tranquility, and the simple pleasures of . . . of . . .

> *—of whatever selfish, arrogant, know-it-all whores do*
> *when they destroy their families for academic success.*

Eyes closed, she sinks beneath the water, trying to wash away the brief betrayal, listening for the two hearts beating within her body to bring her back to center.

A scratching sound on the bathroom door scares her straight up out of the water, spluttering. Mary stays perfectly still to listen, but there's only the sound of water dripping from her trembling body echoing on the ceramic surfaces. The scratching comes again and her eyes bulge with fear when the doorknob begins to turn. The door opens a crack—and a pair of long white, fuzzy ears appear from behind the door, followed by the cute stuffed face of an earlier-than-expected Easter bunny.

Vinny's voice comes from behind the door in his best Bugs Bunny impersonation. "What's up, Mom? My fur's dirty. Can I come in?"

Her fear falling away, no longer valid, Mary decides to play along with her husband, who was not due home until the next day. "I don't know, Bugs . . . Are you alone?"

"Nah, I brought my best pal wit me." Vinny pushes the door open slowly, revealing himself wearing a smile and a pair of thin white cotton boxer shorts.

"Is your pal dirty, too, Bugs?" she says coyly.

"Absolutely filthy," he says, abandoning the Bugs voice and tossing the bunny on the bed behind him. Teasingly he tugs his thumbs in his waistband to show off his honed body parts, before casting the shorts off to join her in some wet, slippery fun.

Saturday
June 4, 1960

The chest of drawers trembles as Vinny slams the top drawer shut. "After Norman died, you begged me to be tolerant of you playing nursemaid to that boy," Vinny growls, forcing the zipper of an overnight bag. "How much longer do I have to put up with this bullshit?!"

"Calm down, Papa Bear!" Mary soothes as she waddles into the bedroom wearing the only dress that still fits her circumference. She presents him with a childbirth reference book, one finger on the appropriate passage, and smiles with confidence at her worried husband. He studies the words on the page closely, not listening or caring for her reasons as she says, "It's just a high-school graduation ceremony. It shouldn't take more than an hour or so. I want to see my friend cross the stage and receive his diploma. He's worked so hard for this moment."

"Did you ask the doctor about this?" Vinny asks, discombobulated, patting himself down for car keys and wallet.

"Yes. He said everything is fine, and that I have hours and hours before I need to be at the hospital. My contractions are only twenty minutes apart right now."

Sitting uncomfortably in her chair, Mary claps enthusiastically when Bobby's name is called. Abandoning his cane, he lifts his rigid left leg and begins the unassisted journey across the stage. His crimson academic regalia hides much of his painful struggle. Bobby extends his right arm and shakes the principal's hand, accepting his long-sought-after prize in his left.

The diploma itself does not fill him with as much joy as the thought of launching off to find his own unique path to success and happiness in the world. Bobby proudly moves the tassel on his mortarboard, relieved after admitting to his dad that he would not be pursuing a career in medicine and that he decided instead to study criminal law and its complexities.

With only three more names on the roster, the graduation ceremony ends.

Mary's contractions are now closer to ten minutes apart.

"Of course his name couldn't be at the beginning of the alphabet," Vinny grumbles, running low on patience as he helps Mary rise to her feet.

Mary chuckles at Vinny's childish pettiness. "You know that isn't his fault!"

Bobby, reunited with his cane, hugs his way through the congratulatory crowd as he moves ever closer to Mary. Vinny steps in front of her and flashes a warning to Bobby before taking his hand for show. No need for words; they both know what this is. There's little fear left in Bobby, now that he is completely prepared for surprise attacks. His cane handle cleverly houses a sharply honed push-dagger blade which he has practiced with extensively for self-defense.

Mary places a hand on Vinny's chest to calm him and let him know it's time to let go. Bobby takes the platonic high-road. "I wanted to thank you both for coming today. It means a lot to me."

Mary touches his shoulder. "I am so proud of you."

"There's a party at my house—please say you'll come," Bobby urges. "My mom made some of her best dishes."

Mary shifts her weight, puts her head down to look at her watch, and grips the back of a chair.

Vinny rubs the back of his neck as if he wishes he could shed his skin. "I'm gonna get the car."

Bobby stoops to see Mary's lingering grimace. "Are you all right?"

"I'm in labor. My water broke earlier today," she explains as this most recent contraction ends. "But I didn't want to miss your moment of glory!"

Bobby stumbles and drops his cane. "Was that wise? Is the baby safe? If I didn't have this bum leg, I'd carry you to the car," he says. He recovers his weapon and makes a path for her through the remaining crowd.

Mary sighs and looks to the ceiling. "As I explained in length to Vinny twice already, it could still be an entire day before I have this baby." She reaches out to pat Bobby's forearm. "I honestly don't know why you guys are making such a fuss about this! I read that women in Nepal have their babies in the field while harvesting vegetables, and right afterward they go back to working. Don't make me out to be some pansy! The hospital's going to give me something for the pain when I get there."

"So let's get you there already!" Bobby hobbles and props the gymnasium door open for Mary to slowly waddle through.

Holding her lower back, she notices many inquisitive onlookers and laughs. "You and I are certainly some kind of spectacle!"

Vinny pulls up in the car and lurches to a stop by the curb. He runs around to open the car door for his wife. Mary slowly lowers herself into the seat, then jumps when Vinny slams the door shut on her dress, leaving the tail of it hanging outside. She waves goodbye to Bobby just as another contraction hits.

She looks at her watch . . . this one only nine minutes after the last.

"Wait here," Vinny says, parking beneath the sheltered drop-off area.

Mary opens the passenger door and watches him run into the hospital. She listens to the loud hum of the building's overhead lights attracting every flying bug in the vicinity.

Vinny rushes back to the car with a wheelchair, trailed by a woman with a clipboard. "Sir, you can't do that!"

"Try and stop me," he says, helping Mary into the wheelchair. He grips the handles and pushes Mary toward the door, paying no mind to the protests of the employee still following close behind. They enter the hospital doors and into the waiting room. Vinny parks Mary in her wheelchair, then snaps at the woman, "Why don't you shut your yap and find my wife a nurse!"

Swallowing hard, she shakily hands him the clipboard and a pen. "Fill out these financial forms. Someone will be right with you."

Vinny sees disapproval on Mary's face for hurting the woman's feelings, and there is a faint flicker of a need to please her, but not strong enough to apologize. He sits in a cushioned chair and lowers his head to fill out the asinine paperwork.

Mary checks her watch at 8:32 p.m., clocking the new contraction at a five-minute interval.

"Mrs. Carlino?" a yellow-haired nurse verifies before stepping behind the wheelchair to begin pushing her down the corridor.

Vinny jumps to his feet. "Wait one goddamn minute!"

The nurse pauses and puts her hand up to stop him. "Now, now, Mr. Carlino. Your job is over. We'll take good care of your wife from here. The doctor is on his way and has given me his explicit directives."

"We're going to have a baby," Mary whispers with excited apprehension.

"Be brave, my darling." Vinny hugs and kisses her a temporary goodbye. "I love you." Feeling suddenly impotent, he stands watching his family turn the corner, with no further need of him. Sitting on his hands is not what Vinny does best; this night is going to be slow and painful for both parents-to-be.

The room the nurse wheels Mary into is cheerless and morgue-like, decorated in white and metal.

"Undress, put on this gown, sit on the bed. I'll be back in a minute." The nurse hands Mary a thin piece of cloth that in no way resembles a decent covering.

Mary does as instructed and sits staring at a tray of sterile implements which look to her like medieval torture devices. She begins to shiver. The temperature of the room reminds her of Mr. Melancon's refrigerated truck; fear creeps in and she feels a rushing violent wish to be that innocent girl once more, hitching a ride with her best friend to the carnival.

The nurse returns with more supplies to add to the tray. Mary answers a few pertinent questions while the nurse evaluates the overall progression of her labor and checks her vital signs for distress.

"Now, don't be shy, but I have to shave you and administer an enema before the doctor comes in to examine your cervix."

Normally this would send a thrill of trepidation through Mary, but instead a stronger contraction rips through Mary's middle and she digs her fingers into the thin mattress for a full sixty seconds.

"I'm going to give you something for that, too, right after your enema," the nurse says. She wields a safety razor and a can of Colgate shaving cream and approaches Mary's nether regions.

Remembering the book that first taught her what an enema was, she asks, "Does the enema have coffee in it?"

"Why in the world would I put coffee in your behind?" asks the nurse. She looks at the capped syringes on the tray to make sure she hasn't already dosed Mary with the twilight sedative. Satisfied, she positions Mary on her side in the Sims' position, hangs a bag of fluid on an IV stand, and rudely inserts the enema tip without any lubrication.

The water that flows into Mary is warm . . . but not at all soothing.

"Relax," says the nurse. "Take deep breaths . . . let the soapy water do all the work, dear." She rolls Mary onto her back to release into a bed pan.

Are these humiliations nearly over?

Post-enema, the doctor arrives and Mary has her answer.

"I hear we're moving along rather nicely—pardon the pun," he says to the nurse, who rolls her eyes while sanitizing and draping Mary for cervical examination. The doctor washes his hands in the sink and snaps into a pair of sterile gloves to accost Mary beneath the sheet.

She whimpers in distress at the prodding. To calm herself, she expels a long breath while looking up at an air vent in the ceiling.

"Seven centimeters, eighty-percent effaced, and station is minus-one now," says the doctor. He peels off the gloves and discards them in a receptacle.

The nurse writes the updated numbers in her chart.

Mary endures another strong contraction and moans deep in her throat.

"I'm coming, dear." The nurse connects a hypodermic needle to a pre-filled glass syringe and taps the side to eliminate the air bubble, along with a tiny spurt of the memory-zapping elixir. She raises Mary's gown to expose her naked hip and roughly swipes the skin with an alcohol-soaked pad.

"What . . . what is that for?"

Before Mary's curiosity can be quenched or she can offer any protest, the nurse pops the business end of the compact pharmaceutical delivery system into her thigh muscle and depresses the plunger.

"Magic potion to make the pain go away, dear," says the nurse in condescension. "Shhh . . . relax. Deep breaths and it'll all be over soon." The nurse covers Mary's quaking body with a blanket to ease the shivers increased by the injection, then flips off some of the bright lights.

Three contractions later, Mary is vaguely aware of another injection—or maybe just a dream of one. She is pulled only partially out of her induced stupor by increasingly stronger episodes at a frequency of three minutes apart.

She writhes, her thin extremities inhibited, bound by leather.

Sunday
June 5, 1960

The brand-new baby girl pierces through the serenity of the womb and into the world with a loud wail at 1:15 a.m.

But Mary doesn't hear her aching cry.

Baby Lisa calls out to her mother, but to no avail.

Poor Mary is moved to a room better suited for convalescing, still lost in the fog of artificial amnesia.

Hours go by before the fog lifts enough for the delicate bundle to reunite with the warmth of a familiar heartbeat. Mary completes the delayed ritual of maternal bonding, counting tiny fingers and toes with no less reverence or wonderment.

"Lisa," she whispers down at her baby girl. "Lisa."

Vinny, unable to stand the surmounting anxiety and arduous pacing, seeks to ease his own agony with the temporary panacea flowing at a local bar.

Allowing his own anesthetic to wear off at home, he arrives back at the hospital freshly showered and mouthwashed to meet his daughter at lunchtime.

In true 1960 American fashion, neither parent is aware of the other's struggle.

Mary's disappointment over missing out on the details of her daughter's arrival is swept away by the joyous love washing over her with Lisa's every new breath, movement, and sound.

"Can I hold her for a minute?" Vinny asks tentatively, sitting down beside his wife and daughter on the bed.

Like a mama bear, Mary flashes him a look as if he has asked to kidnap the sleeping infant. She studies Vinny's face and sees his longing to be included in the circle, the yearning to be a part of the deep bonds being formed. She swallows her selfish instincts and hands Lisa over to him. "Careful with her head."

Vinny falls in love, feeling a rush of fear and strong devotion to this tiny pink being who wraps her hand around his finger with a level of trust that only a newborn knows. A tear drips from his eye and onto the soft afghan surrounding Lisa with cozy warmth and her mother's scent.

A day-shift nurse knocks on the door and enters with a bright arrangement of flowers.

"Who sent those?" Vinny asks, cutting his eyes to Mary.

She looks back at him with a blank face and a slight head shake. "Is there a card?" she asks, squirming uncomfortably at the fullness of her lactating breasts.

"No card, but the gentleman who sent them is waiting in the lobby for visiting hours," the nurse mentions. She sets the vase down on a table near the window.

"You can go take a look," Mary says. "It's time for me to feed the baby."

Vinny stands up, Lisa still in his arms, showing reluctance to give up his turn so soon.

The nurse addresses Mary in a wheedling tone. "Please tell me you're not still set on that breastfeeding nonsense. I *told* you we provide the best nutritional formulas money can buy." The nurse looks to Vinny for help. "Your wife is flying in the face of conventional wisdom."

Lisa grunts and whines as she tries to suckle the back of her own hand. Vinny kisses her sweet-smelling forehead, then tells the nurse, "If you knew how much studying she did for motherhood, you wouldn't question her."

The nurse gives up with a shrug and places an extra pillow in Mary's lap for support. "Press the call button if you change your mind."

"I'm determined to do this," Mary vows, unsnapping the top of her house coat. She reaches for her hungry baby.

Vinny hands over his daughter and marvels at the process of her latching onto her mother's nipple, as if she is performing a new trick.

Mary dislikes being ogled, especially now when she is feeling ugly and inadequate. "This will take about twenty minutes. Go ahead and see who sent the flowers."

Vinny feels like he's being kicked out of the girls' clubhouse before he finds out the secret handshake. Walking down the hospital corridors, he imagines how he'll need to be on his best behavior from now on, so he can be worthy of being included—even if it means putting up with pesky lame-legged rivals. When he turns the corner, he fully expects to see Bobby Vicknair sitting in the waiting area—not the soon-to-be ex-boss he's carefully avoided for months.

"Carlos?" he says, looking around for any ambush that might be lurking, his jaw set. "What are you doing here?"

"It's just me—and I come bearing gifts," Carlos says, lifting a large basket filled with various high-priced knickknacks. "For the new arrival."

"How did you know to come?"

"I keep my eye on you . . . like I always have."

Vinny shifts and thumbs his nose. "You're a regular guardian angel."

Carlos bites the inside of his cheek before he says, "I came all this way to welcome your Junior into the fold. This is how you thank me?"

Vinny snorts. "That eye you keep on me? You need to have it checked. My 'Junior' is a girl."

Carlos looks down at the basket, regretting one or two of the items, then pats his pocket. "I brought us a couple-a Montecristos to celebrate."

"I'm game. We have to burn a few minutes before we can go up, anyway," Vinny says. He takes the basket from Carlos and heads for a courtyard exit.

Sitting outside at a round, wrought-iron table set, Vinny doesn't know if it's the hangover, the cigar, or the company that's turning his stomach, but he tries his best to play nice. He remembers quite well some sage advice about holding your friends close and your enemies closer.

Vinny scrutinizes the items in the basket while listening to Carlos complain about this and that, but interrupts him after finding a transistor radio underneath a bib. "This for a newborn?"

Carlos shrugs noncommittally. "It's for the future."

Vinny covers it with the bib once more. "I'm sorry. What were you saying?"

"I said it looks like JFK is gonna get the nod for Democratic nominee."

"Do we know that for sure?"

"Well . . . no," Carlos replies, drawing gently on his stogie, "but he sure is getting all kinds of attention lately."

"You sound like you're in a forgiving mood."

"Naw, don't get me wrong, I still say *fuck* dem Kennedys. It's not forgiveness you hear. It's patience," Carlos says eerily, the smoke leaking out the sides of his mouth.

Vinny lowers his cigar. He inhales the summer-afternoon air, closes his eyes tight, and exhales, dropping his head. "I'm too exhausted to play games today. I know you're really here to rake me over the coals, so just get on with it."

Carlos jerks his head back and his free hand flies to his chest as if in supreme offense. "So, I'm not supposed to be concerned that I haven't heard from you in forever?" He shoots forward, jutting his cigar at Vinny like a finger. "So, I shouldn't be hurt that you didn't tell me about your firstborn?" Carlos leans back again, studying Vinny's non-reaction, and puffs before resuming. "Games? I'm not the one playing house. I'm not the one shirking the duty to his family that came *first*."

"As you can see, I have my hands full. I need some time."

"Because of our history, I guess you've earned this leave of absence. I will prove that I am patient with my friends as well as my enemies," Carlos says magnanimously.

Vinny stares down at the slow burn of a treasured cigar becoming tall, expensive ash.

As am I, Marcello, as am I.

Monday
July 25, 1960

"**N**o television tonight, guys. We have company," Mary's little sister Sarah says. She finds a safe spot on the floor for the twins to enjoy decorating the pages of their new *Peanuts* coloring books. She hands Jenny and Margene their own separate character books at the table and asks in a teacher's sing-song voice, "What do we say?"

"*Thank youuu, Maryyy!*" they both parrot.

"You're welcome," Mary says proudly of her well-mannered sisters.

Sarah opens two expanded packs of crayons, loving the array of the wax-stick rainbows standing at attention. She selects for each of the twins a fresh-tipped orange-yellow for Charlie Brown's iconic shirt. Margene and Jenny wait their turn at the table with their own colorless character books.

Christmas licks her chops; her tail spanks the table leg as she inches closer for a sniff of the new items, hoping they are edible.

"How about pink for Barbie?" Sarah hands a stick to Jenny, then selects one for Margene. "And a blue for Cinderella."

"Took you two long enough to bring the baby over!" Vivian complains. She opens the box to the new rice cooker Vinny has brought his mother-in-law as a token of good will. "You'd swear you was under some kinda quarantine or somethin."

In the Poche kitchen, the smell of a vanished meal (which yielded no leftovers) lingers in the air. Mary finds herself in an unchanged familiar setting that still somehow seems as foreign as Kathmandu. In unknowing remembrance (more out of habit than anything), Jenny snaps the radio onto NBC News on the hour at seven o'clock.

"Turn that blasted thing off!" Vivian says.

Sarah rises from her spot on the floor to obey when Jenny doesn't.

"Please don't," Mary tells Sarah. "Lisa loves it."

Charlie is holding seven-week-old Lisa. "You do?" he asks, sweetly tapping the end of her button nose.

"It started in the hospital," Vinny explains. "If we changed the radio station when the news was on, she would cry and cry. Doesn't matter if it's the television or the transistor radio—the news is her favorite."

Mary walks up behind Charlie and rests her hands on his shoulders, looking down on Lisa's smiling face. "It looks like our father's legacy will go on. In some respects, anyway."

After an awkward silence among the room's listeners, a news announcement brings Vivian back to her old scoffing self. "Well, go figure. Woolworth's went and gave in," she says.

"I didn't hear . . . what'd they do?" Mary asks.

"They're serving them coloreds up in Greensboro," Vivian answers, making a prime place for the rice cooker to sit in the cabinet below the counter.

Charlie, who has been closely following the plight of the Freedom Fighters, says, "Yeah, but after how many months of protesting?"

"Simple science—adapt or die," Mary says. She unwraps the two pies she brought for dessert. "An evolution, really. They're just deciding to survive."

"Woolworth's or the coloreds?" Vivian asks, fishing a pie knife from the utensil drawer.

Taking it from her mother, Mary sinks the blade into the soft apple pie center. "Both, really. The store will stay open to get their money, and Negros will have the privileges and opportunities we should all have." She places the first slice of pie on a disposable plate.

"I wish we didn't have to discuss these racial issues all the time," Vinny says, grabbing a beer from the pack he stashed in the fridge.

"How can we not?" Mary asks. She rescues a fallen chunk of cooked, cinnamoned apple from the pie plate and pops it into her mouth. "It's all over the news, all the time," she says between chews.

Without further discussion Vinny walks outside, letting the screen door slam behind him.

"What's *his* problem?" asks Vivian. She gives Charlie a slice of pie in exchange for a chance to hold her grandchild for a few minutes.

Mary continues loading plates as if on an assembly line. "Oh, Vin . . . ever since we got married, he's been so sensitive about social ills."

"Could be fatherhood's making him anxious," Vivian says.

"I don't know how," Mary replies. "I'm the only one being a parent twenty-four hours a day."

Vivian snorts.

Friday
January 20, 1961

Vinny, **painfully aware** of his inability to elude his past without risking dire consequences, has returned to doing Carlos's bidding.

At the kitchen table he hides behind a newspaper, shoving his real self and his rage down below the surface of this illusion of normalcy that he insists on maintaining. His repressed emotions are becoming as easy to harness as a cork in water.

"Well, it's official," Mary says. She places seven-month-old Lisa in an upholstered metal high chair and heads for the kitchen counter. "John Fitzgerald Kennedy is the thirty-fifth President of the United States."

Baby Lisa explores the top corner of the orange-flowered upholstery with her mouth, turning to watch her mom smash a ripe banana with a fork.

"You say that as if it's a good thing," Vinny replies. He pats the metal tray of the high chair to get Lisa's attention. She looks at him with a drooling smile and slaps the surface with her own pudgy hands, shrieking with excitement. Some of Vinny's inner agitation wanes, basking in her cherubic zest for life.

"Well, isn't it?" Mary asks, sitting down in front of Lisa, whose eyes fill with delighted anticipation as she watches Mary load the tiny spoon with the sweet mushy treat. "I believe having a forward-thinking President is good for the country, don't you?"

Vinny is back in the Friday headlines. "If you say so, dear," he replies, trying to replicate Chick's obedience training.

Mary can sense a bit of sarcasm and peeks behind his paper curtain. "If the Woolworth's stores were finally able to let it go, so can you."

He peeks back. "Let *what* go?"

"Your prejudice."

"My *prejudice?*" Vinny asks, popping his paper back into place. He mumbles, "Pfft . . . you think *I'm* prejudiced? Well, ain't that rich."

"Aren't you? I just assumed that was why you didn't like Kennedy—because of what he's done for racial equality."

"Someone once told me to never assume, because it makes an *ass* of *u* and *me.*"

Mary narrows her gaze at his insolence, carefully skimming the sides of Lisa's mouth to catch the dollops that try to escape. "All right, smarty, then tell me the real reason you don't like him."

Vinny haphazardly folds the newspaper, leaving himself exposed. "I really don't have anything against the guy. I just don't like to stand too close to anyone who makes his kind of enemies."

Mary mirrors Lisa's cheerful face and glances at Vinny's pensive demeanor. "You mean *political* enemies . . . because Kennedy wants to see positive changes in policy?"

Wearing a sneer, he taps his fingers atop the newspaper askew on the table. "What silly, idealistic *bullshit* notions. You still don't understand how all of this works, do you?"

Mary smiles at Lisa smacking her lips for another bite. "I believe Kennedy has some of those same *silly* notions. That's exactly what will make him a good President . . . isn't that right, my girl?" Lisa slaps the high chair's table in enthusiastic agreement as she takes in another ripe mouthful.

"If your new savior thinks he can change a structure that came way before him . . . that kind of idiocy will make him a *dead* President."

Mary gasps at the thought and the tot's spoon falls to the floor. "Why would you say something so horrible?"

He reaches down to retrieve the spoon. "I know things I wish I didn't."

"What do you know?"

Vinny sets his jaw and doesn't answer as he rinses the spoon under the stream of the kitchen faucet. He turns and hands the spoon back to Mary.

She watches him pass a damp washcloth across the floor at her feet. "I'm not a simpleton," she says. "Talk to me."

He looks up at her with contemptuous pity. "You don't really want to know the truth—no one does." Vinny shakes his head and rises to cleanse the sweet residue from the cloth. "You and everybody else want eloquent speeches given by men in expensive suits to place a bubble around you and make you feel safe from the boogeyman." He drops the cloth in the sink with disgust and lowers his head, bracing his hands on the counter.

"Silly Daddy," Mary says to Lisa. "There's no such *thing* as the boogeyman."

Vinny lifts his eyes and catches his bent reflection in the shiny hide of the metallic toaster. He stares frowning at his own ugly truths and inhales a long, frustrated breath.

Mary turns to him. "Vin? What's wrong?"

"What's wrong?!" he says, astonished and slightly envious of her empirical blindness. An ugly laugh escapes his lips as he reaches to light a cigarette. "Liberty, peace, democratic freedom . . ." He places the cig in his lips and it bobs up and down with his speech. "It's all a pretty lie, sold to you at a premium."

Mary shakes her head sadly. "How can you say that? Look how far we've come, Vin. We live in a country where no one lives in chains."

He raises one eyebrow at her, taking a puff to light his smoke. He holds it in, lest he upset Mary. "Don't we, though? Just because you don't see them doesn't mean they aren't there, Mag. Come talk to me when you can step outside the invisible boundaries of your fancy prison of so-called 'freedom,' " he says as he grabs the keys to leave.

"Wait! Where are you . . ." She jumps from the *pop!* of the screen door slamming behind her husband, launching Lisa into tears.

Tuesday
April 4, 1961

"**M**ay I ask who's calling?" Mary says to the male voice on the telephone.

The exasperated voice pleads, "Mrs. Carlino, can you just tell him it's an urgent call from D.C.?"

Mary puts the telephone handset down on Lisa's empty high chair and runs toward the sound of running water splashing on Vinny in the shower. She reaches in and pushes down the diverter valve so the water now splashes only his feet.

"What the hell?" Vinny says, and turns the water off.

Mary wants to laugh at his confusion, but she knows not to. "You have an urgent phone call from D.C.!"

Vinny wraps a towel around his waist and runs slip-sliding to the phone, nearly taking a spill along the way. Mary hears him loudly ask the voice on the phone if he's joking about Guatemala. She scoots a towel along the floor to mop up his snail-like trail. Before she can complete the task, he backtracks to the bathroom.

"What's going on?" she asks.

With clean undershorts now clinging to his buttocks, Vinny throws random toiletries into a Dopp kit. "Emergency. Have to go out of town."

"I thought you were done disappearing," Mary says, watching helplessly as he rushes to the closet, slips into a pair of dark-blue trousers, and tucks in a bleached-white undershirt.

He exhales, looking at her. "Don't give me a hard time, Mag." He yanks a light-gray shirt off a hanger.

She rests her hands on her hips. "At least tell me if you're going to D.C. or Guatemala!"

He sits on the side of the bed with the unbuttoned shirt, closes his eyes, and tugs at both sides of his damp hair. "You're just never gonna get it through that thick *damn* skull o' yours," he says, low and controlled. The vein in his temple throbs in his anger.

Mary lowers herself onto the foot of the bed. "If you'd just let me in for once, I'll show you I'm stronger and more resourceful than you give me credit for."

His eyes open, hard and cold. "Don't *ever* ask me about my business again."

Lisa wakes from her nap and begins to cry for her lunch.

Mary's chin tremors as she rises up, unusually slow, to answer the cranky call.

"Why don't you worry about what's inside these walls?" he says, irritated by her hesitation. He points in the direction of his child's distress. "*That's* all you need to concern yourself with."

In the days, weeks, months that follow, Vinny arrives and slips away like a tide untethered from the moon's schedule, depositing gifts, doting on Lisa, and keeping true to most of his husbandly promises. He provides a well-above-average existence for his family, leaving them wanting for nothing.

As long as they behave.

Mary, in her increasingly smaller world, learns for the most part to keep any burning questions to herself when he's around. This seems to keep the peace. Despite being well-cared for, however, she can't keep her mind from wandering; she broods about many things inside and outside the walls of her home.

After Vinny's insistence that she stay safely cooped up for her own good, she watches or listens to every news broadcast for information about things like the Bay of Pigs invasion, civil rights riots, missiles in Cuba, and many sad, scary, worldly things. Some of these stick in her mind like the last few pieces of a puzzle that beg to be put in place to make the picture complete. Mary worries about her discoveries, and even more about the things she does not know.

Saturday
June 2, 1962

T he last time Mary was in this venue, she was in labor. Today, a baby two days shy of her second birthday squirms in Mary's lap to see Aunt Gayle happily walk across the stage to say farewell to Terrebonne High School.

Mary squirms a bit, too, reminded all too well that her name is missing from the roster. The green color of her pre-pregnancy dress is almost as dark as the envy she keeps shooing away like a bothersome fly entering her consciousness. When the jealousy creeps into her complexion, stark beneath her long ebony waves, she reminds herself,

I am here to celebrate the accomplishments of my best friend,
and that has nothing to do with me.

Walking in the parking lot after the ceremony, Chick freezes with the recollection of something he heard earlier in the week. "Hey, you feel like going to Rouse's Supermarket with us?" he asks Vinny.

Dumbfounded by the question, Vinny looks at Gayle as if Chick has brain damage.

"Sure, honey," Gayle snarks, " 'cause everyone *loves* to paint the town red at the grocery store." She blows her dangling tassel out of her way.

"Are you hungry?" Mary asks Chick, adjusting Lisa on her hip. "Because I know there's a plate of fried catfish to die for just a mile or two from here."

"Rouse's Supermarket is giving a discount," Chick explains, "this weekend only, to all families with a graduate who wears their nightgown to the store. I'm buying—you guys in?"

"It's not a *night*gown," Gayle says, stretching out her arms to show off her wing span to Lisa.

Vinny looks to Mary, who sets wiggly Lisa down so she can run over to Gayle.

Lisa jumps up and down, claps her hands, and says, "Yayyy, Auntie Gayle!"

"Lisa's in," Mary laughs. "If she's in, I'm game."

Vinny brings his open hands up. "I guess we're going to spank some canned goods."

Gayle dances with Lisa next to the car. "I hope they give S&H stamps. I just received their new idea book and *boy*, did it fill Auntie Gayle with ideas."

"I knew we should have taken separate cars," Vinny says—only half-jokingly—from his place in the backseat on the way to Rouse's.

"It won't take long," Gayle says. "They close in an hour. We'll have you back before your bedtime."

"See? We aren't the only ones." Chick pulls into an unusually active parking lot of other families who, it seems, have also heeded the advertisement.

Seeing some take advantage of the sale with armloads of alcohol for celebrating, Mary asks, "Is the discount only on booze?"

Chick turns off the engine. "No—twenty percent off anything in the store." He rubs his hands together. "Meat department, here I come!"

"Are those Vandebilt colors I see?" Mary asks, picking Lisa up and heading toward the flurry of blue and gold exiting the store with bags of eggs and toilet paper. A tipsy girl's voice calls out from the rear of the pack. "Mush, doggies, mush!" she laughs, making snapping-whip noises behind them.

Mary and Gayle instantly recognize the voice and the mouth it belongs to, too often emitting such meanness to their torment.

Veronica appears in her graduation garb, a drunken grin appearing on her face at the sight of her old enemies. "Well, well, *well*. Lookie what we have here."

In an attempt to fight fire with kindness, Mary says, "I guess you all deserve to revel in catching the big prize."

"The 'big prize'?" Veronica laughs, then steps closer to reach out and touch Lisa's soft curls—but Vinny grabs her wrist before she can make contact. Veronica's eyes flash at Vinny's, and he lets her go.

"We both know only one person here caught the *big prize*, don't we, Mary?"

Lisa wrinkles her nose at Veronica's close encounter. "Lady, your bref stinks," she announces, sending the intoxicated cronies doubled over in laughter.

Veronica glances at Gayle's stunned face and gives Lisa a hard smile. "Perhaps your mommy should teach you some manners," she growls.

"Mommy teached me to brush my teef." Lisa tugs on her bottom lip. "See?"

They watch Veronica stagger away muttering angrily beneath her breath to rejoin her group of hyenas.

Gayle fans herself with the Quick Saver book. *"Well* . . . who knew it was that easy?"

Wednesday
January 23, 1963

It is a quarter to three in the morning when the twirling and flashing lights of the police car arrive.

Mary is still crying, holding a cold compress to her swollen, busted lip over the kitchen sink, next to an unopened First-Aid kit.

"Is this the Carlino residence?" the officer asks Mary through the screen door.

"Yes," she cries into the rag she is using to keep her blood from dripping everywhere.

"Ma'am, is the person who hurt you still on the premises?"

"No . . ." she mumbles, spitting blood into the sink. "He left."

"Can you identify your assailant?"

She drops the rag and turns to open the screen door. "My husband," she sniffs, sweeping her damp, matted hair behind her shoulders.

"Geez—*Mary?*" The officer slips out of his authoritative tone. "Christ—please, sit down." He rinses the rag in the kitchen sink, then wraps it around a piece of ice from her freezer and places it on her left eye, which looks much worse than her lip.

Mary pulls a chair out and sits. "Thanks, Danny. I didn't expect them to send you. Please . . . don't tell your sister. I don't want to suck any more of my friends into this."

"I won't say a word to Jane, promise," Officer Naquin says, moving the First-Aid box to the table. He searches the kit for alcohol wipes, medical tape, and scissors. "But I need you to tell me what happened here."

"I must have said something that made him mad." A hot, stinging tear finds its way from her downcast eyes into the cut in her lip, but she's too numb to flinch at its sting.

"Were you trying to make him mad?" Danny asks, laying out the needed supplies.

Mary watches him pull a chair to face hers. Danny was certainly as handsome as ever, but he still gave her the creeps. "Are you trying to say," she asks him, "that I asked for this?"

He rips open an alcohol wipe packet. "No, but we all know not to poke a bear. Did you poke the bear?"

As he pats her bruised and broken skin with the wipe, Mary inhales quick and sharp and her teeth clinch. She exhales and says, "Even if I had, I certainly did not deserve this." She points at her damaged face. "I need you to do something, Danny."

Instead of replying, he snips and fashions several homemade butterfly closures for Mary's wounds. Each time he pinches her gashed skin, a muffled squeak escapes her throat.

"I want to help . . . I do," he finally tells her. "To be candid with you, Mary, I feel like taking him and wringing his neck right now. But there just isn't a whole lot I can do."

"Can't you arrest him?" Mary watches him pack up the unused items and clamp the lid of the First-Aid kit shut.

"I could ... but how angry do you think he would be after spending a few hours in the tank?"

"If he comes back, can you make him leave?"

Danny shakes his head. "No. If his name is on the deed or the lease, I can't put a man out of his own home. You have to be the one to leave."

"Where would I go that he would not find me?"

"Well, if you can't stay here, how about your mom's? At least there you'd have witnesses—and she could have him removed."

"That might not be the best idea—may not even be an *option*, really." Mary looks to the ceiling to stem further tears. "I'm not sure what to do."

Danny stands up and adjusts his gear belt. "You should go pack a bag. I'll drive you over to your mom's," he says, and then points to the refrigerator. "You mind if I fix myself a sandwich or something?"

"Oh ... uh ... no," Mary stammers at the odd request. "Go ahead and help yourself."

Danny takes notice of a nearly empty bottle of whiskey on the counter and puts the cap back on it. He makes a ham sandwich and washes it down with a glass of milk. When Mary reappears with a bag and a still-sleeping Lisa in her arms, he asks, "Mary, have you been drinking alcohol?"

Mary catches his meaning, and she just barely stops herself from scowling at him. "No, I don't particularly like the stuff. That bottle is what Vinny tore through before tearing into me."

"Well, *there's* the problem, then." Danny ruffles the front of her hair as if she were a shortstop on a tee-ball team. "Just let him sleep it off wherever he went, and it'll work itself out. I'm sure he didn't mean to hurt you."

Mary glares at Danny. "Oh, just like that. Silly me."

In the quiet stillness of the morning, just before daylight floods the Poche household, the beam of headlights crosses the dimly lit kitchen. Vivian is standing watching Charlie form up his first-ever batch of cinnamon rolls. She sees the police cruiser pull up in the driveway. The officer opens the door and the interior light shines on Mary's face in the backseat.

"For the love of God . . . Charlie, go check on the twins," she orders.

"But it's not time. They aren't up yet," Charlie says.

"Don't sass me, boy! Can't you see there's trouble afoot?" she says as she passes through the front screen door. She folds her arms, ready for battle.

Mary steps gingerly out of the vehicle and looks up at her mother with her good eye. Vivian can see the other one is bruised and swollen shut. For a second she has the urge to run to her firstborn, but quickly suppresses it and remains standing on the porch.

Mary perches Lisa on her hip and moves slowly up the steps and past her mother into the house, as if she is a child again, one who has done something terribly wrong and is ready for punishment. Inside, she sets her bag down and retreats upstairs to the bathroom, to wash herself and her child clean of the horrible incident.

On the porch, Vivian silently listens to what Danny has to say before leading him to continue their visit at the boisterous school-morning breakfast table.

"Thank you again, Officer. You sure you don't want another cup of coffee?" she offers him one last time, to which he again declines and then leaves.

Inside, Vivian grabs the phone and dials, paying no attention to the children arguing about who hogged the bathroom during breakfast.

Somewhat refreshed, Mary descends to the stair landing and sits on the bottom step, where she lies in wait for whatever comes next. Lisa drapes from her like a small monkey.

Vivian finally approaches her and says in a strained whisper, "Go up and get yourselves a nap in my room, then, while I figure out how in the hell I'm gonna stretch the food. But after I get some breakfast in you, we're gonna have a little talk."

"I can't rest or eat now," Mary says, standing up beside her mother. "Not until I feel Lisa and I are safe."

Vivian scowls. "We should take this outside before the others find out what you've done." She roughly nudges Mary out and onto the porch. Once outside, Lisa slides down from Mary's arms to explore.

"What have I done?"

Vivian folds her arms again. "You with your high and mighty decisions! Selfish, really."

"Selfish? Mama, he *hit* me. And it's not the first time. I'm scared! What if he gets mad and hurts the baby?"

"Well, then, you had better get yourself together and go right back to put your house in order, young lady!" Vivian continues. "You made your bed—"

"I don't have anywhere else to go," Mary interrupts, her throat full of tears.

Vivian shakes her head. "Nuh-uh, you can't stay here. I have enough mouths to feed on what little I get from the Social Security."

"I'll get a job, Mama."

"Who's gonna watch that one?" Vivian points in the direction of her freshly bathed grandchild. Lisa is sitting on the dirty porch, her head tilted, petting a toy turtle that has been banned from the house for making too much racket when he tiptoes across the floor.

"I could start sewing for hire again," Mary says. "I could watch Lisa myself. She's a good baby."

Vivian starts to pace the porch, looking at her slippers. "Where you gonna get a machine?"

"I can use my old one. I'll make do until I can afford a new one."

Vivian's head pops up. "I sold it, along with the other things you didn't see fit to take with you."

Mary's mouth falls open. "What?" she says, as if her mother's language doesn't make sense.

"I sold that machine and whatever else I needed to to get by. I got bills, you know. Your father left me with nothing but bills."

"Vinny . . . Vinny said he would make sure you were taken care of." Mary's shoulders slump, caught unaware of her mother's predicament.

"He sends a meager check for the house every month. How long you think that's gonna last, with you two at odds? You always was the selfish one, always thinking you're better than all of us, with your grades and your looks. See where it got you? On my doorstep with a fat lip!" Vivian is speaking through gritted teeth. "A smart girl should know when to keep her big trap shut."

Mary stares at her mother, recalling that exact phrase from the most recent row with her husband—right after her lip was busted. "Where did that come from? Have you been talking to Vinny?"

"You darn tootin," Vivian says, unafraid to admit it. "And he'll be here to pick you up in a matter of seconds. So you'd better come to your senses."

"I should've known," Mary says, the tears threatening to return. "My father loved me and wanted me to wait, to give Vinny time to show his true colors . . . but as soon as Daddy was in the ground, you sold me to the highest bidder."

"Daddy!" Lisa claps, seeing Vinny's car approaching in haste.

Mary's heart sinks, knowing it's too late to run. "I'll go back," she tells Vivian, "and when I do, you be sure to remember this one thing: my husband may sign his name on a slip of paper, but it's your daughter who's paying for the things you have." Mary's body fills up with a new level of hate for the woman who gave birth to her.

Vivian smiles with a touch of malice. "You'll be fine, Mary. You'll see."

Vinny runs up onto the porch, scoops Lisa up into his arms, and turns to Mary. "Get in the car," he says calmly, cradling Lisa's head on his shoulder as if he just saved her from some terrible fate.

With her stomach tightly clinched, Mary slinks back to the car, defeated, knowing that no matter what Vivian says, she's nowhere within shouting distance of "fine." She watches Vinny and her mother conversing just as if it were any other visit. Vivian reaches inside the door to retrieve Mary's bag, but Vinny refuses to take it. He carries Lisa to the car, opens the passenger car door, and hands her off to Mary. Lisa is craning over her shoulder, clearly distressed at leaving the bag behind.

"I'll buy Mommy some new stuff," Vinny says to her, and shuts the car door.

Vivian waves goodbye from the porch, blowing kisses at Lisa.

Mary sits against the door, stunned, trying to put herself in her mother's shoes—a poor widow with so many responsibilities, making the hard choices.

Perhaps I would have done the same?

When Vinny slams the driver's door, disturbing Lisa further, Mary thinks,

No way in hell.

For a long while, the car ride is quiet without the radio playing.

Vinny strangles the wheel. "Am I going to have any more trouble with you?" he asks in a flat tone.

"No," she mumbles, barely audible.

"I'm sorry, I didn't quite catch that."

"No, sir," she says obediently, staring out the window at some kids waiting for the school bus, wishing she were one of them.

"That's my good girl." He reaches over to touch her knee.

Reflexively she recoils. "I'm sorry . . . I hurt all over."

"I understand," he says. "Time heals all wounds, and we have the rest of our lives, my Maggie."

There's that name again. Maggie. The name she's beginning to associate with this obedient, enslaved person she became but doesn't want to be, no matter how gilded the cage.

She thinks with all the conviction she can conjure,

I will never forget that my father named me Mary!

Tuesday

June 11, 1963

An hour after lunch, Mary spies a car sitting in the driveway across the street and recognizes it as belonging to Gayle's mother. She jogs across concrete hot enough to melt her shoes and knocks to enter. Shirley opens the door and greets her with a dazzling smile.

"Am I interrupting?" Mary asks, smoothing her haphazardly combed hair.

"Not at all! Please join us." Mary enters the narrow doorway and Shirley pulls her in for a hug, then holds her out at arm's length. "You still look great," she says, turning Mary's chin to the light, looking for signs of any permanent damage.

Mary smiles uncomfortably. "Lisa is still napping and I thought I might come over to say hello, but only for a minute. It's been so long since I saw you!"

"Would you mind if we all went over to your house?" Gayle asks, offering up an embarrassed grin.

"Sure ... I guess so," Mary says, trying to remember if she finished putting away all the dishes and the folded laundry.

"Apparently, my daughter thinks that *Sanka* is the same thing as coffee."

Gayle rolls her eyes at Mary and mouths: *Sorry.*

"Is Community Coffee okay?" Mary asks hesitantly. She steps back outside into the oven of summer, thinking it is way too hot for coffee.

"Perfect!" Shirley says with more than a hint of relief. She slides a container off the counter and follows Mary out. "I brought beignets, made them myself."

The three women cross the street and enter Mary's house, whispering and giggling as if they are sneaking back in after a night on the town, afraid of waking the master of the house. Before the coffee can finish brewing, Lisa is awake, refreshed, and pleased to have company—especially one that is serving up a sugared snack. Mary places her in the high chair and sets her up with a well-powdered beignet.

"When was the last time you saw Vivian?" Shirley asks as Mary hands her a steaming cup.

Mary pauses in pouring a cup for Gayle. "I saw her at Charlie's graduation, but we didn't speak."

"Oh, yes, *Charlie*," Shirley says, adding a nip of milk to her brew. "*So* proud of him getting into Nicholls."

"Mary helped him study for all his midterms and finals," Gayle mentions through a mouthful of beignet, already taking another golden doughy pillow from the open container. "Didn't you, Mary?"

"Yes, I helped," she admits, pouring herself a cold glass of milk. "But he took the tests all by himself, so I can't take any credit for his accomplishments. He's a hard worker." She closes the milk carton and places it back on the wire shelf in the refrigerator.

Shirley sighs. "Just like his father . . . God rest his soul."

"Mommy, I want *down!*" Lisa whines, ready to be free of the long-legged chair.

Mary removes all traces of sugar from Lisa's upper body with a wet paper towel before setting her loose on the rest of the house, then says, "Too bad he never had much to show for it . . . or to leave behind."

Shirley frowns at this. "Sounds like Vivian's been poor-mouthing again."

"The last time we spoke, she was complaining that he left her in a mountain of debt."

Shirley gasps. "That just isn't *true!* Your mom is sitting pretty."

Mary stares at her. She can feel waves of shock begin to numb their way up her spine.

"Sweetie, it's true, I know it for a fact," Shirley says. "Norman had the forethought to use a substantial savings, along with any extra he could spare, to pay off the house before he died! When he and James signed the final paperwork, he was so proud. Wanted to announce it at Christmas."

Gayle and Mary share a look of surprise, and Mary's pulse begins to feel like an express train picking up speed.

"Did he really?" Gayle asks, warily watching Mary's face go from a dismayed pallor to red-hot with angered realization.

Mary's thoughts dive into a deep, sick misery. They scream out,

Blood has no consistency at all!

"Not only that," Shirley continues, "but Norman had a life insurance policy that paid out. I don't know where *that* money went." She takes a sip of her coffee.

Mary battens down her roiling thoughts and says, "She gets a check from Vinny, too." Her voice cracks on the words.

Shirley chokes on both her coffee and Mary's revelation. "Are you *serious?*" she asks with a strained rasp.

"For how much?" Gayle asks, letting Lisa climb up into her lap. Shirley flashes her daughter a look for her impropriety, but Gayle shrugs at her mom. "What? We share everything else."

"I don't know how much, exactly," Mary says, "but I think it's monthly."

"Well, I can tell you she isn't hurting," Shirley declares. "I see deliveries from all *sorts* of places during the week. With the way she flirts nowadays, I had started to think she might be sweet on one of the drivers."

To consider her mother benefitting from her father's death, or as a sexual being, makes Mary's stomach roll. Her fertile imagination ruins her desire for food, drink, even such company as Gayle and Shirley's. Her face begins to mirror her stomach: pinched, sour, and raw.

"Are you feeling okay?" Shirley asks, touching Mary's cheek with the back of her hand.

"It's probably just the milk and the heat."

Shirley picks up the partially consumed contents of Mary's glass to give it a sniff. "Stick your head in the freezer for a minute. It should pass."

Mary tries the remedy. It does nothing but remind her to put Neapolitan ice cream on the shopping list.

Gayle plays with Lisa's soft curly hair and blows on her cute baby neck to make her wiggle. Wistfully, Shirley looks upon the pair of resplendent youth. Gayle notices her mother's watchful eye. "What?" she asks in a tart tone, feeling self-conscious.

"You are so good with Lisa. I'm looking forward to the day when you see fit to make *me* a grandmother."

Without a word, Gayle kisses the top of Lisa's head, sets her down, and stands to leave the room.

"Where are you going?" her mother asks.

"Bathroom. Is that all right with you?"

Lisa, sensing an emotional shift in the room in the way only children and dogs can, climbs into her mother's safe embrace.

Shirley stares back at Gayle, puzzled. "What's wrong with you?"

"I just can't ever do anything right for you, can I?"

Shirley's flustered hand finds the base of her throat. "Whatever do you mean?"

"Let's see . . . I don't act the way you want me to, I don't buy the right coffee, and I can't pop babies out like some Pez dispenser. Just to name a few." Gayle stomps out of the room.

Shirley's cheeks burn with embarrassment. Her mouth opens and closes without finding any words.

Mary sits down at the table, Lisa's arms still encircling her neck. "Gayle has been trying to get pregnant for a while now," she explains, her voice barely above a whisper. "It just hasn't happened the way she'd hoped."

"I had no idea," Shirley replies, also in a whisper. "She never said anything."

Mary leans in closer. "Every month that passes in failure knocks another dent in her spirit. She feels inadequate, somehow thinks she's letting everyone down."

Shirley offers a slow, understanding nod. "That certainly explains the sensitivity. My poor angel . . ." Her hands mindlessly rearrange items on the table.

Mary reaches out to still one of Shirley's hands and holds it. "I believe she's just trying too hard, putting too much pressure on herself. It will happen in time. I'm sure of it."

Shirley sniffs and wipes the corner of her eye with a knuckle of her other hand.

Gayle reenters the room. "Look, Mom, I'm sorry for being so crabby and hurting your feelings and all, but—"

Shirley rushes at her with a hug. "It's okay, sweetheart. I love you. And you're right. Your mother needs to learn to be more flexible."

Gayle looks at Mary over Shirley's shoulder, confused. Mary shrugs and allows Lisa's feet to patter over and join the hug.

Shirley releases her hold and takes a step back, looking at Gayle with motherly commendation. "I believe," she says, "I would like to try a cup of your Sanka now."

"Really?" Gayle asks in disbelief, Lisa still hugging her leg. "Or . . . you could try a Tab soda?"

Shirley steps over to the counter, considering the option while she burps the Tupperware container of beignets. "Sure, why not? I'm hip." She winks at Mary.

After Mary and Lisa say goodbye to their guests, they play on the living room floor with the farm set Lisa received for her birthday. Later, mother and daughter stand in front of the open refrigerator, enjoying the breeze and contemplating what to have for supper.

"Whatcha think, peanut?"

"J-e-l-l-o!"

"We can't have J-e-l-l-o for supper, silly."

"Why?"

"Because J-e-l-l-o is a dessert."

Lisa pushes her bottom lip forward to express her displeasure. Mary doesn't feel much like cooking—or teaching inflexibility—so she negotiates a compromise: they would eat cucumber and tomato salad while watching television, and wait patiently for the Jello to set. Mary snaps on the TV and hears the CBS announcer say the President will soon be making a special address to the nation about the integration of the University of Alabama.

"Good evening, my fellow citizens."

John F. Kennedy's face is visibly perturbed, yet he exhibits quiet strength and decorum in his dark suit and tie. He captivates Mary, bringing back many of the thoughts her father expressed on the subject of human equality across a kitchen table one night long ago.

"Those who do nothing are inviting shame as well as violence. Those who act boldly are recognizing right as well as reality."

Mary absorbs the President's words and repeats this phrase,

Those who do nothing are inviting shame as well as violence, those who act boldly are recognizing right as well as reality,

committing it to memory.

Monday
July 29, 1963

This summer morning isn't turning out to be a good one; the temperature outside is already eighty degrees Fahrenheit, and Mary had an irregular visit from Aunt Flo during the night that left her nylon panties and gown marred with blood. Both items are soaking with a pinch of borax in the bathroom sink.

In the kitchen, Mary is freshly bathed, her long hair pinned up neatly in place, wearing the last of her pad supply under a red, white, and blue plaid cotton dress. She lovingly slides two egg-salad sandwiches into a bag for her husband.

"Do we still have a key to Gayle's house?" Mary asks Vinny when he walks into the kitchen. She folds and hands him the brown bag.

He kisses the back of her neck and sets his empty coffee cup down beside the sink, along with the sack of sandwiches. "Why?" he asks. "They're driving back from Destin as we speak. Whatever reason you got can wait."

Trying not to fret, Mary follows behind him, rushing out the door and onto the driveway. "Vinny, I need something at the store. Can I have some cash?"

"What for? It's not a laundry or grocery day. I approved no list," Vinny states self-righteously.

"I need some feminine napkins," she says. She says this in a whisper, embarrassed at having to plead for the ability to get such a private and basic necessity.

But he barely looks at her. "No—you'll have to figure something else out. I'm late and I don't want you leaving the house. Can't you make them out of paper towels or something?" He gets in the car, no bagged lunch and dressed to the nines.

Mary stands watching as he rolls down the window and cranks up the engine. She searches for the right thing to say to stir some empathy from him. "I've been good," she musters.

Vinny lights a cigarette as he backs the car into the street. "You could use one of Lisa's leftover diapers. She doesn't seem to need them anymore." He says this in a self-amused voice, clearly still resentful that she tried to escape the life he wants to build for her.

Outraged by Vinny's refusal, Mary storms into the house, crying as she discards the fully used pad, and weighs her dwindling options. In a burst of inspiration—or desperation, she can't figure out which—she hastily pretties herself up, places Lisa's pudgy little arms through the straps of a lemon-yellow sundress, grabs her empty purse, and marches down to the local drugstore.

She hasn't the slightest clue what she is going to do once she gets there.

"That's very cute, Gator," Carlos says. His feet are propped up on his huge mahogany desk as he rolls a cigar beneath his nose, enjoying the rich loamy smell.

"What's cute?" Vinny asks, sipping on his cocktail lunch.

"That you think I make all the decisions in these matters," Carlos says. He puts the unlit cigar down on the desk.

"Don't you?" Vinny asks. He looks down into his glass at a swath of lemon rind that has sunk to the bottom, beneath the ice.

Carlos smiles and points to the ceiling. "This one came down from above. Momo brought it to me, knowin I would jump on the opportunity."

Vinny glances up at where Carlos is pointing. "How high we talkin?"

"Don't ask. You wouldn't believe me if I told you, but Jack Kennedy went and bit the wrong tit . . . made him some serious enemies back in June with his executive dick swinging." Carlos leans over his desk. "Do you know what happens when a head lion is ousted from the pride?"

Vinny shakes his head no, waiting for the inevitable answer, rolling an ice cube around in his mouth.

"All his cubs are killed before they can rise to power," Carlos reveals giddily, reaching for a carafe of Vinny's favorite premixed libation—prepared especially for this auspicious occasion.

Vinny offers up his empty glass for the refill. "I will get it done, but I'm gonna need a few of your dog-whistle goons to pull it off."

"A few?" says Carlos, rubbing his face with his knuckles.

Vinny nods. "To do it right, I need a couple crack-shots and an untraceable flight-man to throw the scent. Confusion is a must for this to end well." He rises from his chair and begins to pace. "Since I need more hands on deck, you're going to have to tap a soldier in Dallas for backup. There're too many variables for me to have complete control over the situation."

Carlos considers the complexities. "Gonna take a lot of planning, huh?"

"Yes, and it's going to cost more than money this time," Vinny says. He turns to face Carlos, arms folded, chest out.

Without blinking, his eyes round and wide, Carlos says, "Name it."

Vinny sets his jaw. "My freedom."

"Freedom?" Carlos repeats, as if he doesn't understand the word.

"I want to see if I can change. If I can be better."

"Better? You're the best damn guy I got!" Carlos bangs his fist down on the desk.

"My kid deserves better . . . and my wife—" Vinny stops mid-thought, suddenly wishing he'd peeled a twenty from his wallet for Mary this morning. "You know I got a raw deal as a kid. I don't want that for mine."

"You must be drunk, 'cause I don't know what the hell you're talking about," Carlos says, his face flushed. "We got a good goddamned thing goin here. Your kid is gonna be on Easy Street."

Vinny knows he is flirting with danger here, entering the seemingly bulletproof phase of drunkenness, but he forges ahead nonetheless. "That's my price, Carlos. Freedom, or no deal."

Carlos eyes him, a tentative smile playing on his lips. "Haven't I looked out for you, Gator?"

"It may have been the other way around," Vinny shoots back.

Carlos narrows his eyes. "Tread lightly, boy. I just might lose my humor."

"Like you did with my mother?"

Carlos stiffens and taps his fingers on the desk for more than just a minute. "Answer me this, kid." He is suddenly much calmer than before. "What is it you think you know?"

"I only know two things for sure," says Vinny. "I know my mother is dead, and I know you wanted her that way."

Carlos breaks his calm, throws himself back in his chair with his hands over his face. "I always knew this fuckin day would come. How long have you known?"

"Does that fucking matter? It sure in hell doesn't change a damn thing now, does it? Were you ever even going to tell me?"

Carlos drags his fingers through his hair, bearing down on his skull. "You need to know I cared about her, Vinny. Some things are just impossible to explain."

"Just a necessary part of business," Vinny snarls. "Like Old Joe, right?"

"You gotta learn to let things go, Gator . . . to let the past go," Carlos says, more or less to comfort himself.

Vinny drains his glass. "Do I make your list now?"

"My 'list'?"

"The list of past things that you drop."

Carlos's voice rises to a guttural shout. "Is that what you want? That what you're tryin to make me do?"

"I told you what I want," says Vinny. "I will rid you of this thorn, but afterward I want out."

"That's not a fuckin option."

"Then I guess we don't have anything else to discuss," Vinny says. He leaves his glass on the desk and heads for the exit.

"I don't know what's gotten into you, but I'm gonna pretend this never happened!" Carlos says, loudly enough to follow Vinny down the hall. He sits in the new silence, staring at the nearly empty glass. In a burst of rage, he knocks it off the desk, painting the cinderblock wall with glass shards and alcohol.

Hand in hand with Lisa—sure to look both ways before crossing the intersection—Mary knows she must act quickly, before the folded rag in her underwear soaks through and the blood starts running down her leg.

Gingerly she enters Dupre's Pharmacy, which appears to be empty. With no bell and no sign of an employee on duty, she desperately looks around, hoping that if she can just grab the package before anyone sees, she can dart back out without being noticed and arrested for shoplifting. For one frantic moment, she somehow forgets that Lisa is in tow.

"May I help you, miss?" asks a male voice from behind the pharmacy counter, on a platform level above the checkout register. Only the top of Mr. Dupre's partially balding head is visible. The owner of the store steps down, revealing all five-feet-five-inches of himself to Mary. He is wearing his crisp white lab coat, an exact replica of the photograph that hangs on the wall behind him.

Before Mary can even gather her thoughts, she hears her own voice speaking out with a confidence she has not heard from her own mouth in a long while. "It looks like you are the one that needs help, mister. There should be a bell on this door and a friendly face down here to greet customers as they walk in."

Visibly disturbed by her unhappy tone, Mr. Dupre makes his way to conciliate, pulling a loop-handled lollypop from his coat pocket to give to her child. "I am so sorry. Is there anything I can do for you today?"

"I'm not upset with you," Mary replies, completely improvising now. "I'm sincerely concerned for your establishment, Mr.—" She pauses to look at his name tag. "Mr. Dupre. You see, with competition moving in, and hoodlums on the rise, you are in need of someone to run this floor, so you can stay up there"—Mary's finger points to his nest and his eyes follow—"and do what you were educated to do. If I had walked in here with a mind to steal merchandise from you, I could have been in and out before you ever reached the main floor."

"Hmm," Mr. Dupre grunts. He folds his short arms, smelling a sales pitch. "Go on," he nudges, visually measuring the distance of floor in question.

Mary tenses with the fear of getting tangled in her ruse, and offers a rushed, less-than-eloquent finale. "The point, Mr. Dupre, is that you are in obvious need of help, and I just happen to be in need of a job. Perhaps we can help each other."

He takes a step to the side and gives her a closer inspection, tapping his index finger on his pursed lips. Coming to the conclusion that this man isn't giving up the goods with that lollypop still in his hand, Lisa wanders a few steps to stand in front of a small selection of supplies for creative minds.

Mary senses his wariness of her intentions. Her lips begin to tremble. She clutches her purse and clears her throat. "You wouldn't even need to pay me. All I would need in return is a package of personal hygiene products . . ." Her eyes land on Lisa. ". . . and a pack of paper and some crayons. That's all I intend to leave with today. If by the end of the day you decide you don't need my help, then we can consider our transaction completed with those items."

Stunned by the audacity of this spunky woman using such a bold approach, Mr. Dupre frowns in ratiocination, considering that his current help is lazy, inconsistent, and starting school again in the fall.

"What was your name again, Miss . . . ?"

"Missus," she corrects. "Mrs. Mary Carlino, and this is Lisa," Mary says, looking down at her sweet child's face surrounded by unruly curls. Lisa is smiling, her eyes fixated on the bright green treat Mr. Dupre still holds in his hand.

"I'm this many," Lisa says, holding up three pudgy fingers.

"So . . . do we have a deal?" Mary presses—she knows she is running out of time, feels a rush of blood escape her Kegel hold.

Mercifully, Mr. Dupre nods. "Well, I guess one day couldn't hurt. Go ahead and collect your items and then show me what you have to offer. And what shall we do with this darling little one?" he asks, squatting down and smiling at the patient toddler, who gladly relieves him of the sugary treat he waves in the air as he speaks.

Mary makes a dash to grab what she needs, sets Lisa up with her new art supplies (and opens her lollypop at Lisa's insistence). "Be a good girl and Mommy will make ice cream this evening," she says, then turns to Mr. Dupre. "May I use your restroom before I begin?"

He points her to the facilities and keeps a keen eye on the curly-headed angel on the floor behind the counter. After Mary returns, she immediately gets to work fastening a bell to the door, utilizing a Christmas ornament she found in the storage room, when she sees a familiar face outside on the sidewalk—Mrs. Picou, the dress shop owner.

Mrs. Picou is checking her bangs and her teeth in a small hand mirror. She closes the compact, dropping it into a small purse hanging from her delicate forearm, and snaps the kiss-lock clasp with a look of insecurity. She stomps her foot, inhales deeply, and starts for the door.

Mary has never seen anyone acting so nervous about entering a store before—until she remembers the blood-stained cloth lying in the bottom of the restroom trash can.

"Good morning, Mrs. Picou," Mary greets her. "Can I help you find anything?"

"Why, Mary!" She looks instantly relieved to see Mary's kind face. "How did I not know that you worked here?"

Mr. Dupre scurries over to welcome his patron. "Good morning, Mrs. Picou."

Mary bemusedly watches her new boss become a schoolboy. "You look very pretty today," she says to Mrs. Picou. "Doesn't she look nice, Mr. Dupre?"

"Radiant . . . like the sun," he says, holding his hands behind his back and rocking to his tiptoes and back, twitterpated and unable to hide it.

Mrs. Picou turns away shyly, covering her smile with her long, manicured fingers. Mary notices that she no longer wears any rings on those lovely fingers, but thinks it rude to mention this. Mrs. Picou summons up the courage to say to the pharmacist, "I was hoping we could discuss the benefits of taking a vitamin supplement."

Mr. Dupre nods warmly. "Ahh, yes. Come with me and I will show you a few of my recommendations," he offers, guiding her down the appropriate aisle.

On her way to check on Lisa, Mary is curious to notice Mrs. Picou has abandoned, along with her wedding ring, her stylish heels for a pair of sensible flats. While she absorbs all of the nutritional advice that Mr. Dupre bestows upon his eager novice, Mary dusts every shelf in the store, stopping only to greet new customers as they enter. Mr. Dupre is impressed at Mary's willingness to assist the newcomers in finding what they have come in for. She is cleverly quick to suggest additional purchases, all with charming enthusiasm. He is thinking that indeed this woman will make a fine employee.

Mary, engrossed in her tasks, misses poor Lisa patiently dancing at the door of the little girls' room for a full five minutes before asking for help.

Delighted to be held to wash her tiny hands in the lavatory after her much-needed relief, Lisa lifts her head up and says, "I love you, Mommy."

The guilt that bites at every working mother stings Mary's gut like a swig of acid. "Mommy loves you right back, sweet girl," she says, setting Lisa's small, sandaled feet to the floor and kissing her curly crown. "It won't be too much longer, darling."

Mary returns to the sales floor. The bell on the door rings, and a teen wearing a Terrebonne High gym shirt enters. Mary keeps her face down so the boy cannot examine it. She nervously picks up a broom and begins to sweep the floor she has already swept clean. The boy studies her curiously, knowing he has seen her before, but can't quite place where. Mr. Dupre crosses the store to explain the situation. The boy—also an employee at the drugstore, Mary discovers—nods in agreement with his boss's instructions and heads to the stockroom to unpack the last delivery.

Mr. Dupre approaches Mary with his decision. "I can give you from nine to one Monday through Friday. I simply can't give you full days or weekends, though, because I employ a student saving for college."

For a second, his revelation gives Mary both a sense of relief and a pang of regret, almost bringing her to tears. She thinks,

That used to be me.

but composes herself and says, "I understand, Mr. Dupre, and I believe that would be ideal. Thank you so much for taking a chance on me. I won't let you down." Mary shakes his hand as if he has just liberated her. "I'll be here tomorrow at nine sharp, and I'll be sure to arrange childcare for Lisa."

"You should be proud of raising such an obedient child. I've never seen someone her age so completely occupied with sheets of paper."

"I can't take total credit for that. She's my little prodigy. I don't think she has been a day's trouble since she was born. Smart as a whip to boot."

"I think she deserves that ice cream you promised, and then some," says Mr. Dupre, walking to the register and opening the cash drawer. "Why don't you add this to your items today? You've both earned it." He hands Mary four dollar bills.

"Thank you for being so generous," Mary says. "And please tell Mrs. Dupre that I look forward to meeting her soon."

He lowers his head. "I trust that the late Mrs. Dupre would have enjoyed meeting the two of you."

"Oh . . . I'm so sorry for your loss," Mary says, touching his arm.

"I appreciate your concern, but she has been gone several years now." He reaches for his wallet and pulls out a picture of his lost love.

Mary briefly examines the image of a modest young woman with large, bright eyes. "I know you must miss her plenty," she says thoughtfully, leaning over to gather Lisa and their goods. "After my father died, someone told me that beginnings can sometimes ease the pain of endings."

Mr. Dupre follows Mary, still looking at the old picture and conjuring memories of long ago, and nods in acknowledgment. "That is a wise testament."

Opening the door—the Christmas ornament she fastened above it tinkles in response—Mary pauses. "I know it's none of my business . . . but I think Mrs. Picou is a very nice person."

His attention is immediately drawn away from the photo, but he merely blinks and listens to Mary in the doorway.

She continues, "I know hers are not the best of circumstances, but maybe we all deserve a second shot at love."

Mr. Dupre's eyes blink several times to fight back his emotions.

"Goodbye, hairy," Lisa says, patting his fuzzy hand.

"That's not nice, Lisa Marie," Mary says in embarrassment.

He smiles and bends down to the little girl's eye level. "It was lovely to meet you, Lisa. You are a very observant little girl," he says, shaking her small hand. Rising back up, he offers another handshake to Mary. "Harry. My name is Harry Dupre."

Mary giggles at her own ignorance and lightly shakes his hand. "I shall see you in the morning, Mr. Harry Dupre."

Mary panics hearing the kitchen phone ring as she opens the door.

"Hello, hello," she answers.

"Where were you?" Vinny's voice asks. She can immediately hear his inebriation.

"I . . . we were playing outside," she mumbles.

"In this heat?"

"I took out the sprinkler," she dodges. "Are you okay? You sound funny."

"I'm not feeling well, and I don't want to get my girls sick. I'll be back after work tomorrow."

"I was hoping to talk to you about what happened this morning, but I don't want to do it on the phone," Mary says. "You should come home."

"I'm real sorry about this morning, Mags. I know I can be an ass sometimes," Vinny admits. "I'm going to find a normal job. I want to find a way to make you proud of me . . . of us . . . I want to try," he rambles, then waits for her response, but there is only her breath on the line. "Still there?"

"Yes, that sounds good. I hope you feel better soon. Bye," she says, perturbed, and places the handset back in the cradle.

"I love you," Vinny says to the *click*.

She stares at the idle phone, annoyed at his thin, drunken promises and having to put her own uplifting news on ice.

Just like she promised, Mary scoops a bowl of homemade vanilla love for her little trooper after an early supper, adding a sugar wafer for decoration. She makes special efforts to include Lisa in the process, enjoying her company.

"We had a good day, huh, Mommy?" she says, slurping the puddle in her spoon.

"We sure did, love bug," Mary says. Hoping Gayle and Chick are home from vacation, she looks out the window and sees their car in the driveway.

"Can you do me a favor and let me be the first one to tell Daddy about today, sweetheart?" she asks, then is immediately saddened by recruiting her child into the deception. Still, she grabs the phone to dial Gayle's house.

"Okay, Mommy," Lisa answers, stuffing the last of the cookie in her mouth.

"Am I calling too late?" Mary asks, twirling the phone cord around her finger.

"We were getting ready to hit the sack," Gayle says. "What a trip. You okay?"

"I know it's a huge favor, but . . . can you watch Lisa for me for a few hours tomorrow?"

"No problem," Gayle yawns. "Bring her over after Chick leaves in the morning."

"Oh, thank you. I look forward to catching up. Now get some rest. Oh, and . . . can we keep this between us?"

Gayle sounds intrigued as she responds, "Sounds like catching up might be more fun than a long weekend in Destin."

Tuesday
July 30, 1963

"**Figures! All the** exciting stuff happens when I'm not around," Gayle says, after rummaging through the details of Mary's nerve-racking ordeal. "I thought I had an inkling of how damaged Vinny might be, but maybe none of us really had a clue," Gayle admits, pouring a large bowl of Sugar Smacks from a box wearing a garish clown.

"Is that a good enough excuse? Should I simply accept every abysmal action of his as part of the deal?" Mary asks.

"The vows were for better or worse, in sickness and in health, right?" Gayle reaches into the Frigidaire for a carton of milk.

"Since when are you about following the rules?"

"Since I've been trying to get pregnant. And failing miserably," Gayle admits. She rummages in the unorganized silverware drawer and picks up a spoon. "I don't want Chick to give up on me that easy."

Mary pushes the cereal bowl aside and attacks Gayle with a hug. "None of us will give up easily. Don't worry." She releases Gayle and says, "I don't want to be late on my first official day. But we'll talk more later." She runs over to hug and kiss Lisa, who is eating a bowl of quick oats and raisins and is deeply enthralled by an episode of *Captain Kangaroo*.

"Thanks for sharing this small fry with me," Gayle says, taking a seat next to Lisa on the floor with her breakfast.

"You are a life saver. Thanks so much for taking this on, Gayle. You guys have fun at the library today." Mary heads for the door and looks back at the two of them sitting Indian-style on the large patch of thick nylon pile.

Without turning to look, Gayle says, "Go! It's four hours, for heaven's sake. We'll be fine."

Friday
August 2, 1963

"**I'm sorry you** lost all those dreams you were cultivating . . . but you could still hatch new ones, you know," Mrs. Tisdale tells Mary as they stand in front of the First-Aid supplies. Holding a large box of Band-Aids, Mrs. Tisdale shakes her head. "Peddling adhesive bandages. Such a waste of your talents, Mary."

Mary endures the remainder of the transaction with her former teacher, seizing the chance to show off her astute manipulation of the double-drawered cash register. After pressing an assigned clerk button, her elegant fingers dance across the numbered keys to add up a total sale with tax. The drawer pops open with a *ding!* and Mary quickly exchanges paper for coin, rips off a neatly printed receipt, and deposits the change into Mrs. Tisdale's hand. She folds the top edge of the small brown-bagged purchase and presents it with a plastic smile. "I hope you come again soon. We aim to please at Dupre's," she jingles. But as Mrs. Tisdale exits, the last of her looks of pity strike Mary from the doorway, knocking the last puff of wind from her budding sails. She flies into the storage area, choking back a flood of shame and regret.

Overhearing semi-private conversations in the store is not a new experience for Mr. Dupre—but actively listening and taking an interest *is*. He has never considered himself to be a person who meddles in the personal affairs of others, but as a pharmacologist, he can't seem to let pain go untreated. Stepping cautiously into the storeroom, he says, "Mary, your shift is over. I wanted to tell you what a great job you've done this week. Is everything okay in here?"

"I'm fine," Mary says, looking around for a distraction. "I'm just looking in our box of decorations for something to liven up the place." She settles on a costume crown from the Mardi Gras season, which she places on Mr. Dupre's head, and bows. "My liege."

At first he plans to accept the playful lie, but as she straightens from her bow he feels the need to know what Mary is so desperate to hide behind that counterfeit smile.

"Tell me, milady . . . is it true that you abandoned some bright alternate future to learn the complexities of my fair realm?" he teases, complete with an awkward off-Broadway hand gesture, hoping the humor will make it easier.

Mary laughs, but there are tears in her eyes. "In a way, yes."

He removes the crown and places it back in the box, adopting a more serious expression. "Is there any way that I can help you?"

"You took a chance on me. You *are* helping." Mary drops her eyes. "It's not nearly as bad as she made out—and my Lisa is worth way more than any of the sacrifices I've made."

Mr. Dupre listens carefully to the texture of her words, familiar with the sound of loss behind them. "Mary, the funny thing about sacrifice is that it may be worth it now . . . and maybe even in the long run. Some sacrifices, though, can become regret . . . crippling regret that will claw at you in the dark, when you're trying to sleep. Trying to dream the new dreams."

Mary kisses Lisa's freshly bathed toddler feet, playing "This Little Piggy" and reveling in her sweet musical belly laugh, then tucks her snug into her big-girl bed. This new bed allows Lisa to get up and use the training chair, which is also a fairly new development.

The first evening to fully abandon the plastic barrier of nighttime protection prompts Mary to ask, "Do you need to potty?" before, during, and after each of the three bedtime stories she reads. Finally satisfied, she leaves Lisa to explore some festive colorful dreamland.

Mary's belly gurgles.

Expired ham for dinner may not have been the best idea,

she admits, thankful that Lisa had not wanted anything to do with it. Her insides feel more than a touch of nausea when she enters the kitchen.

Wandering around the house is not an unusual activity for her after Lisa is asleep—especially when the other side of the bed is unoccupied. She has already washed up and made herself ready for bed, sporting a lightweight nightgown and slippers as she searches the pantry high and low for something she can't quite put her finger on. Coming up empty, she moves to the refrigerator, not altogether sure why she is there or what to do about her upset tummy.

Unannounced, Vinny stumbles through the front door, removing his work boots and tossing them aimlessly to the floor. He plops into the nearest chair, nearly missing. In silent fascination and with a menacing grin, he sits watching Mary's figure bathed in the illumination of the refrigerator's interior light as it highlights the naked silhouetted curves of her body.

Trying to seem unaware of her husband's leer, she debates whether or not to add chocolate syrup to her nightcap as she pours the cold white beverage into a small saucepan. She decides against it and replaces the carton, gently spanking the door shut with her hip.

"I'm heating up some milk. Can I make you something?" she asks with practiced nonchalance.

"Nah . . . what I really want is for you to come over here and sit on my lap," says Vinny, patting his thigh.

She flashes him a coy smile. She sets the pan down, and as she reaches to turn off the stove he watches her gown rise several inches, revealing smooth, freshly shaven thighs.

Obediently, Mary goes to him. His roughened hands catch on the silk-like material as they travel over her hips and spin her around. Under his guidance, she drops down onto his muscular lap, and as soon as she does, her nose fills with his bitter stench—a sour mixture of booze and cigarettes strong enough to make her gag. She recoils in disgust. He hugs her close, his haughty lips in search of a kiss, and all she wants is to get away from the rancid smell.

She manages to slip away and says, "Please go brush your teeth and take a shower. Then maybe we can cuddle."

"You high-and-mighty little bitch!" Rising from the chair, Vinny grabs her by the scruff of the neck, lifting her as if she's an ungrateful pup that has just bitten him.

"Please be quiet . . . I just put Lisa down for the night."

"You think I give a shit?!" he says, shaking her in rhythm with each hate-filled word, his white-knuckled talons gripping her by the hair and the skin caught beneath. He points to the hallway leading to Lisa's bedroom and says, "That little whore is keeping secrets from me, just like her goddamn mother!"

Mary whimpers when Vinny brings her face close to his and lowers his voice to a growl. "Did you think I wouldn't find out about your blatant disobedience . . . about this so-called 'job' of yours that you've been hiding from me . . . huh?"

He throws her to the floor.

Her violet-blue, terror-stricken eyes stare back at him.

"Don't act like you don't know what I'm talking about."

"I was going to tell you, but . . ."

"You were going to *TELL* me?!" he yells, then begins to pace a predatory circle around her. "Bitch, you don't *tell* me anything! You *ask!*"

"That's what I meant—I was going to *ask* you," she explains, curling up into a protective ball on her knees. "I needed pads, remember?"

"I remember," Vinny says, pacing above her and rubbing his temples.

"You told me I had to figure something out, so I went to the store." Mary closes her eyes and licks her lips, trying to find the words that will get her in the least amount of trouble.

"And . . . ?" he prompts.

She shudders, hearing the familiar jingle of Vinny removing his belt. She swallows hard then continues in a quivering voice. "So I offered to trade a few hours of work for the things I needed, and he . . . offered me a job."

He folds the belt in half and snaps leather on leather, making her jump.

"I thought you would be proud of me . . . making an effort to help out financially. I'll have my own money now, won't have to ask you every time I need to make a personal purchase." Frantically grasping for a pardon, she adds, "I thought—"

He nods his head and laughs, "You *thought?*" Mary winces at the sound of him airily slapping his knee with the sinister belt. "Well, ain't that something." He places the bend of the stiff belt beneath Mary's chin and cocks her head to an uncomfortably high angle. "Let me tell you something, doll face . . . your thinkin days are long over. They ended the day you left school." He pulls the belt away roughly and lets her head drop. "I'll be the only thinker around this house. You got me?"

She doesn't respond, only looks down at a steady stream of frightened tears falling from her nose and splashing to the floor.

He grabs her by the arms and shakes her. *"You got me?"*

"Yes," she manages to squeak past the resentment lodged in her throat.

"I didn't hear you. 'Yes' *what?*"

"Yes, sir," she snarls between her teeth.

"Good girl." He lets her go and sits back down in the chair. "Now I think you need to come over here and sit on my lap."

"Please . . . I don't feel well."

"You felt fine when you took that job-a yours. I'm not gonna tell you again," Vinny says, unzipping his pants.

She slowly climbs to her feet and retakes her post.

"Now, isn't this better?" he says, holding her hips and grinding against her silky nightgown. He starts to gently caress her breasts, turning himself on, and pulls her back by the hair, breathing that toxic breath into her face.

Mary can't take the smell. She involuntarily lurches forward and tosses her half-digested dinner onto the floor.

When the purge is over, she looks up and sees Lisa in the hall.

Horrified to think of how much of this scene Lisa has witnessed, Mary musters the ability to speak calmly so as not to frighten the child any further. "Go back to bed, sweetheart," she says, a thin line of spit connecting her bottom lip to the floor.

"Mommy?" Lisa says in a frightened voice.

"Go back to bed, baby, and I will be there soon."

Mary's request is followed by Lisa's little bare feet slapping against the hardwood planks on their way back to the bedroom at the end of the hall.

"Get on the rug," Vinny snaps, nudging her with his foot.

"I need to go see about Lisa."

"Not until we've finished our discussion. Now *get on the rug.*"

"I don't want to."

"I'm tired of hearing what you want and don't want!" he yells, whipping her with the belt. He continues the barrage as she yelps in pain and maneuvers clumsily on her hands and knees to the rug in between hits, leaving behind an acrid chunky pool of sick on the floor.

"Now turn over on your back, you frigid bitch."

She starts to cry harder now. "Please don't make me do this."

"Why do you have to be so *difficult?* If you would just relax and enjoy it, I might consider letting you keep that silly-ass job."

She complies—not because she wants to and not to keep the job, but because she knows that if she doesn't, he will become enraged and take it anyway.

"That's my girl," Vinny says as he claws and tears at her delicate underwear. Climbing on top of her, he pins her arms to the floor, preventing her from wiping his aroused, inebriated drool from her face.

She closes her eyes, turns her head, and bites her lip as he violently penetrates. The room fills with his carnivorous grunting. Deep, guttural sounds and putrid scents of half-digested ham blend with the roaring wind of the new air conditioning unit he bought to thwart the first heat wave in June.

The window unit kicks off, and instantly it becomes much quieter. Quiet enough to hear his sweaty body slapping against hers. Even quiet enough to hear the faint pitter- patter of a pair of tiny feet step cautiously down the hall.

There is a very small space between the wall and the couch where the light from the hall can be seen. Mary intensely focuses on that sliver of light, despite the savage rocking of her body beneath his thrust.

Her voice starts with a whisper then works to crescendo as the feet get closer, saying only one phrase over and over: "The baby, the baby, *the baby . . .*"

He puts his hand over her mouth to keep her quiet enough not to distract him from his goal. She struggles for breath, hyperventilating through the cracks in his fingers. The tears fill her eyes and blur her vision—but still, she manages to see that light replaced by a small shadow before she slips into oblivion.

Saturday

August 3, 1963

Mary feels something weighing her hand down as she reenters consciousness. She blinks rapidly before having the nerve to look down to see what that something is.

What she sees fills her with so many emotions that it renders her utterly numb. Frozen. To let it seep into her core and feel it in its entirety would break her into a million jagged pieces.

A small curly head, asleep in her hand. Tiny loving fingers resting upon her bruised thigh.

Mary strains to listen. There is no other movement or sound in the house besides the rise and fall of her daughter's chest with each soft breath. She cautiously slides her hand from beneath Lisa's head, but not without waking her. Unaware of this fact, Mary picks up the torn evidence of the previous night's horrors and wanders down the hall to the bedroom. She sits on the bed, unsure of what to do or where to go, and stares blankly at the undergarment for a long while. With barely a sound, Lisa climbs onto the bed next to her mother. She removes her small beflowered butt-cover and holds it in her hands, trying her best to mimic her mother, in solidarity. They sit there for what seems like an eternity—until Mary hears pounding on the kitchen door, and both are brought into action, quickly replacing their garments. Mary grabs a robe and moves to answer the door, the sound of pattering feet close behind. She thinks,

Vinny wouldn't knock.

"Mary? You all right?" Chick, his voice muffled by the wooden door between them.

She opens the door, standing behind it as if to shield her fragile dignity.

"Oh, thank God!" he says. White as a sheet, Chick enters and takes a seat at her kitchen table, bouncing his knee in rhythm with the distressed thumping of his heart.

Mary sits down as if in a dream; Chick's concerned gestures and frenetic voice somehow sound far away.

"Vinny's at my house. I had to knock him out," he says, scratching his jaw. "Never seen him like that. He was hysterical. Talking about killing himself, talking as if he'd killed *you!* When I asked about Lisa, he wouldn't answer me. He just started rambling about how you don't want him anymore. I came over fast as I could, not knowing what I'd find."

There is a pregnant pause while Mary sits, glazed even more now than before, trying to process this new information on top of what she has been through. Lisa tugs at her mother's robe to get her attention, to hand her a plastic cup in need of juice.

"I know you had a fight about you getting a job, I know he isn't the easiest man to live with, but Mary, he honestly loves you with all his heart." Chick clears his throat. "I don't think he'd survive if you were to stop loving him."

"I haven't *stopped loving* him," she snaps out of frustration, rising from her chair to meet Lisa's needs, wincing from her body's pain.

"Sit down, I'll get it. You sure you're all right? Do you need a doctor?" Chick asks, getting up to fill the small cup with apple juice.

Happy to have her drink-wish fulfilled, Lisa returns to her mother and climbs in her lap to accept delivery. "I can't go to the *doctor*," Mary replies, in wide-eyed distress that somehow everyone would figure out what happened to her.

"I'll pay," Chick offers. With a wrinkled nose, he dumps old milk from a pot on the counter into the sink and turns on the faucet to rinse away the film.

"It's not the money. It's . . . it's just not something I can face today. Maybe tomorrow." She covers her face and looks away to keep Chick from recognizing her shame.

"I don't like to go to the doctor either, Mary, but you look like he may have given you one wallop too many—"

"How many is 'too many,' Chick?" she asks sharply, incensed by such a casual reference to what happened to her only hours before.

After his poor stab at humor, Chick doesn't dare answer without careful consideration, taking a closer look at her disheveled condition.

"How many times have you hit Gayle?" she poses. "Two? Three? Twenty?"

"I could never . . ." He falters, shaking his head at the thought of his own wife sitting there in tears with a small child in her lap, having endured pain in the shape of his hand. "Even one would be too many." He lowers his head to match his voice.

"Yes, one *is* too many from a person who's supposed to care for you," she says. As if to illustrate her point, she presses her lips into silken wisps that adorn Lisa's temple.

He leans against the counter. "What do you plan to do?"

"I'm not sure what my options are. I can't go to my mother's . . . been *that* route before."

"What can I do to help?"

"I need you to keep him away from me for now, so I can think in peace."

"I'll do my best to convince him to give you some space—once he's conscious, that is. How long?"

"I need some time to clear my head."

He straightens up and tugs on his shirt. "Should I take Lisa with me?"

"And bring her where *he* is?" Mary gives a quick, disgusted snort. "No, indeed. She stays. I will call when I'm damn well ready to speak to that man."

Lisa slides down from Mary's lap to investigate a tiny gecko that has erroneously found itself in the middle of the kitchen floor.

Peering out the kitchen window, Chick wears a troubled expression. "I need to tell you something, Mary. Something that might sound like I'm on his side—but believe me, it's for your own good."

"Don't beat around the bush, Chick, it's annoying."

Chick looks away from the window and meets Mary's gaze. "I wouldn't think of skipping town if I were you. He has lots of friends in lots of places. He'll find you, and when he does . . ." Chick squeezes his eyes shut. "I don't even want to imagine it."

"Was that to help me, or to scare me?"

Chick looks away again. "I should have warned you before. I just had no idea he was capable of being like this. Not with you."

Mary stands up, eyes aflame. Lisa scoots under the table to play with her new friend, watching her mother's hands clench and unclench.

"You knew he had violent tendencies and it never occurred to you to fill me in? Some friend you are!" She slams her right hand down on the table. "I need you to leave."

Chick flinches as if she struck him in the face. "Please forgive me. Somehow I thought I was being a good friend by keeping my lip zipped. He was always so protective of Camille . . . I thought he would be the same with you."

"Make it up to me by giving me the time I need to figure this out," she says, pointing to the door. "Is there anything else I should know before you get out? Any other secrets you're keeping for your friend?"

He pauses halfway to the door and turns back to Mary. His mouth makes a failed attempt before he finds his voice. "There are so many things that no one will ever know about Vinny . . . himself included."

"Well," Mary huffs, "thanks for *that* little riddle, Enigma Jones. Everything's clear as *crystal* now." She rakes her hands through her hair in frustration.

His sunken eyes search her hardened features for any sign of absolution.

Mary caves, exhaling hard as her eyes find the ceiling. "I can't forgive you for what he did, because it's not your fault. I know the blame lies with him and him alone—so don't think for a moment that you could have prevented it. Besides, I was too in love to listen to reason. My dad never felt right about him, and even that didn't stop me."

"I'm so sorry Norman's gone."

"I'm not. I can't imagine my father having to witness the situation I'm in. How I've failed him . . . failed myself." Mary crumples. "You really have to go now. I need a bath."

"That's a great idea." He brightens. "The world always looks better after a good soak." Chick offers up a comforting goodbye hug. Mary stiffens and quickly pulls away. Remorseful, he slinks away and out of the door.

She locks the door and pulls back the edge of the curtain to watch Chick disappear around the corner before rushing to the telephone. Fumbling with the handset, she places her finger in the *0* slot and drags the dial clockwise all the way around to the finger stop, releases, and waits for the operator.

"Southern Bell, how may I connect your call?" a whiny voice asks.

"I need the Terrebonne Parish Sheriff's office, please," Mary says, her heart pounding.

"Hold one moment, please."

The line falls silent. The wait is agonizing, but after a sharp click, the line begins to ring.

"Sheriff's Department, what is your emergency?" a young male voice belts into the phone—no doubt a new recruit eager for some exciting small-town mayhem to sink his teeth into.

For a second she wants to hang up, not sure if it is an emergency of any kind.

"Hello?" he tries again, clearly able to hear her quickened breath.

"Is there a woman I could speak to?" she finally manages in a shaky voice.

"I assure you, ma'am, all calls are treated with the utmost respect. What seems to be the trouble?"

"I . . . I have been violated," Mary says, feeling the weight of the words as they pass her parched lips.

"Do you need an ambulance?"

"No."

"Is he still in the area? Are you in any immediate danger?"

"Yes . . . no—" Mary's voice wavers in alarm. "I don't know!"

"Are you able to come in and fill out a report, or should we send someone to you?"

"I'm not sure how to proceed. He could be back this afternoon. I need to get out of here and I have no place to go. I have a small child—"

"Wait, you said he could be back this afternoon—do you know who your attacker is?"

"Yes . . . my husband."

"Your husband?" he asks, followed by a long pause. "I'm sorry, but I'm afraid we can't help you."

"What do you mean? I've been *raped*, and—and I need help!"

"According to the law, it isn't illegal for a man to take advantage of his marital rights."

"Marital rights? What about *my* rights?"

"You could initiate a protective order, but you would need a separate residence—"

"Let me guess, because you can't put a man out of his own home. Why do that when putting women and children on the street is so much easier?!"

"There isn't much we can do from a criminal standpoint, but if you feel strongly enough about it, I can give you the name of a divorce lawyer."

"He raped me when he found out I had a job! What do you think he'll do when I serve him with divorce papers—send me flowers?"

"Lady, I feel for you, I really do, but my hands are tied. I'm real sorry."

"Me too," Mary says, then slams the handset back into its cradle and makes a mad dash for the bathroom.

Lisa looks up from her new pet to see the tail of her mother's robe levitating behind her.

The initial relief of an empty bladder wears thin as Mary lathers her hands and checks her face for damage in the mirror above the sink. The dread she has been repressing comes at her with brutal force as she turns off the faucet.

What in the hell am I supposed to do now?
No money. No safe place to go.
For fuck's sake . . . to stay and endure the tortures of the damned . . .
to tough it out, at least until I can come up with plan B.

"Me and frog want breftist," Lisa says, tugging at Mary's robe.

Mary bends over to inspect Lisa's new friend. "Poor baby," she says, "you and Frog the lizard must be famished." She puts on her mommy face like a Mardi Gras mask, hiding the fear racing back and forth in her mind as she runs all the different scenarios—not one of them viable.

It has been a long time since Mary has overcooked a meal. Under the strain of her emotional state this morning, the bacon is an unfortunate casualty. She doesn't even notice until the smoky smell of singed pork fat assaults her thoughts. The pan of over-sizzled meat heads for the garbage when Lisa decides to intervene—her mission: to save the bacon.

"It's okay, Mommy. I like mine extra crisky," she says, distressed, not wanting the last strips in the house to be fed to the trashcan.

"Baby, I don't think this is edible anymore," Mary tries to reason.

"It's eat-able to meeee . . . pleeease, I want it," Lisa says, tugging at her mother's robe again.

"You can have it if you promise to eat your toast and drink all of your milk," Mary says, setting up the TV tray and snapping on the television to cheerful kid-friendly programming.

Instead of listening to Lamb Chop's knock-knock jokes, Mary opts for the sound of running water. She steps into the tub and lifts her face to the hot spray of the shower to feel herself melting, evaporating . . . the only way to leave and still stay.

Friday
August 9, 1963

Mary could have asked for the Taj Mahal and Vinny would have lain golden keys at her feet. She receives many apologies, tears, promises, flowers, and extravagant gifts in penance. She could have asked anything of him short of a divorce, but all she demands is to keep her job and for there to be peace between them.

At her hard-won place of employment, when no customers are around, Mary sags into the same long face she has repeatedly denied having all week whenever Harry asks. "I'm fine," she insists with a haggard attempt to lift the apples of her cheeks.

"Well, you sure seem sad for someone who's throwing a birthday party tomorrow," Harry says to Mary, while he affixes a label to an amber semi-opaque bottle (filled with several tablets whose monthly recipient lovingly refers to as her *happy pills*). "You look like you could use one of these." He briefly shakes the bottle at Mary, clacking the thirty-day supply of amphetamines around inside.

"I'm just tired, Mr. Dupre. I'm sure I'll be more myself next week," Mary says. She stands stapled bags of already-filled prescriptions in a box, in correct alphabetical order.

Harry moves to her and touches the inside of his wrist to her forehead. "No fever. What seems to be the issue? Maybe I can help."

She offers a weak smile. "Please don't worry about me. I'll be fine."

Suicide is a word and an action which has visited Mary's mind several times over the past week, but she knows it is way too complicated an endeavor to slide off the world in that way.

If killing myself isn't an option . . . what then?
Waking in the morning is painful, having to draw breath is
exhausting . . . so overwhelming to know you'll
have to do it again tomorrow.

"I'm not going to imagine I know what you're going through, nor that I know what's best to do, but I want to be your friend if you are ever in need of one," he says, patting the top of her hand in a way that reminds Mary of her father. Mr. Dupre smiles reassuringly, then walks to a shelf in the dispensary.

Mary could have cried if she hadn't already used up her supply. It takes all of her strength just to maintain the pretenses.

"Are we friends, Mary?" Harry asks, stepping on a stool to reach the next container of magic pills. He rechecks the list of afternoon deliveries on the counter.

"Yes, of course we are," she replies, hoping he won't use their friendship to press her further.

Mr. Dupre braces himself, both hands on the counter, and says something Mary didn't expect. "I have a secret . . . and I feel I can only share it with a friend."

"Is it bad?" Mary asks. "Because I don't think I can handle bad news right now."

"No, it isn't bad, but it *is* scary," says Mr. Dupre, lowering his voice as though someone might overhear. "I have a date tomorrow."

Mary turns to him, bug-eyed, with a genuinely shocked smile. Just at that moment, the bell on the door rings, cutting off the fun news and announcing a nervous young man who scans the shelves with his eyes.

"Can I help you?" Mary asks, following behind the young man, wanting to be rid of him as quickly as possible so she can find out more about this date Harry kept under lock and key. But then her boss discreetly coughs and winks in her direction, and she knows what the boy might be looking for.

It is Friday, after all . . .

Mary goes to the hook where they keep the most popular of the store's prophylactic selection, sure to grab a pack that is supposed to be comfortable for the *female* end of the sexual equation. She cradles the small box in the palm of her hand like a serving platter. "Is this what you are searching for?" she asks coyly.

The young man snatches the box, replacing it with a larger bill than the item warrants, and scurries off to whatever devilment he has planned.

She laughs, and it feels good. Not alone in the laughter, she looks at Harry wiping the corners of his eyes.

"Quick now, tell me about this date before the next one comes in," Mary says with new zest. "Who, where, when?"

He shrugs, diffident. "We're to go fishing in the morning,"

"Fishing?" Mary asks. "On a date?"

He immediately sees it in her expression. "I knew it! It's a terrible idea. I should cancel," he says, scrambling for the phone.

Mary blocks his path. "Not so fast, mister. She said yes to this date, didn't she?"

"Yes," he replies, "she most certainly did."

"Then you're on the right track. Who's the lucky gal?" she asks, temporarily forgetting her sorrows.

"Mrs. Picou ... my sunshine," he admits sheepishly, his cheeks ablaze.

Mary nearly squeals, feeling that child-like giddiness she has missed for so long. "I am so excited!"

"Thank you for giving me the push I needed to ask her."

"I had a feeling about the two of you! Sparks were flying." Mary shakes a finger in his direction. "What kept you from doing it sooner?"

"I guess I felt like I needed permission, like maybe I was betraying my wife," he admits. "Or because people might talk, with Mrs. Picou being newly divorced."

"Don't put your happiness in other people's hands. They'll drop it every time."

"How wise you are, Mary."

"That's not me. Thank my dearly departed father for that little ditty," she says, wishing Norman were still around dispensing his wisdom. "As for your wife, no one who loves you would wish the pain and suffering of loneliness upon you."

"Your father again?"

"Nope, that one is all me." Mary wipes the counter and looks up to see her work relief crossing the street. "Shhh, we have company," she says, and gathers her things.

The bell on the door rings, marking the end of her shift. The young man who takes over barely smiles at her before heading to the box full of deliveries to be made.

Disappointed, Harry waves goodbye to Mary. "Tell your friend Chick 'Happy Birthday' for me tomorrow."

"I will, and I want every detail of your–," Mary begins, sending his eyes wide with terror, "–your *weekend*," she concludes with a wink. " 'Bye, y'all," she adds playfully.

The sun is almost melting the pavement, the steamy air is hard to breathe, but Mary doesn't seem to care, walking home with thoughts of love and hope in the world.

Wednesday
August 28, 1963

This morning, before making the trek across the street to Gayle's, Mary straightens the cushions on the couch and fluffs the two decorative pillows—something that she can easily put right. Once this is done and her world is calmed in measures, she gladly leaves through the door; Lisa climbs into her mother's arms, enjoying the closeness for the few minutes it takes to get to Gayle's kitchen.

"Here, have a carrot." Gayle hands Mary a long, smooth vegetable stick freshly shaved of its flawed epidermis and observes, "You're gaining some weight."

"I know . . . I've been letting myself eat too much lately," Mary confesses. She chomps into the carrot, reading the ingredient list for the cake recipe Gayle is making for the church bake sale. Still tired, Lisa scurries to bury herself beneath a soft puddle of interlocked yarn strewn on the garish velvet sofa.

"Mom and I have started watching that *Jack LaLanne Show*." Gayle scrapes more orange hide into the sink. "She tried to get Dad to participate, but he told her to call me instead. It's actually kind of fun."

"Maybe I should, too. I could use some exercise."

"How would you fit that into your morning schedule, working lady?" Gayle asks, stripping another carrot.

"Oh, it's in the morning? Yeah, that would be tough. How do you watch it with your mom, if you're here with Lisa?"

"We watch it separately—then," Gayle scoffs, "she calls me when it's over so she can go on and on about his outfit."

"What's wrong with his outfit?"

"Nothing really." Gayle giggles. "It's a little too *right* in some areas, you know? Gets Mom all hot and bothered." The conversation yanks something peculiar from her memory bank, and she bounces on her toes. "Ooooh, I saw they have one of those beauty belt-massager things at the women's health club. We should *join!*"

Mary raises her eyebrows. "A club? Yeah, sure, okay," she laughs. "You know Vinny would never let me join a place where I might have fun and meet new people." Her head tilts. "What's a beauty belt-massager, anyway?"

"It's a contraption you put on your rear. Supposed to shake the weight right off."

"You don't think that really works, do you?" Mary asks, munching on the rest of her carrot.

"No," Gayle laughs, "but I'd like to see you try."

Mary picks up a carrot shaving that missed the sink and flings it at her. "I bet you would."

Amused and grossed out, Gayle peels the wet strip from her cheek. "Aren't you gonna be late or something?"

Mary walks to the sofa where Lisa has fallen back to sleep and kisses her cheek. "I do have to go," she says regretfully, petting Lisa's curls. On the way out of the door, she suddenly stops and turns to Gayle. "I think something is happening in Washington today. It might be on the news. Can you ring the store if Martin Luther King makes a speech?"

"Sure, I guess, but why?"

"My dad liked what he had to say, and I feel like I should listen. He would have," Mary says with a shallow sigh, tapping a hand against her heart, and leaves for work.

The Reverend Dr. Martin Luther King Jr. does deliver a sixteen-minute heartfelt speech to a hushed crowd in front of the Lincoln Memorial, his powerful cadence bringing to life his hopeful vision for the future.

Gayle and Lisa spend the day constructing carrot cakes, picture puzzles, and playing "Head, Shoulders, Knees, and Toes" over and over again. She never makes the call.

Thankfully, Mary accidentally catches a rebroadcast of Dr. King's speech on NBC Radio news later in the day, while browning meat in a skillet at home. She is deeply moved by his wishful, booming voice speaking of his dream that "children will one day live in a nation where they will not be judged by the color of their skin, but by the content of their character."

Tears drip from Mary's chin for those who have suffered for lack of so simple an effort. She turns the flame down to simmer, hangs her head, and weeps at the conclusion of Dr. King's speech. She thinks,

So many souls calling for freedom.

"Why you cry, Mommy?" Lisa asks, scratching the side of her small nose.

"Because everyone deserves kindness first, sweetheart," Mary says, taking Lisa's hands. "A cold shoulder must be earned."

"Cuz we should work for sweaters?" Lisa asks, swinging a restless leg around.

Mary laughs through her tears. "Your grandpa used to say that a cold shoulder must be earned. It means you should not go around being mad and cruel for no reason."

"Ohhh . . . like the play rules, Mommy?"

Mary wipes leftover tears from her cheeks and smiles. "Do you remember all the play rules?"

Lisa's eyebrows draw together in concentration as she begins to slowly pace watching her feet. "We gotta *share*, we gotta play *nice*, and . . . and no hitting or hurting," she recites, proud of her expanding skills.

"That's right, sweetheart," Mary says, hugging Lisa tight. "Sometimes the big people forget the rules."

"I'm hungryyy," Lisa says, bouncing.

"Me, too. I'm making us a big pot of dirty rice." Mary resumes her task.

"Why'd you put *dirt* in it?" Lisa asks, wrinkling her nose in disgust.

"It's just called that! I wouldn't make you eat dirt, sweet pea," Mary explains, chuckling at the thought. "Thank you so much. I don't know what I would do without you cheering me up all the time."

"Aunt Gayle says I'm a *silly goose*," Lisa says, skipping around on the linoleum.

"Well, go wash your filthy hands, silly goose. Dinner is almost ready."

The kitchen door opens.

"Daddy!" Lisa cheers and runs into Vinny's arms.

Mary taps the spoon on the steel pot almost hard enough to break the wooden handle in two. Vinny flinches at Mary's hostility.

"Mommy said dinner's almost ready," Lisa says. "We're having filthy rice!"

"I love filthy rice," he laughs, kissing Lisa's cheek.

"Hands," Mary issues a curt reminder.

"Let's go wash our hands and make Mommy happy."

"It's okay, Daddy. She said I make her happy all the time." Lisa takes him by the hand, leading him to the bathroom sink.

Vinny stares at Mary as he passes, waiting for her to look up and acknowledge him.

"Think you could teach *me* how?" Vinny asks.

"Sure," Lisa explains, taking on her serious teacher-tone. "You have to remember to share, to play nice, and no hitting or hurting."

Mary looks up and locks eyes with Vinny just before he is out of sight. She sees a profound remorse in those dark pools.

Later, in the dark, with Vinny's freshly showered scent in her nose, Mary can feel his craving eyes pierce her protective shield of ambivalence, her sensibilities at war with a strong unexpected hunger, the bed alive with two lustful bodies yearning just outside of touch. One tender reach and they are set aflame, an impassioned tangle of souls, limbs, and tongues. The fevered storm somehow cleanses, leaving behind gentle whispers of love, compassion, and forgiveness.

Tuesday
September 24, 1963

Carlos secures the door to the inner sanctum of his office on Airline Highway.

"We should meet at the farmhouse from now on," Vinny says.

Both men carefully sweep the room for listening devices before he uncaps the lid of a cardboard tube and slides out a tall roll of printed paper, rubber bands affixed over the middle and toward each end. The elastic twists and smacks as he rolls the bands off the edges and lets them fly wherever.

"How can you even be sure he'll be in Dallas before Thanksgiving?" Vinny asks. In his head, he is going over a long list of moving parts and things that could go horribly wrong.

Carlos smiles, landing in a chair. "I have it on good authority." He jabs at his well-fed teeth with a toothpick.

"But why so public? The only reason to kill in the light of day is to send a message." Vinny smooths and spreads an enlarged map of the downtown Dallas area across the desk. He frowns, studying the tricky maze of urban terrain.

" 'Tis true." Carlos wiggles his eyebrows and enjoys a loud belch of a superbly dressed muffuletta. "All these doubts, Gator. I've never seen you get chicken-skinned about a job before."

Vinny's face sours as he plucks a pencil from a bouquet of writing utensils on the desk. "Don't mistake my concerns for some kind of yellow streak. I've worked mostly alone all these years, Carlos, and when I ask for a couple goons, you give me half the fucking Louisiana CAP." He hovers over the map and marks a few strategically placed asterisks. "Did you get all the other things I asked for?"

"All that and more," Carlos smiles. He slowly pulls a stainless-steel dog whistle from his pocket and lays the spell-caster on top of the bird's-eye image of Houston Street. "Be careful with this. It's not a toy."

Vinny picks up the silent whistle and holds it up to the light. "I still don't understand how this thing works. You know I don't like surprises on a mission."

Carlos snorts. "People ain't all that hard to control, Gator. Just ask Ferrie. Besides, you don't need to understand it. Just use it like we rehearsed and it'll work." He grips Vinny's shoulder. "This mark ain't just some guy who stole my lunch money. I want dis done right just as much as you do."

"You never told me why it has to be him. I always thought it was Bobby you had a beef with." Vinny shakes off Carlos's hand and locates and employs a wooden ruler to verify distance and position.

"Dis just happens to be the one dat was sanctioned as the sacrificial lamb dis go-round. He's tryin to change an old game without any consent." Carlos's face turns red in a burst of anger.

With heavy breath and cold, flinty eyes he spouts, "Don't worry! Dat kidnappin son-of-a-bitch gonna get his—you can believe dat!"

During the next few minutes of silent measurements, Vinny becomes aware of a bad habit he somehow picked up from his wife, as a question bubbles to the surface. "So who put the pen to paper on this one?"

"Don't go thinking on it too hard, partner." The word came out *pahd-nah*. "Could make your future null and void. It took some effort to convince all the Goombata that you and dem other cogs wouldn't flip under any circumstances."

"That must have been some song and dance, considering this is my big bow."

Carlos turns away, suddenly interested in the contents of a filing cabinet drawer.

Vinny hangs his head, shakes the sand of denial away, and narrows his eyes. "You're not going to fucking let me go."

Carlos closes the drawer, looking down at a jettisoned rubber band. "Can't you do us both a favor and just take a long break, like you've done before?"

The sharp graphite pencil tip collapses and splinters under the weight of Vinny's embittered discontent. He is fully cognizant now that his pact with the devil, sealed by the spilling of someone else's blood, can only be undone with the last drop of his own.

Friday
November 22, 1963

T his should be any ordinary Friday in November, but it isn't. It should be the start to a beautiful long weekend, but it isn't that, either. Vinny is still away on business, and Mary can't seem to shake the feeling that something is amiss. It's the kind of day where you walk around the house checking to see if you turned everything off, like the stove and the iron. You wander the hall scratching your head, contemplating what you could have forgotten to do to prevent some unforeseen disaster.

Is it a missed appointment? The missed shift
I'm used to working?

Half of Mary's morning is spent with a worry-bug in her brain, and it looks like the afternoon will be slipping into much of the same torment. She slides the ponytail holder out of her hair and attacks her scalp, trying to rub away the anxiety.

What is nagging me so bad that I can't
relax and enjoy my day off?

She regathers her hair and secures it into an even tighter ponytail. "We need to get out of this house!" she says to Lisa, who is at the table eating a mid-morning snack of peanut-butter-covered crackers.

Standing by the window, Mary wonders if maybe it's the soft, steady breeze or the shining sun which has been calling to her all morning. At an abrupt thought, she gasps with giddiness, putting her hand on the phone to call Gayle. "You've never flown a kite! We could go out to the air base and have a picnic!"

"*Yayyy!*" Lisa exclaims, putting her hands up. "The tunnel!"

Mary holds the receiver to her ear and smiles at Lisa. Going through the tunnel would be a little out of their way, but she lifts her hand loosely and says, "Yay, the tunnel."

"I'm so glad you called. It's such a nice day to be out," says Gayle, basking on a blanket beside a short stack of magazines.

Mary is perched on her knees, noisily flipping through stations on a pocket-sized transistor radio—a present given to Lisa before she ever met the outside world—and finally settling on WTIX out of New Orleans.

"What's with the ugly black kite?" asks Gayle, her hand shielding her eyes from the sun.

Mary shrugs half-heartedly, looking up to see the mischievous red-eyed kite attempting to cause its small pilot some trouble. "It's the one she wanted." She sets the radio down next to Gayle and hops to her feet. "Here, let Mommy reel it in a little."

"Whyy?" asks Lisa, wanting to exert her big-girl abilities.

Mary tugs and wraps the nylon string of the new kite around the plastic handle. "Because it's getting too close to the power lines."

"Whyy?"

"Because it's dangerous, sweetheart, and I don't want you to get hurt."

"Ohhh." Lisa is eager to once again have lone command of the flying baby bat in the wind. A strong cross-breeze steals the kite before the transfer is complete, whipping it around so hard that it dives into a tree behind them.

"Oh, no, it's *stuck!*" Lisa shrieks.

Gayle surveys the altitude of the dejected kite. "Honey," she tells Lisa, "let's wait until Uncle Chick gets back with the food."

"No worries," Mary says, "I climbed many a tree in my day. Granted, it's been awhile." Nimbly, she pulls herself up the trunk and lower branches, reaching the kite where it sits tangled around an upper bough.

"Oh, I *love* this song!" Gayle squeals, turning up a tune by The Chiffons.

"Dance with me, Auntie Gayle!" Lisa has now entirely forgotten her suspended toy. "Wanna dance, too, Mommy?" Lisa asks, twirling around to "One Fine Day."

"Sure, baby. I've almost got this tangle beat." Mary smiles as she looks down at them, loosening the last of the knotted mess. She releases the kite, and as it floats to the ground slowly, gently, like a fallen leaf, an emergency tone breaks into the song.

"We interrupt this program to bring you a special bulletin from Dallas, Texas."

Mary freezes, intently listening for the ominous voice of the announcer.

"In downtown Dallas today, three shots were fired at President Kennedy's motorcade. The first reports say that this shooting has seriously wounded President Kennedy and Governor Connally. I repeat, there has been an attempt on the life of President Kennedy, wounded in a vehicle while in downtown Dallas today. The Secret Service is casting a wide dragnet in search of the shooter. They are searching for a white male, approximately twenty-five years of age, slender build, weighing about one hundred sixty-five pounds."

The announcer continues, but Mary can no longer hear what he is saying. All she hears is the description of the assailant, over and over—

"—white male, approximately twenty-five years of age, slender build, weighing about one hundred sixty-five pounds—"

—as she tries to make her quaking legs cooperate.

Chick arrives on the scene with a grease-stained sack of fried chicken, which he promptly sets beside the radio to help her get down from the tree. "Mary, are you all right?"

"I—" Before she can finish her sentence, she blacks out and tumbles out of the tree, gashing her calf open on the way down, landing with a *thud!* in a limp heap on the ground.

"Holy shit!" Gayle yells, and runs off to get help.

Chick takes his shirt off and ties it around Mary's bleeding leg. As gently as he can, he picks her up and moves her unconscious body onto the blanket.

"*Mommyyy!*" Lisa screams, crying and clawing at her delicate face.

Mary's concussed eyes flutter open. Her head pounds, her ears ring, her dazed eyes focus on the wispy, fast-moving clouds high in the baby blue. She doesn't respond to Chick's voice calling her name, or his nervous fingers snapping near her face. The peaceful sky becomes intermittently vivid and fuzzy, before an overwhelming sleep drags her under again.

Mary half-wakes to the whirring sounds of a heavy cart being rolled down a hall and the jarring clatter of clipboards coming from a nurse's station right outside her curtained area.

She's spent enough time in a hospital for her heavy hand to automatically search for the button to call for answers to the questions swirling around in her achy head. Upon finding it, she presses it repeatedly.

A pleasant and rather plump nurse enters the area, heading straight for Mary with a pressure cuff. She wraps it smooth and snug around Mary's feeble upper arm, places the small cold disc of the stethoscope in the crook of her elbow, and furiously pumps the inflation bulb until the cuff is tight enough to occlude the artery, making Mary's hand tingle.

"Ouch," she says hoarsely, flinching with a furrowed brow.

"Shush," says the nurse, concentrating on the noise in her earpieces.

Mary works her cottony mouth to produce some saliva as the nurse props her up.

"Here, let me get you some water." The nurse pours a small cup from the pitcher on the bedside tray.

Mary takes the cup and pours the room-temperature liquid down her parched throat. She repeatedly blinks, trying to get a clear focus on the nurse's face looking down at her chart. When she leans to return the empty cup to the tray, a pain rips through her left leg.

"It seems you took a nasty spill from a tree earlier today," the nurse says, in a much too perky octave.

"My baby—" Mary croaks with wild eyes, looking for signs of Lisa.

The nurse's free hand settles on Mary's shoulder. She begins again in a more pacifying tone. "Relax, honey. The doctor says the baby will be fine. Our examinations haven't shown any signs of harm done." The nurse raises the covers to check the state of Mary's loosely mummified leg. "It's this poor thing that needs your immediate attention. We put thirty stitches in your left calf." Satisfied with her dressing, the nurse tucks her patient back in. "And that means some bed rest for you."

Mary stiffens and winces, wanting to slap her away.

The nurse puts her fists on her hips and sighs. "I suppose it's almost time for your pain medication. I'll let the doctor know you're awake. He'll be in shortly to answer any more of your concerns." The nurse abruptly walks away, recording her findings in the chart, before Mary can muster a clear, coherent exchange, leaving her with a confused and frightened imagination.

A girl not much younger than Mary enters the curtained room wearing a red-and-white striped pinafore dress. Unlike the nurse, she has a hushed quality to her voice. "Hi, I'm here to get you some hydration." The candy-striper empties the pitcher into Mary's cup and adds a flexible straw so Mary can sip water without strain. "Now isn't that better? The doctor will be here in a minute. He's talking with your family in the waiting area." Mary's eyes perk up as she drinks, and the volunteer continues. "You were the talk of the whole floor. Everyone was on pins and needles, waiting to hear results on your baby. It gave them something else to think about besides the President."

"My baby? Was she hurt?"

The candy-striper smiles. "They said everything is A-OK. You really shouldn't skip meals when you're pregnant, though. It's not good for either of you."

"Pregnant?" Mary says, placing her hands on her secret-keeping belly.

"Almost sixteen weeks gone now." She gives Mary a sympathetic smile. "You must have hit your head."

"Maybe." Mary touches her temple. "Glad I'm not just fat."

"Did you hear about the President before your accident? I would hate to shock you twice in one conversation."

"He was shot at. Is he okay?"

"I wish I could give you happier news, but I heard he expired about one o'clock this afternoon. It's such a shame. At least they caught the guy who did it."

Mary's panic returns as she jerks her head back up at the candy-striper.

"—white male, approximately twenty-five years of age, slender build, weighing about one hundred sixty-five pounds—"

"They did?" she asks.

"Yep, about an hour after it happened."

"Do they . . . know his name?"

"Osbald, Osward, or something like that," the candy-striper reports, oblivious to Mary's intensity.

"Oh, thank God."

"Yeah, it'd be hard to sleep knowing there was some crazy killer on the loose out there. Well, I have to go tend to other patients, but I'll bring you some ice water later. Can I get you anything else?"

"No, you've made me feel so much better, thank you."

The candy-striper places both hands over her heart. "I just *love* helping people. Rest and heal up fast! Chasing after little ones will require both of those legs," she says with a wink.

"I'll do my best," Mary whispers, her hands still caressing her small baby bump.

"Tootles!" The girl waggles her fingers and disappears, forgetting to pull the curtain shut.

The next thing into view of the opening is a man in a white coat at the nurse's station, poring over paperwork handed to him by the same nurse who strangled Mary's arm earlier. She studies the details of the man's concerned face and sees what Bobby will look like when he is an older man. She has not realized she is staring at him until he looks up and breaks the spell. He smiles at her and she returns the gesture as best she can, considering the pain in her leg is beginning to bust through whatever local anesthetic was administered. He walks into her curtained room, still flipping through the chart, closing it when he reaches her bedside. "I wish we'd met under better circumstances than these, Mary." He offers up a deep sigh and a thoughtful expression.

"Dr. Vicknair, I presume?" Mary says with nervous impulse, feeling like a helpless Humpty Dumpty.

"That's what it says on my nametag, anyway," he replies with a smile. "You had yourself quite a fall. I don't want to be rude, but what possessed you to climb a tree in your condition? And on an empty stomach, to boot?"

"Long story short, Doctor, I was waiting for food when my daughter's kite decided to climb the tree before me. As for the pregnancy, I had no clue."

"Had you not missed a cycle or three?"

"Not a one. They were much lighter than usual, but were still spot-on." Mary grimaces and adds, "Pardon the pun."

But the doctor doesn't even chuckle. "That's not abnormal," he says. "I had a peek at your bloodwork and everything seems to be in order. You'll need to make an appointment with an obstetrician and let him know you're taking these." Dr. Vicknair rips a page from his prescription pad, which has appeared out of nowhere like a magic trick at a birthday party.

Mary doesn't take the proffered slip. "I don't like to take medicine."

"Just a low dose of hydrocodone to dull the pain."

"I doubt I can take them, regardless. I have a pretty sensitive constitution."

He insists the paper upon her. "I'd like to see you tell me that a half-hour from now. Can I take another look at my work?" he asks, pointing at Mary's leg. "That is, if you don't mind."

Mary braces herself and pulls the covers back for him to see. "You gave me the stitches?" she asks, shaking her head in pain and disbelief. "I don't know why I always thought you were a general practitioner . . . cold and flu stuff."

He begins to loosen the outside wrap. "I cover the emergency room, so I'm trained in all areas of medicine, a good bit more than just your average cold and flu. Take your leg, for example." He peels back the oozy gauze. "A work of art, if I do say so myself."

" 'Art'? It looks pretty scary right now." Mary looks at the gory, orange-stained zipper of sutures holding the meaty part of her calf together.

"The betadine wash makes it look much worse than it is, but it helps to prevent infection."

She marvels at the complex network of thread and barbs. "I do a bit of sewing myself, but I just can't imagine," she says, and adds, "Thank you so much."

Bobby's father nods humbly, a practice he has passed down to his son. "It may leave a scar, but the beauty of it is that you will walk again. This wound was deep in the muscle. Any deeper and the prognosis might not have been so promising. Cleaning and closing the tissue properly was my contribution. The other half of your recovery will be up to you. You may have to attend some type of rehabilitation."

"Like Bobby did?" Mary asks, remembering the suffering he endured.

"Nothing quite so intense—just some stretching and movements to help you regain the use of it faster."

Mary rubs her face, feeling overwhelmed. "So many things to do and remember. What a day this has been."

"Don't worry. I've given all my written instructions to your husband—all the when's, where's, and how's have been discussed."

Mary looks up, suddenly conscious of the still-open curtain. "My husband is here?"

The doctor's eyebrows pull down in concentration as he removes and clicks a penlight from his breast pocket. "Follow my finger, please," he says, to examine Mary's pupils.

"Is . . . something wrong?"

"No, I just want to be sure. I'm going to have the nurse dose you, place a more secure sterile dressing on your leg, and send you home," he says, replacing his penlight. "Any more questions for me?" He widens his stance and his hands form a steeple pressed to his lips.

"Hmmm." Mary squints, looking inward, her thoughts seeming only to register the throbbing in her wound. "Maybe not."

"You have my contact information in your paperwork if you think of anything," he says, taking and encasing her hand in his.

"I can't thank you enough for putting me back together, Dr. Vicknair."

"Tell me that when you see the bill," he says, patting her hand and leaving it to rest on the bed.

He starts to leave, but turns back to say, "Bobby is on his way home from school for Thanksgiving. Shall I keep this under my hat? He'll ask about you. He always does."

"He's one of the best friends I've ever had. I don't want to worry or distract him."

"Well, then, I won't say anything unless he asks directly," he says, slyly tapping the side of his nose before closing the curtain.

Pleasantly medicated, Mary is rolled toward the exit, where a raw-eyed Chick wrinkles his brow, jumps from his seat, and nervously rubs the tops of his thighs when he sees her approaching. Mary realizes that he was probably mistaken for her husband.

She raises the small page bearing the recommended medication. "Can we pick this up on the way home?"

"Sure, anything you need." He tucks the slip, written in doctor-scratch, in the pocket of his jeans and takes helm of the wheelchair.

"The list he gave me says to get bandages, crutches, and some vitamins, too."

She looks up at the underside of his chin. "Where are Lisa and Gayle?"

"I brought them to the house to lie down. They were both so upset."

Chick parks Mary's wheelchair outside on the curb. "I'll go get the car."

"Any word from Vinny?" she asks his back as he walks away.

He stops, half-turns, and shakes his lowered head "no" before shoving his hand in his pocket to retrieve the car keys.

Her head begins to throb again, and she thinks,

White male, approximately twenty-five years of age,
slender build, weighing about one hundred sixty-five pounds.

Sunday
November 24, 1963

"**Girls, I'm home!**" Vinny calls out.

It is a little after four in the afternoon. Mary rises from a post-hydrocodone nap and struggles to get up onto the cushioned crutches. Once steady on her feet, she has no trouble coordinating ambulation.

"I've got presents!" he bribes.

Stealthily, she arrives in the kitchen to see his disappointment after lifting the lid of an empty pot on the stove.

"Supper is at Gayle's tonight," she says.

When his bright eyes find her, his excited smile evaporates and is replaced by pallid fear. "Did someone hurt you? Did they threaten you?" he asks, erasing the distance between them as he rushes to check her condition.

She raises a crutch-supported arm to ward him off. "A threat? No." She shakes her head. "I fell out of a tree."

"A tree?" he asks, dropping into a chair.

Mary's face melts into the heat of a rising swirl of emotions. She wails, "It's been *days*, Vinny! Where were you when I needed you?"

Vinny's cheeks burn, his throat bobs, and he lowers his blinking eyes. His chin quivers. "Tell me what happened?" he asks, and looks up. "Where's Lisa?"

"Why should I answer your questions when you won't answer mine?"

He rises from the chair.

With wide, frightened eyes, she lifts her right crutch, wielding it like a weapon.

"I'm not going to hurt you." His voice cracks. "I want to hold you and tell you how sorry I am."

She pauses, searching his eyes for sincerity. Visibly shaking, she lowers the crutch and allows him to come closer. He slowly reaches out to smooth the hair from her face, to cradle her head in his hands, to lovingly kiss away the tears, to kiss away the pain, the worry, the fear. Secure in his passionate embrace, she lets the crutches clatter to the floor. Gingerly, he lifts and delivers her to the soft altar of their bedroom. Avoiding her injured calf, Vinny soothes and nourishes Mary's wounds, providing the kind of relief no bottle of pills has to offer.

"We were supposed to be at Gayle's at six," Mary says, lying on Vinny's chest in a warm post-coital cocoon. She caresses his playfully reciprocating hand, enjoying the blissful closeness.

"Just a few more minutes," he whispers, and kisses her forehead.

Mary nuzzles deeper into her spot by his side, and sighs.

Vinny lies in repose until his brain begins to itch. "What the hell were you doing in a tree?"

Mary giggles, covers her face, and buries her head in his armpit.

He says, "I was out of town making sure we'd have enough money to send Lisa to any college she wants."

Mary's head pops up. *"Really?"*

"Yes, really. Now you."

"I was in a tree making sure Lisa's brand-new kite would—"

"And where was Chick?" Vinny interrupts, as if he'd been her hired babysitter.

"What does Chick have to do with anything? It was your fault for not being here—and for being completely unreachable."

Vinny ignores this. Instead, he pulls the covers back and unwraps her bandages to inspect her leg. "Yikes," he says, pulling air between his bared teeth as he stares at the thirty overlapping sutures. "So . . . how is this my fault?"

"The President was shot—"

"And I suppose you want to blame that on me, too," Vinny says, rewrapping her bandages with more care than he'd displayed in their unwrapping.

Mary shrugs and pulls her dress back on over her head as he does so. "They caught the guy, didn't they?"

"Yeah, they caught a guy," Vinny says with faraway eyes. *"And then the spider ate the fly."* He bites the aluminum-toothed clip into the skin of her Ace bandage and lightly pats her foot.

"Whatever *that* means." Mary rolls her eyes and swings her legs over the side of the bed. "I'm starving. Can you bring me my wooden legs?"

Vinny hops up and snaps the elastic on his boxers, then heads to the kitchen. "I know I ought not mention it," he calls, "but I picked you up earlier, and sweetheart . . . you ain't starvin."

"Are you suggesting I put your unborn child on a diet?" she asks, followed by a loud clatter as the crutches fall to the kitchen floor for the second time that evening.

Mary smooths the bodice of her dress with a satisfied grin.

Tuesday
February 25, 1964

"**Fourteen! I still** can't believe it," Mary says, hugging Sarah tight in the Poche kitchen. A box on the counter contains only rich crumbs of a once wickedly dark chocolate birthday cake.

"How far along is the baby now?" Sarah asks. She bends down to place her ear to Mary's pregnant belly, hoping for a message from her future niece or nephew.

"Last Friday the doctor said I was around twenty-nine weeks," Mary answers, massaging her lower back with her fingertips.

In reaction to a report on the television, Vivian booms from the other room, "How horrible!"

The younger Poche children—Jenny, Margene, Brandon, and Barbara—sit in a square on the front room carpet, attempting to organize and interlock five hundred oddly shaped pieces together in the hopes of seeing Snoopy and Woodstock before bedtime.

Sarah and Mary join the others gathered in the front room. "What happened?"

"I told y'all being up in the sky just ain't natural," Vivian cries. She places both hands over her mouth and begins to rock, so Jason decides to explain.

"They still can't find large portions of an airplane that crashed in New Orleans early this morning. Only bits and pieces of people and plane floating around. They're sending divers down to look."

With sleep-deprived eyes, Jenny jumps and bites at her bottom lip when someone outside pops the seal on the front door and it stands ajar. Her rigid body relaxes slightly when she hears Lisa's voice talking to the dog.

Mary rubs the circulation back to her left calf, still on the mend. "Did anyone hear what airline it was?"

"Eastern Flight 304," Vinny answers, wiping his feet as he enters the house and brings in a blast of crisp, cool air along with Lisa and Christmas the dog.

Smelling like stale hay, Christmas turns around in a labored circle and whines as she lowers her creaky arthritic parts down onto an old folded blanket on the floor. She rests her gray-specked muzzle on Lisa's welcoming knee.

Mary looks at Vinny suspiciously. "How did you know that?"

He shrugs and moves, careful not to mash any fingers or toes of the kids littering the floor, to land on the couch. "I heard about it several times today while I was out and about."

Mary—who isn't quite sure she's convinced by her husband's answer—turns her attention back to Jason. "Where did it go down?"

"Looks like the Pontchartrain swallowed it nearly whole, somewhere east of the Causeway." Jason gnaws on the inside of his cheek.

Mary stares down at the framework of the puzzle under construction, listening to the children—whose biggest concern is finding the last yellow pieces of Woodstock to connect the first isthmus of the picture contrasting against the blue sea of carpet. She yearns for their childlike insouciance.

"Was it full?" she asks her brother.

Jason sweeps strands of hair in need of a trim from his forehead. "I don't know about full, but it looks like a total loss. I believe they said fifty-eight altogether."

Vivian shakes her head, still in shock over the news. "That huge bird fell right out of the blasted sky."

"What did you just say?" Mary asks with knitted brow, stirred by those words, resurrecting the faintest of memories playing in the periphery of her mind . . . some odd phrase of eerie prescience that Mambo Beulah spoke to her so long ago. In this mnemonic reverie she can almost feel the Creole psychic woman's urgent fingers wrapped around her wrists.

"A fallen bird . . ." she mutters slowly.

Monday
June 1, 1964

"What are you doing? You don't have to come back so soon. It's barely been a month!"

Mr. Dupre says this to Mary as she unexpectedly charges through the pharmacy door at five minutes to nine. She is briefly startled by the harmonic chime of a new electronic doorbell, installed in her absence. He rushes to her, biting his lip, and she instantly recognizes a new smell about him: Mrs. Picou's Windsong perfume. The chime plays again as someone exits through the back door. Harry freezes, his face squinched, regretting the tattletale wiring.

Mary grins, rolls her eyes, and waves him off. "Four weeks and two days, to be exact," she announces proudly, slipping into an apron with ample pockets for dusting paraphernalia. "I'm only going to be here long enough to stock shelves and tidy the place up. I'll be home in time for her next feeding." Feather duster in hand, she begins to dust and straighten bottles and cartons, starting with the top of the cough-syrup section.

"How is our sweet baby Tina?"

"She is fine, thank you. Napping with her dad right now."

"And how is big sister Lisa?"

"She's a helper—and she'll be four years old on Friday."

"Is that so," he chuckles, and rubs his chin. "And what, pray tell, made you decide to come back in today?"

Mary smiles as she cleans. "Gayle gave me something for energy this morning, and now I just can't be still."

Harry frowns, watching her work furiously, but says nothing more. He decides to go check that his darling properly secured the back door on her way out.

Two hours later, finished and ready to skedaddle back home, Mary stops long enough to gulp several cones of water from the cooler, beads of sweat on her forehead. "I'm headed out, but I'll be back in the morning to make the orders," she says to Harry as he passes by. "Unless you have other plans?" She chuckles, refilling the flimsy rolled-rim paper.

"Hardy, har, har," he says in ersatz mockery, hiding his warm, rosy cheeks behind the register as he rummages beneath it. "Before you go, there's a present here for the baby." Harry places a white, glossy department-store box on the counter.

"You've done so much already," she says, dragging her arm across her forehead.

"This one isn't from me. A nice young man brought it for you about a week ago."

"Oh?" Mary wipes her wet hands on the sides of her pink high-waisted shorts and sweeps the mystery gift off the counter to place beneath her arm for the stroll home. *"Harry and Ms. P sittin in a tree,"* she sings as she exits the store into the balmy afternoon.

Harry shakes his head, unable to tame his wide grin.

Approaching the house, Mary sees Vinny lift the hose and spray a fan of water at Lisa, followed by her piercing squeal. "Where's the baby?" she asks.

"I'll give you three guesses," Vinny says. He angles his head in the direction of Gayle's house. "We traded. The baby-stealer will be over soon."

"I see." Mary giggles, watching Lisa run through rainbowed sprinkles.

Vinny glances at her. "What's in the box?"

"Another baby gift."

"Hope it's not another damn blanket," Vinny says, shaking his head. "You'd think we lived in Minnesota or something."

Mary hears Lisa's little voice lilting, *"Theee itsy bitsy spiiiderrr went out the waaater spout,"* when she pops the sealed tabs at each end with her thumbnails and slides the lid open, revealing an envelope neatly centered atop a soft green satin-edged blanket, her name carved in Bobby's bold print.

Mary's first instinct is to tear into the card, but fear inhibits her fingers. A cowardly reluctance to find out if his affections for her have not faded and he still painfully longs for her heart, a longing she can't possibly alleviate ... or worse to find some cheesy prefabricated message with a whimsical *on-to-greener-pastures* signature. With powerful restraint and reverence she lifts the fold and places the envelope of his unknown intentions in the blanket's interior to hide the pain it causes. She lowers the lid back down and presses on it, causing the box to bend and crease, hoping to smother the past, to quell the yearning she still has for Bobby's friendship. To avoid confronting his sentiments, she conceals the gift on a high shelf in a dark, private place where most well-kept secrets are hidden . . . in the closet.

Thursday
July 2, 1964

Laughter and applause fill the intimate wood-paneled belly of the Elks Lodge. The hall, pre-draped and decorated in red, white, and blue for a Fourth of July potluck dinner, serves well enough for the nearly impromptu and understated second nuptial celebration under way. Mary sits rejoicing in the smoke-filled room amongst friends and acquaintances, unaccompanied by Vinny, who was too stubborn, moody, and full of excuses to attend.

"To the happy couple!" shouts a cheerful voice, and everyone around the large banquet table happily raises a glass of champagne for the toast.

Mr. and Mrs. Dupre sit beaming at one another, surrounded by the people of their inner circle as they celebrate a second chance at wedded bliss.

"Speech! Speech!" someone cheers, followed by several sets of hands drumming on the table in rowdy endorsement. With eyes that sparkle, Alene Picou Dupre conveys extra encouragement and support by patting her new husband's arm.

Harry nods to the call reluctantly and raises his hand to calm the small, insistent crowd. He stands, straightens his suit, and clears his throat, waiting for the hush to fall.

"On behalf of my lovely bride Alene and myself, I would like to thank you all again for coming to share this night with us. After this beautiful creature agreed to marry me, I didn't want to give her the chance to change her mind."

He sighs, skimming along her jawline with his fingertips. Seeing Harry's chin quiver, Alene offers up a warm hand for him to hold, and he clutches it to his hitching chest.

"I . . . uh," he sniffs, and starts again, a bit slower than before. "For those of you who don't know how the journey to this moment began, the story opens with kind words from my friend and associate, Mary Carlino."

"I'm an 'associate' now?" Mary calls out, and everyone laughs.

"She reminded me a while back," Harry says as the merriment dies down, "that love is forgiving and blind . . . that it doesn't mind when we're over twenty and our hearts have dents. She often says that I should remember to live while I'm still alive."

"Amen to that!" someone hoots enthusiastically.

Harry picks up his champagne flute. "So let's all lift our glasses to Mary, and to living, laughing, and loving while we still can!"

After glasses have been clinked and drained several more times, Mary smiles, fondly watching her friends take the room's center to swing and sway to The Fabulaires, their first song as a married couple. When conversation is exhausted, livelier music fills the hall, blaring beats out of large portable speakers. With no desire for late-night dancing, Mary is ready to say goodbye to the mingling group and make her exit.

Before she can get up from the chair, however, her body freezes—petrified by the sudden grip of two strong hands upon her shoulders.

"Is that the guy?" Vinny slurs, his hot breath in Mary's ear. He lifts one hand from her shoulder and points to Alene Dupre's handsome cousin.

"Guy?" Baffled, Mary shakes her head. "What guy?"

Vinny violently jerks her chair and raises his voice. "Is *he* the reason you like workin so much?"

"I don't know what you're talking about," she says. "You're embarrassing me."

The scene draws the attention of one of the larger male guests. "Hey, buddy, you ever think she might like working to get away from you?"

Vinny grabs Mary by the wrist and yanks her out of the seat.

The big guy raises a hand up to Vinny. "Okay, pal. I think you need to take it outside."

"Maybe you and I should take it outside!" Vinny taunts the man, banging on his own adrenaline-bloated chest. "Can't you see I'm celebrating my brand-new civil rights?"

"That's hilarious!" The big man laughs, finding Vinny to be a kindred drunkard. "We should raise a big toast to 'em, then . . . I'll go get us a bottle."

"A law against segregation and discrimination is of great significance. Today was a watershed moment for our country. You guys shouldn't make fun of that sort of thing," Mary says, trying to yank her wrist from her husband's grip.

"Why, lady? You some kind of nigger lover?" the big man asks.

Mary cuts her angry eyes into him.

"Yeah, Mary," Vinny half-teases, his heart pounding. "You some kind of nigger lover?"

Unamused, Mary heads for the door, dragging Vinny as far as she can. When he won't budge any more, she places her arm around Vinny's waist and his around her neck. "You are sloshed. Let's get you home."

"Home?" Vinny sniffs, staggering alongside her into the night air.

"Yes, home."

"What if I'm not sure where that is anymore?"

Disgusted, Mary rolls her eyes and shakes her head. "Wow, you're truly pickled this time." She leans his loose body against their car to fish the keys out of his pocket. When she glances into his drunken eyes she is startled by the sad, boyish face staring back at her in distress. Mary studies his somber face for a moment with pursed lips and he looks away. She sighs, opens the passenger door, and says, "Home is where your heart is, *coo yon*."

Vinny climbs in the seat and the door slams behind him. He presses his cheek against the coolness of the window. "I don't know where *that* is, either," he mutters before she opens the driver's-side door.

Saturday
July 4, 1964

Mary wakes early to the angry hoot of an owl warning of a sun not yet on the rise. She stretches out, her limbs finding no barrier—she's alone in the bed. No sounds of Lisa scurrying about in her nightclothes attempting to be quiet. No cry from the now bottle-fed angel, a sardonic thanks to her uncooperative breasts. Both girls most likely sound asleep.

Tiptoeing out of bed, she senses a foreign vibration in the house: not at all unpleasant, something more like an ineffable unfolding, like being vaguely aware of the push, pull, and spin of the celestial clockworks. She hears an echo of tinkering in the kitchen just above the whir of the air conditioner that never seems to shut off in the summertime.

Vinny must have stayed up after feeding Tina.

Wrapped in only a thin robe, Mary sneaks down the hall and peers into the kitchen. Vinny stands shirtless over the stove cracking eggs into a pan. She remains partially hidden, marveling at the rare sight of him cooking; how could she have remained unaware of these talents for so long? Since Vinny does not often partake of a morning meal, she guesses the effort is for her. His next trick is to flip the fried eggs with his agile wrist and slide them onto a plate alongside a small mound of grits. He flinches as a pop of grease lands on his bare skin.

A girlish giggle of amusement escapes Mary's lips, giving her presence away. Afraid the slip has wrecked his generous mood, expecting harsh words or punishment, she retreats backward down the hall a few steps.

"Get your toosh in here," Vinny says with a smile. He gestures with the plate, inviting her to join him at the table. "I would have brought this to you in bed if you'd stayed there," he says, verging on playful as he places her princess-style breakfast on the table.

Sheepishly, she takes a seat and inhales the fragrant steam. A *meal*, prepared especially for her.

"Sarah's here," he says, sipping his coffee.

With just two words, Mary's morning crumbles around her. Her face is panic-stricken. "When? Why? What happened?"

"Calm down, don't wanna wake them up. I arranged for her to watch the girls. I want to spend the day—just you and me. I borrowed a boat, the car is already packed, and we're going fishing," he says matter-of-factly.

Her panic morphs to puzzlement. "We've never been fishing. What do we know about fishing? And you know I'm not wild about boats and water . . . I don't understand."

He rises from his chair. "What's there to understand? You always say that we don't spend enough time together. So I go out of my way to get a babysitter you'd trust, and a boat to take you out for some fun in the sun." He tosses his empty ceramic mug into the sink, where it just manages not to shatter. "Fuck me for tryin!"

"I'm sorry. Please don't be mad. It's a great idea. I was just being a silly worrywart again," she backpedals, wanting to rewind his mood. "As soon as I'm done with my skillfully prepared breakfast, I'm going to get ready for a super-fun outing with my super-sweet husband." To further prove this, she stuffs a huge bite of egg and grits into her mouth.

He stands with his hands wrapped around the outer lip of the kitchen sink, staring out into the yard. "Forget it. It's ruined now."

She swallows and stands. "Don't say that. I won't take long. All I need is a few minutes to brush my teeth and get a suit on. I don't even need to fix my hair—I'll grab a hat! Please, I'll be a good girl for the rest of the day, I promise," she says, embracing him from behind, tenderly kissing across his smooth, hairless shoulders.

Loosening his grip on the sink, he turns to kiss Mary on the lips. "Maybe we have time to . . ." He trails off, kissing her again, pulling her hips toward the bulge that has formed from her pleading. "It *has* been a while."

"I did say I'd be a good girl, didn't I?" she says, leading him back to the unmade bed. She pushes the small amount of comforter that managed to hang on throughout the night to the floor.

Watching her do this on all fours only arouses him more. He locks the door.

She spins around, upright on her knees, teasingly peeling off her robe to reveal a naked shoulder, slowly passing her hand lower until her left breast pops out from beneath the silky material. He sheds his pajama bottoms as quickly as he can, no longer wanting to be an inactive participant in her game. After eight weeks of abstinence, it doesn't take long before they are both made greedy, bathed in each other's saliva and sweat, fiercely pumping on a carnal path to ecstasy. With Sarah and the kids in the house, Mary buries her teeth into Vinny's neck to prevent vocalizing any delight at the height of her excitement, and digs her nails into his back, causing him to explode deep within her.

Weakened, he rolls off and pays due homage to her honey hole with a small towel from a drawer in his bedside chest. Both satisfied and both still out of breath, he spanks her bare ass with a *thwack*.

Vinny peeks out the bedroom window at the waking sun. "We must hurry! Daylight is burning," he says, jumping into a pair of shorts.

With the prospect of handling icky fish in a boat, Mary slips on a swimsuit and a pair of shorts, keeping her prep time to a minimum, briefly brushing her teeth. The mirror's reflection of her wild hair begs for time she simply doesn't have, reminding her to grab the sunhat Mrs. Shirley gave her years ago. During a quick peek in the girls' bedroom at the three sleeping beauties, two snuggled in the bed and one in the crib, she hears the car start and runs for the driveway.

"You should wear hats more often," Vinny says, impressed at her Daytona-worthy finish time.

She narrows her eyes at him as she slides into the seat. "Did you leave the feeding schedule and formula directions?"

"I thought of everything," he says with confidence.

"Did you grab towels?" Mary stretches over the bench seat, taking inventory of what is packed in the back as he pulls out of the driveway.

"Trust me, if I didn't bring it, you won't need it," he says.

She glances uneasily at the ice chest several times.

"There's no beer in there, I swear," he says, seeing her gaze. "I'm trying to apologize for the other night at your boss's wedding, if you haven't noticed. I feel terrible for the way I acted. You don't have to worry about me drinking today."

"What a beautiful day," Mary says, watching the last of the early-morning mist burn away. The sun shines down on her as she looks out over the fairly calm water from the sturdy wooden planks of the wharf at the marina. "Looks like a good day for fishing," she says to self-motivate and soothe her screaming insides, once again faced with an irrational fear of boarding a boat.

Vinny looks at home on the borrowed vessel, the custom Chris-Craft's fiberglass-coated meranti grain winks at her handsomely as he readies it for the trip. Considering she's never known him to be an outdoorsman in any sense of the word, this strikes Mary as odd. She rubs the chill-bumps on her upper arms, anxiety on the rise, threatening to become an intense itch, the kind you can't rid yourself of no matter how much you scratch. Maybe it's the water—the way it laps up reaching for your ankles to pull you under—or the sweep of purple martins tweeting out a warning to stay safely ashore. Maybe it's the unusual twinkle in Vinny's eye as he reaches out for her hand to help her board.

"Come on, Maggie the Scaredy-Cat." Sensing her trepidation, he points at a bright-orange vest. "I have a life jacket here with your name all over it."

For the first few steps, her footing is a challenge. Mary slides across the deck of the boat like a clumsy deer on ice skates. "I guess I grabbed the wrong shoes," she says, holding onto Vinny as she looks down at her leather sandals.

"You can take them off now. You won't need them." He adjusts the straps on her new bright-orange accessory. "Have a seat and get comfortable."

He moves to release the rope from the cleat, freeing the sport boat from its captivity. She chooses a seat in the rear of the seventeen-footer, feeling safest there. He falls down into the driver's seat, turns the key, and the inboard V8 engine roars to life. *Blub, blub, blub . . .* The boat idles loudly, drifting out of the slip.

Mary takes a last look around, noticing the lack of activity at the marina.

Seems strange that on a summer holiday,
more boats aren't on the water.

"I wonder where all the people are on such a pretty day," she says, trying to take her mind off the disquietude in her veins.

"Probably gathering with family at crab boils and barbecues, getting drunk and waiting for the fireworks," he says over the engine.

The prop maintains a firm bite on the water past the no wake sign. At a safe distance, he opens the engine up until they are almost flying, barely skimming the top of the water.

They are going so fast that Mary has to hold onto her hat with both hands, surrendering her grip on the boat. "Slow down!" she cries, cheeks billowing and eyes squinted from the force of the air pelting her face.

He must hear her, because the speed decreases and the boat sinks a little lower.

Now I'm not quite so apt to get bugs caught in my teeth,

she thinks to herself—which immediately brings little Jenny of yesteryear to mind. She laughs out loud, putting herself at risk of swallowing one, and this only makes her laugh harder.

Perplexed, Vinny turns to see what's going on behind him. "What's so funny?"

"It's nothing," she says, wiping her teary, wind-shorn eyes.

He continues at a reasonable clip until they arrive in what he deems a sweet spot, and kills the engine as if he actually knows what prime conditions to look for.

Mary listens to the estuarine current sloppily licking against the boat's fiberglass skin. She looks over the side into the dark, brackish pool of inland sea, wondering where each adventurous drop has been.

Vinny raises up two pushbutton fishing rods pre-equipped with spoon lures.

"Hmmmm." Mary's throat betrays her lack of confidence. Growing up, she only ever fished from a bridge with a stick, using worms or chicken livers.

Vinny smiles. "These are easy kid reels. Just relax and I'll show you."

Following the simple-enough instructions, Mary still finds it difficult to let go and enjoy the day that he has gone to such trouble to spend with her. She feels learning to fish has turned what is supposed to be fun into a fruitless chore.

Vinny casts his line, and eyes her stiff posture. His shoulders slump and he lowers his head. "I have a confession to make, Mag . . . but I need you to promise you won't get mad."

"I promise," she says, reeling in her line.

"I told you I didn't bring any beer, and I didn't, but—" He reaches into the ice chest.

She feels her heart sink and does a poor job of hiding the disappointment on her face when he pulls out Lisa's Flintstones thermos.

"I brought a nip of rum," he says, then adds quickly, "but not for me. Just enough for you. I know how nervous you get around water, so I thought it might loosen you up a bit. I'll mix it with some Coke and you'll barely notice the taste. Wanna give it a try?" He pours the mixture in a cup before she has a chance to answer.

At this point, she sure doesn't want to start an argument—not when there is nowhere for her to run or hide. So she takes the cup like a good girl and sips the concoction, even winking at the bartender for good measure. Vinny smiles, thankful for her good humor and cooperation—so much so that he quickly refills her drink every time it is halfway gone. Casting and drinking with a bulky foam vest on proves to be difficult, so she removes it temporarily.

Thirty minutes pass with no bites, not even a nibble. Vinny huffs in frustration, tugging on his line.

The rum brings out the philosopher in Mary. "A true fisherman finds joy in just getting a line wet and basking in the peaceful outdoors."

Nature, in fickle declaration, pulls a sinister cloud across the sun, still shining brightly in the distance. The gentle sway of the boat becomes more of a rocking, shaking up the contents of Mary's belly, which the heat has turned rancid.

She looks up at the darkening sky. "Maybe we should head in. It looks like bad weather is rolling through."

He reaches for her hand and gives it a soft squeeze. "We just got here. I'm sure it will blow over."

"Not soon enough." Mary grimaces, her face tinged in green. "I think I'm going to revisit my scrambled eggs."

"Let's give it a few more minutes." Vinny throws his line out in vain. "If it doesn't get any better soon, we'll head in, okay?" He tucks the pole between his knees and lights a cigarette.

Oh, what a fertile cast we leave when
first we're baited to upheave,

Mary thinks to herself, giggling—and just as she predicted, she suddenly feels a strong need to throw her own liquid contribution into the waters of the Pontchartrain.

Unaffected by her heaving and retching, Vinny leans and exhales, watching his cigarette smolder between puffs. "Maybe now the fish will bite," he jokes, sending her into hysterical laughter from where she still leans over the gunwale. Vinny hands Mary some fresh water to wash out her mouth and rehydrate.

Strength returning, she shivers at a slight temperature dip and takes another look around. "I don't want to be out here if the rain comes. There might be lightning to follow."

"You would think you had someone waiting for you somewhere, as much as you're bellyachin to leave. I thought we were having fun," he says, flicking the cigarette butt into the water.

"We are. I'd just like to take our fun indoors somewhere," she says, conjuring up images of earlier that morning.

"Was there somewhere in particular you need to be—like work, for instance?"

Mary flicks her gaze skyward. "Please say you're kidding, Vin. I just threw up, it looks like a hurricane is brewing out here, and you're going to act like I want to leave because I'm having an affair?" She sits down and crosses her arms.

He hands her the orange safety vest. "Are you?" he asks with a curled lip and cold, flat eyes.

She throws the vest back at him. "I'm not even going to dignify that nonsense with an answer."

Vinny preps the boat to leave, deploying a look or two of accusation at Mary.

Exasperated, she throws her hands up. "Oh my *god!* I cannot believe how ridiculous this is—for you to come at me again with this paranoid song-and-dance from the other night."

"Okay, okay, okay," he says, his palms facing her. "Calm down. I didn't mean to start a fight with you." He points over the windshield. "You see that pretty spot over there?"

Relieved he's moved on to something else, she looks where he is pointing and is instantly mesmerized by the ethereal rays of light stretching into the water, seemingly only a mile or so away. "Yeah . . ."

"We are going to catch some redfish over there, I'm sure of it."

"If you say so." Mary purses her lips.

"I'm calling a truce." Vinny slides into the driver's seat. "Why don't you come sit up front next to me?"

"I'm fine where I am, thank you very much." She crosses her legs and lifts her chin.

Vinny turns the key and shrugs. "Suit yourself." He puts the hammer down slow and steady in a large, graceful arc, heading for clearer skies.

Mary, rattled and damp with spray, decides she wants the vest after all. Seeing it on the port side just a leg away, she reaches out with her foot to get it, but only pushes it out farther. Determined, she stands low and reaches for the vest. The boat suddenly bounces hard and pivots, catapulting Mary from the deck.

Why didn't I learn to swim?

is the first thing that pops into her head while flying through the ungraspable mid-morning air. The blow her hip sustained on the portside railing is already throbbing when the water slaps her in the face. The brackish water embraces her and pulls her close as if to apologize. Now submerged, her ears fill with the vicious buzzing of the propeller as it just misses her head. In a soundless scream, she loses the last of her air. Frantically, she scratches her way through the underwater flora to follow her bubbles to their destination, barely breaching the surface before her lungs betray her. Through ragged chokes she greedily gulps the air—there may not be another chance.

Must stay calm and float,

she thinks, attempting to tread water. As she bobs up and down in the boat's wake, everything becomes intermittently vivid and fuzzy—

a feeling quite familiar to her, one that conjures swirling thoughts of death, new life, and falling from trees.

Slow breaths . . . slow breaths . . .

she pleads with herself, a litany to fight the ebb of consciousness, and once again she finds herself hearing Mambo Beulah's words—

"When de water comes, stay calm and float, child,
or you will surely drown."

—echo to her from so long ago. She's vaguely surprised at her ability to stay afloat, to keep her nose just above the waterline until she feels the reason beneath her bare feet: something below, beneath the murky waters, something odd . . . unyielding, covered in a layer of slime; something which has risen from the depths to greet her bare toes in the water, shocking her into complete sobriety. Unable to see what it is, she recoils and pulls her limbs from its clutches—but has a change of heart when she sinks far below the surface. This forced underwater meeting with her interloper brings some relief from being ravaged by an unseen carnivore. It turns out to be a large algae-coated protrusion, like a colossal shark fin, lying in a way that allows her to rest on its fortuitous ledge between swells. Its assistance is surely crucial to her survival, and so she is willing to endure the sick, squishy feeling underfoot.

The panicked thumping of blood in her ears subsides enough for her to think beyond drowning and she begins to survey the situation, bouncing from her slimy springboard to get a better look, each time trusting her feet will again land in the same spot.

What the hell just happened?
A fine July fourth outing this turned out to
be—my hip is killing me!
Where is he? He has to have realized that
I'm not in the boat,

she thinks impatiently, despite the fact that the boat seems to be turning around in the distance. Out of the corner of her eye Mary spots her sun hat floating, sneaking away on the shallow ripples that remain from the boat's wake.

How I've always loved that bright pink hat.
It came with a matching sundress that no longer fits.

The hat is too far away, but she reaches out in vain. Considering her swimming skills—or lack thereof—she decides to stay put. Perhaps the hat can be retrieved later.

Does he not see me?

she thinks, realizing that the boat is heading toward the hat, which has now drifted even farther away.

Maybe he saves the hat first?

Her foot slips. Mary scrambles to find her mysterious platform. Just as her nose once again breaches the surface, she sees the boat speed up, raging through the water, aiming, shredding her favorite hat under its angry hull.

Mary blinks, wide-eyed. Could this mean what it implies?

Did he . . . did he mean for me to fall out?

A brand-new kind of panic washes over Mary. The pounding of her heartbeat in her ears is almost deafening; so much so that it prevents her from hearing the hungry propeller return. Terrified, Mary strategically ducks and hides, holding her breath as Vinny brings the boat sweeping through the water like a fine-toothed comb. After the fourth pass he stops the boat, turns off the engine, and from the other side of the boat, for the first time, calls out for her.

"Maggie . . . Maggie!"

Paralyzed with suspicion, she watches him without answering.

Just before he cranks the engine to abandon the search, something brushes against her thigh and she stifles a yelp. Her knees buckle, ducking Mary beneath the churning surface and away from Vinny's hawk-eyes. In case he noticed the sudden disturbance, she stays submerged, stuck between the slimy thing beneath her and the slimy man above, unable to breathe.

Just when her breath is about to rip a seam in her lungs, she hears the engine start and pull away, muddled and thudding under the water. Mary bursts through the surface, chest heaving in distress as she watches the boat get smaller and smaller.

Now what?

"A fine mess, indeed," she says aloud, looking around for any available options to consider, no matter how implausible.

Soon the clouds dissipate and the sun returns.

"Just as he predicted," she says sourly.

After an hour, Mary is blinded by the glittery, glistening water that surrounds her for miles. She can even see sparkles and spots when her eyes are closed, like some massive, blazing kaleidoscope.

She hears a boat's engine approach closer and closer . . . but not close enough.

I'm going to fucking die out here!

"Here! *I'm over here! HELP!*"

Mary yells this over and over until her voice is gone and so is the thrum of the engine.

The sun moves ever westward, and an ebbing tide brings Mary a fleeting relief from having to bounce for every full breath. To distract herself from the muscle aches, the bruises, her crispy pink face, and the possible monsters lurking about in the water, Mary ponders the fact that it is actually the earth that moves and not the sun after all, and how very much she wants to have many scientifically enlightened conversations with her children if she survives.

Several speeding boats pass by, heading for home—but without a strong voice, all she can do is wildly wave her arms to no avail.

Later, as the tide begins to rise again, a screaming red peony crackles overhead, delivered by someone ashore who is too excited in their patriotism to wait for a black backdrop. Perhaps it is a test run, or a signal for spectators to gather. Mary's weary eyes follow the pyrotechnics' ashy fingers as they rake through the early evening sky and fade over the water.

A small white-and-red stripe appears to hover, coming closer, dancing just above the water. Mary looks hard, trying to focus on the fuzzy hallucination—until it sounds a long, deep blast of a horn.

A rescue boat!

"I'm here! I'm over here!" Mary calls out with her painfully raw vocal chords, jumping and waving and slapping the water.

A spotlight turns in her direction, sweeping slowly back and forth. In the twilit sky, the white light looks like an evil cyclops searching for a meal. The bright beam stops and shines directly in her face as if she were suddenly on stage. Tears of relief flood her eyes when the engine cuts off and the large boat drifts closer. A tethered floatation ring lands in the water a few feet away. In her eagerness to get out of the water, Mary leaps after it without hesitation. The tether pulls her closer to the side of the boat, the beam of light still shining her way. She hears the splash of a rope ladder being deployed. Exhausted and shivering, she finds just enough strength in her drained reserves to hoist herself up onto the ladder, and takes the outstretched hand of the uniformed Coast Guard officer.

"Are you sure? And she's okay?"

Mary's eyes bulge.

Vinny!

His voice came from somewhere on the boat. She immediately lets go of the officer's hand and plunges back into the drink, still clutching the flotation device.

"Try again—take my hand," the patient rescue officer says, reaching out to her as far as he can.

Mary shakes her head and yells in a hoarse voice, "He tried to kill me!"

"Ma'am, you have been in the water far too long," the officer replies, his hand still outstretched to her. "You will surely drown if you begin to cramp, not to mention the likelihood that you are suffering from some degree of hypothermia and could go into shock at any moment. We must get you dry and warm. There are several officers on this boat. I promise you will be safe. Now please take my hand."

Too feeble to argue, she reaches for the ropes a second time, but adds, "I don't want to see him!"

"Detain him in the rear," the officer shouts, giving a harsh hand gesture to his fellow crew member, and stretches out, making contact with her wrist.

On board, Mary looks back at the water. "There's something down there . . . I think it's a plane."

The officer wraps her in a thick blanket, touches her fevered head. He lifts her and carries her inside the cabin, setting her down in front of a heater.

Teeth chattering behind her blue lips in rhythm with her shivers, skin thoroughly pruned, Mary asks, "Why is it that we drive on a parkway and park on a driveway?"

The officer pauses to scratch his head and laughs. "I really don't know. I never thought about it before." He gives Mary a medical trauma assessment before flooding her with plenty of hot soup and fresh water.

A young shipmate steps into the cabin and smiles at her, touching the brim of his cap. "I sure am glad we found you safe and sound. That fella back there was coming out of his skin."

The officer in charge glares at the young man and slaps his own hand with a clipboard. The mate jerks to attention, waiting for further instructions.

"Take us home nice and slow," the officer says. "I think we have enough paperwork for today."

The mate nods curtly and sets about his orders, leaving Mary alone with the officer.

With a look of deep concern, the officer sits and leans toward Mary with the thickly papered clipboard and a pen. "I want you to take your time," he says, "but you need to explain to me what happened here. What you tell me may help me decide to radio the police and have your husband arrested as soon as we hit land. I've already recorded his statement." The officer casually hits the stack of papers with the pen.

She cranes her neck to see Vinny through a rear cabin window, sitting bent over with his fists glued to either side of his head.

"Oh, yeah?" she asks, already gaining strength back in her voice. "And what did that liar have to say for himself?"

"I can't discuss all the details in his report, but I do have some questions for you regarding what I was told." He leans back, holding up the top papers and revisiting some notations.

"Go right ahead, Officer. I'd be glad to answer any of your questions."

"He said you refused to wear your safety vest, even though you are not a strong swimmer. Is this true?"

Mary's mouth falls open. "Well, I wouldn't say 'refused.' " Her eyebrows furrow. "I was irritated, and forgot to put it on."

"He said you were consuming alcohol this morning. Is this true?"

Her face tightens. "Yes, but he wanted me to—and it made me sick."

"He said you have a history of taking pills that can alter your state of mind. Is this true?"

"I've only taken pills a dozen times in my life, and that includes aspirin."

"And the other pills, what were they for?"

"I took some for pain when I hurt my leg." She turns her calf to show him her dented scar.

"Any other times that you can remember?"

Mary's cheeks burn. "No," she lies, not wanting to have to explain the daily hardships of being a mother of small children.

"He says you got up from your seat while the boat was in motion. Is this true?"

"Did he tell you that he swerved on purpose to knock me out of the boat?"

"No." The officer shifts in his chair. "He said there was some bad weather causing a small waterspout that he was trying to dodge at the time of the accident. Did you see a waterspout?"

"A waterspout?" She repeats the question slowly and shakes her head in disbelief. "No."

"So is he lying about the waterspout?"

"I can't say for sure—I wasn't looking. But he did try to run me over with the boat. Did he tell you that?"

"He says he came unglued, frantically looking for you, and couldn't find you. Without his forethought to note the approximate position on a map, we would not have found you until tomorrow, if at all."

"You see? There's the lie to cover his deed," she says, determined to prove her sanity. "If he were unglued, would he have that kind of presence of mind?"

Pow!

Mary flinches, eyes wide and round with fear at the gunshot noise.

Scree . . . pop! pop! pop!—the fireworks announce their official arrival. Her whole body sighs with relief seeing the vigorous display of color slash across the dark indigo sky.

The officer raises his eyebrows, sits back in the chair, and rubs his smooth chin. "A classic case of 'he said, she said.' "

The police and an ambulance are waiting at the south shore search-and-rescue facility. Beneath the additional scrutiny of the police's questioning, Mary lies limp and confused on a stretcher, a tube pushing life-sustaining fluids into her veins, as the medics slide her into the back of a hearse-like ambulance.

Vinny rushes to her, but he is blocked by a police officer and the Coast Guard officer who promised to keep her safe.

"Maggie, please!" he cries from behind the barricade. "Do you honestly believe I would try to kill the mother of my children?"

"Ma'am, do you want to press charges?" the police officer asks, with one hand on Vinny and the other on his handcuffs.

Mary stares at Vinny with her languid, bloodshot eyes—he looks distraught, with his tear-stained, sunburned face.

She sags in surrender and answers: "No."

Wednesday
August 5, 1964

emale patient presented with *signs of prolonged weather exposure, dehydration, hematoma on left hip. Administered 1000cc normal saline IV. Upon initial evaluation patient exhibited acute paranoia brought on by possible intoxication. Patient denies any history of substance abuse. No documented history of schizophrenia. Suggested to husband to have the patient follow up with a mental health professional.*

These are the doctor's notes, hastily typed on the hospital release form that Vinny tucks in his shirt pocket with satisfaction and pats twice for good measure on the afternoon of July the fifth, 1964.

One solid month has passed since the accident, thirty-two days of Mary counting intertwining loops of cognitive distortion. Unable to trust her own intuition or logic, she begins to see collusion everywhere. Fallacies abounding in the Gulf of Tonkin, in the state of Mississippi, along with the dear old Pontchartrain, or perhaps not.

Am I going mad?

Mary wonders if the initial error shaping all the subsequent assessments was hers and not his.

A simple misinterpretation?

she wonders, unable to distinguish fact from fiction, the truth from the lies. The seeds of doubt have been planted in the fertile soil of her mind, but Mary knows to keep the tangled vines of theories beneath the surface. Under threat of men in white coats, she adheres to Vinny's suggestion of a hiatus from Gayle, and many other warmly offered decrees given in his grand benevolence. She tells herself it is—

For my own good.

No one is the wiser to Mary's inner turmoil, as she has concealed it beneath a placid demeanor. Not even Harry seems to notice the stormy blue of her eyes—eyes that comb incessantly through the pages of thick, recondite library books, looking for an answer or at least an equation.

"What are you reading now?" Harry asks, looking at her hands wrapped around the latest two-pound checkout.

"*Modern Algebra and Trigonometry, Structure and Method,*" Mary says, as if it were a riveting novel. She tucks the book away.

"Last week it was science, this week math. Have you always been so hungry to learn?" he asks curiously, watching her tear four strips of clear tape and hang them on her left inner forearm.

"Ravenous," she says, picking up an end-of-summer specials poster and moving it around on the window until she is satisfied with the placement. She smooths the small advertisement and restrains the middle with a splayed hand, using the tape strips to invisibly keep each side flush against the brittle pane.

Harry smiles at her attention to detail. "Have you considered going back to school?"

"And leave all of this?" Mary asks flatly, just before stepping outside to admire her work. She rushes back in, feet moving so fast her upper body struggles to catch up. "Man your battle stations, here comes the Queen of Cocodrie," she says, running to hide all the loose counter displays.

Harry pulls a board down over the open bins of lozenges and cough drops, created for just such occasions where there are too many small fingers to keep out of products mistaken for candy (such as the Ex-Lax chocolate bars). Even before Harry can see their white rubber shrimp boots in the window, he can hear the vociferous Fontenot clan coming up the walkway, led by the loudest of them all: matriarch Enola Fontenot.

"Behave you-self, heathens, or I'm gonna pass you each a slap!" she warns her five preschool-aged grandsons when she opens the glass door. She is carrying the youngest, and sets the small, runny-nosed boy down. "Dat two-year-old like ta t'row my back out," she groans.

"Good morning, Mrs. Fontenot," Mary says, her eyes on the boys loose in the store at play. She keeps track of all the merchandise the rowdy boys displace like four petite tornadoes.

"Ooh-*wee*, Sha! You as pretty as a picture, like always," she says to Mary, and flashes a wide, toothless grin.

"What can I get for you today?" Harry says, hoping to expedite the errand.

"I'm in town to make me a grocery bill, and I t'ought I should come down here an' see if I could get me a subscription of the pain relief for my authoritis . . . mais, my knee, she is swolle."

"Let me check if we still have a refill for that one," he says, rushing to his dispensary.

Enola turns to see one of her boys climbing a shelf. "Oh yi yi!" she hollers. "Get down from dere, you *coo yon*, you gonna break you fool neck! You all best behave or I'm gonna tell pretty Mrs. Mary here how many of you still sleep wit da rubber sheets."

The boys all scramble around her and settle down like good little cross-legged Indians. They wait for Mr. Dupre to hand their grandmother a bottle of hydroxychloroquine pills, leaving the aisles tousled, antagonizing Mary's essential need for order at the end of an elongated shift.

As soon as the Fontenot clan exits, she moves around the store picking up the randomly disturbed boxes of Ipana toothpaste and jars of Dippity-do. "Vinny wants to know when the new guy starts. He's been giving me grief about theses extra hours," she says, finding a tube of Unguentine with teeth marks in it and handing it to Harry.

Harry sighs and tosses the tube in the garbage. "Tell him one more week. Hey, did I ever tell you he called to apologize right after the wedding?"

Mary stiffens and blinks in disbelief. "Did he really?"

"Yeah, and he asked me for advice on what he could do to get closer to you."

"And what did you say?"

"I bragged about my first date with Alene and how we went fishing."

Mary briefly squeezes her eyes shut. She blows out a breath that rattles her lips and picks up the borrowed book. "Well, what an entropic force you turned out to be."

Unenlightened to the scientific reference, he smiles with pride and shrugs. "I do what I can."

Friday
September 18, 1964

Each flip of the synchronous numbers on the bedroom alarm clock demands Mary's attention, reminding her that time is not as forgiving as her boss was when she called in sick, or as she has been of her husband's absences.

Late is not an option. The doctor's office is nearly an hour's walk away.

Can't wait around much longer for a ride that may not come.

Mary picks up the phone and dials, still hoping to hear the car pull up.

"Good morning. Is there any way I could get a taxi? Yes, please, the corner of Liberty and Point, as soon as possible."

Mary packs her purse with items she may need to nurse and entertain her sickly bundle of joy (and mucus) while waiting for the hired ride.

Four-year-old Lisa sits quietly next to her mother atop the cracked vinyl backseat of the taxi, stroking the red yarn hair of a small rag doll, her windbreaker zipped, hair neatly in place, and both feet buckled snug in her Buster Browns. Holding sniffling baby Tina,

Mary watches intently through the windshield to make sure the driver doesn't stray off route. When a deep pothole sneaks up on the car, her head bumps the door's window glass and she suddenly sees the unexpected up ahead. She leans over and squints hard in disbelief—surely her eyes are lying, postulating!

"Pull over, please," Mary says, rereading the LSU Centennial license plate. Her eyes have not deceived her: it is their family car, which is parked haphazardly in front of a small, squatty cinder-block building with no visible windows. Fuming and conflicted, she studies the weathered face of the taxi driver, who kindly blinks back at Mary while awaiting further instruction.

She checks her watch ticking off the seconds—another reminder of time's unrelenting march—and clutches the seat; her face contorts, asking the universe for help.

"It's just a bad stretch-a road, ma'am . . . we can go another way if you want," says the driver, reminding Mary of a conversation she once had with her sorely missed father.

"Can you wait a moment here with the girls?" she asks him, depositing Tina in the arms of a big sister who welcomes the chance to snuggle the baby, happily putting her doll aside.

Mary opens the cab door as if she is about to step into a corridor leading into an alternate universe. She has never set foot near this building before, but is pretty damn sure it's a bar, noting the stench of liquor and vomit surrounding the place. She stares down at a broken beer bottle and breathes hard, as if preparing herself for some great feat of courage or physical endurance. Quickly, before she can change her mind, Mary raises herself out of the car and into the unknown.

Like an angry bull, Mary charges inside, where she witnesses Vinny perched on a stool and leaning way too close to, of all people, Veronica Babin, covering his face as if he is telling her a closely kept secret.

Mary grabs the car keys and Vinny's fat wallet from the counter, knocking over a dish of germ-ridden peanuts in the process. She pulls a stack of cash out of the wallet and hurls the leather carcass back at him.

With his booze-addled brain, Vinny fails to respond fast enough to stop her or the wallet from slipping away. He scrambles, slurring, "It's not what you think!"

Uninterested in hearing Vinny's worthless lies and excuses, Mary leaves as quickly as she came in, marching back to the cab with her hollow victory in hand. She thanks the driver monetarily for the abandoned trip, and quickly loads her precious cargo into the 1960 Dodge Polara for the remainder of the journey, too shocked and numb to feel or to answer any of Lisa's questions.

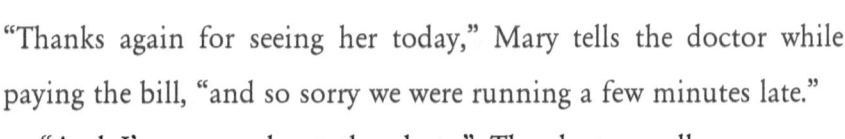

"Thanks again for seeing her today," Mary tells the doctor while paying the bill, "and so sorry we were running a few minutes late."

"And I'm sorry about the shots." The doctor pulls an orange lollypop from his pocket and hands it to Lisa, who is now sporting a Band-Aid over a brand-new boo-boo on her bicep. "But we can't be too careful."

As the nurse gives Mary a receipt, she says, "We already called in the prescriptions to the pharmacy. You can pick them up on your way home."

Outside, Mary is opening the door to the car when Tina sneezes a greenish-yellow glob onto her blouse.

"Yucky," Lisa says, and gags, throwing up orange candy on the pavement.

On a desperate expedition for napkins, tissues, or anything resembling the like, Mary reaches into the car and opens the glove box. A gun pops out into her hand. She shoves it back in and slams the door shut as if it were the lid on a demonic jack-in-the-box—but it is too late. Puke, tears, snot, hurt, fears, and rage, all the evils of the day let loose.

Harry is stunned to see three of his favorite females enter the pharmacy distressed, crying, and painted in germy goo. "We need the restroom," Mary says through tears of frustration. "Don't ask," she adds, trembling, only deepening the worry lines on Harry's face.

For nearly ten anxious minutes, he hovers outside the restroom door, before deciding to knock. "Everything all right in there?" he asks. "I have your scrips out here."

Cleaned up and more composed, the trio exits the small room. Mary doesn't make eye contact when she accepts the small bag of remedies. "Thank you" is all she says.

Harry recognizes her agitation as she shrinks away; she is swaying, hiding behind her sickly baby. "When you are ready to talk, I'm here," he offers, picking up Lisa, who looks ready for a nap. Lisa lays her heavy head down on his shoulder.

Mary freezes, forces her sad eyes to meet his earnest gaze, and nods in silent agreement, holding her lips in a stubborn, tight line. She lowers her head and turns to leave. Harry follows her outside, putting his cheek to Lisa's forehead to check for fever.

"What can I do?" he asks, placing Lisa in the front seat of the car.

Dragging her feet through emotional quicksand, Mary looks at him over the hood of the car and shakes her head, unable to utter a word about her predicament just yet.

In the driver's seat, traveling the few blocks it takes to reach her driveway, Mary rests at a stop sign; her hands writhe on the wheel as she considers a radical turn that will take her far away in another direction.

"Are we home yet?" Lisa asks with closed eyes.

Mary sighs, pressing down slowly on the gas pedal. "Almost, sweetheart, almost."

When they enter the kitchen, Vinny is waiting to pounce with commodious explanations for his latest escapade. Mary raises a hand and flashes her *stay-away* eyes at him. He stays zipped, cooperating long enough to see the girls are changed, medicated, and put safely in their beds.

After half-listening to a tall tale about coincidences and Veronica, Mary sits across from Vinny at the kitchen table, eyes closed, rubbing her temples. "You didn't even bother to show up last night," she says. "You knew Lisa was excited to watch *The Flintstones* with you."

He grimaces and scratches his head. "That was last night?"

Mary drops her hands to the table and opens her eyes. "You're always so busy putting your own needs first."

Vinny stares at her with sunken eyes. "My life was simple before you. I'm not used to all this hassle." He reaches for a cigarette and a lighter.

"Are you trying to say that I *forced* this life upon you? Because, mister, I remember it being the other way around."

"Can't you see I'm upset?" he says, and hurls smoke at her.

"And what? You think *I'm* happy?" Mary coughs, waving away the toxic cloud. "It's now to the point where I'm excited to know when you're going away. At least then we have some peace around here."

He jams his partially smoked cigarette into a small porcelain dish. "I promised I would keep my cool, but you're making it real hard to keep that promise. I think it's best if I go."

"Go where?" she asks, folding her arms, imagining the Babin Inn on Highway 90.

Vinny stands up, pushes his chair in, and leans forward. "Anywhere that ain't here."

"It makes me terribly sad that our love is so fragile that it can't even endure a real conversation."

Vinny drops his head and squeezes the chair. "This isn't easy for me."

"You think it's easy to process the fact that I have a dishonorable husband? I don't even know what I'm supposed to do with that information."

"For the last time, I wasn't cheating!" he says, shoving the chair in disgust. "How about this? You *had* a husband. Now you'll be single in this mess without anyone to blame but yourself. You should have just left it alone, Maggie. Always too nosy for your own good." He scrapes his keys off the table, turns to the door, and pauses with his hand on the knob, taking a long, ragged breath. "If you must know, I've lost something very important to me," he says, then lets out an anguished sigh, slapping his keys against his leg. He looks up as if to speak to the heavens, stormy turmoil roiling in his eyes. "My life turned out so differently than I had originally planned."

"Join the fucking club!" Mary says sharply. She flinches when he slams the door behind him.

The car engine roars, tires squeal. Vinny speeds off, angry, rejected, and ashamed. Mary rushes to the window in time to see his tail lights refuse to brake at the stop sign.

I should have left him alone when my dad wanted me to.

I should have left when he hit me the first time.

I should leave right now . . .

She looks down at feet that dare not move.

Saturday
September 19, 1964

The doorbell jerks Mary out of the deep sleep she entered just two short hours ago. She looks at a clock that says seven o'clock on a morning slated for her to rest.

"Ugh!" she says when the bell chimes again. Reluctantly she peels her exhausted, fully clothed body from the mattress to make the racket stop. "I'm coming, I'm coming," she mumbles, dragging her slippered feet across the floor, fully prepared to rip some Electrolux salesman to shreds if Tina wakes before her next feeding.

Mary opens the door to find two uniformed state troopers standing outside. They bear an odd resemblance to the vaudevillian duo Abbott and Costello, and wear expressions which suggest they pulled the short straw at roll call.

"May I help you?" she asks subserviently, as if she were the one on the clock.

"Are you Mrs.—" The thin officer, Abbott, pauses to check his well-fed partner's handwriting. "Carlino?"

"Yes, I'm Mrs. Carlino. Is there a problem, officers?"

"Just for verification," Abbott asks nervously, adjusting his hat, as if this protocol is new to him. "Your husband's first name is Vincent?"

"Yes. May I ask what this is about?"

Abbott looks to Costello, who takes over. "Is he home? May we speak with him?"

"No, he isn't home right now." Mary bites her lip.

"Do you know if he has a 1960 beige Polara registered to his name?"

"It's fawn. I picked the color," Mary says, as if in apology, "but yes, that sounds like our car."

"When was the last time you saw the vehicle?"

"When my husband left in it last night. Around ten."

"Do you know where he was headed?"

"No."

"Do you know if he was upset?"

"Why? What's going on? Is he in some sort of trouble?"

"Do you think he had any reason to . . ." Costello pauses to clear his throat. ". . . to harm himself?"

At his words, an image flashes in Mary's mind.

The gun!

"Oh my God! Did he shoot himself?" Mary's hand covers her mouth, wide open in horror as her body clumsily tries to find the floor.

The officers—who seem to have abandoned their apprehension now that they have been given something they are used to, a lady in distress—help her inside and carefully place her in a chair.

"Is he dead?" she asks meekly through a tightening throat.

"We're here to help the local police investigate. Frankly, Mrs. Carlino, we aren't sure what's happened to your husband."

Mary scrunches up her face tight then releases it, trying to stay calm. "Can you fill me in on what you do know . . . before I lose every one of my marbles?"

Sweat springs up on Costello's face. "We were called out to a train accident near Schriever involving your husband's vehicle. The sheriff's department has been combing the area trying to locate him since the sun came up."

She looks up to both of them with huge saucer eyes. "For a body?"

"For his whereabouts," Abbot says to mitigate her assumption.

"I want to see the car."

"I don't think that's a good idea."

"I want to see the goddamned car!" Mary screams, followed by an irascible shriek from Tina.

Leaving Gayle in charge of the girls, Mary steps out of the cherry-top cruiser and walks zombie-like until she is shoulder-to-shoulder with newly appointed Deputy Sheriff Danny Naquin. Near the glass-littered railway intersection, they stand morose in the bright, unforgiving light of day, watching a large-platform tow truck load what is left of the twisted, fawn-colored metal that will remain in many fond Carlino family memories—but not this one . . . no, not this one.

It looks so much like my heart,

Mary thinks,

a pile of seemingly irreparable damage.

Danny glances at Mary. He sees her worried eyes, bulging and unable to blink. He sighs and rubs his face. "Sorry about sending the troopers. I just couldn't face you—not without knowing where he is."

The air feels suddenly thin. Mary bends over with a deep ache in her chest, her hands gripping her knees, and takes a few raspy breaths. A gold chain bearing a small dented kitten pendant dangles from her neck.

"Not finding him is a good thing," Danny says, rubbing her back. "It means he must have wandered off."

"Surely he must be injured!" she cries, sweeping her arm to Exhibit A: the demolished scrapheap being hauled away to some local junkyard. "Did you find out anything? Did you search the car?"

"Yes. Follow me, I have a stack of things from the glove box for you."

"Did you find a gun?"

"No, there wasn't a gun in his possession. Couldn't be." Danny stops and turns back to her with squinted eyes. "Why? Do you know something about a gun?"

She shrinks away.

"He's a felon, Mary."

"A felon?" She sniffs in disbelief.

"Yes, and that means he can't legally own or be in possession of a firearm."

"And how do you know all of this?"

"I ran a background check on Vinny and, Mary, he's no angel. I believe he did a stint in Angola for armed robbery."

Her breath catches and she shuffles back a step in disbelief.

"I take it you didn't know," says Danny.

Mary swallows hard and shakes her head. "There's obviously very much I don't know right now, Danny. I need a minute." She holds one hand up to him, covers her mouth with the other, and walks away. She trudges clumsily on the shells and rocks alongside the tracks, smelling leftover fumes of oil and gas on the ground, avoiding shreds of whitewall tires with so many miles of tread still left on them. She hasn't the slightest idea where she is going, but she's too dazed and disturbed to stay still, as if moving farther away from the scene will prevent her mind from leaking out onto the pavement. She wanders through a quagmire of fear, eyes searching the trackside and foliage for any missed clues, when a little voice in the far-back dour reaches of her mind suggests a concept so vile, she chokes on the whisper.

If he's gone . . .

Behind Mary blares the scream of a police siren. She spins around to see Danny waving her back to the road from the window of his car.

She runs to him with leaded feet.

"We got him!" Danny yells as she comes closer, a corded two-way radio in his hand. "We got him!" he repeats to her with relief.

"Are you sure?" Mary asks, jumping into the patrol car's passenger seat, too afraid to celebrate just yet.

Danny lowers the volume on the radio chatter. "Found him a couple miles from here. He admits to being drunk when he left the stalled car on the tracks. Says he was walking to find a pay phone when he fell into a ditch and went to sleep."

"So he's okay," she says, a rattled hand patting the hollow base of her throat.

On the side of the shoulderless parish road, Mary arrives to see Vinny's eyes beg her for amnesty, full of a liquefied, vulnerable love. After imagining him dead, guilty of having a pang of disloyalty, she chooses to ignore all the bad blood between them for now, to enjoy the still-alive feel of his warm, muscular body.

"I'm so sorry. I love you so much, Mary," he says, shuddering beneath her forgiving touch.

"I know. I love you, too," she says.

As they embrace, she sees a swollen pink slash on his neck behind his collar.

Instead of dying, he almost walked away without a scratch.

Wednesday
September 23, 1964

Vinny is bored, waiting for a secret pow-wow rendezvous with David Ferrie and Charles Rodgers. He wanders too far and feels the sole of his buffed leather shoe squish down into the deceptive surface of a spongy patch of marshland. He frowns, removing his footwear from the suction of the thick, sticky mud.

"I told you not to worry about that goddamned Warren report," Carlos says to him. The squatty man smiles and breaks a skinny branch in half as if it were a Kennedy's neck. walking behind Vinny in a discreet area of his vast, undeveloped investment property. "Trust me, it wouldn't come out any better for us if we had written it ourselves. Besides, you got bigger fish to fry."

"And what exactly would that be?" he asks Carlos, still inspecting the caked mess on his shoe. He wonders how much longer they have to wait for Clown Face and Frenchy to show.

Carlos turns his face from the sunlight, squints a suspicious eye, and says, "Someone in enforcement has been sniffing up your skirt, pal . . . and Nofio's nephew, too. You have any idea who might've put dat together and set dat nose into action?"

With a look of concern, Vinny halts in mid-drag of his shoe across a thick cypress knee and frowns again, calculating any possible collateral damage.

"Just might be that curvy tail you went and married," Carlos says, radiating superiority. "Better find a way to shut that shit down, or I might have to amputate that pretty ball-and-chain from your ankle."

Vinny cuts Carlos with dagger eyes for such audacity.

Carlos raises his hands in immediate surrender. "Just making sure you heard me. I know you'll handle it."

Irritated, teeth clenched, Vinny begins to slowly prowl, like a tiger in a zoo ready to escape or pounce at any given opportunity. "We were supposed to meet twenty minutes ago. Where the fuck are they?"

"If I know dem two, dey stuck at the Tastee Donuts talking to that Copeland kid again."

"We wouldn't even be having this meeting," Vinny says, "if I'd been called in on this lady doctor clean-up in the first place. I could've staged it better. I would've called in Liggett and put this whole Doctor Sherman fiasco to bed."

Carlos scrubs the stubble on his cleft chin and says, "Because her name was Mary, I thought—"

"Since when does a name get in the way of a job?"

"Well, anyway, that apartment was dismantled last month by the cops and dey found a bunch a nuttin."

"With the investigation still open, 'nothing' means a loose end."

"I thought you said once that it's best to leave no real evidence behind."

"Nothing that'll come back to haunt *me*, is what I meant."

The two men brood in silence, long enough for Vinny to watch a great blue heron come into view, creating a shadow much like a prehistoric pterodactyl, large slate-azure wings spread in a slow-flying glide, land, and walk in a cool, confident strut near the water's edge. The bird stabs his beak with deadly precision into the water below an innocent insect, flips an unlucky fish into the air, and slides it easily down his throat without even bothering to chew or swallow. The smug, satisfied bird takes another arrogant step and disappears below the waterline. There is a wild, violent thrashing of feathers and teeth for a brief few minutes, and then, after the last ripple vanishes, everything is as it was: still, serene water, with no trace that the bird had ever existed.

Vinny hears the *snap, crackle,* and *pop* of a car arriving behind him. He doesn't turn until he hears the car doors shut in succession.

He knows the terrain.

He knows the game.

He knows you can choose to be the bait, the fish, the bird, or . . .

I will always be the gator.

Monday
September 28, 1964

It has been ten days since Vinny's drunken belligerence put the family car out to pasture, but tonight he is coltish in private celebration of the Warren Commission report, its release desiccating all worries of any boomerang repercussions.

The girls have already had their baths and are now wearing matching-print nightgowns Mary fashioned with her clever sewing skills. Lisa patiently retrieves the slobbery teething toys Tina knocked out of reach beyond her blanketed borders while watching the opening to *The Andy Griffith Show*.

Mary folds the clean laundry at the kitchen table with angry jerks of her hands as she watches through the large archway into the den, not *The Andy Griffith Show*, but her husband drinking his fourth beer of the night. She pairs up socks and tosses them into designated baskets as if she were trying out for the Harlem Globetrotters. Next she snaps the bed sheets, making crisp, expert folds, but taking her frustrations out on the sheets has not made her feel any better . . . so on to the towels.

The "Things Go Better with Coke" commercial plays. Whistling along with the tune, Vinny gets up from his dent in the couch to throw away this most recent empty can. As he passes the folding station, he reaches over to grab at Mary's behind. She swats his impetuous hand away.

He shakes his paw, feigning injury. "What's *your* problem?" he asks.

"Which one? Your drinking, the fact that you never help me, the fact that we haven't had a real conversation in two weeks, or that you think it's okay to maul me out of the blue?"

"Whoa! Someone has the scarlet fever tonight. Don't they make a pill for that now?" Vinny says, trying to act playful.

Mary slams a folded towel atop its brothers. "Why can't a woman have an emotion without being accused of having a hormone issue?"

"All right, all right, let's talk. I'll fix you a drink," Vinny offers. "You could use one to relax."

"I want a real conversation, not one you'll forget in the morning."

He sets the empty can on the table and steps behind her. Gently he moves her hair to the side and whispers, "How about I give *you* something to remember in the morning?" placing a wet, lustful kiss on her neck.

It is so damned hard for Mary not to melt beneath his opium touch—but it is time to abnegate and deal with the maladies between them. She pulls away and says, "We pass each other like strangers for weeks on end and you expect *that* to melt all the ice? I need more."

"I really don't know what you want from me," Vinny says, throwing his hands up.

"I'm not sure what I want, either, but I know this isn't it," she replies.

He picks up a clean towel, folds it sloppily, and places it atop her sharply squared stack. She picks it up and shakes it out to refold. He frowns and swats the empty can off the table.

"Real mature," Mary says. She picks the can up and grabs a kitchen rag to mop the last stinky sip that spilled out onto the floor.

"I just can't do anything right for you, can I?"

"You could let me go," she says without pause.

Vinny's throat bobs. "Go where? Please tell me we're not having this back-to-school bullshit again. Let it go, already! You're a mother, for Christ's sake." He turns away from Mary's wounded eyes, wraps his hands around the edge of the counter, and lowers his head.

Mary begins to shake; she's simply unable to hold her tongue any longer. "You know, there was a time I felt our love was pure and strong, like some precious gem. You have slowly chiseled and eroded away my love for you, to the point where it no longer has a shape or a purpose. What's left is deformed . . . ugly, even." She pauses to think and blink back her angry tears. "To stay here with you is to allow myself to succumb to this sick, twisted world we've tolerated for too long. It isn't good for any of us—especially the children. They deserve better. They need to grow in a stable environment. All you have to show them is turmoil and violence."

"What are you trying to say with your fancy fuckin words?" Vinny asks, snarling like a panther. "That you want to leave? That you don't love me?"

"I don't feel safe here. My children are not safe here."

Vinny jerks back, offended. "Have I ever hurt the kids?"

Mary doesn't answer.

"Well? Have I?"

"No . . ." she says, retreating back to her laundry at the kitchen table, "but—"

"That's right! I never hurt the kids," he says. He gives Mary a dismissive nod and heads for the fridge, his victory followed by the hiss of another can of Schlitz.

"You think all this anger isn't upsetting them?" Mary throws her exasperated arm out in the direction of two small, helpless bystanders. "Just look at them," she pleads.

Hearing a whimper, Vinny peers into the living room to see Tina with wide eyes, lying on her side, savagely biting a fabric book, and Lisa peeking out behind the arm of the couch, wiping her worried face in perfect imitation of her mother.

"I didn't start this," Vinny tells the girls, and shakes his head. "You know I love you and I would never hurt you, don't you, my darlings?"

Lisa begins to mirror the pain in her father's face.

"Your mother is trying to destroy this family," he says, pointing at Mary. He knocks back a swig to numb himself further, knowing this fight is now quicksand: the more he tries to wiggle out, the deeper in he'll sink.

Mary grabs the phone. Her finger furiously tugs at the dial and she waits for someone to pick up. "Can you please come and get the girls for a bit?" Mary asks, then listens to Gayle at the other end. "No, it's definitely not for a good time," she says, and hangs up.

Leaning against the counter, Vinny gives her a heavy-browed dirty look. She has completely ruined his celebration buzz.

"Please put this on, sweetheart," Mary says to Lisa, holding up a lavender crocheted sweater. "Auntie Gayle made Jell-O."

"Don't *you* like Jell-O, Mommy?"

"Yes, but me and Daddy need to talk some more," she explains.

Even though it's sixty-five degrees outside, Lisa slips her short, obedient arms into the cozy sweater her mommy made for the upcoming fall weather. Mary lovingly wraps Tina up in a matching blanket, demonstrative motherly precautions for weathering a storm she provoked, now spinning and brewing in the turbulent convection of the kitchen, much like tropical storm Hilda now crawling south of Cuba.

The darkish sky ignites the streetlamps, and her friend's porch light follows suit. Mary watches through the window as Gayle takes her sweet-assed time crossing the street. The screen door opens without a peep, having been silenced with WD-40 the day before. Gayle winks, reaching for the baby, and takes Lisa's hand without a word, recognizing the fed-up look on Mary's face.

"I saw some frogs on the way over. Wanna see?" Mary hears Gayle ask Lisa on the stoop through the thin mesh door.

Vinny glares at Mary staring back at him—an intense standoff long enough and worthy of a whistling spaghetti-western theme song. He swallows a sip of beer hard, baring his teeth, then huffs, dropping into a chair. "I've got to be away for work all next week," he says. "Why don't you stay here, and I'll find somewhere else to be while you figure out how to love me again."

"You are simply not listening to me!" she cries, framing her face with her hands. "I can't– I won't– I *don't* want to do this with you anymore."

He sees the finality of the decision firming, cementing, deep in her clear blue eyes. "But it will get better . . . it always gets better . . . *I* will be better," Vinny pleads.

"Yes, it does–for a while," Mary says, "and then it gets bad again. It's those times I can't go through anymore. I don't want the lies and the secrets, Vinny. I need to live in the truth!"

"The 'truth'?" Vinny gives a disdainful snort, staring at the shiny can he spins with his fingertips. "People die with the truth on their lips."

Mary rolls her eyes and shakes her head at his ugly smirk. "I'm so sick of you men with your arrogant idiotic riddles . . . do you even know what the truth is anymore?"

His cold eyes flash up at her. "I could tell you truths so full of fire and brimstone they'd melt the flesh off your bones!" he growls, erupting to a boil. His powerful fingers wrap around the thin, crackly skin of the aluminum can and squeeze hard until ale and blood drip from his fingers.

"I'm tired of being afraid." She takes a cautious step backward. "Of always living under your cruel thumb."

"If you leave, I will hunt you down and I will kill you," he seethes, rising up from his seat and slamming his damaged can down on the table. He rocks unsteadily in his drunken state.

Instead of scaring Mary, this time he seems a weak and cartoonish version of himself. She covers her mouth with her hand, but it does not hide the fact that she finds him amusing.

"You think I'm kidding?" Spittle flies from his bared teeth and his angry gestures cause him to stumble backward. He falls back down into his chair.

Mary can't hold back this time—she crumples to the floor, eyes squinted shut, consumed by her laughter. His face turns red at her impudence and he lunges at her, cocking his arm back, ready to release a hard backhand to her face.

Neither of them is prepared for what happens next: that slap comes careening down, surely powerful enough to break bone, and strikes the innocent face of little Lisa, who has somehow escaped her Auntie Gayle and returned, still running and breathless, wielding small bold fists to defend her mother.

Vinny's assault launches Lisa across the kitchen floor.

"MY BAAABY!" Mary screams. Horror clogs her throat as she rushes to her child, but she swallows it down. *"Please be okay please please oh please please please,"* she cries, her fingers whispering against the curves of Lisa's face to check for damaged bones. Luckily there are none, but there will likely be a nasty bruise.

Vinny sits on the floor with his head in his hands, writhing from sobs ripping through his body. But Mary feels no pity for him this time. She suddenly feels the rage of every bad turn of this marriage filling her veins, making her large and fearless. She lays her baby's precious head back down on the ground, trying to send comfort telepathically to those wounded eyes looking up at her—Lisa does not cry through any of this, just stares with a sense of acceptance no child of four should grasp—and she stands, looming larger than ever before. Her eyes now firmly on her still-sobbing husband, she grabs the vase that came to her the same day that Vinny did and holds it high above her head with both hands, preparing to kill him with it. No sunlight spilling rainbows from it tonight, just an ethereal hint of amorous light from inside its many-colored glass—a light she means to extinguish.

"Mommy?"

She looks down at Lisa, still lying beneath her, and blinks through her blind rage. In that moment, with her child's eyes gazing up at her, Mary realizes that he has driven her to act like him and recalls Beulah's haunting words from so long ago: *Your steps will lead smaller feet, so walk a careful line.*

She brings the vase down hard—not on her husband's skull, but on the linoleum floor of the kitchen—and it shatters at his feet, along with all the fragile hopes and dreams she once held dear.

This ends here!

"Get out, you son of a bitch!" she screams at the top of her lungs. "You get out, and I don't ever want to see you again!" Her voice blends with the sound of a ringing phone, but she doesn't hear it call to her.

Vinny scrambles to his feet and out the kitchen door without looking up to meet her gaze or knowing the full outcome of what he has done.

By the second phone ring, alarm bells go off somewhere inside her now, chilling her spine, and she remembers,

He has a gun!

Her mind races.

*He could be retrieving that unregistered gun
from his brand-new car's glove box right now!*

Without another second's thought, she scoops Lisa off the floor and makes a mad dash through the living room and out the back door, as far away from Vinny as possible. She doesn't look back, hearing the screen slam behind her on the third ring, not knowing if he may be at her heels. Her legs are in full sprint now, leaving the rest of her to catch up as her bare feet thud, first on the hard-packed grass lawn, then on the still-warm pavement. The grip she has on Lisa is so tight, she will surely have to apologize if she ever finds her breath again. Lisa instinctively knows this is no time to complain, staying as loose as her Raggedy Ann doll so as not to hinder her mother's pace.

Gayle is half out of her open kitchen door, phone in hand, puzzled, when she sees Mary running as if she is being chased, and instantly knows this is worse than bad. With terror-filled eyes, Mary mows her down. Gayle shuts and locks the door behind her, blockading it with her petite frame. Mary staggers, gasping for breath, in a kitchen that seems unnaturally still compared to the nightmare from which she has just fled. Her heart pounds a panicked rhythm in the dimly lit space. A television commercial jabbers soft in the background. Tina, recumbent and unaware of the commotion, is sprawled atop her lavender blanket on the floor, losing interest with her feet, becoming fussy for attention.

Lisa stays still while Mary performs a more thorough inspection of her small body and checks her pupils for signs of head trauma. A single soundless tear leaks from Lisa's eye, not from what has happened, but out of fear for the unknown repercussions they will surely face.

"My god, what's happened? I couldn't find her!" Gayle falls to her knees to beg her friend's forgiveness. Mary cries vocally along with baby Tina, and kisses her eldest child's undamaged cheek.

"It's my fault . . . it's all my fault," Mary repeats, rocking Lisa the way she did when her oldest child was younger.

"Don't cry, Mommy," Lisa says. Softly, she puts a small, brave hand on her mother's worried face. "I'm all right."

"This is not all right." Mary shakes her head. "None of this is all right," she whimpers, and turns her face to Gayle. "My babies aren't safe!"

The phone draws everyone's attention, screaming a loud, annoying cadence, a painful sound to announce its being left in limbo, abandoned off the hook.

Gayle rises to her feet. "You're staying right here until we can figure this out," she says, placing the hanging receiver back in its cradle. It immediately jumps to life, ringing in her hand. She looks squarely at Mary, eyes wide, raising the phone to her ear. Gayle listens to Vinny's determined voice rattle off a desperate, heartfelt apology to keep her from hanging up. "Fine . . . shoot," she says.

Mary flinches at her poor choice of words.

Gayle listens a while, hearing out his Machiavellian spiel before raising her voice. "You damn sure better keep to that promise, mister! We have all endured way too much of this shit from you."

Gayle sets the phone back down in the cradle and watches it, her leery eyes rapidly blinking. This time it stays still and silent.

"Well?" Mary asks. Lisa stops playing peekaboo with Tina to hear Gayle's answer.

"He said that he will give you what you asked for and not to worry, because he is going to stay away and give you your space," Gayle says. Her eyebrows draw together. "What was it you asked for?"

Mary lets out a huge breath of relief, letting her head fall back. "I asked for him to let me go."

"Like, out of town?"

"I don't know yet. I have no clue what to do now and I'm—" Mary looks at the girls and spells, "I'm s-c-a-r-e-d."

"I know." Gayle kneels down beside Mary and takes her hand. "I'm just selfish and don't want to lose you. I've missed you. Besides, who is going to help me with *my* baby?"

Mary gasps and Gayle squeezes her hand. As the news sinks in, Mary's tentative smile builds and she squeals, "Oh, Gayle, it finally happened! I'm so happy!" She embraces her best friend and asks, "How far?"

"I'm not for-sure sure yet. I go to the doctor tomorrow morning. I didn't want to tell you until I had his confirmation. I haven't even mentioned it to Chick yet."

"No!" Lisa cries, with her hair tangled around Tina's grabby fingers.

Mary taps on Tina's pudgy hand to let go, but instead of cooperating, she laughs with sparkling eyes, squeals with delight, and tugs again.

"*Ouch*, lemme go!" Lisa cries.

"See what you have to look forward to?" Mary says, unwinding the delicate, rooted strands from the baby's tenacious grip and thinking,

Her father's child.

Tuesday
September 29, 1964

arly morning, the kids still asleep, Mary stands in the yellow-orange light of dawn, staring harshly through Gayle's kitchen window across to her own neatly mowed lawn. As her mind relives every disappointment, every mistake she has ever experienced, her glazed-over expression hardens and her eyes focus, spotting a dandelion rebelliously standing in a sunlit beam, virtually untouched, somehow having survived the sharp deadly blades of the mower. She taps her nails on the green ceramic sink, barely registering the sound of the radio as it warns of a storm swirling into the Gulf of Mexico and gaining strength with each passing hour.

My ass might be grass, but I'm going to
take it to a much safer lawn.

Mary pushes away from the counter and leaves Gayle's house, her bare feet landing on cold dewy grass and slapping on the concrete street as she heads back into the place she no longer wants to call her home. Tearing through the house, she grabs only what she deems a necessity and quickly stuffs it into a garbage bag. She saves the closet for last, flinging open the door, and her indelicate search sends a long-forgotten box spilling onto the floor, revealing a baby gift for Tina, given months ago.

The sorrow of lost time comes as she picks up the small luxurious blanket and presses it to her face. Something tucked safely inside falls out, landing at her feet—a white envelope with her name written in Bobby's bold handwriting.

At first, Mary looks at it as if it's a bomb that might go off. Then, without another thought, she picks it up and rips it open to read his words inside the card.

My dearest friend Mary,

Here is a small token from me to the new love in your life: a gift of warmth and safety. I am graduating soon from LSU. I've been accepted to all three of the law schools I've applied to, so I don't know yet where I'll be in the fall, but if you and your children ever find yourselves in need of warmth and safety, please contact my friend and mentor Mr. Aycock. I have included all of his contact information below. He will know who you are if you call. He has a file in his desk with all of your transcripts, courtesy of Mrs. Tisdale. He is a kind, learned man of the law and will know how to help you and keep you safe.

Sincerely concerned,
Bobby

Mary presses the card to her chest, closes her eyes, and says, "I need to make some phone calls."

Wednesday
September 30, 1964

After two busy days of preparation, several enlightening conversations, a trip to the bank to close a Red Sock account, and a trip to the bus station to buy three one-way tickets, Mary feels an unexpected wave of optimism break over her, washing away the dread. She is ready for the future, and happy to settle down and spend her last night in Houma celebrating Gayle's confirmed baby on the way.

Camping out on the living room floor, everyone else asleep, Mary and Gayle lie relaxed next to one another, looking up at the ceiling, holding hands in the gentle glow of a Mickey Mouse face plugged into a nearby socket.

"I can't believe how fast today went," Mary sighs.

Gayle watches Mary's wandering gaze in the soft light. "Thanks for all the baby stuff you gave me."

"It was a relief to not have to pack it."

"What's left to do tomorrow?"

"Not much. I'm taking a few boxes to Harry on my way out. He'll send them later when we're settled."

"Will you tell me where you are when you get there?" Gayle asks.

"I'll send word to the pharmacy when we're safe. I don't want you in the middle of my mess anymore. You have to be more careful now."

"I'm going to miss you so much," Gayle says, and chews on her lip.

"We will see each other again, I promise."

Gayle's eyes prickle with tears. "And you won't forget about me?"

Mary chuckles softly and nudges Gayle with her shoulder. "How could I ever forget about you?"

Gayle snuggles in closer. "We had some good times, didn't we?"

"Yes," Mary admits, reassuringly stroking Gayle's hand with her thumb. "We had some pretty good times." Mary smiles, remembering long summer days, the countless afternoons filled with laughs, dancing, and so many thrilling truths and dares. Most of all she recalls the delightful myriad of sleepless nights spent talking and dreaming of the exciting things to come.

"What time is it?" Gayle whispers.

"It's Big Bopper time," Mary whispers back, and a tear slips from her eye.

"Chantilly lace and a pretty face and a ponytail hanging down . . ."

They whisper-sing the words to their favorite songs with girlish giggles and grown-up tears late into the night.

Thursday
October 1, 1964

"**We brought the** boxes," Chick calls out to Mary from the kitchen while she performs one last walkthrough. "Why are we back here again?" His voice bounces off the walls without the kids and their belongings strewn across the rooms of the soon-to-be abandoned home. Chick shuffles from one foot to another, becoming antsy surrounded by history and her awkward silence. "If you're gonna leave, now is as good a time as any," he announces. Desperately not wanting to be there, feeling like an accomplice to a crime, he blurts out, "That storm is on the move. Hurricane Hilda will be here tomorrow night and she just might pack a punch." He jingles his keys, lowering his volume when Mary suddenly walks into the kitchen. "By the sound of the weather reports, anyhow," he trails off with a shrug, and moves out of her way.

Mary is too focused, too far away in her myopic thoughts to hear him. After foraging through the kitchen drawers for anything important, she takes one last nostalgic look around the room before her eyes land on her pet dictionary sitting on the table.

She drapes a necklace across it and perches the cat pendant delicately atop an envelope addressed to Vinny, inside of which she has written:

I'm leaving you with the first book my father ever gave me because its contents hold no magic for me now. I used to love all the words in this dictionary. I used to trust in them. Now I find them to be useless sounds to fill the air, no purpose whatsoever— so save all of your dishonest words for someone who can still believe. Please release me and my girls from whatever hell that surrounds you and let us find the calm that we deserve. If you don't understand, look up the meaning of "equanimity" and the definitions for all its synonyms. That is what I am searching for. Look at the inside cover. We both need to remember that my name is Mary. I used to know who that was before becoming your possession. I will search my shell until I find her again. As for the necklace, I took off my golden collar to show you that Maggie the Cat simply does not exist in me—not for you, nor anyone else. I give it back because all the shiny things in the world will not tempt me to stay.

Feeling exorcised, she brushes her hands free of the demon dust. "All done here," Mary professes with a sigh of relief, and turns to face Chick.

Finally having her full attention, Chick deflates under her gaze. "I want you to know that I'm going to miss you . . . and I'm so sorry about everything. I should have—" he chokes, and reprimands himself by hitting the side of his leg with his fist.

"I understand friendship, Chick," she says, putting a hand to his shoulder. "Don't worry. I won't ask you to choose."

"But you can't possibly understand my friendship with Vinny," he says, lowering his eyes to the floor. "I don't always understand it myself."

"I get it," she says. "All relationships start with a set of circumstances that cross our paths, and sometimes it can bond us together for a minute, a month, a year, or forever."

"He saved my life, Mary," he cries, rubbing the side of his head. "He was the only reason I survived prison."

Mary stands wide-eyed and stiff, wondering how she had not put that together before.

"Do me a favor," he sniffs. "Don't tell me where you're going. That way he can't beat it out of me."

Mary wraps Chick up in her arms, sharing his pain, knowing very well the thin, blurry lines between love and fear when it comes to Vinny.

The Impala's horn blasts at them impatiently from the driveway. "It's time to go," she says, pulling away and blotting her eyes with her fingers.

Chick, Gayle, Mary, and the girls ride in the car to the bus station with what Mary has salvaged of their belongings. They have a quick farewell-round of ice cream before the Greyhound Scenicruiser begins to load at twenty minutes till noon. Chick ignores the judgmental grunt from the bus driver when he hands him a heavy suitcase and an overstuffed garbage bag of clothes to put in the luggage compartment. Mary hugs Gayle tight, deeply inhaling her Prell-scented hair, not wanting to let her go.

"Come on, Mommy," Lisa says, struggling to climb the steps to board the bus after demanding to carry the diaper bag that weighs almost as much as she does.

Holding sleepy Tina on her shoulder, Mary's heart twists in her chest, her hand heavy with sadness as she waves goodbye to her friends from the high bus window, watching Chick and Gayle through a veil of warm, salty tears.

When the bus starts to move, Mary presses her shaking hand to the window. Gayle panics, following behind, waving, blowing kisses until the engine growls and labors the wide carriage onto the road. Gayle doubles over, crying and screaming, *"I love you, I love you!"*

Powerless, Mary gasps. She covers her mouth, watching Chick rush over to console his pregnant wife and carry her back to the car.

"I love you, too," Mary cries softly behind her hand, as Gayle disappears from view.

Overwhelmed and weary, she melts down into her seat next to Lisa. Several minutes of listening to Tina's slow rhythmic breathing lulls Mary, making her eyelids heavy.

"EEEEKKK!" Lisa screeches, climbing up and standing on the bus seat.

Mary rouses in alarm. "What's wrong, honey?"

"A spider . . . he's gonna get me . . . kill it!" Lisa points to the floor with her eyes tightly shut.

Mary stands up, finds him, and without hesitation brings her shoe firmly down on the eight-legged intruder. "You don't need to be afraid anymore," she says, heavy with determination. She sits back down, pulling her children in close. "It's over. Mommy's here now. I will protect you." She gently strokes the hair of both her girls, gaining strength with each passing mile.

Together they leave a violent storm two days behind them in the rearview mirror.

The torrential winds and rain follow Mary's path, the storm's fingers reaching out over to the eastern coast, but she only looks forward with hopeful eyes as a nervous energy builds, filling her head with fantasies of what may lie on the road ahead.

My story's just beginning,

she reminds herself, as the bus picks up speed, hitting the open interstate to her new life.

Monday

May 3, 1965—Chapel Hill, North Carolina

Humming and hovering over a stack of envelopes on a cheerful kitchen counter, Mary practically jumps out of her skin, her hand flying to her chest, when the phone rings, interrupting her bill-sorting ritual.

Only three people have this unlisted number: Gayle, Harry, and her new protector, Mr. Aycock. Her brow creasing, she puts down the mail she was prying open and grabs the phone. She holds her breath and braces for whatever news awaits her on the other end of the line.

"Hello?" she asks warily.

"Hey, it's me," Gayle's voice announces from far away. "Am I gonna make you late for class?"

Mary's shoulders relax. "No, summer semester starts next week. I dropped the girls off at daycare. I thought I would get some cleaning and grocery-grabbing done before I pick them up." Mary tilts her head to steady the receiver while she gathers her hair up with an elastic band and a quick twirl of the wrist. "How's our baby boy?" she asks, smiling.

"Our precious Junior! He's good. I just fed him," Gayle says with pride, and yawns. "I lost track of my days and realized that Tina's birthday was yesterday, so I thought I would call and check up."

Mary laughs. "Wow, you really *are* sleep-deprived. You didn't forget! Mr. Aycock said there's a birthday gift with the monthly money you sent to his office."

"Pfft, *what* money?" Gayle asks.

"Don't be silly. I've been keeping track, and I'll pay you back. I only need help until my next scholarship comes through."

"Mary, I'm not trying to be coy. We didn't send any money."

Mary pauses. "Someone is sending me cash . . . I just assumed it was you."

The doorbell rings and she freezes.

"Someone's at the door!" Mary whisper-screams, lowering herself into a squat.

In the eight months she has been here, no one has come to the door of her small rented house. No one knows where she lives—not even Gayle. Mary has all of her mail go through Mr. Aycock's office, not putting her current physical address on anything. Aware of the dangers, he knows to go to the police with Mary's recorded statements and gathered evidence should Vinny ever catch up to her.

"Don't answer it," Gayle suggests. "Maybe they'll go away. It's probably one of those persistent Jehovah's Witnesses."

"Okay," Mary says cautiously, making herself comfortable on the floor. "Talk to me. I'm freaked out."

"Are you excited about Eshelman in the fall?"

"I have to finish proving myself by passing all these undergrad board tests first."

"Look at all you've accomplished so far. You'll do fine and become the best pharmacist there ever was."

"If you say so. I think I'm more nervous about Lisa starting kindergarten in the fall than I am about myself."

"Oh yeah—that first week is going to be a tough one, no doubt."

The doorbell rings again.

"Oh god, they're back," Mary squeaks, curling up into a ball.

"Yikes," Gayle frets, wanting to come through the phone. "Call the police!" she demands.

"I would have to hang up to call the cops," Mary says, her pulse racing. "Stay on the line while I check who it is. If something happens, call Mr. Aycock. I don't trust the police to protect me." She stretches out the cord, places the receiver down on the floor, and inches closer to the danger.

There is a loud rapping on the entry door.

She can hear Gayle's faint voice from the phone, yelling various threats to whoever it might be: "Leave her alone, you son of a bitch!"

Mary listens, wiping her sweaty hands on her shorts, working up the fortitude to peek through the door's little spy window. Squarely in front of the door stands a flower arrangement with legs.

Male legs.

He lowers the purple flowers as if he is considering whether or not to leave, revealing his face.

"Bobby!" Mary yells, instantly flooded with relief as she scrambles to unlock the deadbolt. "I can't believe it's you!"

He brightens when she appears in the wide-open doorway, happy to see him. For a moment or two, they just stand smiling at one another, as if their eyes have to readjust to details, like after staring into a bright light.

"I hope I'm not disturbing you. I tried to call ahead from the corner, but your line was busy," Bobby says.

"How did you get my number?"

"Gayle."

"So much for keeping secrets," she says loudly to the still-occupied receiver.

Mary sees Bobby's cane leaning against the house. "This is such a surprise, and with flowers, no less," she says, relieving him of the arrangement with a casual laugh.

"I—" he starts with a shaky voice, clears his throat, and picks up his cane. "I wish I could say they are from me, but they were already here when I walked up," he admits.

Mary frowns. She looks around suspiciously, pulls him inside, and locks the door.

Meanwhile, sitting in silent brooding observation in a car parked on a rise across from Mary's house, is a man with a healing face, a face that has spent the last few months wired shut, in pain, and deep in thought. His eyes are trained on the front door of the woman he has been tracking for two hundred and fifteen days, waiting for the asshole at her door to move ever so slightly so he can catch another glimpse of her beauty. One more peek, no matter how brief, will be enough to sustain him for now . . . the sparkle in her violet-blue eyes . . . those plump, rosy lips . . . He lowers the brim on his hat, starts the car, and rolls past the house. His ears ache with the sound of her laughter, a welcomed torture.

He will return.

He will return to her again and again.

Because the Gator leaves nothing behind.

The story unfolds, questions are answered,

and fate will not be denied in . . .

THE DISTURBING
HISTORY SAGA

MORE SECRETS REVEALED . . . 2018

. . . coming soon, sign up for pre-order information and extras at

www.boleybooks.com.

AFTERWORD

History has always fascinated me—my own included. In this book, I was able to delve into both. There have been many, many books written in the years since JFK was assassinated; I didn't want my book to feel like it was covering the same tired ground as all the others, so I added layers of other histories (and an ounce or two of make-believe). I stacked them carefully for you, like a deck of trick cards.

As I studied and delved into research for my first series of novels, The Disturbing History Saga, I was inspired to include many historical facts and plausible morsels. I felt by stirring in several real-world ingredients that it would make the story more delicious. Wrapping my fiction up in some truth would add more fun, color, and depth. I read countless blog posts, news articles, and books in order to have them blend together well—some areas perhaps a little too well; please don't confuse the two. Not every factual detail was easy to find or easy to corroborate (but you may be surprised to learn that 98 percent of it *was*—tirelessly hunted down by me, my fans, my editors Nicole and Spencer, and Lee Alessi as mentioned in my acknowledgments), and we know now that not everything is Google-able. So many were gracious enough to help me during this odyssey, but I had the last call in what went in and what didn't, and I apologize if I missed the mark—I promise it wasn't for lack of trying. I never had any intention of offending friends, relatives, history buffs, or any other people with these flights of my imagination; what you hold in your hands is simply (or perhaps not so simply, considering the ten-plus-years it took to get here) my artistic interpretation of the past, written entirely for your entertainment. Please enjoy!

If you would like to take a deeper look behind the scenes and learn more about the history that inspired my books, sign up for my email list and you will receive a free gift filled with the insider's scoop. If I didn't address something that you are interested in, you find an error, or you have more questions about these or any of my work, please email me at kami@boleybooks.com and I will answer as quickly as I can.

ACKNOWLEDGMENTS

As you may know, it takes more than one person to make a book come to life. I wanted to take a moment to thank the people who helped make this dream come true.

First and foremost, I would like to thank my daughter, **Kirstie Rae Schieffler**, and my husband, **James Boley**, for changing my life, and all the other wonderful miracles they perform (like having the compassion and patience to put up with me on my toughest days).
I also owe a debt of gratitude to the following:

Nicole Eva Fraser—For her expert guidance and steadfast belief in me, for being a dear friend and my biggest fan. I lay all of my tangled first-draft work at her feet. I honestly could not have finished this or any book without the care and support of this lovely lady. She gave my book the wisdom of her experience as an editor and a strong female perspective. Nicole's books are also available on Amazon.

Spencer Hamilton—For getting my jokes, for understanding the soul of my stories, for smacking some words out of my hands even when I resisted, helping me dig for that one right word, for polishing my story to a high shine, and for all the hand holding. This man assisted me in dividing a huge monster of a story into two delectable parts—he deserves a standing ovation. He runs a freelance editing service—Nerdy Wordsmith Ink—at www.nerdywordsmith.com, and has a book of his own launching in 2018.

Lee Alessi—For his shared love of details and history, for kindly helping me track down those hard-to-find nuggets of information.

Toni Palermo—For kindness and willingness to share her honesty as a reader when combing through my clumsy first completed draft. I don't trust people easily; she has earned it.

K.M. Weiland—For her friendship, allowing me to annoy her often and tap into her infinite genius. I appreciate all of her contributions to the writing world, including her books, blog, and podcasts—Helping Writers Become Authors.

Angela Ackerman and Becca Puglisi—For their collection of thesauri aiding authors in their descriptive writing efforts and online resource, Writers Helping Writers.

Damonza—For delivering another gorgeous book cover I can be proud of, and a special thanks to Chrissy.

Sandeep Likhar—For being a kind soul who often contemplates the world with me, as well as formatting all of my prose to make it an enjoyable experience for my readers. He's the best.

Beta Readers—A special thanks to all the brave readers who agreed to scan my pages for mistakes, so that I wouldn't embarrass myself in front of the world, and for their honest opinions.

All the clients of **Koncepts Salon & Spa in Prairieville, LA**— For all of their support, patience, encouragement, and kind words.

The many members of **Tribe Writers, SPS**, and other Indie authors who have reached out to assist me—For not letting me struggle alone.

My peeps who interact with me often on Facebook and other social media platforms, especially those who assist with difficult research issues—I appreciate your valuable feedback and efforts!

. . . and last but not least, **I THANK YOU!**

Readers breathe life into a writer's words, so I wanted to take this opportunity to thank you for your purchase and for the support in making my dream of being an author a reality.

I am an **Independent Author**, a tiny voice in a big world. If you enjoyed this book, please leave a review, and help me spread the experience to others.

The next book will be out soon . . . **DON'T MISS IT!** Please follow my writing journey at www.boleybooks.com.

About the Author

The author **Kami Boley** was born in Houma, Louisiana, in 1973. At a young age, she discovered a deep passion for books and writing.  As a young adult, she put that dream on hold to devote her time and energy to working as a cosmetologist so she could provide for a new love in her life, her daughter, Kirstie. Now that Kirstie is grown, Kami is ready to share her stories. Some stories will be for children, some will be for adults—but as she creates them, you will be able to find them all at www.boleybooks.com.

www.ingramcontent.com/pod-product-compliance
Lightning Source LLC
Chambersburg PA
CBHW020507260626
47156CB00006B/1903